Contents

PUFFIN BOOKS

The Invisible Dog

Dick King-Smith served in the Grenadier Guards during the Second World War, and afterwards spent twenty years as a farmer in Gloucestershire, the county of his birth. Many of his stories are inspired by his farming experiences. Later he taught at a village primary school. His first book, *The Fox Busters*, was published in 1978. Since then he has written a great number of children's books, including *The Sheep-Pig* (winner of the Guardian Award and filmed as *Babe*), *Harry's Mad*, *Noah's Brother*, *The Hodgeheg*, *Martin's Mice*, *Ace*, *The Cuckoo Child* and *Harriet's Hare* (winner of the Children's Book Award in 1995). At the British Book Awards in 1991 he was voted Children's Author of the Year. He has three children, a large number of grandchildren and several great-grandchildren, and lives in a seventeenth-century cottage only a crow's-flight from the house where he was born.

Some other books by Dick King-Smith

ACE
THE CUCKOO CHILD
DAGGIE DOGFOOT
DODOS ARE FOREVER
DRAGON BOY
FIND THE WHITE HORSE
THE FOX BUSTERS
HARRY'S MAD
THE HODGEHEG
HOW GREEN WAS MY MOUSE
LADY DAISY
MAGNUS POWERMOUSE
MARTIN'S MICE
THE MERMAN
THE MERRYTHOUGHT
THE MOUSE BUTCHER
NOAH'S BROTHER
PADDY'S POT OF GOLD
PRETTY POLLY
THE QUEEN'S NOSE
THE ROUNDHILL
SADDLEBOTTOM
THE SCHOOLMOUSE
THE SHEEP-PIG
THE STRAY
TREASURE TROVE
THE WATER HORSE
THE WITCH OF BLACKBERRY BOTTOM

Dick King-Smith

The Invisible Dog

Illustrated by Ann Kronheimer

PUFFIN BOOKS

PUFFIN BOOKS

Published by the Penguin Group
Penguin Books Ltd, 80 Strand, London WC2R 0RL, England
Penguin Putnam Inc., 375 Hudson Street, New York, New York 10014, USA
Penguin Books Australia Ltd, 250 Camberwell Road, Camberwell, Victoria 3124, Australia
Penguin Books Canada Ltd, 10 Alcorn Avenue, Toronto, Ontario, Canada M4V 3B2
Penguin Books India (P) Ltd, 11 Community Centre, Panchsheel Park, New Delhi – 110 017, India
Penguin Books (NZ) Ltd, Cnr Rosedale and Airborne Roads, Albany, Auckland, New Zealand
Penguin Books (South Africa) (Pty) Ltd, 24 Sturdee Avenue, Rosebank 2196, South Africa

Penguin Books Ltd, Registered Offices: 80 Strand, London WC2R 0RL, England

www.penguin.com

First published by Viking 1995
Published in Puffin Books 1997
Published in this edition 2003
18

Set in 15/18.5 Perpetua

Made and printed in England by Clays Ltd, St Ives plc

British Library Cataloguing in Publication Data
A CIP catalogue record for this book is available from the British Library

ISBN-13: 978–0–14–131603–1

www.greenpenguin.co.uk

One
The Lead and Collar

Rupert died when Janie was only two, so she didn't really remember anything about him.

She knew what he looked like, of course – there were lots of photos of him: on his own, or with Mum or Dad, and one she specially liked of herself as a toddler sitting on the lawn with Rupert standing beside her. She was just sorry she'd never known him.

'Mum,' Janie said one day, 'how long ago did Rupert die?'

'Oh, let's see,' her mother said. 'He died when you were two and now you're seven. So – five years ago.'

'And how old was he?'

'He was eight.'

'That's not very old for a dog, is it?' Janie said.

'Not for most dogs,' her mother said, 'but then Rupert was very big, a giant really. Great Danes don't usually live as long as smaller dogs.'

'What did he die of?'

'Kidney failure.'

'Were you and Daddy sad?'

'Terribly.'

'Is that why we've never had a dog since?'

'I suppose it is, really. We talked about getting a puppy, but somehow it seemed as though no other dog could replace Rupert, so we never did.'

'What kind of puppy would you have got?' asked Janie.

'Oh, a Great Dane again, I think. We wouldn't want any other sort of dog. But they're awfully expensive to buy and awfully expensive to keep.'

'Shall we ever have another one, d'you think?'

'I don't know, darling,' Janie's mother said. 'We'll see.'

'We'll see', Janie knew, always meant

'probably not and don't go pestering me about it or it'll be certainly not'. So she thought she'd better drop the subject.

However, the spirit of the late great Rupert must have decided otherwise, for only a few days later Janie came by chance upon something she'd never set eyes on before.

She was hunting about at the back of the garage, where her father had his workbench, looking for an oil can to oil her bike, when she saw something hanging high on a nail in a dark dusty corner.

It was a dog collar with a lead attached.

Janie climbed up on to the bench and took it down.

The collar was a very big, broad, brass-studded one with a round metal disc

attached to the buckle. She rubbed the disc clear of dust and there, scratched on the face, was the name RUPERT and, underneath, their telephone number.

Janie put the collar to her nose. It smelt of leather and dog, and just for a moment it made her feel sad to think that this faint smell was all that was left of the creature whose great neck the collar had encircled. How many hundreds of times in his eight years of life would he have gone for a walk wearing it, with Mum

or Dad holding the end of the thick plaited lead?

Janie went out of the garden gate and wandered up the lane, the loop of the lead in her left hand, the empty collar dangling. She looked down at the thick leather circlet and imagined the shape and sweep of the great neck, the Great Dane neck, within it. She saw the dog clearly in her mind's eye as it walked beside her.

Lost in a daydream, she almost bumped into Mrs Garrow, an elderly widow who lived alone in one of the cottages at the top end of the village.

'Hullo, Janie! Where are you off to then?' said the old lady with a loud laugh. Mrs Garrow's laugh sounded like nothing so much as a duck quacking.

'I'm taking my dog for a walk,' Janie said.

'I can see that,' said Mrs Garrow, and she put out a hand and patted the air behind the dangling collar, just where the dog's back would have been.

'Who's a good boy then?' said Mrs Garrow. 'He's looking ever so well, Janie; you must be proud of him. Make sure you keep him on the lead, mind; there's a lot of traffic in the lane these days,' and she went on her way, quacking loudly.

Some people never grow too old for games of make-believe, thought Janie. That's nice. And two can play at that.

'Heel!' she said, and she walked on, the invisible dog pacing at her side.

Two
The Name

After Janie had gone to bed that night, her parents were talking.

'I see Janie's got hold of old Rupert's collar and lead,' her father said.

'Yes,' her mother said. 'She's been carrying it around all day. It's lying beside her bed now.'

'When I arrived home from work,' her father said, 'she was so engrossed with it I

don't think she even heard the car. She was walking round the lawn, dangling the collar and talking away to an imaginary animal. Every now and then she'd stop and say, 'Sit!' and then after a bit she'd say, 'Heel!' and walk on again.'

'I know. I can only think she must have a very vivid imagination to play a game like that for so long.'

'Has she been pestering you to get a puppy?'

'No. It would be nice though, David, wouldn't it? One day.'

'Another Great Dane?'

'Of course.'

'Oh, come off it, Sally,' Janie's father said. 'They're awfully expensive to buy and awfully expensive to keep. I mean, these days a decent Dane puppy costs over three hundred pounds.'

'You know that, do you?'

'Well . . . yes, I just happened to notice an advertisement. And as for feeding a growing pup – well, you can reckon on over six hundred pounds a year.'

'So we can't afford one?'

'No. You weren't seriously thinking of getting one?'

'No.'

'Right then.'

At breakfast next morning they both noticed that the loop of the lead was round Janie's left wrist as she ate, the collar on the floor beside her.

'Do we have to have that dirty old thing at the table?' her father asked.

'He's not a dirty old thing,' Janie said.

'He? I'm talking about the collar and lead.'

'Oh sorry, Dad, I thought you were talking about my dog.'

'It's a funny thing,' her mother said, 'but Daddy and I can't actually *see* a dog.'

'You wouldn't,' said Janie. 'He's invisible.'

'I see.'

'No you don't, Mum.'

'I mean, I hear what you're saying. By the way, what do you feed him on?'

'Invisible food.'

'In an invisible dish?'

'Naturally.'

'Think of the money you're saving,' Janie's father said, 'never having to fork out for dog meat or biscuits. Can't cost you a penny.'

'Of course it does, Daddy. When we go shopping today, you wouldn't believe how much I shall have to spend.'

'Invisible money?'

'Of course.'

'Has he got a name, this invisible dog?' her mother asked.

'Well, no, not yet,' said Janie. 'I haven't decided.'

'Have you decided what breed he is?' her father said.

'Oh honestly, Daddy!' said Janie. 'I

should have thought that you'd have known a Great Dane when you saw one.'

'You could just call him Rupert,' her mother said. 'That's what's written on his collar, after all.'

'No,' said Janie. 'I think this dog ought to have a different name, don't you?'

'Oh yes,' they said.

'I mean, he's quite a different colour, isn't he?'

'Is he?' they said.

'Rupert was a fawn dog, with a black mask,' Janie's father said.

'Whereas this one,' Janie's mother said, 'is . . . um . . . well . . . what would you say, Janie?'

'Black with white splodges,' said Janie.

'Or white with black splodges, whichever you like to say.'

'A harlequin Great Dane!' they cried.

'Of course.'

'So he really needs a sort of black-and-white name, doesn't he?'

'Like Magpie, you mean?' said her mother.

'Or Zebra,' said her father.

'Or Panda.'

'Or Penguin.'

'Yes,' said Janie, 'but I don't like any of those names. I think I'll just call him Spotty.'

'You can't!' they cried with one voice. 'You can't call a harlequin Great Dane "Spotty". It's not dignified enough.'

'He's my dog,' said Janie, and she put

down a hand and stroked an invisible back, 'so I can call you Spotty if I want to, or Tom, Dick or Harry.'

'He liked "Harry",' said Janie's father, looking down at the collar lying on the floor. 'He wagged his tail a bit when you said "Harry".'

Janie's mother raised her eyes to heaven.

'Oh honestly, David!' she said. 'You're as bad as she is. No doubting where she gets it from.'

'Harry,' said Janie. 'I quite like that.'

'Or perhaps Henry,' said her father. 'That's a bit more dignified.'

'Henry?' said Janie. 'Henry! Yes, you're right, Daddy. He's wagging his tail like mad now. Henry it is!'

Three
The Price

All this happened towards the end of the holidays and, as the new term approached, Janie's parents began to wonder if Henry would be taken to school.

They worried at the thought of their child doing lessons or playing games or eating her lunch, always attached to the lead and collar. It was all very well to make-believe at home, but whatever would the teachers think?

They waited, a little nervously, for the first day of term.

'Got all your school things ready?' her father said at breakfast.

'Yes.'

Her mother drew a deep breath.

'You're not taking Henry, are you, darling?' she said.

'Oh honestly, Mummy!' said Janie. 'You know we're not allowed pets at school, not even a gerbil, let alone a Great Dane. But he can come in the car with us, can't he?'

'Oh. Yes. Of course.'

'And then he can go back home with

you once you've dropped Daddy off at the station.'

'All right.'

'You'll have to exercise him, Mum.'

'Take him for a walk, d'you mean?' her mother asked nervously.

'No, just let him out for a run in the garden. Mind you take his lead off or he'll trip over it. Just let him out at lunch time, that'll be enough. After all, we don't want Henry making a mess in the house. Specially an invisible mess.'

'I wonder what it would be like,' said her father thoughtfully, 'stepping in an invisible dog mess?'

When, however, her mother drove to fetch Janie at the end of the school day, she found that she had forgotten something. As they came out of the playground and reached the car, parked at the roadside, Janie looked in at the back seat and made a little noise of disappointment.

'Oh, Mum!' she said. 'You left Henry at home.'

Janie's mother stopped herself on the verge of saying, 'No, he's there all right, it's just that he's invisible.' From then on she was always careful, whenever she collected Janie, to have put the collar at one or other end of the back seat and the lead ready for Janie to clip on when they arrived home.

'Have you told them at school?' Janie's mum said, a few days later.

'Told who?'

'Your friends.'

'What about?'

'About Henry.'

'No. But I told our teacher,' said Janie.

'What! That we'd got a Great Dane?'

'No. Just that we might have one, one day. Another one, I mean, as well as Henry.'

'What makes you think that?'

'Well, we might, Mum, mightn't we? You never know what's going to happen.'

'I do,' her mother said, 'and we aren't. Your father wouldn't consider it.'

'How d'you know?'

'You ask him.'

So when her father came home from work that evening, Janie did.

She didn't for one moment think that he'd say yes, though she half hoped for a 'We'll see', which would mean there might be a chance, but he simply said, 'No, of course not. Can't afford it.'

'How much would a puppy cost then?'

Janie said. 'A Great Dane puppy, I mean. A harlequin Great Dane.'

Her father stopped himself on the verge of saying 'three hundred pounds'. Possibly that was a guess on the low side, he thought, and probably harlequins are more expensive than other colours, and anyway, if I say a really high price she'll forget the whole silly business.

'Five hundred pounds,' he said.

Janie looked down at the collar, dangling as usual from its lead, and patted an invisible head.

'D'you hear that, Henry?' she said. 'Just think what you must be worth.'

'You stick to Henry,' her father said.

'I could save up my pocket money,' Janie said.

'Take you about ten years.'

'Just think! I'd be seventeen,' said Janie, 'nearly eighteen, and then I'd be grown up and you wouldn't be able to stop me buying a Great Dane puppy.'

'I'm not stopping *you* buying one now,' her father said. 'Just so long as you've got the money. You come along with five hundred pounds and then . . .'

'And then what, Daddy?'

'Then we'll see.'

Four
The Show

Janie's birthday was in the early part of January, and for a treat each year she was always taken to London – to the Zoo, or Madame Tussaud's, or the Tower, or the Natural History Museum.

'What shall we do for Janie's birthday outing this year?' her mother said. 'Can you think of something a bit out of the ordinary?'

'As a matter of fact, I can,' Janie's father said.

'What?'

'Cruft's.'

'Cruft's Dog Show?'

'Yes. Might be rather fun, don't you think?'

'Which day? It's a four-day show, I seem to remember.'

'Oh, the fourth day, I think.'

'Why? No, don't tell me, David; I can read you like a book. Great Danes are judged on the fourth day. That's it, isn't it?'

'Well, yes. I mean, I know they're your favourite breed, Sally.'

'Not by any chance yours too?'

'Well, yes. But I just thought it might be fun for Janie.'

'I see. Don't you think it might be a bit hard on the child? She may not be satisfied with an invisible Great Dane. It isn't as if you had any intention of buying a puppy.'

'No,' said her husband. 'Though I told Janie *she* could buy one.'

'You did *what*?'

'I said that if she came along with five hundred pounds clutched in her hot little hand, then I wouldn't stop her buying a Dane puppy.'

'You say the stupidest things sometimes. Next thing you know, she'll be robbing a bank.'

'Well, shall we go to Cruft's or shan't we?'

'Ask Janie.'

'A dog show?' Janie said when the idea was put to her. 'What dog show?'

'Cruft's. The biggest of them all. There'll probably be something like twenty thousand dogs there altogether. Of every breed.'

'Great Danes?'

'Of course.'

'Harlequin Great

Danes like Henry?'

'Sure to be some. Though they'll look a bit different from Henry.'

'Why?'

'Well, you can't see him too well.'

'Can he come to Cruft's?'

'No.'

'Poor old boy,' said Janie, fondling an invisible ear.

'I'll tell you all about it afterwards.'

*

Apart from those old snapshots of Rupert, Janie had never in her life set eyes upon a Great Dane until that unforgettable day shortly after her eighth birthday. They had walked into the great hall of Olympia and made their way past the judging of a whole lot of other breeds – terriers and collies and gun dogs and many more – and suddenly there were the giants, a ring full of them.

Black and blue, fawn and brindle and harlequin, they stood and

showed themselves in all their majestic dignity.

The judge was a little woman, small enough, it seemed to Janie, to have gone for a ride on any one of the great dogs whose points she was so carefully examining.

Janie and her mother and father watched at the ringside as class succeeded class, and handlers stood their charges before the little judge, or walked or ran around the ring, the huge

dogs striding out beside them. Tall men or short men, thin ladies or fat, old or young, they each had something in common, thought Janie – a Great Big Beautiful Dane. If only we could have one some day, she said to herself.

A man beside them noticed the rapt expression on Janie's face.

'Bet you wish you had a dog like one of those,' he said with a smile.

'Actually,' said Janie, 'I have. He's called Henry.'

'Imagine that!' said the friendly man.

'Henry's rather out of the ordinary,' Janie's mother said.

'Out of this world,' said her father.

They stayed and watched till the end of the judging, till the little woman had made her choice between Best Dog and Best Bitch. Both appeared equally beautiful to Janie – every one of the Danes there, it seemed to her, was faultless; she couldn't see any difference between them except colour. But she desperately wanted the dog to win Best of Breed because, just by chance, he was a harlequin. And her wish was granted.

'He's beautiful!' Janie said.

'Isn't he just!'

'They all were.'

'Weren't they just!'

Afterwards they went round the benches, and there

he was, with his rosettes and his prize cards and his proud owner.

Janie pushed between a small crowd of admirers to get a closer look. The dog, she could see, knew just what a clever fellow he was. He had a kind of smile on his great face and his long tail wagged slowly and majestically.

'He's called Champion Larkmeadow Nobleman of Merlincourt,' she told her parents.

'Gosh! What a mouthful.'

'But his owner called him Bob. I heard him.'

'That's better.'

'Funny thing though,' said Janie.

'What?'

'He looked just *exactly* like Henry.'

Five
The Tea Leaves

The postbox was at the top end of the village, not much more than a hundred yards from Janic's front gate. It was, in fact, set into the low garden wall of Mrs Garrow's cottage, and Janie sometimes wondered how the old lady posted any letters she might write. Did she come out into the lane and post them from the front like everyone else, or did she stay inside her garden and stretch over the wall, then feel for the opening in the box and post them, so to speak, upside down? No, she wouldn't be tall enough, would she?

One day she found the answer.

'Take this letter up to the post for me, Janie, will you, please?' her mother had said, and Janie set off, the letter in one hand, the lead in the other, the collar around Henry's invisible neck.

She was approaching the postbox when she saw Mrs Garrow come out of her front door, also carrying a letter, and walk across her little bit of lawn to a spot directly behind the bright red box.

She'll never be able to do it; she's too short, Janie thought, but then Mrs

Garrow seemed suddenly to rise higher, and she leaned right over the top of the wall and posted her letter.

Straightening up, she saw Janie and let out a burst of quacking laughter.

'Bet you thought I wasn't tall enough to do that!' she said. 'And I wouldn't be if it weren't for these,' and Janie could see that the old lady was standing on top of a little pair of wooden steps positioned behind the wall.

'I always enjoy doing that, Janie,' Mrs Garrow said. ''Specially as I always feel somehow that the postbox is mine, seeing as it's set in my wall.'

'Oh,' said Janie. 'Is it all right if I post my letter in it?'

'Course it is!' cried Mrs Garrow with another volley of quacks. 'Though I'm surprised to see *you* carrying it.'

'What d'you mean?' Janie asked.

'Well, I'd have thought that great animal of yours would be carrying it for you in his mouth. Some dogs do, you know. My! He's a size, isn't he? What's his name?'

'Henry,' said Janie.

'Well I never!' said Mrs Garrow. 'D'you know what, Janie? That was my late husband's name.'

'Oh,' said Janie. 'I'm sorry,' she added.

'No need to be sorry, dear,' said Mrs Garrow. 'He's been dead and gone these twenty years, though never a day passes when I don't think of him. And you know what? There's a lot in common between your Henry and mine.'

'How d'you mean?' Janie said.

'Well, my Henry was a great big chap too – he didn't need a stepladder to post a letter – and another thing, he was quiet, just like your dog. He doesn't bark much, does he?'

'No,' Janie said.

'Saw one just like him on the telly, couple of weeks ago,' Mrs Garrow said. 'Some big dog show it was.'

'Cruft's!' said Janie. 'We went there!'

'Did you take Henry?'

'No, but there was a dog there just exactly like him and he won the prize for Best of Breed. Another harlequin Great Dane, he was.'

'A harlequin Great Dane, eh?' said Mrs

Garrow, and she looked down from her perch at the dangling collar and nodded.

'I see,' she said.

'And Daddy says I can have a real one – I mean, another one – but only on one condition.'

'And what's that?'

'I have to have five hundred pounds.'

'That's a lot of money.'

'It's a fortune!'

Mrs Garrow looked down at Janie and her invisible dog, and her wrinkled face creased some more, into a smile.

'Talking of fortunes, Janie,' she said, 'how would you like me to tell yours?'

'Oh, could you? Oh yes, please,' said Janie.

'Come in and have a cup of tea then.'

'I'd better ask Mum,' said Janie.

'You do that,' said Mrs Garrow. 'I've got some nice cake.'

When Janie returned, permission granted, Mrs Garrow called from her front door, 'Come on in.'

'What about Henry?' Janie said.

'He'd better stay in the garden,' Mrs Garrow said. 'My old black cat doesn't like dogs.'

'All right,' said Janie, and she came in through the gate and dropped the collar and lead on the lawn. 'Down, Henry,' she said, and, 'Stay.'

'Now,' said Mrs Garrow when they had drunk their tea, 'let's have a look in your cup.'

For a long moment she studied the tea leaves in the bottom of the cup, very carefully.

Then she said, 'Janie, I think you're going to be lucky.'

'Why? What can you see?' Janie asked.

'Look,' said Mrs Garrow, handing the cup back.

Janie looked in, but all she could see was a scatter of black tea leaves at the bottom of the white cup.

'I can't see anything,' she said.

'You've got to know what you're looking for,' said Mrs Garrow. 'There's a shape there all right – a great big shape it is, no doubt about it, and what's more, it's black-and-white.'

'A harlequin Great Dane!' cried Janie. 'Is that what it is?'

Mrs Garrow smiled her crinkly smile.

'I shouldn't be surprised,' she said. 'And

now you'd best get off home.'

Out on the lawn, Janie picked up the end of the lead.

'Heel, Henry!' she said, and, 'Thank you for the tea, Mrs Garrow. I hope the tea leaves were right.'

'Talking of leaves,' said Mrs Garrow, 'this lawn's covered in them. I'd better sweep them up. Bye-bye, Janie dear.'

'Goodbye,' Janie said.

For a moment she stood in the lane by the postbox, looking over the low wall. On the lawn old Mrs Garrow was sweeping away with a long broomstick of birch twigs, watched by her black cat.

Six
The Money

'I'm bankrupt,' said Janie's mother.

'And I soon shall be,' said her father. 'I don't think it's fair. Whoever heard of a dog playing Monopoly?'

''Specially an invisible dog,' his wife said.

Janie sat grinning, a great stack of money in front of her. She patted the unseen head at her side.

'You played well,' she said.

It had been Janie's idea that Henry should take part in the game. She threw the dice for him, of course, and moved his symbol round the board, and collected the rents from all his properties as well as her own. As always, she played with the top-hat, her mother with the flat-iron and her father with the car. Henry's symbol, naturally, had to be the dog.

'OK,' said Janie's father as the car landed on Henry's Park Lane hotel. 'I've had it too. You win, Janie. You and Henry.'

'Cheer up, Daddy,' Janie said. 'I've got a nice surprise for you,' and from a wad of money she peeled off a five-hundred-pound note and held it out to him.

'What's this for?' he said.

'For my Great Dane puppy. Remember what you said? "You come along with five hundred pounds," you said . . .'

'Oh, no you don't,' her father said. 'It's got to be real money if you want a real

dog. Five hundred pounds of Monopoly money indeed – you'll be lucky!'

'I think I will be,' Janie said.

*

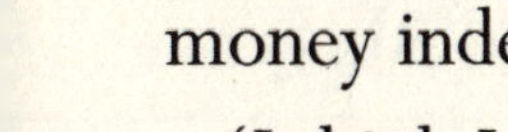

Later, Janie's mother said, 'I wish you hadn't done that silly thing, David.'

'What silly thing?'

'Telling Janie she could have a puppy if she had five hundred pounds. You saw the look on her face just now – she genuinely believes she's going to be lucky. It's not fair on the child – there's no way she could find that amount. Either put up the money yourself or shut up about it.'

'I just might,' Janie's father said.

'Might what? Shut up?'

'No, put up the money. Ever since Janie brought out that lead and collar, I've found myself thinking of dear old Rupert and what a super dog he was and wondering why we never replaced him.

And what with Cruft's – well, I must admit I'm getting quite keen on the idea. After all, Sally, we are the right sort of people to have a big dog – we've a sizeable house and garden, we live in the country and we can afford it.'

'You told Janie we couldn't when she first asked you.'

'Yes, I know; it's all the fault of that invisible dog of hers. The more she plays that game, the more I find I want to see an actual living, breathing, flesh-and-blood Danc on that lead.'

'A harlequin.'

'Does that matter? Surely any colour would do.'

'Not for Janie it wouldn't. And it may not be easy to find exactly what we want.'

'*We*?' said her husband. 'You go along with the idea then?'

'We'll see.'

'We will,' said Janie's father, and he grinned, slyly it seemed to his wife.

'What have you got up your sleeve?' she said.

'Not up my sleeve,' said Janie's father. 'In my pocket,' and he took something out of it.

'What's that?'

'An advertisement. I cut it out of the local paper.'

'You don't mean . . .?'

'Yes. Listen. 'Great Dane puppies for sale. Blacks, blues, one harlequin.' '

'Price?'

'Doesn't say.'

'Where?'

'Not all that far away. Extraordinary, isn't it? I had no idea there was a Great Dane breeder anywhere near here. And there's a harlequin in the litter too. What a bit of luck!'

'Janie said she'd be lucky, didn't she?'

'I know. All it needs now is for five

hundred pounds to drop out of the sky and land in Janie's lap and I shall begin to believe in witchcraft.'

At that instant they heard a loud noise outside.

'What on earth was that?' Janie's father said.

Her mother went to look out of the window.

'Oh, it's only old Mrs Garrow going down the lane,' she said. 'She has the most peculiar laugh.'

'I'll say! I thought it was a duck quacking.'

'She's chatting with Janie. And she's flapping her hand up and down. Oh no, I see what she's doing – she's patting Henry.'

'That,' said Janie's father, 'has really made my mind up. If it's got to the stage where Janie's playing her invisible dog game with people like Mrs Garrow, it's high time we got a visible one.'

'Will you tell Janie?'

'No, not yet. The harlequin pup may be sold, or it may be a bitch, or it may just be a poor specimen. We must go and see the puppies.'

'When?'

'As soon as you've taken Janie to school tomorrow morning.'

'But you'll be going to work.'

'No. I'm taking the day off. I've fixed it at the office. Urgent business.'

'David! You are a slyboots!'

The postman came just as Janie was getting ready to go to school next morning, and by the time their car reached the top end of the village his van was parked outside Mrs Garrow's cottage while he collected the outgoing mail from the postbox.

Mrs Garrow was chatting to him and she waved at Janie as they went by.

'Your friend,' said Janie's mother.

'She's nice,' said Janie, waving back.

'Did you enjoy going to tea with her?'

'Yes, it was interesting.'

They drove on, while the postman got into his van and drove away, down towards their house.

Seven
The Kennels

Back home again, Janie's mother found her husband still sitting at the breakfast table, looking very pleased with life. He waved a letter at her.

'What's up?' his wife said. 'You look as if you've won the pools.'

'*I* haven't won anything,' Janie's father said. 'Janie has. Do you remember when

she was very small I bought some Premium Bonds for her? Well, they've won her some money – quite a nice sum. Here's the letter telling me so.'

'Don't tell me it's five hundred pounds!'

'No, that would be an unbelievable coincidence after what I said about buying a Great Dane puppy.'

'How much then?'

'Two hundred.'

'It won't be enough then,' Janie's mother said.

'Enough for what?'

'Why, to buy one of those puppies. For Janie to buy one, I mean, with her own money.'

They looked at one another.

'We might have to add a bit to it,' Janie's father said.

They looked at one another again, and they smiled.

'Ring up the kennels,' Janie's mother said, 'and see if they'll keep the harlequin until we get there.'

She listened anxiously to her husband's share of the conversation.

'Good morning. I'm inquiring about the pups you advertised. Are they sold?'

'I see. But you still have the harlequin?'

. . .

'Dog or bitch?'

. . .

'Oh, good. That's the one we're interested in. Can you keep him for us?'

. . .

'Yes, I understand. We must take a chance on that. We'll be with you just as soon as we can. By the way, how much are you asking for him?'

The answer to this last question seemed to take some time, but at last Janie's father put the phone down.

'The harlequin is a dog puppy,' he said, 'and he's not sold. The woman said she couldn't guarantee to keep him for us. She's sold a couple of the others but hasn't had anyone after the harlequin yet.'

'How much?' Janie's mother said. 'She seemed to take a lot of time answering when you asked her that.'

'That's because she was giving me a long spiel about how well bred this litter is, and what the mother had won, and the fact that the father is Champion

Thingummy Nobleman of Wotsitsname – you know, the dog that won at Cruft's.'

'So, how much?'

'Five hundred pounds.'

'I'm awfully sorry,' the breeder said when they arrived. 'No sooner had you rung off than someone turned up, wanting the harlequin puppy. He's just this moment driven off; you probably passed him on your way here.'

Janie's parents looked at one another once more, and they sighed a joint sigh.

'There are still two blacks and a blue left,' said the breeder.

'No,' Janie's mother said, 'thanks all the same. It has to be a harlequin or nothing.'

'Leave me your address and phone number then,' said the breeder. 'I might hear of something.'

'At least Janie doesn't know anything about it,' said one to the other as they drove home again, 'so she won't be disappointed.'

'And she's got a nice surprise waiting for her when she gets back from school this afternoon.'

*

'I didn't even know I had a Premium Bond,' Janie said when they showed her the letter and the cheque. 'You never told me.'

'We don't tell you everything,' her father said.

'Two hundred pounds!' Janie said. 'Nearly enough to buy half a harlequin Great Dane puppy!'

'Has it really *got* to be a harlequin?' her mother said.

'Yes. She said so.'

'Who said so?'

'Mrs Garrow.'

'What on earth has Mrs Garrow got to do with it?'

'She saw it.'

'I don't know *what* you're talking about,' her father said.

After tea Janie took the invisible dog for a walk up the lane. As she passed Mrs Garrow's cottage, the old lady looked over the garden wall and said, 'Hullo, Janie. Better luck next time.'

I don't know what you're talking about, Janie thought.

'Ask your mum

and dad,' Mrs Garrow said, just as though she'd read Janie's mind.

'Ask them what?'

'Where they went this morning.'

'Where did you go this morning?' Janie asked when she got home again.

'How d'you know we went anywhere?' her father said.

'I just do.'

There was a pause.

'Tell her,' her mother said.

At that moment the phone rang. It was the Great Dane breeder.

'I've just this minute had a thought,' she said. 'Since you just missed that puppy this morning and are set on having a harlequin, I've had an idea, if you're interested. I have a nine-month-old harlequin dog that might do you. He's a good typical specimen, with a lovely nature, but he has a fault that spoils him for the show ring.'

'What sort of fault?' Janie's mother said.

'He's got a kink in his tail – a little sort

of twist near the end of it. He was born like that, but I've kept him on because he's such a lovable

character. Would you like to see him?'

They arrived once more at the kennels, this time with Janie. The breeder looked at her as she stood, lead in hand, collar dangling. 'That's a biggish collar,' she said. 'Have you had a Dane before?'

'We had one called Rupert,' Janie said, 'when I was very small, but he was fawn, not a harlequin like this one.'

'Which one?' said the breeder.

'Janie has an invisible dog,' her father said. 'He goes everywhere with her. He's never any trouble.'

'Sit, Henry!' Janie said.

'Did you say Henry?' said the breeder. 'How extraordinary! Hang on half a tick, I'll fetch the dog.'

Of course they all fell in love with him at first sight. Already he seemed enormous, with feet like soup plates. He did not squirm or wriggle as a puppy would have done, but stood steady in black-and-white dignity as befitted someone who was almost grown-up.

'His nose is partly black and partly pink!' Janie's father said as the young dog sniffed at them.

'That's all right,' the breeder said. 'A harlequin's allowed a butterfly nose.'

'And he's got one brown eye and one

blue!' said Janie's mother, as he smiled at them.

'A wall eye. That's all right too. He's a good typical specimen, with a lovely nature, but, like I said, he has a kink in his tail – that little sort of twist near the end of it.'

As if he understood, the dog slowly wagged his tail.

'I like that,' Janie said. 'I want to buy him, please.'

'*You* want to?' the breeder said, smiling. 'Have you got enough money of your own, d'you think?'

'I've got two hundred pounds,' Janie said.

'I won't charge you that much,' the breeder said. 'As I told you, he's no good for show, with that fault. But I don't think

I can give him to you – he's cost me a lot to rear. On the other hand, I feel sure that you'll give him a really good home. So shall we say a hundred pounds?'

Janie put out a hand.

'It's a deal,' she said. 'What's he called?'

'You aren't going to believe it,' the breeder said. 'In fact I must confess that there's something very strange about all

this. But he's called Henry.'

Janie nodded. It was as though she had expected this news.

Carefully she unbuckled the collar from the invisible dog and fastened it again around the neck of his successor.

'Good boy, Henry,' she said.

Eight
The Twist

About a week later Janie came out of the front gate and turned up the lane, the lead in her right hand, her dog walking steadily at heel with his long strides, his great head not far below her shoulder. From the buckle of his collar hung a new round metal disc that said, above the telephone number, HENRY.

They walked up the village until they came to Mrs Garrow's wall, with the red postbox set into it, and Janie opened the garden gate and went in. Inside the porch of the cottage were Mrs Garrow's wellies and, leaning in the corner, the long broomstick that she used for sweeping up leaves. Her cat sat on the mat.

'My old black cat doesn't like dogs,' Mrs Garrow had said, but to Janie's surprise it stood up and began to rub itself against one of Henry's long legs, purring loudly. Henry looked embarrassed.

Janie knocked on the front door, and after a moment old Mrs Garrow opened it, smiling her crinkly smile.

'Hullo,' Janie said. 'This is Henry.'

'I know that, dear,' said Mrs Garrow. 'You showed him to me before, lots of times, don't you remember?'

She patted the dog.

'Who's a good boy then?' she said. 'He's looking ever so well, Janie. You must be proud of him.'

'I am,' Janie said. 'D'you see, he's got a butterfly nose and a wall eye? There's only one thing meant to be wrong with him though I don't think it matters a bit, and that's the twist in his tail.'

'It was all in the tea-leaves,' Mrs Garrow said.

'I don't understand,' Janie said. 'How can you know these things?'

Mrs Garrow let out her usual volley of quacks.

'Aha, Janie my dear!' she said. 'That's the twist in the tale.'

Winner of the

Guardian Children's Fiction Prize

Here's what the judges had to say about

The Sheep-Pig

★ 'Perfect'

★ 'Thrilling'

★ 'Funny'

★ 'The Best'

★ 'Charmer'

★ 'Suspense'

★ 'Breathless'

★ 'Delight'

Ace

Ace is a very special pig.

He loves watching television and gradually makes himself at home in the farmhouse, much to the annoyance of Megan, the corgi. Megan is determined to keep Ace out, but Ace is the great-grandson of Babe the sheep-pig, and he's full of surprises.

The Hodgeheg

The story of Max, the hedgehog who becomes a hodgeheg, who becomes a hero!

Max's family dreams of reaching the Park. But no one has ever found a safe way of crossing the very busy road. Can Max really solve the problem?

PUFFIN BOOKS

The Mouse Family Robinson

Dick King-Smith served in the Grenadier Guards during the Second World War, and afterwards spent twenty years as a farmer in Gloucestershire, the county of his birth. Many of his stories are inspired by his farming experiences. Later he taught at a village primary school. His first book, *The Fox Busters*, was published in 1978. Since then he has written a great number of children's books, including *The Sheep-Pig* (winner of the Guardian Award and filmed as *Babe*), *Harry's Mad*, *Noah's Brother*, *The Hodgeheg*, *Martin's Mice*, *Ace*, *The Cuckoo Child* and *Harriet's Hare* (winner of the Children's Book Award in 1995). At the British Book Awards in 1991 he was voted Children's Author of the Year. He has three children, a large number of grandchildren and several great-grandchildren, and lives in a seventeenth-century cottage only a crow's-flight from the house where he was born.

Books by Dick King-Smith

ACE
BLESSU
DINOSAUR SCHOOL
DINOSAUR TROUBLE
DUMPLING
FAT LAWRENCE
FIND THE WHITE HORSE
THE FOX BUSTERS
GEORGE SPEAKS
THE GOLDEN GOOSE
HARRY'S MAD
THE HODGEHEG
THE INVISIBLE DOG
THE JENIUS
MAGNUS POWERMOUSE
MARTIN'S MICE
THE MOUSE FAMILY ROBINSON
POPPET
THE QUEEN'S NOSE
THE SCHOOLMOUSE
THE SHEEP-PIG
SMASHER
THE SWOOSE
UNDER THE MISHMASH TREES
THE WATER HORSE

The Mouse Family Robinson

Dick King-Smith

Illustrated by Ben Cort

PUFFIN

PUFFIN BOOKS

Published by the Penguin Group
Penguin Books Ltd, 80 Strand, London WC2R 0RL, England
Penguin Group (USA) Inc., 375 Hudson Street, New York, New York 10014, USA
Penguin Group (Canada), 90 Eglinton Avenue East, Suite 700, Toronto, Ontario, Canada M4P 2Y3
(a division of Pearson Penguin Canada Inc.)
Penguin Ireland, 25 St Stephen's Green, Dublin 2, Ireland (a division of Penguin Books Ltd)
Penguin Group (Australia), 250 Camberwell Road, Camberwell, Victoria 3124, Australia
(a division of Pearson Australia Group Pty Ltd)
Penguin Books India Pvt Ltd, 11 Community Centre, Panchsheel Park, New Delhi – 110 017, India
Penguin Group (NZ), 67 Apollo Drive, Rosedale, North Shore 0632, New Zealand
(a division of Pearson New Zealand Ltd)
Penguin Books (South Africa) (Pty) Ltd, 24 Sturdee Avenue, Rosebank, Johannesburg 2196, South Africa

Penguin Books Ltd, Registered Offices: 80 Strand, London WC2R 0RL, England

puffinbooks.com

First published 2007
Published in this edition 2008
4

Set in Perpetua
Typeset by Palimpsest Book Production Limited,
Grangemouth, Stirlingshire
Made and printed in England by Clays Ltd, St Ives plc

British Library Cataloguing in Publication Data
A CIP catalogue record for this book is available from the British Library

ISBN: 978–0–141–32062–5

www.greenpenguin.co.uk

Chapter One

John Robinson and Mr Brown were next-door neighbours. That is to say, they both lived under the kitchen floor, for John Robinson and Mr Brown were housemice.

John was a young chap. He was respectful towards his neighbour, who was very old, and always addressed him as 'Mr Brown'. Mr Brown, John knew, now lived alone because his wife had been eaten by the cat.

There came an evening when John's young wife, Janet, told him that he was to become a father for the first time. She was tearing up bits of newspaper to make a comfy nest.

'Gosh!' said John. 'You mean you're going to have a baby?'

'Babies,' said Janet.

She has got fat lately, come to think of it, said John to himself.

'When?' he asked.

'Very soon.'

'Gosh! How many?'

'How do I know, you stupid mouse,' said Janet. 'Now push off, do, and leave me in peace.'

As John was hurrying under the kitchen floor, he met his neighbour coming back home.

'Good evening, Mr Brown,' he said.

'Evening, John,' said Mr Brown. 'How's life?'

'Wonderful!' replied John. 'I am going to be a father.'

'For the first time, eh?'

'Yes, I believe you've had a large number of children, Mr Brown, haven't you?'

'Dozens. So many that I've gone and forgotten most of their names. My late wife and I used to rely on the alphabet.'

'The alphabet?' said John.

'Yes. Start with A – Adam, let's say, or Alice – and keep going till you get to Z. That gives you twenty-six names.'

'You mean you've had twenty-six children, Mr Brown?'

'Seventy-eight, actually, John. We went through the alphabet three times.'

'Gosh!' said John.

'Xs and Zs,' said Mr Brown, 'are the hardest ones to put names to, but we managed. Why don't you try the same trick?'

'I will, I will,' said John. 'Thanks, Mr Brown, that's a good idea.'

The young mouse and his elderly neighbour chatted for a while, mainly about food. A nest under the kitchen floor, as both knew well, is the best place for mice to live. Those clumsy giants called humans were always dropping bits of food on the floor, and if a mouse was bold enough, there were lovely things to eat in the larder.

Talking about food made John feel hungry and after a while he said, 'I must be going, Mr Brown, if you'll excuse me.'

'Of course, John,' Mr Brown replied, 'and I'm so pleased to hear your good news. Please give my regards to your wife.'

'I will,' replied John, 'and thank you.'

Poor old fellow, he thought, remembering what had happened to Mrs Brown.

Now evening had turned to night, and the giants had all gone up the stairs to bed. John Robinson popped out of a mousehole and began to search the kitchen floor, all his senses alert, especially for the squeak of the cat flap.

He was in luck. Someone had spilled half a dozen cornflakes: not much for a giant, but a feast for a mouse.

His hunger satisfied, he made his way home.

Will Janet have had the babies yet? he wondered. How many will there be? How many will be boys, how many girls?

The answers to these questions, John found, were 'Yes', 'Six' and 'Three of each'.

'What shall we call them?' John asked.

'You can choose, if you like,' said Janet.

I'll use Mr Brown's alphabet method, thought John. Six kids, that's A to F. Let's see now, I must think up some unusual names because I'm sure my

children will grow up to be unusual mice.

John Robinson spent the rest of the night deciding what to call his newborn sons and daughters. As dawn broke, he knew he had found six perfect names. 'And,' he said to himself, 'I must tell Mr Brown. I'm sure he'd like to know,' and he hurried along one of the runways beneath the kitchen floor.

'Mr Brown,' he said, when he had found his neighbour, 'Janet's had six babies. I thought you'd like to know.'

'Congratulations, John!' said Mr Brown. 'Got names for them?'

'I have,' said John. 'Ambrose, Beaumont, Camilla, Desdemona, Eustace and Felicity. What d'you think?'

'Brilliant!' said Mr Brown.

‘Three boys and three girls, eh? It’s a start. Twenty more babies and you’ll have finished your first alphabet of names.’

‘Gosh!’ said John to himself. To think that his neighbour had seventy-eight kids!

Even as he thought this, they heard, through the floorboards above their heads, the squeak of the cat flap.

Chapter Two

At the sound the two mice froze, even though they were quite safe under the kitchen floorboards. They looked at one another and Mr Brown sighed deeply.

I know what he's thinking, said John to himself. How dreadful if such a thing ever happened to my Janet. If only that horrible cat didn't live here.

'I must be getting back to my family, Mr Brown,' he said after a while.

'Of course,' replied Mr Brown. 'I'd love to come and see them when they're a little older. Could I?'

'Please do,' said John.

The mousekins had been born naked and blind but later on, when they had grown coats of fur (grey, of course) and had opened their beady little eyes, John invited Mr Brown round. Proudly he and Janet stood on either side of their six children while the old mouse looked them over.

'They're lovely!' he said. 'I do congratulate you both.'

'Thank you,' replied Janet, and 'Thank you, sir,' said John.

'When they're a bit older,' said Mr Brown, 'perhaps they'll come and visit me?' and, a few weeks later, one of them did.

Beaumont was the brightest and the most adventurous of the six mousekins, and he was the first to venture out of the nest and start to explore the spaces under the kitchen floor. Soon he came upon a mouse run that led upwards and, following it, stuck his head out of a hole in the skirting board. He found himself staring across the kitchen floor. Beside the cooker, he could see, was a basket.

Beaumont was not only bright and adventurous, but also curious. I wonder what's in that basket? he thought.

He was halfway across the kitchen floor when two things happened. First, he heard a voice coming from the hole he'd just left, a frantic voice that cried, 'Come back! Come back! Quickly! Quickly!'

Then he saw a face, a face that rose above the rim of the basket, a fearful furry face with yellow eyes that were fixed upon him.

Beaumont turned and dashed back towards the hole in the skirting board just in time. Above him, he heard the scrabble of the cat's claws as it scratched at the mousehole. Before him, he saw an old mouse.

'Oh!' squeaked Beaumont. 'Was it you who called me back?'

'It was,' replied Mr Brown. 'That was a narrow squeak, young fellow. What's your name?'

'I'm Beaumont Robinson.'

'One of John's children?'

'Yes. Who are you?'

'I'm Mr Brown.'

‘Oh, you’re Dad’s friend.’

‘I like to think so.’

‘The one that came to visit us?’

‘Yes.’

‘Have you got any children?’

‘Seventy-eight,’ replied Mr Brown. Though goodness only knows how many are still alive, he thought.

‘Gosh!’ said Beaumont (a word he had learned from his father). ‘My dad told us your wife got eaten by the cat.’

‘She did, Beaumont,’ said Mr Brown. And so would you have been, he thought, if I hadn’t happened to look out just in time. Yours would have been a very short life.

‘Well,’ said Beaumont, ‘isn’t there

any way we can get rid of the beastly thing?'

'Alas, no,' said Mr Brown. 'Cats can

kill mice but unfortunately, mice can't kill cats.'

'Oh,' said Beaumont. 'So we've got to wait till it dies of old age, have we?'

'That might be a long time,' said Mr Brown.

'What can we do, then?'

'Nothing, I'm afraid, Beaumont. The giants have got a cat and we have got to live with it.'

Have we? thought Beaumont. What if . . . ? No, I'd better ask Dad first.

'Got to go,' he said. 'Nice talking to you, Uncle Brown.'

When he got home, he said, 'I've been talking to Uncle Brown, Dad.'

'Have you indeed?' said John. I bet the old chap's pleased at being called that, he thought.

'Yes,' said Beaumont. 'He saved my life, Dad. I went up into the kitchen and the cat nearly got me!'

'Gosh!' said John.

'Uncle Brown says we've just got to live with the beastly thing.'

'Well, he's right, Beaumont. We've got no choice.'

'Yes we have, Dad,' said Beaumont. 'If the cat won't leave us, we can leave the cat.'

'What d'you mean?'

'We can move to another house, one without a cat. We can emigrate, Dad,' said Beaumont.

Chapter Three

'Emigrate?' said John to Beaumont.

'Yes, Dad.'

'But . . . how shall I know if another house has a cat or not?'

'If it has, it'll smell of the beastly thing. If it hasn't, it won't. Simple, Dad.'

'It'll take me an awfully long time to inspect every house in the street.'

'It would if it was just you, Dad,' said Beaumont, 'but what if we all helped, eh, Mum?'

'I certainly will,' said Janet, 'but you kids are too small to take the risk.'

'We're not,' said Beaumont, turning to the other five mousekins, 'are we?

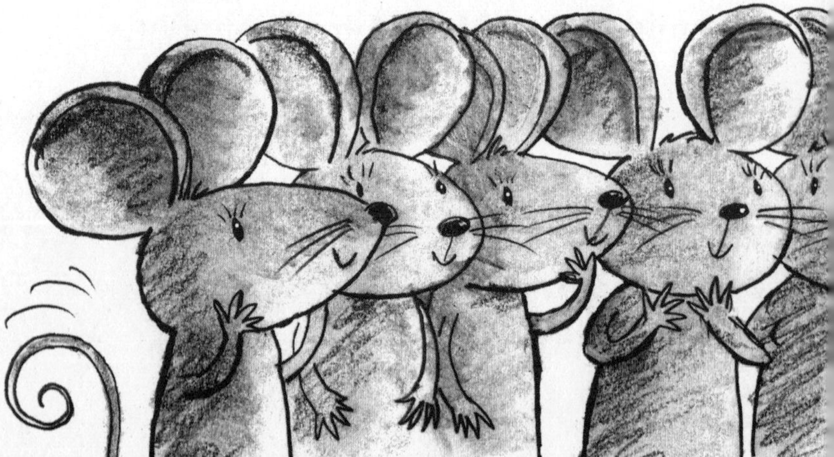

We can help, can't we?' and with one voice Ambrose and Camilla and Desdemona and Eustace and Felicity cried, 'Yes!'

Janet looked proudly at her six children.

'All right,' she said, 'but not just yet. Wait till you've grown a lot bigger.'

'And a lot faster on your feet,' added John. 'There'll be other cats in other houses in the street, and dogs too, and then there's all the traffic. Wait till you're as big as Mum and me.'

'But that'll be ages, Dad!' said Beaumont.

'Do as your father says,' said Janet sharply, and in unison Ambrose and Beaumont and Camilla and Desdemona and Eustace and Felicity muttered, 'Yes, Mum.'

In fact a month went by before John and Janet allowed the six mousekins out of the house.

John had established a route – from under the kitchen floor through a runway that led down into the cellar, and from the cellar up and out through a grating on to the pavement outside.

Janet made a plan of action. Their house was Number 24, even-numbered like all those on that side of the street. Each night she and the three girls would work their way down the road, somehow making their way into Number 22, then Number 20 and so on, while John and the three boys would be inspecting each house up the street – Numbers 26, 28, 30 and so on.

'Let's just hope they don't all have cats in them, Janet,' said John. 'I don't fancy having to cross the road.'

But luck was on their side.

On the fourth night Janet and the girls explored Number 16 and came home excited and delighted to report that there was no smell or sign of cat or dog in that house.

'All we could smell,' said Janet, 'was mice!'

'Great!' said John. 'We'll emigrate there.'

Five of the mousekins squeaked with joy but Beaumont said, 'What about Uncle Brown?'

'What about him?' said the others.

'He'll be lonely without us.'

'Beaumont's right,' said Janet. 'He might like to come too, don't you think, John? Why don't you ask him?'

Of course we must, thought John. He saved Beaumont's life.

So one of the girls – Felicity, it was – was sent to fetch Mr Brown.

'We're moving house, Mr Brown,'

said John when the old mouse arrived. 'To get away from the cat.'

Just what I was thinking, said Mr Brown to himself.

'We're going to Number 16: there's no cat there,' said John.

'We wondered if you'd like to come with us,' said Janet.

'It's very kind of you, Mrs Robinson –'

'"Janet", please,' she interrupted.

'– very kind of you, er, Janet, as I was saying, but I'm sure you'd rather be on your own as a family. I shall miss you, of course.'

'No, you won't, Mr Brown,' said John in a masterful voice. 'I insist that you come with us. Please do.'

'We can't go without you, Uncle Brown,' said Beaumont quietly.

Uncle, thought the old mouse. How nice. Some of my seventy-eight children must, I hope, be alive and well but I never see any of them. They've all pushed off somewhere, so why don't I push off too?

'Please come, Uncle Brown!' squeaked the other mousekins.

'Pleeeease!' and then they heard the sound of the cat flap as the cat, attracted by all the noise, came into the kitchen.

Mr Brown looked at Janet and John and at Beaumont and the other five youngsters.

'Thank you,' he said. 'I'd love to.'

Chapter Four

Number 16 Simple Street did indeed smell quite strongly of mice, and the family who lived there wouldn't have dreamed of having a cat.

There were three giants (as mice thought of them): Mr Black, Mrs Black and their son, a boy called Bill.

Bill Black had always been keen on pet animals, especially mice and, once he was old enough, his parents let him keep some. These were pet mice, fancy mice, of course, not ordinary housemice like the Robinsons and Mr Brown.

Bill had mice of several different colours: he had white ones with pink eyes and white ones with black eyes and chocolate ones and fawn ones and plum-coloured ones and mice with special black markings called Dutch.

By the time Bill was ten years old, he had so many pet mice that his father and mother let him use a little spare room (which he called the Mousery) to keep all his different-coloured mice in their neat cages. By the time that Janet Robinson and her daughters had come into Number 16 to have a sniff around, there were thirty pet mice in the Mousery, not counting babies, so that the smell of them was pretty strong.

No matter, thought Janet. There's not the faintest smell of cat.

At the next full moon all the migrants made their move down the street from Number 24.

John Robinson – after politely asking the advice of old Mr Brown – had decided that though travelling in bright moonlight might be risky, it would alert them to any cats or other dangers on the way, and at midnight the emigration began.

John led the file of mice: behind him came Beaumont and Eustace and Ambrose. Next came Mr Brown, followed by Felicity and Desdemona and Camilla, while Janet brought up the rear.

After they'd gone a little way Beaumont said to his father, 'I'm just going to drop back to make sure Uncle B's all right.' It was just as well he did, for at that very moment a dog barked loudly from inside Number 22, and Mr Brown, frightened by the sudden noise, slipped off the pavement. He seemed to be about to cross the road.

'Come back! Come back! Quickly! Quickly!' cried Beaumont, and the old mouse obeyed just in time, for a car came roaring down the road, only just missing Mr Brown.

'Oh, thank you, Beaumont, my boy!' he panted as he scrambled back over the kerb. Another narrow squeak, he thought. I save him from the cat, he saves me from the car.

After that, they passed Numbers 20 and 18 – cat smells coming from both these houses – and mercifully arrived safely at Number 16 and made their way in. The scent of mice was everywhere but the nine travellers from Number 24 soon found the room where it was strongest: the Mousery.

The cages in which Bill Black kept his fancy mice stood on top of two long low tables. John Robinson shinned up the leg of one of them and found himself in front of the first cage, staring into the red eyes of a mouse that was otherwise pure white. It was a buck, John could tell from its scent, and a bad-tempered buck at that. Coming close to the bars of its cage it said in a sneery voice, 'Push off, you. We don't want common housemice in here. These cages are for well-bred fancy mice only, so sling your hook, ugly mug.'

'Don't talk to me like that!' said John angrily. 'Come on outside and

we'll see who's the better mouse.'

Calm down, John,' said Mr Brown from the floor below. 'He can't come out anyway, he's in a cage.'

'Just as well for him,' said John.

'Yes, but just as well for us too,' said Mr Brown.

He turned to Janet.

'You've been very clever in your choice of house,' he said. 'One of the giants here keeps mice as pets, it would appear, so the place has got to be free of cats. Well done, my dear Janet.'

'Thank you, Mr Brown,' Janet replied. I can't call him by his first name, she thought, because I don't know what it is and I don't really like to ask him. Perhaps we'll never know what it is.

'There's lots of food about too,' she said.

'Which means,' said John, 'that there'll be lots of other housemice about,' and at that very moment a mouse came out through a hole in the skirting board.

'Too right, mate,' he said to John, 'but there's plenty for all of us. The giants here are lovely people, specially the smallest one of the three. No cats – as you can smell, no dogs, no traps, no poison, and they leave food all over the place. You've struck lucky, you lot. Welcome to Liberty Hall!'

Chapter Five

'He seemed a happy sort of chap,' said John to Janet as the mouse disappeared down its hole. 'Don't you think so, Mr Brown?'

'I think,' said Mr Brown, 'that he and his fellows have plenty to be happy about. He's right – we have struck lucky.'

For the rest of that night they all explored the Mousery. None of the fancy mice were as rude as the first pink-eyed white buck had been but all were a bit stand-offish.

'Hadn't we better be moving?' asked Janet as the first light of dawn came in through the window. 'We don't want one of the giants to come and find us in here.'

'Why not, Mum?' asked Beaumont.

'Because they might not wish to have nine more mice in their house,' said Janet. 'Let's all go down that hole in the skirting board and find where it leads to.'

So they all did. As they made their

way down, their sharp ears heard a lot of mouse noises. There were runways through which came sounds of mice, above and below them. They came at last to the cellar of Number 16 in which there were a good many mice, all of whom greeted the newcomers in a friendly fashion.

Above their heads, Bill Black came into the Mousery in his pyjamas (his bedroom was next door) to give his pets their breakfast. He filled the feeding pot in each cage with canary seed, made sure that all the mice had clean water to drink and, of course, talked to the occupants of every cage. Bill was sure that pets like dogs and cats enjoyed being talked to, so why should mice be any different?

In the last cage was a chocolate doe, all by herself because she was soon to have babies. Bill took a very small bit of broken biscuit from a tin and put it down in front of her nose.

'D'you know,' he said to her, 'what I'd love to do? I'd love to tame a wild mouse. Shouldn't think anyone's ever done that. I'd have to catch one first though, a young one.' Even as he said these last words Bill heard a little scratching noise, and there, coming

out of the hole in the skirting board, was a young housemouse.

Beaumont, the brightest, most adventurous, and now indeed the boldest of John and Janet's six children, had heard the sound of Bill's voice from the cellar below and had scuttled back up the runway to see what a giant looked like. Never in his short life had he seen one before.

How strange! thought Bill. Just the kind of mouse that I need, but how do I catch it?

Very slowly, he took another bit of biscuit from the tin. Very slowly, he moved towards the young mouse, who

crouched by the hole below, whiskers twitching. Very slowly, Bill Black offered the bit of biscuit to Beaumont Robinson.

They looked into each other's eyes and each had much the same feelings. They liked the look of one another.

This is a very bold little housemouse,

thought Bill. Could I make a pet of him?

This is a very nice giant, thought Beaumont. I'm not afraid of him at all.

He took a bite of biscuit.

'Delicious!' he said.

All Bill heard, of course, was a squeak, but it sounded like a happy squeak. Suddenly, the young mouse turned and disappeared down the hole.

'Dad!' cried Beaumont as he reached the cellar. 'There's ever such a nice giant up above us. He gave me a lovely bit of biscuit. Come up and see him!' and he turned and dashed up the runway again, followed by Ambrose and Camilla and

Desdemona and Eustace and Felicity.

After them went Janet, calling, 'Come back, children!' and after her went John, calling, 'Come back, Janet!'

To his surprise Bill found himself looking at five more mousekins, and then to his astonishment two adult mice emerged from the hole.

Mum and Dad and six kids, he thought, and crumbled more biscuit on the floor. They were all feeding greedily when another mouse came up out of the hole, a mouse that, Bill could see, looked very old and was a bit wobbly on its legs. Immediately the mousekins surrounded it, squeaking happily.

Must be the grandfather, thought Bill. How could he know that they were all saying, 'Come on, Uncle Brown! Have some biscuit!' or that Janet and John were saying, 'Yes, help yourself, Mr Brown'?

The mice listened as the giant made noises. How could they know that he was saying, 'What a lovely family! Wherever did you come from? Would you like me to make you a special home, here in the Mousery? I don't mean a cage, I don't want to shut you up, but somewhere comfy and warm for you? How would you like that?'

Chapter Six

In fact the Robinson family and their friend Mr Brown never did get to live in the Mousery at Number 16. To be sure, they came up from the cellar whenever they heard the sound of Bill's voice as he talked to his pet mice. They knew he would always give them something to eat. Beaumont was the first of them who actually took food from the giant's hand but the others soon did too.

I wanted to tame a wild mouse, thought Bill, and now it looks as though I've tamed nine! And I dare say there'll be more before long. I must make a proper home for them.

So one day when the Robinsons and Mr Brown came up from the cellar, they found a large shallow box on the floor of the Mousery. Bill had put bedding in it, over which he had scattered a lot of canary seed, and by the time John Robinson and his family and his old friend had eaten it all, they felt quite at home.

So that when Janet said, 'Well, I suppose we'd better get back down to the cellar,' John said, 'Why?'

'It is very comfortable here, Janet,' said Mr Brown.

'Come on, Mum, let's stay,' said Beaumont.

'Yes, let's!' chorused Ambrose and Camilla and Desdemona and Eustace and Felicity.

So they did. But not for long because soon two things happened. First, the rapidly growing mousekins decided that living with the pet mice was a bit boring, so they went back to the cellar where they could play with their wild friends. Only Beaumont stayed. He liked being with his friend the giant, and he was interested in getting to know the pet mice. He talked politely to them, and some of them responded in quite a friendly way.

The second thing to happen was that Janet had another lot of babies – nine this time: six boys and three girls.

Gilbert, Hermione, Inigo, Julius, Kingsley, Lindsay, Marmaduke, Niobe and Olivia.

'Only eleven to go, John,' said his old friend, out of Janet's hearing.

'What d'you mean, Mr Brown?' John asked.

'Eleven more and you'll have

finished your first alphabet of names.'

'Gosh!' said John, and 'Gosh!' echoed Beaumont.

'I only hope,' said Mr Brown, 'that I'm still around to see the alphabet completed.'

'Why shouldn't you be, Uncle Brown?' asked Beaumont.

'Well, I'm not as young as I was.'

'You'll go on for ages yet, Mr Brown,' said John.

But he was wrong.

One morning a few days later, Bill woke up and went into the Mousery to look at what he thought of as his 'tame wild mice'. There were two boxes on the floor now, for Bill had supplied a small one as a single room for the mouse he thought of as 'Grandad'.

In the big box Bill could see Janet suckling her newborn nine, watched

by John and Beaumont. In the small box Grandad lay comfortably, having breakfast in bed. Not wanting to disturb anyone, Bill tiptoed away.

Mr Brown spent a lot of his time asleep, but he still had some appetite and John and Beaumont brought him choice bits of food.

As they had been collecting it that morning, Beaumont said, 'You always call Uncle Brown "Mr Brown", don't you, Dad? Why don't you use his first name?'

'I don't know it.'

'Can't you ask him?'

'I don't like to. He'd have told me if he'd wanted to.'

I'll ask him, thought Beaumont. I'm sure he wouldn't mind. He's nice, Uncle Brown is. He'll tell me his first name.

'Uncle Brown,' said Beaumont, climbing into the small box that afternoon. 'Will you tell me what your first name is? I'd like to know.'

The old mouse did not reply.

He has got a bit deaf lately, thought Beaumont, and more loudly he said, 'Uncle Brown! Can you hear me?'

But there was no answer.

With his nose Beaumont touched

the body of the old mouse. It was stone cold.

Just then Bill came into the Mousery with some bits of biscuit that he'd saved as a treat for his tame wild mice. He saw that one of the youngsters was in Grandad's box. It looked up at him and squeaked.

'He's dead!' cried Beaumont. 'Look, giant, Uncle Brown is dead!'

Oh dear, thought Bill as he stood and stared down. Poor old Grandad.

Chapter Seven

All up and down, in both the even and the odd-numbered houses in Simple Street, mice were being born. Mice were dying too, in the jaws of cat or trap or of poisoning or simply – like Mr Brown – of old age.

But never before had a mouse been

given such a funeral as he was.

'One thing I do know,' said Bill Black as he fed his fancy mice, 'and that is – I'm not just going to chuck poor old Grandad in the dustbin. He shall have a proper burial in the garden.'

Heaven only knows how Beaumont knew what was going on in the brain of his friend the young giant, but the fact remains that when Bill had dug a hole, he suddenly realized that there were seven little mourners at the graveside. Only Janet could not come out to pay her last respects.

'I can't leave the babies unprotected. Mr Brown wouldn't

have wanted me to,' she said to John.

But when Bill had carefully put the body in the grave, John and Ambrose and Beaumont and Camilla and Desdemona and Eustace and Felicity all crept to the edge for a last look at their old friend – 'Uncle' to them, 'Mr' always to John and Janet, and, had they known it, 'Grandad' to the giant who was shovelling the earth back over him.

That night Bill cleaned out the small box on the floor of the Mousery but left it where it was. It'll do for a spare room, he thought. When these nine new mousekins get too boisterous, their parents can get a bit of peace in it.

Time passed, and at Number 16 Gilbert, Hermione, Inigo, Julius, Kingsley, Lindsay, Marmaduke, Niobe

and Olivia went down to join their older brothers and sisters in all the fun and games that went on in the cellar.

John came out of the spare room and settled himself comfortably beside Janet in the big box.

'D'you think we shall have any more babies, dear?' he asked her.

'I shouldn't be at all surprised,' she replied.

The one member of the family who was different from the rest – as he always had been – was Beaumont. Once his father had left the spare room, he took it over, so as to be near his new friends.

Because he had grown so close to the young giant, Beaumont had seen a good deal of the fancy mice. He would go up and down the cages on the low tables in the Mousery and chat with them through the bars – the pink-eyed whites, the black-eyed whites, the chocolates, the fawns, the plum-coloured mice and the Dutch mice. Most were civil to him (even the bad-tempered pink-eyed buck) and, had he known it, quite a few of the young does rather fancied this friendly talkative young buck.

Bill noticed that his tame pet housemouse spent a lot of time looking and squeaking at one very pretty plum-coloured doe. He offered a bit of food to Beaumont, who came on to the palm of the giant's hand as usual, and then he popped him into an

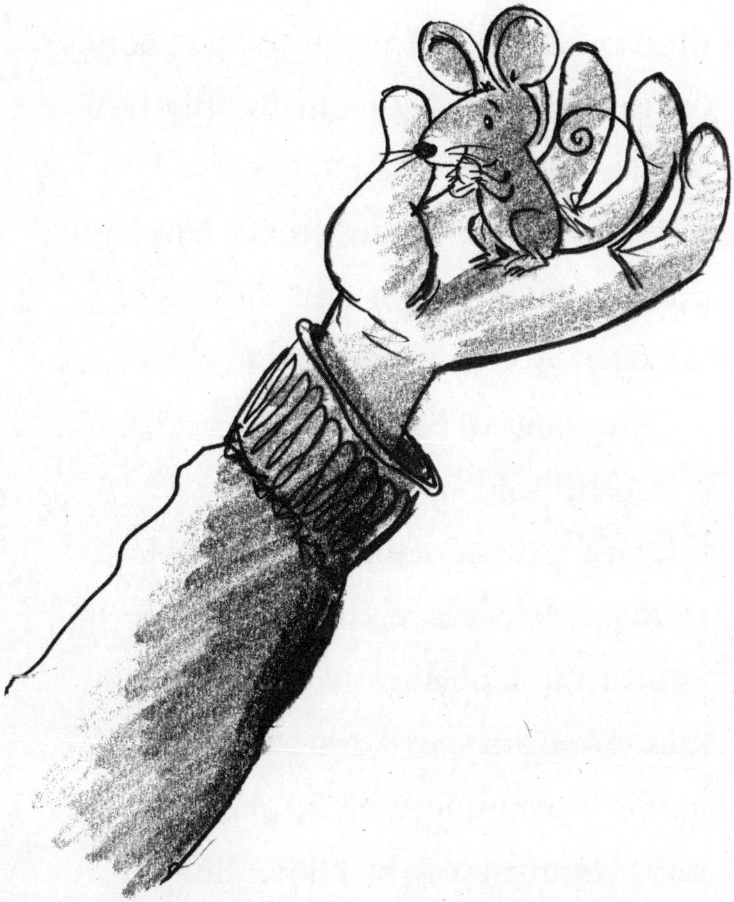

empty cage and, catching the pretty plum-coloured doe, put her in too.

One morning Bill woke to the sound of much squeaking from the big box on the Mousery floor.

'I want to be alone, John,' Janet was saying. 'Go away, please.'

'Why?'

'I'm going to have some more babies.'

'Gosh!' said John.

Don't have more than eleven, he thought, because then we'll reach the end of the alphabet, like Mr Brown said. How on earth am I to think of names beginning with X or Z? I'll ask Beaumont, he might know. But there was no sign of his son.

John climbed up and went along the tables, looking into each cage. In the

last one of all was a pretty little fancy doe, a plum-coloured one, but she was not alone.

'Beaumont!' cried John. 'What are you doing in that cage?'

'Just having a chat with a friend, Dad. I'll be out soon. How's Mum?'

'Having babies,' said John.

'Gosh!' said Beaumont.

When John returned later to the big box, Janet had had the babies.

'How many?' asked John.

'Eleven,' replied Janet.

As they spoke, Bill was letting his pet housemouse out of the fancy plum-coloured doe's cage, and soon Beaumont appeared.

'How on earth,' his father said to him out of Janet's hearing, 'am I going to think of names beginning with X or Z?'

'Easy, Dad,' said Beaumont. 'Just call it "Ecks" or "Zed", boy or girl. By the way, Dad,' he went on, 'I think you might like to know something, something that I guess Uncle Brown would have been pleased about.'

'What?' asked John.

'Before very long,' said Beaumont, 'I am going to be a dad, Dad.'

'Gosh!' said John Robinson. 'My whiskers! Fancy that! And you're right, Beaumont – Uncle Brown would have been very pleased. Gosh!'

PUFFIN BOOKS

The Hodgeheg

Dick King-Smith served in the Grenadier Guards during the Second World War, and afterwards spent twenty years as a farmer in Gloucestershire, the county of his birth. Many of his stories are inspired by his farming experiences. Later he taught at a village primary school. His first book, *The Fox Busters*, was published in 1978. Since then he has written a great number of children's books, including *The Sheep-Pig* (winner of the Guardian Award and filmed as *Babe*), *Harry's Mad*, *Noah's Brother*, *The Hodgeheg*, *Martin's Mice*, *Ace*, *The Cuckoo Child* and *Harriet's Hare* (winner of the Children's Book Award in 1995). At the British Book Awards in 1991 he was voted Children's Author of the Year. He has three children, a large number of grandchildren and several great-grandchildren, and lives in a seventeenth-century cottage only a crow's-flight from the house where he was born.

Some other books by Dick King-Smith

ACE
THE CUCKOO CHILD
DAGGIE DOGFOOT
DODOS ARE FOREVER
DRAGON BOY
FIND THE WHITE HORSE
THE FOX BUSTERS
HARRY'S MAD
HOW GREEN WAS MY MOUSE
LADY DAISY
MAGNUS POWERMOUSE
MARTIN'S MICE
THE MERMAN
THE MERRYTHOUGHT
THE MOUSE BUTCHER
NOAH'S BROTHER
PADDY'S POT OF GOLD
PRETTY POLLY
THE QUEEN'S NOSE
THE ROUNDHILL
SADDLEBOTTOM
THE SCHOOLMOUSE
THE SHEEP-PIG
THE STRAY
TREASURE TROVE
THE WATER HORSE
THE WITCH OF BLACKBERRY BOTTOM

Dick King-Smith

The Hodgeheg

Illustrated by Ann Kronheimer

PUFFIN BOOKS

PUFFIN BOOKS

Published by the Penguin Group
Penguin Books Ltd, 80 Strand, London WC2R 0RL, England
Penguin Putnam Inc., 375 Hudson Street, New York, New York 10014, USA
Penguin Books Australia Ltd, 250 Camberwell Road, Camberwell, Victoria 3124, Australia
Penguin Books Canada Ltd, 10 Alcorn Avenue, Toronto, Ontario, Canada M4V 3B2
Penguin Books India (P) Ltd, 11 Community Centre, Panchsheel Park, New Delhi – 110 017, India
Penguin Books (NZ) Ltd, Cnr Rosedale and Airborne Roads, Albany, Auckland, New Zealand
Penguin Books (South Africa) (Pty) Ltd, 24 Sturdee Avenue, Rosebank 2196, South Africa

Penguin Books Ltd, Registered Offices: 80 Strand, London WC2R 0RL, England

www.penguin.com

First published by Hamish Hamilton Ltd 1987
Published in Puffin Books 1989
Published in this edition 2003
21

Set in 15/18.5 Perpetua

Made and printed in England by Clays Ltd, St Ives plc

British Library Cataloguing in Publication Data
A CIP catalogue record for this book is available from the British Library

ISBN-13: 978–0–141–31602–4

www.greenpenguin.co.uk

Penguin Books is committed to a sustainable future for our business, our readers and our planet. The book in your hands is made from paper certified by the Forest Stewardship Council.

Chapter One

'Your Auntie Betty has copped it,' said Pa Hedgehog to Ma.

'Oh, no!' cried Ma. 'Where?'

'Just down the road. Opposite the newsagent's. Bad place to cross, that.'

'Everywhere's a bad place to cross nowadays,' said Ma. 'The traffic's dreadful. Do you realize, Pa, that's the third this year, and all on my side of the family too. First there was Grandfather, then my second cousin once removed, and now poor old Auntie Betty . . .'

They were sitting in a flowerbed at their home, the garden of Number 5A of a row of semi-detached houses in a suburban street. On the other side of the road was a Park, very popular with local hedgehogs on account of the good hunting it offered. As well as worms and slugs and snails, which they could find in their own gardens, there were special attractions in the Park. Mice lived under the Bandstand, feasting on the crumbs dropped from listeners' sandwiches; frogs dwelt in the Lily Pond, and in the Ornamental Gardens grass snakes slithered through the

shrubbery. All these creatures were regarded as great delicacies by the hedgehogs, and they could never resist the occasional night's sport in the Park. But to reach it, they had to cross the busy road.

'Poor old Auntie Betty,' said Ma again. 'It's a hard life and that's flat.'

'It's a hard death,' said Pa sourly. 'And that's flat too – talk about squashed, the poor old girl was . . .'

'Ssssshhhhh!' said Ma at the sound of approaching footsteps. 'Not in front of the children,' as up trotted four small figures, exact miniatures of their parents except that their spines were still greyish rather than brown. Three of them were little sows, named by Ma, who was fond of flowers, Peony, Pansy and Petunia. Pa had agreed, reluctantly, to these names but had insisted upon his own choice for the fourth, a little boar. Boys, he said, needed noble-sounding names, and the fourth youngster was therefore called Victor Maximilian St George (Max for short).

Almost from the moment his eyes had opened, while his prickles were still soft and rubbery, Max had shown promise of being a bright boy; and by now his eyes, his ears and his wits were all as sharp as his spines.

‘What are you talking about, Ma?’ he said.

‘Nothing,’ said Ma hastily.

‘You wouldn’t be talking about nothing,’ said Max, ‘or there wouldn’t be any point in talking.’

‘Don’t be cheeky,’ said Pa, ‘and mind your own business.’

‘Well, I suppose it is their business really, Pa, isn’t it?’ said Ma. ‘Or soon will be. They’re bound to go exploring outside our garden before long, and we must warn them.’

‘You’re right,’ said Pa. ‘Now then, you kids, just you listen to me,’ and he proceeded to give his children a long lecture about the problems of road safety for hedgehogs.

Max listened carefully. Then he said, 'Do humans cross the road?'

'I suppose so,' said Pa.

'But they don't get killed?'

'Don't think so,' said Pa. 'Never seen one lying in the road. Which I would have if they did.'

'Well then,' said Max, 'how do they get across safely?'

'You tell me, son. You tell me,' said Pa.

'I will,' said Max. 'I will.'

Chapter Two

Max began his research the very next day. He slipped out of the garden at dusk, ambled along the path by the side wall of Number 5A and crept under the front gate. Immediately, he found himself in a sea of noise.

It was the evening rush-hour and the home-going traffic was at its heaviest.

Cars and motorbikes, buses and lorries thundered past, terrifyingly close it seemed to him, as he crouched outside the gate, and he was confused and dazzled by their lights. The street lamps too lit up the place like day, and Max, nocturnal by nature, made for the darkest spot he could find, in the shadow of a tall litter-bin, and crouched there with hammering heart.

Gradually, he grew a little more accustomed to the din and the glare and, though he dared not move, began to observe the humans, for numbers of pedestrians passed close by him. They were all walking on the narrow road on which he sat, a road raised above the level of the street itself by about the height of a

hedgehog. 'They're safe,' said Max to himself, 'because the noisy monsters aren't allowed up here.'

He looked across the street, and could see that at the far side of it there were other humans, also walking safely on a similar raised road. He did not, however,

happen to see any cross the street.

'But they must cross somewhere,' said Max. 'There must be a place further along the street.'

A part of him, for he was very young,

said that he would find out about that another time and that it would be nice to creep back under the gate to his family. But then another part of him determined to set off to see if he could find this human crossing-place. The street was on a slight slope, and perhaps because of this Max chose to go in the downhill direction. He moved very slowly, keeping close to the outer walls of the front gardens where there was some shadow, and he froze, stock-still, whenever a human passed. No one noticed him.

Soon, the houses gave way to a short row of shops, one of them that very newsagent's opposite which his Great-Aunt Betty had breathed her last, and here his progress was more difficult. The shops were still open, and Max had to choose his moment to make a dash across each brightly lit entrance.

'Phew! This is tiring. Perhaps I should go back home . . .' he said, but then suddenly, not far ahead, he saw what he was seeking. There were humans crossing the street!

Sometimes singly, sometimes in twos and threes, sometimes in quite large groups, they stepped down from the narrow raised road and walked straight across the street with hardly a look to left or right, and stepped up again on the far side, and off they went. And every time that anyone wanted to cross, all the traffic stopped, and waited respectfully until the way was clear again.

This, then, was the magic place! Here humans could cross in perfect safety! 'If humans can, why not hedgehogs?'

reasoned Max. But how do people know the exact spot? How do the cars and lorries know when to stop?

Cautiously, he shuffled nearer, keeping close to the wall, until he found himself beside a tall chequered pole on top of which was a glowing orange globe. Across the street, he could see, was a similar pole, and between these two poles the humans walked while the traffic waited.

Biding his time till a moment when there was no one about, Max crept forward to the edge of the raised road and peered down at the surface of the street. It was striped! It was striped, black and white, all the way from one side to the other. This was the secret!

Chapter Three

By now it was quite late. The rush-hour was over. The shops were shut. All was quiet. I'll wait, thought Max, and then when a car or lorry comes along I'll cross in front of it.

Soon he saw something coming. It was a lorry. He was halfway across when he suddenly realized that the lorry hadn't slowed up at all and was almost on top of him, blinding him with its brilliant lights, deafening him with its thunderous roar. It was not going to stop! Lorries only stopped for people – not hedgehogs!

The lorry driver, who, until he was almost upon the crossing, had been quite unaware of the tiny pedestrian, did the only possible thing. With no time to brake or swerve, he steered so as to straddle the little animal. Looking back in his wing-mirror, he saw that it was continuing on its way unhurt, and he grinned and drove on into the night.

The sheer horror of this great monster passing above with its huge wheels on either side of him threw Max into a blind panic, and he made for the end of the

crossing as fast as his legs would carry him. He did not see the cyclist silently pedalling along close to the kerb and the cyclist did not see him until the last moment. Feverishly the man twisted his handlebars, and the front wheel of the bicycle, suddenly wrenched round, caught Max on the rump and catapulted him head first into the face of the kerbstone.

The next thing that Max recalled was crawling painfully under his own front gate. Somehow he had managed to come

back over the zebra crossing. He had known nothing of the concern of the cyclist, who had dismounted, peered at what looked like a small dead hedgehog, sighed and pedalled sadly away. He remembered nothing of his journey home, wobbling dazedly along on the now deserted pavement, guided only by his sense of smell. All he knew was that he had an awful headache.

The family had crowded round him on his return, all talking at once.

'Where have you been all this time?' asked Ma.

'Are you all right, son?' asked Pa.

'Did you cross the road?' they both said, and Peony, Pansy and Petunia echoed, 'Did you? Did you? Did you?'

For a while Max did not reply. His thoughts were muddled, and when he did speak, his words were muddled too.

'I got a head on the bump,' he said slowly.

The family looked at one another.

'Something bot me on the hittom,' said Max, 'and then I headed my bang. My ache bads headly.'

'But did you cross the road?' cried his sisters.

'Yes,' said Max wearily. 'I hound where the fumans cross over, but –'

'But the traffic only stops if you're a human?' interrupted Pa.

'Yes,' said Max. '*Not* if you're a hodgeheg.'

Chapter Four

'D'you suppose he'll be all right?' said Ma anxiously.

It was dawn, and they were about to retire for the day. The children were already asleep in a thick bed of fallen leaves.

'I should hope so,' said Pa. '"Hodgeheg" indeed! His brains are scrambled.'

Max slept the clock round and halfway round again; he did not stir till the evening of the following day. The shock had sent him into a kind of short, early hibernation.

When at last he woke, his sisters rushed to nuzzle at his nose (the safest nuzzling place for hedgehogs) with squeaks of concern, and his parents left their snail-hunting and came trotting up.

'How are you feeling, dear?' said Ma.

Max considered this. His headache was almost gone, and he was thinking straight, but his speech, he found, would still not behave properly.

'I'm a bet bitter, thanks,' he said.

'You had a nasty knock,' said Pa.

'You need rest,' said Ma. 'Why not get

back into bed? We will bring you some nice slugs.'

'I don't want to bed into get,' said Max. 'I feel quite wake awide. In fact, I feel like walking for a go.'

Pa took a moment to work this one out. Then he said firmly, 'You're not going anywhere, son, d'you hear me? You stay home in the garden for a while. Get your strength back, understand?'

'Yes, Pa,' said Max. 'I'll say what you do.' And he did do what Pa had said, for a week or more.

Peony, Pansy and Petunia fussed over their brother. They brought him the fattest, slimiest slugs they could find, and encouraged him to play their favourite game, Hide-and-Seek. However, this didn't work. When they hid, Max forgot to go and look for them; and when it was his turn, he forgot to go and hide, so busy was he thinking about the business of road-crossing. The girls would count to thirty with their eyes shut, but when they opened them, Max would still be sitting there thinking. Striped bits were no good – he didn't intend trying that again – but maybe, he thought, there were other methods.

His determination to find out was increased when Pa came back early one morning from a visit to the Park, with more bad news. Max overheard him telling Ma.

'Another one gone,' Pa said.

'Not a relation?' said Ma fearfully.

'No,' said Pa. 'Chap from Number 9A just up the road, I didn't know him well, you understand, but he always seemed a decent sort of hog. He was crossing just in front of me, not ten minutes ago. Misjudged it. Motorbike got him. Leaves a wife and six kids.'

That evening Max waited until he was sure that Pa was out of the way, in the garden of Number 5B. The people in 5A always put out bread and milk for Max's family, but the people in 5B often provided something much better for

their hedgehogs – tinned dog food.

Every evening, Pa crept through the dividing hedge to see if he could nick a saucerful of Munchimeat before his neighbour woke from the day's sleep.

'Ma,' said Max, 'I'm walking for a go.'

Ma was quick at translating by now.

'Did Pa say you could go?' she said.

'No,' said Max, 'but he couldn't say I didn't,' and before Ma could do anything he trotted off along the garden path.

'Oh, Max!' called Ma. 'Are you sure you'll be all right?'

'Yes, of course,' said Max. 'I'll be quite KO.'

Once outside the garden gate he turned left and set off up the road, in the opposite direction to his previous effort. By now he was used to the noise and the

brightness, and confident that he was safe from traffic as long as he did not step down into the road. When a human passed, he stood still. The creatures did not notice you, he found, if you did not move.

He trotted on, past the garden of Number 9A with its widow and six kids, until the row of houses ended and a high

factory wall began, so high that he would not have been able to read the notice on it beside the factory entrance: Max Speed 5 mph it said.

Max kept going (a good deal more slowly than this), and then suddenly, once again, he saw not far ahead what he was seeking. Again, there were people crossing the street!

This time they did not go in ones and twos at random, but waited all together and then, at some signal he supposed, crossed at the same time. Max drew nearer, until he could hear at intervals a high, rapid peep-peep-peeping noise, at the sound of which the traffic stopped and the people walked over in safety.

Creeping closer still, tight up against the wall, he finally reached the crossing-place, and now he could see this new magic method. The bunch of humans stood and watched, just above their heads, a picture of a little red man standing quite still. The people stood quite still. Then suddenly the little red man disappeared and underneath him

there was a picture of a little green man, walking, swinging his arms. The people walked, swinging their arms, while the high, rapid peep-peep-peeping noise warned the traffic not to move.

Max sat and watched for quite a long time, fascinated by the red man and the green man. He rather wished they could have been a red hedgehog and a green hedgehog, but that was not really important, as long as hedgehogs could cross here safely. That was all he had to prove, and the sooner the better.

He edged forward, until he was just behind the waiting humans, and watched tensely for the little green man to walk.

Chapter Five

What Max had not bargained for, when the bunch of people moved off at the peep peep-peeping of the little green man, was that another bunch would be coming towards him from the other side of the street. So that when he was about halfway across, hurrying along at the heels of one crowd, he was suddenly confronted

by another. He dodged about in a forest of legs, in great danger of being stepped on. No one seemed to notice his small shape and, indeed, he was kicked by a large foot and rolled backwards.

Picking himself up, he looked across and found to his horror that the green

man was gone and the red man had reappeared. Frantically, Max ran on as the traffic began to move, and reached the far side just in front of a great wheel that almost brushed his backside. The shock of so narrow an escape made him roll up, and for some time he lay in the gutter whilst above his head the humans stepped on to or off the pavement and the noisy green man and the silent red man lit up in turn.

After a while there seemed to be fewer people about, and Max uncurled and climbed over the kerb. He turned right and set off in the direction of home. How to re-cross the street was something he had not yet worked out, but in his experience neither striped bits nor red and green men were the answer.

As usual he kept close to the wall at the inner edge of the pavement, a wall that presently gave place to iron railings. These were wide enough apart for even the largest hedgehog to pass between. Max slipped through. In the light of a full moon he could see before him a wide stretch of grass and he ran across it until the noise and stink of the traffic were left behind.

'Am I where?' said Max, looking round him. His nose told him of

the scent of flowers (in the Ornamental Gardens), his eyes told him of a strange-shaped building (the Bandstand), and his ears told him of the sound of splashing water (as the fountain spouted endlessly in the Lily Pond).

Of course! This was the place that Pa had told them all about! This was the Park!

'Hip, hip, roohay!' cried Max to the moon, and away he ran.

For the next few hours, he trotted busily about the Park, shoving his snout into everything. Like most children, he

was not only nosy but noisy too, and at the sound of his coming the mice scuttled under the Bandstand, the snakes slid away through the Ornamental Gardens and the frogs plopped into the safe depths of the Lily Pond. Max caught nothing.

At last he began to feel rather tired and to think how nice it would be to go home to bed. But which way was home?

Max considered this, and came to the unhappy conclusion that he was lost. Just then he saw, not far away, a hedgehog crossing the path, a large hedgehog, a Pa-sized hedgehog! What luck! Pa had crossed the street to find him! He ran forward, but when he reached the animal he found it was a complete stranger.

'Oh,' said Max, 'I peg your bardon. I thought you were a different hodgeheg.'

The stranger looked curiously at him. 'Are you feeling all right?' he said.

'Yes, thanks,' said Max. 'Trouble is, I go to want home. But I won't know the day.'

'You mean . . . you don't know the way?'

'Yes.'

'Well, where do you live?' asked the strange hedgehog.

'Number 5A.'

'Indeed? Well now, listen carefully, young fellow. Go up this path – it will take you back to the street – and a little way along you'll see a strange sort of house that humans use. It's a tall house, just big enough for one human to stand up in, and it has windows on three sides and it's bright red. If you cross there, you'll fetch up right by your own front gate. OK?'

'KO,' said Max, 'and thanks.'

As soon as he was through the Park railings, he saw the tall, red house. He trotted up close to it. It was lit up, and sure enough there was a human inside it. He was holding something to his ear and Max could see that his lips were moving. How odd, thought Max, moving very close now, he's standing in there talking to himself!

At that instant the man put down the receiver and pushed open the door of the telephone booth, a door designed to clear the pavement by about an inch, the perfect height for giving an inquisitive young hedgehog – for the second time in his short life – a tremendous bang on the head.

Chapter Six

Meanwhile, back at Number 5A, Pa had had a bonanza. Sneaking next door and finding a full saucer of dog food and no sign of his neighbour, he had scoffed the lot.

He came staggering back, very full of himself and Munchimeat, and fell into a deep, bloated sleep.

Ma woke him just before dawn. 'Pa,' she said. 'Wake up. Max hasn't come back.'

Pa opened his eyes and saw her worried face and the three smaller but equally worried faces of Peony, Pansy and Petunia.

'He's been gone all night,' said Ma. 'Oh,

Pa, do you think something's happened to him?'

Pa got to his feet. 'I don't know,' he said, 'but don't fret, Ma. I'll find him.'

'But he could be anywhere. How are you going to know where to look?' Before Pa could answer, he heard a strange voice, coming from the hedge that divided 5A and 5B.

'Excuse me,' said the strange voice, and out poked the head of their neighbour. Pa bristled, his spines standing on end. It's that Munchimeat, he thought. He's found his empty saucer and he's going to cut up rough about it. Well I can play rough too. I don't like the look of him anyway and if he wants a fight, he can have one. We'll soon see who's the better hog.

But before he could think of anything to say, the hedgehog from 5B came out of the hedge and said again, 'Excuse me.'

'Well?' said Pa.

'I couldn't help overhearing what you were saying.'

'Family matter,' growled Pa.

'Exactly. You're worried about your little lad.'

'Oh!' cried Ma. 'Have you seen him?'

'Yes, I have. At least I met a young chap in the Park who said he was lost and looking for the way back to 5A. Unless of course it was a 5A in some other street.'

'Did you notice anything . . . different about him?' asked Ma quickly.

The neighbour looked a trifle embarrassed.

'Well, yes,' he said, 'now that you mention it. He seemed to be having a little bit of difficulty with his speech – muddled some of his words now and then.'

'Like "hodgeheg"?'

'Yes.'

'That's our Max!' cried Ma.

'Was he all right?' asked Pa. 'Not hurt or anything?'

'No, he was fine. I told him the best way to go home. He'll be along soon, I'm sure. Try not to worry.'

Pa cleared his throat awkwardly. His neighbour's kindness greatly added to his feelings of guilt.

'It's very decent of you,' he said.

'Glad to help. That's what neighbours are for.'

'Can we offer you something?' said Ma. 'Some bread and milk?'

'Oh, no thanks,' said the neighbour. 'I had a pretty good night's hunting in the Park. Just as well, because when I got home I found that something had eaten all my Munchimeat.' He looked directly at

Pa, and his eyes were twinkling. 'It was a cat, I expect,' he said, and back through the hedge he went.

'Wasn't that nice of him!' said Ma, and Peony, Pansy and Petunia chanted, 'Nice! Nice! Nice!'

Pa grunted. A part of him thought that he should confess his sin to his neighbour. But then another part of him, for he was very worldly-wise, thought that least said was soonest mended. Life was full enough of headaches without inviting any extra ones.

The same thought occurred to Max when at last he came to his senses. The door of the telephone booth had knocked him out cold, and the neighbour from 5B had not noticed the still, small figure as he hurried to cross the deserted street before the morning rush-hour began.

Oh, thought Max, has any hedgehog ever had a more horrible headache? The last bang I got made me talk a bit funny and I expect this one's made things even worse. I'd better try saying something.

'Oh,' said Max, 'has any hedgehog ever had a more horrible headache?' Max considered this. It sounded fine. Suddenly he felt fine. Even the ache already felt much less.

'My name,' he said softly, 'is Victor Maximilian St George, and,' (he said more loudly), 'I have three sisters called Peony, Pansy and Petunia and I live with Pa and Ma at Number 5A, and,' (he shouted at the top of his voice), 'I am a very lucky

HEDGEHOG!' and without thinking, without listening, without a single glance to left or to right, he dashed across the street, straight in front of the first of that morning's vehicles – the milk van.

The noise that followed was enough to wake the whole street.

First there was a screech as the milkman braked and swerved, and then came the shattering sound of

dozens and dozens of bottles smashing. Lastly came the sound of the milkman's voice cursing every hedgehog ever born, as he danced with rage in a sea of Gold Top and Silver Top, of Semi-skimmed and Skimmed, of Orange Squash and Grapefruit Juice and Fresh Farm Eggs.

Ma and Pa had sent the girls to bed and were waiting up in the growing light of dawn. They were crouching side by side listening, when suddenly the dreadful racket burst upon their ears.

'Sounds like something's got run over,' said Pa heavily. 'Brace yourself, old lady. It could be our Max.'

Ma buried her head and rolled herself into a ball of misery.

At that moment they heard a cheery voice.

'Now, now!' it said. 'What's all the fuss about? There's no point in crying over spilt milk!'

Chapter Seven

What a happy scene of grunting, snuffling, squeaking joy there was in the garden of 5A as the girls were woken to be told the good news! And what a jolly crunching of snails there was as the family celebrated with a feast!

After it all, Max slept heavily, and by evening, when he reappeared, the

neighbour had come through the hedge twice, once to enquire if Max was back and again to ask if he was quite well.

At first Ma and Pa felt a little uncomfortable at these visits, Ma because she knew what Pa had done, Pa because he knew that the neighbour knew. But the matter was not mentioned.

They had been wrong, they found, in

supposing that a family of hedgehogs lived next door. The neighbour had never married and, as elderly bachelors often are, he was rather lonely and very fond of children. He had already invited Peony, Pansy and Petunia to come and play in his garden whenever they liked and, seeing that they were not sure how to address him, had asked them to call him 'Uncle'.

'Uncle what?' they said.

The neighbour scratched his head thoughtfully with his hindfoot.

'Let's see now,' he said. 'I live in the garden of Number 5B. How about "Uncle B"?'

After dark the family were worm-hunting on the lawn when there was a rustling in the dividing hedge and the three girls ran towards it, crying, 'Uncle B! Uncle B! Uncle B!'

'Who's Uncle B?' asked Max.

'Our next-door neighbour,' said Ma. 'That's what the girls call him. They've been playing in his garden.'

‘But, Pa,’ said Max, ‘I thought you couldn’t stick him?’

Pa was saved from replying by the approach of Uncle B, and now Max recognized him.

‘Oh hello, sir,’ he said politely. ‘You’re the gentlehog I met in the Park. Thank you very much for your help.’

'Don't mention it, Max,' said Uncle B. 'Glad to hear from your parents that you're, um, totally recovered.'

'You should stay in the garden, son,' said Pa. 'You're safe in here.'

Max considered this. He had no intention of giving up his research. The neighbour had helped him once. Maybe he could do so again. As if reading his thoughts, Uncle B said, 'Well, I must be running along now. Any time you feel like having a chat, Max, you just pop over.'

The next night Max popped over.

'Hello, young fellow,' said Uncle B. 'Have some Munchimeat. They always give me more than I can manage.'

'No, thanks. It's your advice I need,' said

Max, getting straight to the point.

'Shoot,' said Uncle B.

He listened carefully while Max told him everything that had happened so far in his efforts to find a safe hedgehog-crossing. 'I must say,' he said when Max had finished, 'I admire your spirit. And your ambition. Finding a really safe way to cross roads would benefit the whole of hedgehogkind. But the two methods that humans use don't seem to be suitable for us. No better, it appears from your experiences, than the old time-honoured way – look right, look left, look right again, before going across. One thing strikes me, however.' Uncle B paused.

'What's that, Uncle B?'

'All your research so far has been at night-time because hedgehogs are nocturnal. But humans aren't. They don't see at all well at night, which is why they keep on clobbering us. Now if you could only find a place to cross in broad daylight, then at least they could see us coming. It might pay us to change our habits. Better to lose your sleep than your life, that's what I say.'

'Well,' said Max, 'I suppose that either of the two ways I've tried would work in daylight too. Trouble is with either of them, you've got to get across so quickly. Now if only there was a human who could stop the traffic and make absolutely sure it didn't move till you were safely over.'

'There are humans like that,' said Uncle B. 'I saw one once, when I was out during the day – not something I often do. He was a big man dressed in blue, with a tall domed hat on his head. He just held up his hand and everything stopped while some small humans crossed the street.

Once they were safely on the other side, he waved the traffic on again.'

Max pondered this. 'So,' he said, 'there might be lots and lots of small humans who have to cross the street by day?'

Uncle B nodded.

'And the big humans,' Max continued, 'would worry about the small ones getting across safely?'

'Oh, yes. Just like hedgehogs.'

'So there simply must be a special perfectly safe daytime crossing-place for small humans – now where on earth could that be?'

'You tell me, Max. You tell me,' said Uncle B.

'I will,' said Max. '*I will!*'

Chapter Eight

Max could hardly wait for the next dawn. Something inside him said that today he would at last be successful in his quest; and outside him every one of his five thousand spines tingled with excitement. The more he thought of his conversation with Uncle B, the more he felt convinced that the answer to the problem lay with the small humans. Their crossing-place must be the safest. Follow them and he would find it.

He waited until the family were fast asleep, and then, blinking in the unaccustomed sunlight, he went along the path by the side wall of Number 5A to the front gate. He did not go under it but waited, watching beneath it. Already he had learned that you could tell the age of humans from the size of their feet, and he settled himself to wait patiently until a pair of small ones should come past. When at last they did, he was about to go out and follow but then another pair went by and then several pairs, and then, as the pavement filled up with school-going children, dozens and dozens of small feet

went walking, dancing, skipping, hopping past his gate.

All of them were going in the same direction, to his left, up the road, which would take them, he knew, to the end of

the row of houses and past the factory to the red man and the green man. Was that, after all, where all small humans crossed? He must follow, he must know for sure.

At last, when it seemed to him that no

more feet were coming, Max crept under his gate and set out. Some way ahead he could see the tail of the procession and he hurried after. He had passed the last of the houses and reached the factory entrance when he saw that the crowd was taking no notice of the changing red and green men. They were going to a spot further on. And they were crossing over the road there!

He ran on (under the notice 'Max Speed 5 mph'– and he wasn't far short of it) until he was close enough to see exactly what was going on. And oh, what a scene it was!

'Oh, what a scene it was!' he told the family and Uncle B that evening. 'There was this great big human (it was a female, I could tell by the voice) and she was dressed in a long white coat and she had a black cap with a peak and she carried a long pole and on the top of the pole was a big white round disc with an orange rim and black marks on it – a magic wand it must have been, because she walked out into the middle of the street and held it up and all the traffic stopped dead!'

He paused for breath.

'Then what?' said Pa.

'Then all the small humans went across and the great big female just stood there until the very last one reached the other side safely. And all that time everything stood absolutely still. Buses, lorries, cars, motorbikes, not one of them dared move an inch for fear of the great female and her magic wand!'

'Where did the small humans go, Max?' asked Uncle B.

'Into a huge building,' said Max. 'And I hid myself and watched all day, and at the end of the afternoon they all came out of the building again and there was the great female waiting for them, in her white coat and her black hat, and she waved her wand again and saw them all safely back across. I tell you, it's the ideal place for us – the huge building's right next to the Park. Nothing would ever dare touch us if we were under the protection of that great powerful human!'

'But I don't want to spend the daytime in the Park,' said Pa. 'Setting out in the

CAUTION
CHILDREN
CROSSING

morning and coming back in the afternoon – that's no good to me. I need a good day's sleep.'

'You could still get that, old hog,' said Uncle B. 'You could go over in the morning, find a nice place to lie up – under the Bandstand, let's say – get your eight hours, have a good night's hunting, and come back the following morning. Do it once a week perhaps. You could take your wife and the girls – it'd make a nice outing.'

'Oh please, Pa! Please! Please!' cried Peony, Pansy and Petunia.

Pa considered this. 'One of us ought to try it first. See if it works,' he said. 'And if anyone's going, it's me.'

'Not without me,' said Ma stoutly.

'Why not let me go,' said Uncle B. 'After all, I've had a good long life and if anything goes wrong, there'll be no one to miss me.'

'Oh yes there will!' cried all the family.

'Look,' said Max. 'You don't know which way to go, how to get there, where exactly it is. None of you can go without me.'

'Well, then,' said Ma, 'why don't we all go?'

Chapter Nine

Very early the following morning seven spiny shapes emerged from under the front gates of Numbers 5A and 5B. They set off up the road, passing garden after garden from many of which (like 9B) a hedgehog had set out on a journey to the Park, never to return. If only they could succeed today! Henceforth the street

would be forever safe for all hedgehogkind!

They passed the factory and the automatic crossing with its little red and green men, and came at last to the spot where Max had seen the great female with the magic wand. Opposite them across the street, the school clock showed

six. The hedgehogs concealed themselves in a doorway and settled down to wait.

At a quarter past eight, the lollipop lady arrived. Even the earliest children never appeared before half-past, but she liked to be in good time. She stood stamping her large feet, for it was a crisp morning. She smoothed down her long white coat. She settled her black cap firmly. Then, grasping her staff of office, its circular disc bearing the words 'Caution. Children crossing', she stood at attention at the kerbside, ready for the firstcomers, while the early rush-hour traffic roared past.

Never, for the rest of her life, did the lollipop lady forget the sight that now met her eyes. Coming along the pavement towards her were seven hedgehogs in single file.

'Surely you're not going to school?' said the lollipop lady when they reached her.

The noise she made meant nothing to Max, but he advanced to the edge of the kerb, his nose pointing eagerly across the street, the others lined up behind him.

CAUTION

'We wish to go to the Park,' he said. 'Kindly stop the traffic.' The noise he made meant nothing to the lollipop lady, but his intention was as clear as the day. Raising her magic wand on high, the great female strode into the middle of the street and at the sight of her the traffic meekly halted.

Then, before the astonished eyes of those fortunate enough to witness this historic occasion, there walked across the street a slow, solemn dignified procession – of hedgehogs.

At the rear was Uncle B, shepherding before him Peony, Pansy and Petunia. In front of them was Ma. In front of her was Pa. But at the head of the file there marched that pioneer of road safety, Victor Maximilian St George, a name to be remembered forever by hedgehogs the world over.

*

'Tell us the story of the First Crossing, Mummy,' little hedgehogs would plead at bedtime, and then they would listen, enthralled, to the tale of Max, the hedgehog who became a hodgeheg who became a hero. Always the mothers ended with the same words: '. . . and they all crossed happily ever after!'

Dick King-Smith

Born: Bitton, Gloucestershire
27 March 1922

Jobs: Soldier, farmer, salesman, teacher,
TV presenter and author

When did you start writing?

Started my first book for children, *The Fox Busters*, in 1976, got it published in 1978. Since then I have written so many books that I think I have rather lost count!

Where do you get the ideas for your stories?

Things I've done, people I've met or known, animals I've owned or know, but mostly it's just a question of sitting and thinking.

What are your hobbies?

Writing books for children. Sitting in the garden on summer evenings with a nice drink. Talking to my dogs. Washing up. You'll never catch me buying a dishwasher; it would take all the fun out of it!

Will you give your three top tips on becoming an author?

- Read as widely as you can. Try not to read rubbish, but soak up all sorts of good stories.
- Practise. No good saying, 'I'm going to be a writer'. Get on with it. Write about whatever you fancy.
- Show what you've done to someone whose opinion you respect – Mum, Dad, your teacher. Listen to their comments: don't get upset by them, think about them.

And finally, if you hadn't been a writer, what do you think you would have been?

A farmer still. I'm glad I'm not now, I'm too blooming old to be humping sacks of corn or pitching bales; and I shouldn't like to go back to milking cows. I wish I still had some pigs though...

PUFFIN BOOKS

The Swoose

Dick King-Smith served in the Grenadier Guards during the Second World War, and afterwards spent twenty years as a farmer in Gloucestershire, the county of his birth. Many of his stories are inspired by his farming experiences. Later he taught at a village primary school. His first book, *The Fox Busters*, was published in 1978. Since then he has written a great number of children's books, including *The Sheep-Pig* (winner of the Guardian Award and filmed as *Babe*), *Harry's Mad*, *Noah's Brother*, *The Hodgeheg*, *Martin's Mice*, *Ace*, *The Cuckoo Child* and *Harriet's Hare* (winner of the Children's Book Award in 1995). At the British Book Awards in 1991 he was voted Children's Author of the Year. He has three children, a large number of grandchildren and several great-grandchildren, and lives in a seventeenth-century cottage only a crow's flight from the house where he was born.

Books by Dick King-Smith

ANIMAL STORIES
BACK-TO-FRONT BENJY
CLEVER DUCK
GEORGE SPEAKS
THE GOLDEN GOOSE
THE HODGEHEG
THE INVISIBLE DOG
JULIUS CAESAR'S GOAT
THE JENIUS
THE MAGIC CARPET SLIPPERS
KING MAX THE LAST
MR POTTER'S PET
SMASHER
THE SWOOSE

Colour Young Puffins

BLESSU
DINOSAUR SCHOOL
DUMPLING
FAT LAWRENCE
POPPET
THE GREAT SLOTH RACE

Dick King-Smith

The Swoose

Illustrated by Ann Kronheimer

PUFFIN

PUFFIN BOOKS

Published by the Penguin Group
Penguin Books Ltd, 80 Strand, London WC2R 0RL, England
Penguin Group (USA), Inc., 375 Hudson Street, New York, New York 10014, USA
Penguin Books Australia Ltd, 250 Camberwell Road, Camberwell, Victoria 3124, Australia
Penguin Books Canada Ltd, 10 Alcorn Avenue, Toronto, Ontario, Canada M4V 3B2
Penguin Books India (P) Ltd, 11 Community Centre, Panchsheel Park, New Delhi – 110 017, India
Penguin Group (NZ), cnr Airborne and Rosedale Roads, Albany, Auckland 1310, New Zealand
Penguin Books (South Africa) (Pty) Ltd, 24 Sturdee Avenue, Rosebank 2196, South Africa

Penguin Books Ltd, Registered Offices: 80 Strand, London WC2R 0RL, England

www.penguin.com

First published by Viking 1993
Published in Puffin Books 1994
Published in this edition 2005
5

Set in 17/22.25pt Perpetua

Made and printed in England by Clays Ltd, St Ives plc

British Library Cataloguing in Publication Data
A CIP catalogue record for this book is available from the British Library

ISBN-13: 978–0–14–131824–0

www.greenpenguin.co.uk

One

'Mum,' said Fitzherbert. 'Why do I look different from all the other goslings on the farm?'

He did, there was no denying it. He was larger than the rest, his feet were bigger, and his neck was longer.

'You *are* different,' said his mother.

'Because I'm an only child, d'you mean?'

The other geese all had five or six goslings apiece, but Fitzherbert alone had hatched from his mother's clutch of eggs.

'An only child in more ways than one,' she said. 'I doubt if there's another bird like you in the whole wide world. All these other youngsters will grow up to be ordinary common or garden geese, but not you, Fitzherbert my boy.'

'But I'm a goose like you, Mum, aren't I?' said Fitzherbert.

'No,' said his mother, 'you are not.'

She lowered her voice.

'You,' she said softly, 'are a swoose.'

Fitzherbert coiled his long neck backwards into the shape of an S.

'A what?' he cried.

'Sssssssh!' hissed his mother, and she waddled off to a distant corner of the farmyard, away from all the other geese.

Fitzherbert hurried after her.

'What did you say I was?' he asked.

His mother looked around to make sure they were out of earshot of the rest of the flock, and then she said, 'Now listen carefully. What I am about to tell you must be a secret between you and

me, always. D'you understand?'

'Yes, Mum,' said Fitzherbert.

'You are old enough now to be told,' said his mother, 'why you are unlike all the other goslings on the farm. They are the children of a number of geese, but all of them have the same father.'

'The old grey gander, you mean?'

'Yes.'

'But isn't he my father too?'

'No.'

'Then who is?'

'Your father,' said Fitzherbert's mum, and a dreamy look came over her face as she spoke, 'is neither old nor grey. Your father is young and strong and as white as the driven snow. Never shall I forget the day we met!'

'Where was that, Mum?'

'It was by the river. I had gone down by myself for a swim, when suddenly he appeared, high in the sky above. Oh, the music of his great wings! It was love at first flight! Then he landed on the surface in a shower of spray and swam towards me.'

'But I don't get it, Mum,' said

Fitzherbert. 'What was he? Another sort of goose?'

'No,' said his mother. 'He was a swan.'

'What's that?'

'A swan is the most beautiful of all birds, and your father was the most beautiful of all swans.'

'What was his name?'

'He didn't say. He was a mute swan.'

Fitzherbert thought about all this for a while.

Then he said, 'So I might be the only swoose in the world?'

'Yes.'

'There aren't any other swooses?'

'Sweese.'

'Eh?'

'When there's more than one goose, you say geese. So more than one swoose would be sweese.'

'But there isn't more than one. Just

me. You just said so, didn't you?'

As mothers do, Fitzherbert's mum became fed up with his constant questions.

'Oh, run away and play,' she said.

But playing with the other goslings wasn't a lot of fun for Fitzherbert. Already they had noticed that he was different. They poked fun at him, calling him Bigfeet or Snakyneck, and they wouldn't let him join in their games.

Time passed, and Fitzherbert began to grow his adult feathers. Often, as he thought of his father swooping down from the sky on whistling wings, he flapped his own and wished that he too could fly. Farmyard geese like his mother

and the rest couldn't, he knew – they were too heavy-bodied to get off the ground. But swans could. How about a swoose? And the more he thought about his father, the more he wanted to meet him. So one day he decided to go down to the river by himself. He would say nothing to his mother about it, but just set off when she wasn't looking.

He had never before been out of the farmyard, and he was not at all sure

what the river looked like, let alone where it was, but luck was on his side. He walked across a couple of fields and there it was, in front of him!

Fitzherbert looked at the wide stretch of water, winking and gleaming in the sunlight and chuckling to itself as it flowed along. Never in his life had he swum upon anything but the duckpond at the farm, but this – this is the place for swimming, he thought, and he

waddled down the bank and pushed off.

He paddled about in midstream, looking up at the sky, hoping that a snow-white shape would come gliding down to greet him.

Instead he suddenly turned to see a whole armada of snow-white shapes sailing silently downstream towards him. There must have been at least twenty swans, all making for this stranger who dared to swim upon their river. Their wings were curved in excitement, and the look in their black eyes was far from friendly.

Oh, thought Fitzherbert, as the fleet of swans approached, all now grunting and hissing angrily, oh dear, I really must fly!

Two

As Fitzherbert swam hastily away from his pursuers, he spread his wings and beat them madly on the water in an effort to increase his speed. Harder and harder he flapped, and then he felt his body lift a little so that now, instead of swimming, he was slapping his broad webs on the surface in a kind of clumsy run.

Suddenly he was airborne, and the swans, satisfied that they had seen off the stranger, did not trouble to follow.

It wasn't much of a flight, that first effort. For perhaps a quarter of a mile, Fitzherbert laboured along only a few yards above the water, and then, tired out by his efforts, flopped back down into the river. He looked anxiously around, but to his great relief, there was no sign of the swans. Nasty, bad-tempered creatures, he said to himself. I wasn't doing them any harm. Why, my dad might have been one of that lot. I don't know that I want to meet him after all.

He swam on, looking about him with interest. He could see other birds on the

water – different sorts of duck, and moorhen, and coot – and there was a sudden brilliant flash of colour as a kingfisher darted across. There were people on the river too, in rowing boats and punts, and one very long thin craft shot by with eight large young men pulling at their oars, while a ninth much smaller man steered and shouted at them through a kind of tube held to his mouth.

'In! Out! In! Out!' he called, and the blades dipped and rose as one.

Fitzherbert drifted dreamily with the current, enjoying the sunlit scene, when suddenly a sharp voice cried, 'Avast there, you landlubber, or you'll run us down!'

Startled, the swoose looked down to meet the angry gaze of a small water vole.

'Oh, sorry!' said Fitzherbert. 'I'm afraid I wasn't looking where I was going.'

The vole did not answer, but swam to the bank. Fitzherbert followed.

'I suppose you couldn't tell me?' he said.

The vole turned at the mouth of his burrow.

'Tell you what?' he said.

'Where I'm going?'

The vole stared beadily at the swoose.

'Are you feather-brained?' he said.

'No, I'm Fitzherbert.'

The water vole shook his blunt head as though to clear it.

'Tell us something,' he said. 'You come sailing along without any regard for the rule of the river, and then you go and

talk a load of rubbish. Anyways, I never in my life set eyes on a bird like you before. What are you?'

'I'm a . . .' began Fitzherbert, and then he thought, oh no, I promised Mum I wouldn't tell.

'I can't really say,' he replied.

'You don't know what you are,' said the vole. 'You don't know where you're

going. Next thing, you'll be telling me you don't know what river this is.'

'No. I don't.'

'Then you don't know the name of that town you can see, down at the end of the reach?'

'No.'

'Nor the castle on the hill above it?'

'No.'

'Nor who lives in that castle?'

'No,' said Fitzherbert. 'I've never been outside our farmyard before. But I'd be very grateful if you'd tell me.'

'You're lucky, young fellow,' said the vole. 'You've come to the right chap. Now, if you'd asked a moorhen, or worse, a duck, you'd have been wasting your breath. But there isn't much that I

don't know about this here stretch of the Thames.'

'The what?'

'The Thames. That's the name of this river. Most famous river in all England, I'd say. And that town yonder is Windsor, and that's Windsor Castle above it. Now then, surely you know who lives there?'

'No.'

'Why, the Queen, of course.'

'Oh,' said Fitzherbert. 'What's a queen?' he said.

The water vole sighed deeply.

'You're a bright one,' he said. 'She's only the most important person in the land, that's all.'

At this point a pair of swans appeared in midstream.

Fitzherbert backed into a clump of reeds and kept his head down.

'Now d'you see those swans?' said the vole. 'They belong to the Queen, they do, like every other swan in the country. Royal birds, swans are.'

Oh, thought Fitzherbert, I wonder if sweese are? I bet she's never seen one.

'This queen,' he said. 'What's she called?'

'Victoria. She's been Queen for donkey's years, she has.'

'Donkey's ears?' said Fitzherbert.

'Why, 'tis ages ago she lost her husband.'

'Couldn't she find him again?'

The water vole sighed and continued.

'And ever since she's shut herself up in that castle. Always dressed in black, she is. The Widow of Windsor, they call her.'

'How do you know all these things?' asked Fitzherbert.

'I keep my ears open,' said the water vole. 'Windsor folk come out boating on the river and I listen to all the latest gossip.'

'She doesn't sound very happy, this queen,' said Fitzherbert.

'She isn't. Grumpy old thing, from all accounts.'

'Perhaps she needs cheering up.'

'Easier said than done. Anybody tries making a joke, she says, "We are not amused",' said the vole, and with that he vanished into his burrow.

A moment later he stuck his head out again.

'She might be amused at you,' he said. 'Why don't you pay her a visit?'

Why don't I? thought the swoose.

'I will,' he said, 'and I'll come back and tell you all about it.'

Then it occurred to him that there were probably a great many water voles living beside the Thames.

'So can you tell me your name, please?' he said.

'Alph,' said the vole, and he disappeared once more.

Three

Dressed all in black, Queen Victoria stood at an upper window in Windsor Castle and looked down at the courtyard below. In the centre of this courtyard was a perfect square of brilliantly green grass, a lawn that was not only personally mown by the Royal Head Gardener, but afterwards finely manicured by a number of under-gardeners. No other feet were allowed upon this lawn, save those of the Queen's pet dogs and of the footman who tidied up after them with an elegant brass shovel.

But now it seemed there was a large shape, right in the centre of the square of green.

The Queen held out a hand.

'Our pince-nez,' she said to her Lady of the Bedchamber, and when these were brought, she fitted them upon the bridge of the Royal nose.

For some moments she stared down, and then she said, 'And what, pray, is that?'

'It is a bird, ma'am,' said the Lady of the Bedchamber.

'We can see that,' said Queen Victoria. 'We are not blind. See that it is removed immediately. Whatever is it doing on our grass?' and she turned away from the window.

The Lady of the Bedchamber heaved a sigh of relief that she'd avoided having to answer the Queen's last question. She

could see plainly what the bird had that moment done on the grass.

'That's better!' said Fitzherbert as he waddled away from the large squelchy mess he had just made.

He was feeling pretty pleased with himself. Everything had gone swimmingly. He had swum on down the Thames, keeping well away from swans, and stopping every now and then to feed on juicy water-plants. It was late in the day before he came to the town, so he decided to

wait till next morning before visiting the castle.

At dawn Fitzherbert looked up to see its looming walls and towers. Good job sweese can fly, he thought, and he took off and flew up the hill.

The town of Windsor was still asleep and its streets were as yet empty of the busy horse-drawn traffic. Only a milkman driving his cart with its load of brass-bound wooden churns noticed a large bird fly up Castle Hill and over the

turrets of the Henry VIII Gate.

This, Fitzherbert's second flight, was altogether a much more successful effort. Even so, he tired rapidly, and, seeing a square of grass in an inner courtyard, he landed thankfully upon it. It was a crash-landing that knocked the wind out of him, and for some time he lay and gasped for breath.

Finally recovered, he looked about him. Then he saw a movement at an upper window. Someone was looking down at him. He could not see the figure clearly, but it appeared to be dressed in black!

If that's the Queen, thought Fitzherbert, I'd better make myself comfortable before I meet her. He stood up and

suited his actions to his words.

'That's better!' he said, and he waddled off slowly towards the nearest door. The Lady of the Bedchamber lost no time in contacting the Lord Steward of Her Majesty's Household.

'There's a large bird,' she said to him, 'in the Queen's private courtyard, and she wants it removed immediately.'

'What sort of a bird?' asked the Lord Steward.

‘I don’t know,’ said the Lady of the Bedchamber. ‘It was something like a swan. But, then again, it was something like a goose.’

The Lord Steward of Her Majesty’s Household sent for the Ornithologist Royal, the man who looked after the Queen’s birds.

‘There’s a large bird,’ he said, ‘in Her Majesty’s private courtyard. Get rid of it, will you?’

‘What sort of a bird?’ asked the Ornithologist Royal.

‘Part swan, part goose, apparently.’

‘Part swan, part goose!’ murmured the Ornithologist Royal excitedly to himself as he hurried to do the Lord Steward’s bidding. ‘Could it be . . . ?

Could it be?'

When the door into the courtyard opened, Fitzherbert was disappointed to see a man emerge. He seemed a nice man, however, for he produced some pieces of bread which he offered to the swoose. But no sooner had Fitzherbert begun to eat them than he was grabbed, his wings pinioned to his sides, and he was carried, kicking and struggling, away.

'It is! It is!' said the Ornithologist Royal as he listened to his captive's cries of protest, a blend of the grunting bark of an angry swan and the cackling of an outraged goose. He carried Fitzherbert to the Royal Menagerie, where all manner of creatures were housed, presented as gifts to the Queen by visiting foreign rulers.

'It is!' said the Ornithologist Royal again as he feasted his eyes upon Fitzherbert, now shut in a large cage. 'I had heard tales of such a bird, but never thought to see one! It is a swoose!'

'That bird,' said the Lord Steward of Her Majesty's Household later. 'Have you dealt with it?'

'Yes,' said the Ornithologist Royal.

'What was it?'

'It is a swoose!' said the Ornithologist Royal. 'A cross between a swan and a goose! A *rara avis* indeed! Her Majesty should be told.'

The Lord Steward of Her Majesty's Household remembered enough of his Latin to say to the Lady of the Bedchamber, 'It's a rare bird, the one that was in the Queen's courtyard. Called a swoose apparently. Her Majesty should be told.'

Nervously, for the Queen did not like to be told things, preferring that people should not speak until they were spoken to, the Lady of the Bedchamber approached her sovereign.

'Forgive me, Your Majesty,' she said, 'but that bird that you saw earlier this morning . . .'

'Well?' said the Queen, her face set in its usual grim mode.

'I am given to understand, ma'am, that it is a swoose.'

'A what?'

'A swoose, ma'am.'

To the great astonishment of the Lady of the Bedchamber, something that might almost have been called a small smile appeared on the Royal face. Never

in all the many years she had served at court had the Lady of the Bedchamber seen such a thing.

'A swoose,' said Queen Victoria. 'Why, surely that must be part swan, part goose!'

'Perhaps Your Majesty might care to see the creature?' said the Lady of the Bedchamber.

'We would,' said the Queen.

So it was that Fitzherbert, puzzled and angry at being shut in, saw the doors of the Royal Menagerie opened by a pair of

bewigged footmen and a procession enter.

Followed by the Lord Steward, the Ornithologist Royal and the Lady of the Bedchamber, and attended by the Lord Chamberlain, the Comptroller of Her Majesty's Household, the Master of the Horse and several Ladies-in-Waiting, came a short dumpy figure, dressed all in black.

For some time Queen Victoria stared

at Fitzherbert without speaking. Naturally no one else spoke.

Then the Queen said, 'Are we right? Is this bird indeed half-swan and half-goose?'

'Your Majesty is perfectly correct,' said the Ornithologist Royal.

'And it is a rarity?'

'Indeed, ma'am.'

'We do not like to see it so imprisoned. Open the door of its cage.'

'But, ma'am . . .' began the

Ornithologist Royal, fearing that the bird might misbehave itself in some way, might even (dreadful thought) peck the Royal ankles.

'Do as we say,' snapped the Queen, 'and look sharp about it,' and the Ornithologist Royal looked very sharp indeed.

Fitzherbert could, of course, understand nothing of the medley of sounds that the humans made. However, it was clear to him that, thanks to the Queen, he was to be a prisoner no longer, and he thought that he should show his gratitude.

With measured tread he walked out of the cage and stood at attention before

the Queen. Then he slowly uncurled his long neck and laid his head upon the ground at the very feet of the monarch in a gesture that was the nearest he could come to a courtly bow.

To the amazement of the Lord Steward of Her Majesty's Household and the Ornithologist Royal and the Lady of the Bedchamber and the Lord Chamberlain and the Comptroller of Her Majesty's Household and the Master of the Horse and the Ladies-in-Waiting and the two bewigged footmen, none of whom recalled ever seeing such a sight before, Queen Victoria looked down at the swoose and smiled broadly.

'We are amused,' said the Widow of Windsor.

Four

The news that something had made the Queen smile for the first time in a quarter of a century, or, in other words, since the death of her husband, Prince Albert, spread like wildfire among the courtiers at Windsor Castle. Not only had she smiled once, but had continued to do so, and had even spoken quite pleasantly to

a number of people. More, she had exchanged her widow's cap of black for one of white lace, and all because of that swoose!

'It's all so beautifully timed,' the Lord Steward of Her Majesty's Household said to the Lady of the Bedchamber. 'Next year it's the Queen's Golden Jubilee as you know, when the whole kingdom will be celebrating her fifty years on the throne, and she will have to go about and show herself to the people. How pleased they will be to see her wearing a happy face again after all those years of gloom. The greatest care must be taken of that bird.'

Unfortunately, it wasn't.

The very next morning, the

Ornithologist Royal came in armed with a large pair of scissors. He intended to clip the flight feathers of one of the swoose's wings, a painless operation which would render the bird incapable of flight. Little did he guess that Fitzherbert had plans of his own.

First, despite having been released from his cage the previous evening on the Queen's orders, he had been shut up again as soon as she had gone, and this he did not like.

Second, he was longing to tell the water vole all about his audience with Queen Victoria.

So the moment the Ornithologist Royal opened the cage, Fitzherbert pushed past him and made his way as fast

as he could along a corridor and out through a door.

'Stop! Stop!' cried the Ornithologist Royal, hurrying after him, scissors in hand, and then could only stand and watch in horror as the swoose took wing and flew away towards the Thames.

Fitzherbert flew upriver, trying to remember whereabouts it was that he had met the vole, when suddenly he saw him swimming across a little backwater.

'Alph!' he cried, and swooping down, landed with a great splash. He looked around, but could only see a couple of moorhens that squawked angrily at him from the rushes.

Then he saw a blunt brown head break surface.

'Alph!' he cried again. 'Remember me?'

'How could I forget you?' said the vole sharply. 'First time we met, you nearly ran me down, and now you drop out of the sky almost on top of me. You're a clumsy great hummock and no mistake.'

'Sorry, Alph,' said Fitzherbert. 'I was in a hurry to tell you. I've seen the Queen! And what d'you think – she smiled at me!'

'Fancy!' said Alph.

He swam to the bank, and climbed out and shook himself.

'Wonder why?' he said.

'I don't really know,' said Fitzherbert. 'She seemed to like me. And they were all very pleased. Everyone was ever so nice to me.'

'They didn't shut you up then?' said Alph.

'Well, yes, they did, but I escaped.'

'What for?'

'Why, to come and find you and thank you.'

'What for?'

'For suggesting I should visit the Queen. It was a great idea. I must be getting back now, I dare say Her Majesty's missing me, wouldn't you think?'

For a moment the water vole did not answer. He sat on his haunches, combing his very small round ears with his forepaws. Then he fixed his very small beady eyes on the swoose.

'I hope you know what you're doing,

young fellow,' he said. 'It's all very well being the Queen's pet, but what if she gets fed up with you, eh?'

'Well, then I suppose she'd just let me go.'

'She might,' said Alph. 'Or she might not. There's plenty of meat on you from

what I can see. You don't want to end up like that, do you?'

'End up like what?' asked Fitzherbert.

'Eaten,' said Alph. 'At Windsor,' and down his burrow he went.

Five

Meanwhile, back at the castle, panic reigned.

Everyone now knew that the swoose had flown away. Everyone, that is, except the Queen, and all were waiting, horrified, for the moment when she would find out.

The Ornithologist Royal in particular

was in a cold sweat. He had let the bird escape. He, everyone agreed, would lose his job.

So it was with a great sigh of relief that the worried man saw Fitzherbert come winging back over the battlements to

land once more in the inner courtyard. Armed with his scissors, he hurried out.

As he did so, an upper window was flung open and a commanding voice called out, 'Stop! And wait for us!'

The Ornithologist Royal stopped and waited, his heart in his mouth. What if the bird should take off again?

But Fitzherbert had no intention of doing so. To begin with, the flight to Alph and back had been quite tiring, and secondly, though he did not understand

the words, he recognized the note of command in the Royal tones.

In a little while Queen Victoria emerged from a side door into the courtyard, leaning upon the arm of the Lady of the Bedchamber.

The Ornithologist Royal was a tall man, but he felt very small at the sight of the dumpy little Queen's frowning face.

'What,' she said, 'are you doing with those scissors?'

'If you please,

Your Majesty,' said the Ornithologist Royal, 'I was intending to pinion the bird.'

'To pinion it?'

'To cut the flight feathers of one wing, ma'am.'

'With what object?'

'To prevent the bird from leaving you.'

'Leaving *us*?' said the Queen. 'Flying away, from *our* presence, do you mean? What an absurd idea! You will put those scissors away, sir, or it will be you who is leaving.'

Soon the whole court knew that, far from being chopped off, the feathers of the Queen's pet swoose must on no account be so much as ruffled. He was

to have the choicest food, such as fresh young vegetables from the kitchen gardens, brought to him by the Royal Head Gardener in person, and Scotch oatmeal porridge served by the Queen's manservant, John Brown.

In addition, the Royal Head Gardener's little daughter was appointed Swoosegirl-in-Waiting, to take Fitzherbert for daily walks in Windsor Great Park. By night, however, he was still shut in the Royal Menagerie for his own safety (for foxes, the Ornithologist Royal was sure, would be no respecters of sweese), but the Queen came in each evening to see her pet. Fitzherbert would make his bow, the Queen would smile, and everyone would heave a sigh

of relief at the welcome change that had come over the crusty old lady.

At first Fitzherbert found the nights trying. By day there were so many people making a fuss of him, but at night he was lonely. None of the other inmates of the menagerie such as parrots or monkeys bothered to talk to him, and he thought how nice it would be to have a chat with someone like Alph.

How pleasant it was then to hear a friendly voice one evening, just after the Queen and her company had left.

A cultured voice it was, a little singsong in tone, and altogether quite unlike the country voice of the water vole, though in fact it belonged to another rodent.

'How are you settling in, may one ask?' said the voice, and Fitzherbert looked up to see that the speaker was a rat.

He had come across rats before in the farmyard, ugly-looking creatures with rough brown coats, but this one was quite different.

To begin with, it was smaller and slenderer than a farm rat, with large thin ears and the

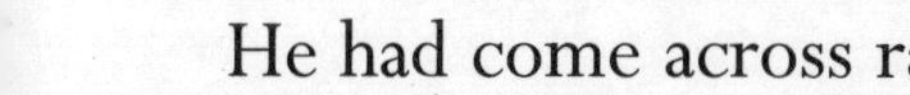

longest of tails, longer even than its whole body. And second, that body was clothed in the glossiest of blue-black fur.

Altogether it was the most elegant animal, Fitzherbert thought, and he answered politely, 'Quite well, thank you.'

'Allow me to introduce myself,' said the black rat. 'My name is Maharanee.'

'Fitzherbert,' said the swoose.

'A noble-sounding name,' said Maharanee.

'So's yours,' said Fitzherbert. 'It sounds foreign.'

'So it is,' said the black rat. 'Her Majesty, as you may know, is also Empress of India, and her loyal subjects within the raj often send her gifts of animals. I stowed away with such a shipload, believing my proper place to be at court.'

'I don't quite understand,' said Fitzherbert.

'I myself am of Royal blood. I was

born in a palace, so it is fitting that I should associate myself with Her Majesty. Maharanee, you see, means "Great Queen".'

'Oh,' said Fitzherbert. 'So you're a favourite of hers too, are you?'

'I wouldn't exactly say that,' replied Maharanee. 'The English, you know, are less than friendly towards our brown

cousins and are apt to tar black rats with the same brush. I tend therefore to keep a low profile. But you certainly seem to have taken Her Majesty's fancy. You're quite the Royal pet.'

Until she gets fed up with me, thought Fitzherbert, and then suddenly remembered that that was what Alph had said.

'Look here, Maharanee,' he said. 'You

don't suppose she'd ever . . . eat me, do you?'

The black rat looked at the swoose consideringly, and strangely, she too echoed Alph's words.

'She might,' she said. 'Or she might not. But if you are ever to be on the menu, I shall hear about it. I spend a good deal of time in the castle kitchens. Rely upon me to give you warning, Fitzherbert my friend.'

So the time passed pleasantly for the swoose. Not only did he enjoy the favour of the Queen, with all the benefits that came with it, but now he had two friends.

At night he had long and interesting

conversations with the much-travelled Maharanee, and as often as he liked, he flew upriver for a chat with the home-spun Alph. To see the swoose go gave the Ornithologist Royal fifty fits at first, but gradually he became confident that the bird would always return.

All went well until the Head Cook and Bottlewasher at Windsor Castle reached retirement age and was replaced.

The black rat arrived in Fitzherbert's cage one evening in high excitement.

'What do you think!' she said. 'There is a French chef in the kitchen! No more stodgy, unimaginative English cooking. Now we shall see food fit for a Queen and leftovers fit for a Maharanee! There is nothing that a good chef cannot cook.'

Except sweese, I hope, thought Fitzherbert.

Six

Soon after this, some foreign cousins of the Queen were due to stay at the castle, and the new chef was instructed to plan a modest ten-course dinner for the visitors.

'And make sure that the main course is something really spectacular, said the Lord Steward.

The French chef sought the advice of the Queen's Butler.

'Is there something,' he asked, 'that only Royalty may eat, *monsieur*?'

The Queen's Butler thought for a moment.

'Why, yes,' he said. 'There is. Swan. Royal birds, swans are. No one else is allowed to eat them. There are plenty down there on the Thames.'

Roast swan and all the trimmings, thought the chef. That will indeed be *spectaculaire*!

All might yet have been well had not the chef lost his way in the many halls and corridors of the castle. One morning he took from his knife-rack the largest of his carving knives, closely watched,

10,000
ECIPES

though he did not know this, by an elegant blue-black creature crouching beneath a dresser.

He fingered the knife's edge, and then, shaking his head at its bluntness, set off to have it sharpened at the Armoury. However, he failed to understand the directions given him, and became confused in the maze of passages.

Opening a door, he found himself in an

enclosed courtyard, in the centre of which was a perfect square of brilliantly green grass.

Right in the centre of it was a large shape.

The chef's hand tightened on his carving knife.

'*Voilà*!' he said softly. 'No need to go to the river. The bird has come to me!'

Fitzherbert was dozing, a little tired

after his daily walk. The Swoosegirl-in-Waiting had gone home to tea, and the Ornithologist Royal had not yet arrived to take the Queen's pet to the menagerie for the night.

Suddenly the swoose was woken by the voice of Maharanee.

'Fly, Fitzherbert, fly!' squealed the black rat.

Opening his eyes, the swoose saw a man approaching, a man dressed all in white and wearing a tall white hat, a man brandishing a huge knife!

At that very moment, a door opposite opened, and out of it, supported by her Lady of the Bedchamber, came Queen Victoria.

In his terror, Fitzherbert totally

disregarded Maharanee's instructions. Indeed, he completely forgot that he possessed his wild father's powers of flight and reverted to his mother's farmyard waddle.

Grunting, barking, cackling at the top of his voice, he hastened towards the Queen and turned and stood in front of her, his eyes fixed in horror on that dreadful knife that was destined, he was sure, for his throat.

Then, drawn by the terrible noise that the swoose was making, a host of people appeared and fell upon the wretched chef and dragged him away.

Later that evening, when all had been explained (and the luckless chef sent hurriedly back to France), the Queen came with her company into the menagerie. They brought a gilded chair for her, and she sat and looked at her swoose.

'What courage!' she said quietly. 'Not only did he sound the alarm, but he stood before us, thinking that we were to be murdered. He believed that he was saving us!'

Everyone looked at everyone else, but nobody said anything.

'We shall reward him for his bravery,' said the Queen, and those nearest could see that her old eyes were twinkling.

'Open the door of the cage,' she commanded, and they opened it.

Fitzherbert stepped forward and stood at attention before the monarch's chair, and then, as always, lowered his head to the floor.

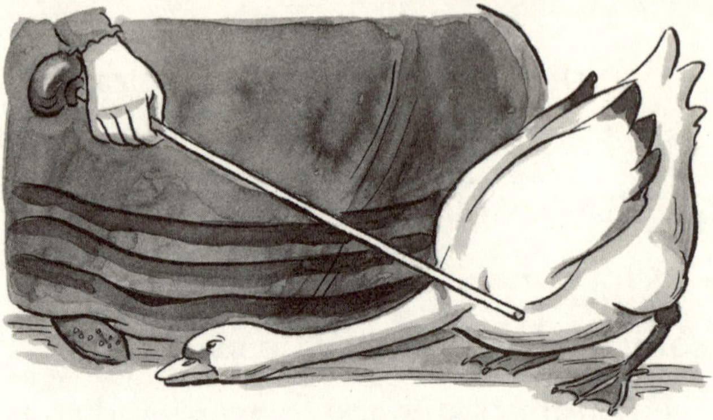

The Queen looked round at her courtiers and she positively grinned.

Then she raised her silver-headed, ebony walking stick and with it she lightly touched Fitzherbert upon one shoulder.

'I dub thee Knight!' said Queen Victoria in a loud voice. 'Arise, Sir Swoose!'

And slowly, proudly, to a burst of clapping from the smiling company of watchers, Fitzherbert arose.

PUFFIN BOOKS

The Golden Goose

Dick King-Smith served in the Grenadier Guards during the Second World War, and afterwards spent twenty years as a farmer in Gloucestershire, the county of his birth. Many of his stories are inspired by his farming experiences. Later he taught at a village primary school. His first book, *The Fox Busters*, was published in 1978. Since then he has written a great number of children's books, including *The Sheep-Pig* (winner of the Guardian Award and filmed as *Babe*), *Harry's Mad*, *Noah's Brother*, *The Hodgeheg*, *Martin's Mice*, *Ace*, *The Cuckoo Child* and *Harriet's Hare* (winner of the Children's Book Award in 1995). At the British Book Awards in 1991 he was voted Children's Author of the Year. He has three children, a large number of grandchildren and several great-grandchildren, and lives in a seventeenth-century cottage only a crow's flight from the house where he was born.

Some other books by Dick King-Smith

ACE
THE CUCKOO CHILD
DAGGIE DOGFOOT
DODOS ARE FOREVER
DRAGON BOY
FIND THE WHITE HORSE
THE FOX BUSTERS
HARRY'S MAD
HOW GREEN WAS MY MOUSE
LADY DAISY
MAGNUS POWERMOUSE
MARTIN'S MICE
THE MERMAN
THE MERRYTHOUGHT
THE MOUSE BUTCHER
NOAH'S BROTHER
PADDY'S POT OF GOLD
PRETTY POLLY
THE QUEEN'S NOSE
THE ROUNDHILL
SADDLEBOTTOM
THE SCHOOLMOUSE
THE SHEEP-PIG
THE STRAY
TREASURE TROVE
THE WATER HORSE
THE WITCH OF BLACKBERRY BOTTOM

Dick King-Smith

The Golden Goose

Illustrated by Ann Kronheimer

PUFFIN BOOKS

PUFFIN BOOKS

Published by the Penguin Group
Penguin Books Ltd, 80 Strand, London WC2R 0RL, England
Penguin Putnam Inc., 375 Hudson Street, New York, New York 10014, USA
Penguin Books Australia Ltd, 250 Camberwell Road, Camberwell, Victoria 3124, Australia
Penguin Books Canada Ltd, 10 Alcorn Avenue, Toronto, Ontario, Canada M4V 3B2
Penguin Books India (P) Ltd, 11 Community Centre, Panchsheel Park, New Delhi – 110 017, India
Penguin Books (NZ) Ltd, Cnr Rosedale and Airborne Roads, Albany, Auckland, New Zealand
Penguin Books (South Africa) (Pty) Ltd, 24 Sturdee Avenue, Rosebank 2196, South Africa

Penguin Books Ltd, Registered Offices: 80 Strand, London WC2R 0RL, England

www.penguin.com

First published 2003
16

Set in 15/18.5 Perpetua

Made and printed in England by Clays Ltd, St Ives plc

British Library Cataloguing in Publication Data
A CIP catalogue record for this book is available from the British Library

ISBN-13: 978–0–14–131618–5

www.greenpenguin.co.uk

Mixed Sources
Product group from well-managed forests and other controlled sources
www.fsc.org Cert no. SA-COC-1592
© 1996 Forest Stewardship Council
FSC

Penguin Books is committed to a sustainable future for our business, our readers and our planet. The book in your hands is made from paper certified by the Forest Stewardship Council.

Chapter One

Farmer Skint was a poor unfortunate man.

He was poor because he was not a very good farmer. He always sold things for less than other people did, and he always paid more than other people for whatever he bought.

He was unfortunate because nothing

ever seemed to go right for him. At haymaking or at harvest time, it always seemed to rain. His cows often got foul-in-the-foot, his pigs often got swine fever, and his chickens were always being eaten by foxes.

There came a time when Farmer Skint had lost nearly all his animals. He'd had to sell his remaining cows and pigs and what chickens were left, and all he had now on Woebegone Farm was a

pair of geese: a gander called Misery and a goose called Sorrow.

'I'm sorry, Janet,' he said to his wife, 'but things have got so bad that we shall have to sell the farm.'

'Oh no, John, no, John, no!' cried Mrs Skint. 'What shall we do then? The children have to be fed and clothed.'

Farmer Skint looked sadly at his two children, a little girl named Jill and a baby boy named Jack. Both looked very hungry. 'I don't know about clothes,'

said the farmer, 'but at least we've still got something left to eat.'

'What?' asked Mrs Skint.

'The geese.'

'Oh no, John! Not poor Misery and Sorrow!'

'Well, Misery anyway,' said Farmer Skint. 'Not Sorrow. Not yet. She's sitting on a clutch of eggs. I'll have to let her hatch them out first.'

Later that day he went into his orchard where there was an old hut. Inside it, Sorrow was sitting on her eggs. Misery the gander was standing guard outside and he cackled angrily at the farmer.

'Sorry, old chap,' said Farmer Skint, 'but you may be for the chop one of these fine days.'

Then he went into the hut and carefully lifted Sorrow off her eggs. She pecked at him furiously but he was so low-spirited that he took no notice.

But he took notice quickly enough when he peeped in the nest.

He'd had a look the day before and there

had been four eggs, four dirty-white goose eggs, and he was expecting to see a fifth. He was right. There were now five eggs.

But what made Farmer Skint gasp with surprise, what made his heart race and his breath come quickly, what made his eyes nearly pop out of his head, was the colour of that fifth egg. Dirty-white it was not.

It was golden.

In the weeks that followed, Sorrow sat steadily upon her five eggs, while Misery mounted guard outside the hut. At nights, Farmer Skint shut him inside for fear of the fox.

Then there came a morning when the farmer went into his orchard and was about to open the door of the old hut to let Misery out. But then he thought that the time had come to sacrifice the gander. 'At least,' he said to himself, 'we can have one really good square meal before we all starve,' and he made ready to catch up the bird as he undid the bolt on the door.

Yet it was not Misery who came out first, but Sorrow, and behind her came five newly hatched goslings, and behind them marched their proud father.

Out of the darkness of the hut into the brightness of a lovely May morning they all came, and what he now saw made Farmer Skint catch his breath.

Four of the downy goslings were a pale yellowish colour, like most goslings are, but the fifth one was a wonderful bright gold, all over. Even its beak was gold, as were its little webbed feet.

Out of the golden egg, thought Farmer Skint dazedly, has come a golden gosling that will grow into a golden goose!

As the geese stood around him, waiting for the food in the bucket that the farmer was carrying, the golden gosling waddled right up to his feet and stood looking at him with eyes that were not only bright with intelligence but also golden in colour.

Something made poor unfortunate Farmer Skint squat down on his heels and put out a hand and stroke the gosling's golden back. Had he tried to do this to its brothers or sisters, they would surely have backed away, but the golden gosling stood quite still and even nodded its little head as though it was enjoying his touch.

But more than that, much more than that, as he stroked, Farmer Skint began gradually to feel happier. He looked at his little family of geese and knew,

with certainty, that even to feed his own family he could not possibly kill Misery. It was his own misery, he felt, that had suddenly received its death blow.

He looked around his orchard and at his fields beyond and decided he could not possibly sell them. He looked up into the sky and saw what a glorious morning it was, with a sun as golden as his gosling.

Quickly he tipped the food for the geese out of the bucket and ran back to the farmhouse, calling for his wife. When she came out, carrying baby Jack and holding Jill by the hand, she wore a worried face.

'Oh, what is it now, John?' she cried. 'What has happened? What has gone wrong?'

'It's Sorrow,' he said.

'Oh no, John! Not more bad news?'

But then Mrs Skint looked more carefully at her husband and saw that he was smiling. It's ages since I saw him smile, she thought. For that matter, it's ages since I did.

'Come along with me, Janet,' said Farmer Skint, and he led the way out into the orchard, where Misery and Sorrow were finishing their breakfast while their five children pottered about in the sunshine.

'Now then,' said the smiling farmer to his worried wife, 'what d'you think of that, eh?' and he pointed to the golden gosling. 'Just look at the colour of it!'

Mrs Skint looked in wonder, and then, letting go of Jill's hand and holding Jack in her other arm, she bent down and stroked that downy golden back. As she did so, the look of worry gradually left her face and she too began to smile.

Husband and wife looked at one another.

'D'you feel as happy as I do?' asked the farmer.

'Oh yes, John, yes, John, yes! I felt it the moment I touched her.'

'Her?'

'Yes. Something tells me it's a little goose, not a gander.'

'Well, we'd better think of a name for her,' said Farmer Skint. 'She may be the daughter of Misery and Sorrow but she'll have to have a happier name than that.'

'How about Joy?' suggested his wife.

'Joy,' said Farmer Skint. 'That's perfect. Just what we need.'

Chapter Two

As they walked back up to the farmhouse, they met the postman, who had parked his van by the garden wall and was just about to walk up the path to the front door. Instead, he handed the letters to the farmer.

'Thank you! Thank you very much!' said Farmer Skint. 'It's a beautiful morning,

isn't it? Makes you glad to be alive!'

Whatever's come over him? thought the postman as he drove away. Usually he's a miserable sort of fellow. In fact, I've never seen him smile before, but just now he was grinning like a Cheshire cat.

Farmer Skint ate his breakfast, the letters lying unopened on the table beside him. It was his habit not to look at anything the postman might have brought until he'd finished eating. By then he'd feel more able to deal with the post, which consisted mostly of bills.

'A good dish of bacon and eggs for breakfast,' Farmer Skint's father had been used to say, 'and a man can face up to anything. Bacon and eggs give a good lining to the stomach.'

But now there were no pigs or chickens on Woebegone Farm, so the poor unfortunate farmer had to make do with toast and a scrape of jam. Unfortunate he may have been, and poor, at that moment, he still was, yet he ate his food with gusto. Then he took a paper-knife and slit open the three envelopes which the postman had brought.

The first two contained bills and for a moment his smiles were replaced by a frown, but then he opened the third envelope and the frown vanished, to be replaced by a look of total amazement.

After a while he raised his head and looked around the kitchen table, at baby Jack in his high chair, at little Jill, at his wife.

'Would you be*lieve* it!' said Farmer Skint in a hoarse whisper.

'Believe what, John?' asked Mrs Skint, her smiles now changing to a frown.

'I've been and gone and won the

Premium Bonds, that's all,' said her husband.

'What d'you mean?'

'Well, years and years ago, when I was a boy, my old dad bought me a Premium Bond. A one-pound bond it was. It never won anything of course. Till now.'

Farmer Skint looked at his wife and his face broke into the biggest smile you can imagine.

'Till now,' he said again. 'Now it has won something, Janet, that old one-pound bond has. Guess how much.'

'Oh, I don't know, John,' said Mrs Skint. 'Ten pounds perhaps?'

'A lot more than that.'

'A hundred pounds?'

'Not enough noughts.'

'Oh no, John, don't tell me – you've never won a thousand pounds, have you?'

'No,' said Farmer Skint. 'This letter is to say that that old Premium Bond that my old dad bought me has won ten thousand pounds! Look, here's the cheque,' and he waved it in front of his wife.

‘Oh John!’ gasped Mrs Skint in a choked voice. ‘Our luck has changed at last.’

‘Looks like it,’ said the farmer. ‘We shall have money in the bank again. Or we shall have once I’ve paid this cheque in. There’s still a drop of petrol left in the old car, so leave the washing-up – we’ll all go straight into town.’

‘And buy some new clothes for the children,’ Mrs Skint said.

‘And food, all sorts of food, specially bacon and eggs. We’ll have a second breakfast when we get back.’

‘And we’ll get sweets for the children.’

‘And petrol for the car.’

‘And new shoes for the children.’

‘And, Janet, you could have a new washing machine.’

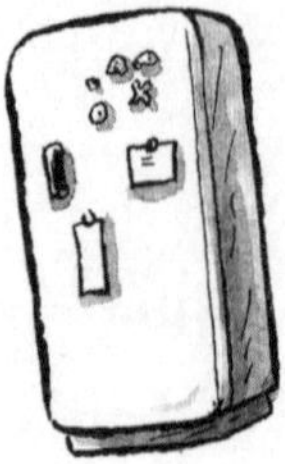

'And a new fridge.'

'And a new telly.'

'And toys for the children.'

'And it's Market Day tomorrow. I could buy a couple of cows.'

'And some hens.'

'And a pig or two.'

'And perhaps a pet rabbit for the children. Oh John, everything in the garden is lovely, and you know why, don't you?'

'Yes. I've just won ten thousand pounds.'

'Yes, but why have you? What's happened to change you from a poor unfortunate man to a rich and lucky one? Who is the cause of all this luck?'

'It must be Joy,' said Farmer Skint.

Chapter Three

What a shopping spree the Skints had that day! As well as buying some of the things they'd talked about, Farmer Skint bought a big sack of corn for the geese and a few sacks of meal and bran which he would mix together to make their daily mash. Misery and Sorrow had been living on rather poor rations recently and they were obviously delighted to be given much more food.

'Kark! Kark!' they cried in their pleasure.

But one morning, after the farmer had given them their breakfast and was eating his own (a good dish of bacon and eggs), he suddenly heard them making quite a different noise – a loud, urgent honking which meant, he knew, that were was danger about. Geese are good watchdogs, which is why the ancient Romans kept them to guard their most important temple. They knew the geese would make a great din if enemies approached.

Farmer Skint was neither ancient nor a Roman, but as soon as he heard the row that Misery and Sorrow were making, he jumped up from the breakfast table. On his way out of the farmhouse, he grabbed his gun, for he had a pretty good idea of what the approaching enemy was.

He was right. Sneaking among the orchard trees was a red bushy-tailed figure.

Misery and Sorrow stood bravely side by side facing the fox, their children grouped behind them. Farmer Skint ducked down behind the low wall of the orchard. His

two geese would, he knew, do their best to protect their family, even at the cost of their own lives, but the goslings would be easy meat for the red raider, who was by now very close.

Long muzzle pointed ahead, eyes fixed upon its intended prey, the fox was poised for a final deadly rush, when Farmer Skint fired both barrels.

The alarm cries of the geese now changed to shouts of triumph as the farmer came forward to pick up the limp body of their enemy.

'And d'you know what, Janet?' he said to his wife later. 'Misery and Sorrow and four of the goslings just went off down to the pond as though nothing had happened. But the golden one –'

'Joy,' said Mrs Skint.

'Yes, Joy – she stood looking at that old

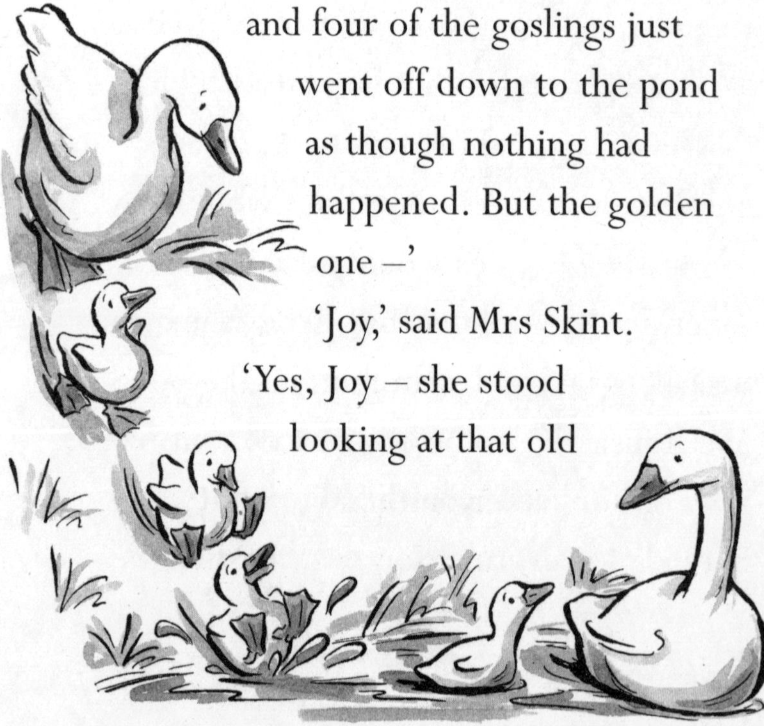

dead fox and then she looked up at me, and it seemed almost as though . . .'

'What?' asked Mrs Skint.

'As though she was saying thank you.'

'Well, you saved her life.'

'Thank goodness,' said Farmer Skint. 'I couldn't bear to lose her.'

'I suppose we could shut them all up in the daytime,' said Mrs Skint.

'Shut them up? Where?'

'Well, in the empty cowshed. Then, if another fox comes, they'd be safe.'

'But the old ones would be miserable, Janet. You know how they like grazing the orchard grass and swimming in the pond. We'll just have to be on the look-out from now on, or rather on the listen-out, because Misery and Sorrow will give the alarm if there's any danger in the daytime. I wouldn't worry all that much if it wasn't for Joy.'

'Well, put *her* in the cowshed.'

'All on her own? No, no. But I don't know what to do. It's a problem.'

But that very afternoon the problem was solved. Farmer Skint had just given the geese their midday mash and was standing, watching them eat. He was thinking, as he so often did, how beautiful the golden gosling was. She's safe at night, he thought. If only I could be sure that she'd be safe by day.

As he walked back up to the farmhouse, he had a sudden feeling that he was being followed. He looked round, and there was Joy, pattering along at his heels. He stopped. She stopped. He went on again. She came after him.

Reaching the door of the farmhouse, Farmer Skint opened it and, turning, said to Joy, by way of a joke, 'Do come in, won't you?'

She did.

'Oh look, Mummy!' cried little Jill, and she ran forward and began to stroke the gosling's golden back. As she did so, she broke into a huge smile.

Then baby Jack came crawling across the floor and touched Joy. As he did so, he began to chortle with delight.

'Look at them!' said the children's

mother. 'They love her, don't they? I don't know what we'd do without her now.'

'She'd be quite safe in here,' said Farmer Skint.

'In here, John?' asked his wife. 'Whatever do you mean? You're surely not thinking of having her live in the house? Only dogs and cats live in people's houses. She's a goose. Just think of the messes she'd make.'

'I could house-train her, Janet,' said Farmer Skint.

'What, to go outside to do her business, like you'd teach a puppy to do?'

'Yes, or better still, we could give her a litter tray, like you would for a kitten. I bet she'd soon learn to use it. Come to think of it, there's an old plastic seed tray in the greenhouse that would do fine. I'll get it now,' said the farmer, and he went out. Joy followed him. Before long he came back with the seed tray, in which he'd put a layer of peat. Joy was still following him.

He placed the tray in a corner of the room.

'Now then,' he said to the golden gosling, 'if you want to do something, you do it in there, OK?'

Mrs Skint laughed. 'Don't be silly, John,' she said. 'How could the poor little thing possibly understand what you're saying?'

Hardly were the words out of her mouth when Joy waddled over to the seed tray, climbed into it and did a poo. Somehow neither of the Skints was all that surprised to see that, instead of the usual dirty-white colour that birds' droppings are, these were golden.

'Clever girl!' said Farmer Skint to his gosling, and to his wife, 'I bet you she would, didn't I?'

He sat down and looked at his watch. 'It would have been time for afternoon milking now,' he said, 'after I'd fed the pigs and the chickens. But now there are no animals left, so there's no hurry to do anything. I could get used to a life like this, Janet.'

'That Premium Bond money's not going to last us forever, you know,' his wife said.

'You're right,' said her husband. 'But then, you never know, Joy might bring us another bit of luck. So shall I put the kettle on? We'll have a cup of tea while I have a look at today's paper.'

While Farmer Skint was sitting at the

kitchen table, Joy was standing beside his chair, looking up at him.

'She's certainly taken a fancy to you, John,' said Mrs Skint.

The farmer put down a hand and stroked the gosling. Then he opened his newspaper. By chance it fell open at the sports pages, and by chance his gaze fell upon the runners and riders for the afternoon's racing at Ascot.

'Well, would you believe it!' he cried loudly.

'What?' asked Mrs Skint.

'Look here! Just look at this! I'm not a gambling man, Janet, you know that, but don't you think I ought to have a bet on this one? It's running in the four-thirty – I've just got time to get some money on it,' and he pointed at the name of one particular horse.

Chapter Four

'Goodness!' said Mrs Skint. 'You'll have to have a flutter on that, John, won't you!'

Farmer Skint looked at his watch again.

'I'd better get down to the betting shop straight away,' he said.

'But John, your tea?'

'When I get back. It's ten past four

already. I've got to get there before the race starts. I must find my wallet.'

Farmer Skint had never been inside a betting shop before and didn't know quite what to do. He went to the counter and said, 'Excuse me, I want to put some money on a horse.'

The clerk handed him a slip.

'Fill in the horse's name,' he said, 'and the name of the meeting and the time of the race and the amount of your stake.'

'Stake?' said Farmer Skint.

'How much money you're going to bet.'

How much money am I going to bet? the farmer asked himself. He took out his wallet, bulging these days thanks to the Premium Bond win. Then he filled in the betting slip.

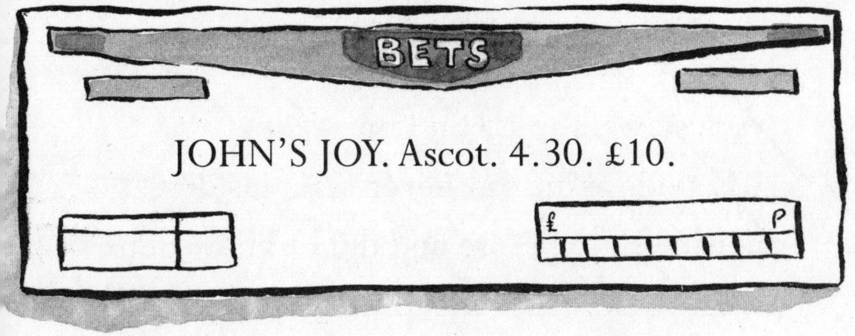

He took a ten-pound note from the wallet.

'Better hurry, sir,' said the clerk. 'They're going down to the start now.'

But then Farmer Skint suddenly thought, If I'm going to have a gamble, I'll have a real gamble. After all, I'm backing the golden gosling, aren't I? She'll make it come right. He took nine more notes from the wallet and altered the ten pounds to a hundred pounds. The clerk took the betting slip and the money without saying anything, but he couldn't

help raising his eyebrows. Whatever's this country bumpkin up to? he thought. Never had a bet in his life before by the look of him, and now he's going to chuck away a hundred quid on a horse that hasn't got a hope of winning. He looked at the starting prices:

JOHN'S JOY 50–1.

He looked at Farmer Skint and he shook his head sadly.

'They'll be off in a minute, sir,' he said, 'if you'd care to watch.'

'Watch?' said the farmer.

The clerk pointed to the rows of television screens on the walls of the betting shop.

Farmer Skint watched open-mouthed as the runners in the four-thirty at Ascot burst from their starting stalls.

'The early leader,' came the voice of the commentator, 'is Sweet Thursday by a couple of lengths from Guardian Angel in second, followed by Merry Music. The rest are fairly tightly bunched, with the exception of John's Joy, who is bringing up the rear.'

Farmer Skint watched the galloping horses, not knowing the number or the colours of John's Joy, let alone the odds against it winning. But he could see that there was one horse behind all the others. Before he could begin to worry, he heard the commentator saying, 'They're coming to the halfway mark now and Sweet Thursday's dropping back. Merry Music takes up the running by a length from Guardian Angel, and the rest are getting a bit strung out as the leader passes the three-furlong post. The early front-runner, Sweet Thursday, has faded and John's Joy is beginning to make good

progress through the field. In fact, as they reach the two-furlong post John's Joy is only a couple of lengths off the lead and going well. Will there be an upset here, I wonder? Is the outsider going to get into the frame? John's Joy is on Merry Music's shoulder now at the furlong post – now they're neck and neck – fifty yards to go – it's John's Joy! John's Joy's the winner! It's John's Joy by a length – the outsider's beaten the lot of them!'

She did it! Farmer Skint said to himself. Joy did it! and he went to the counter and handed over his betting slip.

'My horse won,' he said. 'How much do I get?'

'The starting price,' said the clerk in a strained voice, 'was fifty to one.'

'I'm no good at arithmetic,' said Farmer Skint.

'You've won five thousand pounds, sir,' said the clerk, and he began counting from a wad of fifty-pound notes.

'. . . A hundred . . . a hundred and one . . . a hundred and two,' he finished, and handed over the thick packet of notes.

'Wait a minute,' said Farmer Skint. 'You said I'd won five thousand pounds but you've given me a hundred and two fifty-pound notes. That makes five thousand, one hundred. You've given me too much.'

The clerk sighed.

'No, sir,' he said. 'Your stake was a hundred pounds – that's what you bet – so, because you won, you get that back. Five thousand pounds plus one hundred equals five thousand, one hundred.'

'So it does,' said Farmer Skint. 'I'm

much obliged,' and out of the betting shop he went.

Country bumpkin my foot! thought the clerk. He knew what he was doing all right.

Farmer Skint did not go straight back to Woebegone Farm. He went first to a wine merchant's, then to a toyshop, and then to a jeweller's. As nearly as he could (for he was not good at arithmetic), he spent the hundred pounds that he had staked on a horse –

and very much enjoyed doing so.

When he came into the farmhouse, laden with parcels, his wife took one look at them and cried, 'Oh John, you must have won!'

'I did,' said her husband, 'or rather John's Joy did. So I've bought you all presents.'

He put the parcels down on the kitchen table and said to his little daughter, 'This is for you, Jill.' It was a beautiful doll.

Then he said to his baby son, 'And this is for you, Jack.' It was a big teddy bear.

And to his wife he said, 'There are lots of good things in small parcels, Janet,' and watched as she undid a very small packet. In it was a pretty necklace.

'Oh John,' she said, 'how lovely! Fancy

buying all these things for us. You must have won a lot.'

'I did.'

'Well, you'd better have that cup of tea then.'

'No,' said Farmer Skint, 'I think we'll have something a bit special, to celebrate,' and he unwrapped a large bottle of champagne. Mrs Skint and her children and the golden gosling all watched as he eased off the cork, and all jumped when it came out

with a very loud pop. Then Farmer Skint poured the golden wine into two glasses.

'Cheers, Janet!' he said.

'Cheers, John!' she replied. 'My goodness me, you must have won an awful lot of money to be able to buy all these presents.'

'I did,' said her husband, and he took from his wallet that thick wad of fifty-pound notes and laid it on the table.

'Count those,' he said.

Mrs Skint did so, looking more and more amazed.

'There's a

hundred of them!' she said in a dazed voice.

'Quite right,' said Farmer Skint. 'That's what I won. Or I suppose I should say, John's Joy won it,' and he poured a little champagne into a saucer and set it on the floor before the golden gosling.

'She won't drink that, John!' laughed Mrs Skint.

'She will,' said Farmer Skint.

And she did.

Chapter Five

At first Farmer Skint only allowed Joy to be a house-goose by day. At night he shut her in the old hut with her family. But one evening he thought to himself, she's so good, never makes a mess in the house, always uses her litter tray, doesn't make a noise – she's no trouble at all. I'll let her stay in the kitchen tonight.

After the children had been put to bed and it was beginning to get dark, Mrs Skint said, 'Have you shut the geese up, John?'

'Yes, I have.'

'But you've forgotten Joy.'

'No, I haven't. I thought she could stop in with us.'

'Oh John, you make a fool of yourself over that bird!'

'Maybe, Janet, but that bird's made a new man of me.'

And it was true. Not only was it due to Joy, Farmer Skint thought, that he had won on the Premium Bond, and the horse-race, but also, he thought, she had somehow changed him from a loser to a winner.

Before May was out, he had bought a bunch of good-quality heifers, and a couple of well-bred sows, and a flock of handsome young chickens (which he housed in a fox-proof enclosure).

He had not paid more than other people for this livestock, as he once would have done, but less. And later in the year, when he came to sell his eggs and his piglets and the occasional bull-calf, he did not sell for less than other

people, as he once would have done, but for more.

That bird has made a new man of him indeed! Mrs Skint thought now. And a new woman of me, for that matter, and the children love her. It's almost as though I had another child in the house.

'All right, John,' she said. 'Try keeping her in the kitchen tonight, but mind – any messes, she's out.'

'There won't be any,' said Farmer Skint.

And there weren't.

So Joy became a full-time house-goose. To be sure, she saw her parents every day, for she always followed the farmer down to the orchard when he went to feed them (he'd sold the other four goslings – for a handsome price, what's more), and Misery and Sorrow were always noisily pleased to see this golden child of theirs.

But Farmer Skint was careful not to take Joy outside unless he was sure there was nobody about. As things were now, he no longer worried too much about foxes, but human thieves would be a different matter. If a dishonest person were to set eyes on his extraordinary bird, she might be stolen.

Really, the only person likely to see Joy was the postman. Nobody else much ever came to the Skints' isolated farmhouse. When the new flock of chickens began to lay, Mrs Skint took the eggs she had for sale to the market in town. She didn't want people knocking on her door.

The postman didn't usually knock, he just shoved the mail through the flap of the letter box in the front door – unless he had a parcel too big to go through the flap, in which case he'd press the bell.

One morning towards the end of June, when Farmer Skint was making hay (no rain about now, the weather was glorious and stayed so throughout haymaking and, later, harvest), the postman came to Woebegone Farm with a biggish parcel and pressed the bell. Mrs Skint didn't hear the ring because she was hoovering,

but Jill did and went to the front door. She was not tall enough to open it, but just the right height for talking through the flap of the letter box.

'Who is it?' she asked.

'Postman, dear,' said the postman. 'I've got a parcel for your mummy.'

'I can't open the door. I'm not tall enough.'

'Well, don't worry, I'll leave it on the step and you'll tell her, will you?'

'All right,' said Jill.

'Bye-bye then,' said the postman.

'We've got a golden goose,' said Jill.

'You've got a what?'

'A golden goose. She's called Joy.'

'Fancy!' said the postman. Kids! he thought. They say some funny things. And he got in his van and drove away.

Chance plays a great part in the lives of people, and of geese for that matter.

If the postman hadn't had a parcel to deliver, he wouldn't have rung the bell.

If Mrs Skint hadn't been hoovering, she'd have heard it and gone to the door instead of Jill.

If the postman hadn't sounded so nice

through the flap, Jill might not have told him about the golden goose.

But the biggest 'if' was to do with one of the Skints' nearest neighbours. Not that any of them lived very close to Woebegone Farm, but a couple of miles away there was a large country house that was also on the postman's rounds.

It was called Galapagos House, and it belonged to a famous naturalist and broadcaster called Sir David Otterbury.

And the final strange chance that came about that morning was that when the postman arrived at Galapagos House and knocked on its front door (for here too he had a parcel to deliver), the door was opened by Sir David himself.

The postman knew him of course, as did millions of people who had watched his many television programmes about all sorts of animals in all parts of the world, and it struck him that the great man might be amused to be told what the Skints' child had said.

'Good morning, sir. Parcel for you,' he said.

'Thank you,' replied Sir David Otterbury.

'I heard a funny thing this morning, sir,'

said the postman. 'You know all about geese, I'm sure.'

'I know a bit about them.'

'Well, you know the Skints, sir? Woebegone Farm?'

‘I don’t know them, but I had heard they’d fallen on hard times.’

‘Oh, their luck’s changed,’ said the postman, ‘so folk say. But anyway, what I was going to tell you was that I was talking to the Skints’ little girl this morning, through their letter flap.’

‘Through their letter flap?’

‘Yes, she’s not tall enough to open the door – and you’ll never guess what she said to me. She told me they’d got a golden goose. Funny the things kids say, isn’t it?’

‘A *golden* goose?’ said Sir David Otterbury.

‘Don’t suppose you’ve ever heard of such a bird, sir,’ said the postman. ‘I thought you’d be amused.’

After the postman had driven away, Sir David went to his study to open his parcel and to read the rest of his mail. But all the time, as he was always interested to hear about different beasts and birds, he kept thinking about what the child had said. A golden goose? No such bird, surely.

Yet the phrase rang a bell in his mind. Was it a story he'd heard on his travels? Was it something he'd heard as a child – a fairy story, perhaps? No, don't be so silly, he said to himself. The little girl was talking nonsense or perhaps just talking about one of her toys. Maybe she'd got her birds muddled and it was a golden pheasant that the Skints had. But a golden goose! Rubbish! Still, thought Sir David, I'd quite like to go and have a look and see what bird it is.

Chapter Six

Sir David Otterbury was, of course, a very busy man. He was abroad a good deal, making nature programmes in various parts of the world, and even in England he was often away from Galapagos House on business of one sort or another. So it was in fact many months before he was reminded of the postman's story of the little girl who said she had a golden goose.

But then one day he was driving along a country road not too far from his home and there was the signpost for WOEBEGONE FARM. It pointed up a very narrow lane.

Ah, thought Sir David, the golden goose!

I'll have a peep and see if I can spot this ridiculous bird. I'll pretend I've come to buy some hens' eggs. And he turned up the lane.

Nearing the farmhouse, he saw an orchard with an old hut in it and a pond and a pair of geese, grazing side by side.

Ordinary white geese, thought Sir David. No more golden than I am. Why am I wasting my time? I'll turn round and go back.

But just at that moment Farmer Skint came out of the farmhouse and approached the car.

'Looking for me?' he asked, and then he recognized the face of the driver – a face that he had seen so many times on his television set. The driver smiled at him.

'Good afternoon,' he said. 'My name's David Otterbury.'

'Yes, sir, I know,' said the farmer. What's he want? he thought.

'Could you sell me a dozen eggs? I'd be most grateful.'

'Certainly,' replied Farmer Skint. 'I'll fetch them right away.'

Thought for a moment he might have heard about Joy, he said to himself as he went to get a tray of eggs. Don't see how he could have done, though. But then he suddenly thought how interested Sir David Otterbury would be. Of all the people in the land, he'd be the one who'd be the most interested. Shall I let him see her? thought Farmer Skint. But then he'd tell the world about her, wouldn't he? Not if I swore him to secrecy, though – if I made him promise not to tell.

Farmer Skint still hadn't made his mind up what to do when he came back with the tray of eggs.

'Here you are, sir,' he said to Sir David, who had got out of his car and was leaning on the wall of the orchard, looking at Misery and Sorrow.

'Thank you, Mr Skint,' he said.

'You know my name, Sir David?'

'Yes.'

'Everybody knows yours,' said the farmer. He looked at that pleasant smiling face, and made up his mind in a flash.

‘You know all about geese, I’m sure,’ he said.

‘I know a bit about them. You’ve got a handsome pair out there. Have you bred from them?’

‘Yes, sir, I have,’ said Farmer Skint. He took a deep breath. ‘I’d like to show you what I’ve bred from them, if you’ve got a minute.’

‘Certainly.’

‘There’s just one thing, sir. I don’t want anyone else to know. Will you promise not to breathe a word of it to anybody else?’

Don’t tell me, thought Sir David, that your little daughter was telling the truth to the postman! Golden goose indeed! It’ll just be a brownish sort of bird, I expect. But I would like to see it.

'Certainly, Mr Skint,' he said. 'I promise not to tell a soul.'

Farmer Skint went back into the farmhouse and a few minutes later came out again, followed by Joy.

Never, for the rest of his life, did Sir David Otterbury forget the thrill of delight he felt at the sight that met his astonished eyes. For walking sedately at the heels of Farmer Skint of Woebegone Farm was a full-grown goose, a goose that was a wonderful bright gold colour all over. Even its beak was gold, as were its large webbed feet, and it stared up at him with its golden eyes.

'Ever seen one like this before?' said Farmer Skint.

Sir David Otterbury had, in his time, met many different sorts of geese. Aside from ordinary farmyard geese, he had seen barnacle geese, and Canada geese, and white-fronted, and pink-footed, and lots more. But never had he set eyes on such a goose as this.

'Did I understand you to say, Mr Skint,' he said, 'that you had bred this bird?'

'Yes, sir. From Sorrow and Misery out there in the orchard. Sorrow hatched four normal goslings and this one. Give her a stroke, Sir David. She likes that.'

The naturalist bent down and ran the palm of his hand gently over the

feathers of the golden goose, and as he did so, he began to smile broadly.

'It's a funny thing, Mr Skint,' he said, 'but touching this extraordinary bird of yours has made me feel on top of the world! Do you find she has that effect on you?'

'I do, sir. We all do.'

'What is she called?'

'Joy.'

'That,' said Sir David, 'is exactly what I feel.'

Chapter Seven

In the weeks that followed, life went on very pleasantly at Woebegone Farm. Farmer Skint's new dairy cattle milked well, his sows gave birth to large litters of piglets and his hens produced masses of eggs.

However, life at Galapagos House was less serene. Not that Sir David Otterbury was unhappy – how could he be when he had touched the golden goose? – but he was in a worried state of mind. It was very hard to know that this wonderful and unique bird was within a few miles of him and not to be able to tell the world about it. But he couldn't say a word – he had promised Farmer Skint that he would not.

Now that he had seen Joy, he began to feel sure that somewhere, in some book or other, at some time or other, he had once read something about a golden goose. It was an old story, he was sure, that he had come across. He searched through the dozens of bird books in the library of Galapagos House but could find nothing.

Then one night he had a strange dream,

and when he woke up he remembered two strange words from this dream.

Sir David realized, first, that these two words were in Latin and, second, that what they meant in English was

GOOSE OF A GOLDEN COLOUR.

The Romans! he thought excitedly. That was it, that was what I came across once! The Romans had something to do with a golden goose. And he bolted his breakfast and jumped in his car and raced off to the nearest large public library.

After a great deal of searching through books on Roman stories and legends, he found what he had been looking for.

The Legend of the Golden Goose

During the reign of the Emperor Nero (AD 37–68) there began a belief that one day there would be hatched, from a golden egg, a golden gosling that would grow into a golden goose. This bird would be possessed of magical powers, which would bring happiness, contentment and good fortune to anyone who touched it. As it grew older, however, the bird, though keeping its magic gifts, would gradually lose its distinctive colour. Eventually it would look exactly like an ordinary farmyard goose. At no time during the period of the Roman Empire (27 BC–AD 476) was there ever any report of such a bird, and therefore the legend of the golden goose was gradually forgotten.

'But not by me!' said Sir David to himself. 'Those old Romans were right – Joy does have magic powers, I'm sure. But what if they were also right about her losing her colour? Somehow I must try to persuade Farmer Skint to release me from my promise, to allow me to show his wonderful bird on television before she becomes as ordinary to look at as Misery and Sorrow. What if she's already begun to change colour?'

Hastily he jumped in his car again and whizzed off to

Woebegone Farm. He found the farmer mucking out his cowshed.

'Good morning, Mr Skint,' he said.

'John's the name, Sir David,' replied Farmer Skint.

'Right,' said the great naturalist. 'John it is, and you can drop the "Sir'. I get enough of that. Now then, tell me, how is Joy?'

'She's fine, sir,' said Farmer Skint.

Sir David Otterbury held up a finger. 'Now, now,' he said, 'what was I just saying?'

'Oh, sorry, er, David,' said the farmer. 'She's fine.'

'Still that glorious golden colour all over, eh?'

'Oh yes. Though there is one funny thing I noticed. Only this morning I saw it.'

'Saw what?'

'Well,' said John Skint, 'I told you, didn't I, that Joy is house-trained? She does her business in a litter tray, like a cat would. But I don't think I told you that her droppings are always gold-coloured too. And this morning they weren't. They were just dirty-white, like her mum's and her dad's.'

Oh, misery and sorrow! thought Sir David. It's started!

Chapter Eight

It's now or never, said Sir David to himself, and to Farmer Skint he said, 'John, my friend, will you do me a great favour?'

'Of course, sir – I mean, of course, David,' replied the farmer. 'What is it?'

'Will you release me from my promise to you to say nothing about Joy? Will you allow me to tell two other people – two people I have worked with for many years and would trust to keep the secret of your golden goose?'

'Who are these two people?' John Skint asked.

'One is a cameraman, the other a sound recordist. If you will allow me, I will arrange for them to come here, to Woebegone Farm, and film Joy as soon as possible.'

'For the television?'

'Yes.'

'But that's the last thing I want,' said Farmer Skint. 'Why, if you showed her on the telly I'd have the whole world knocking on my door. We'd never have any peace – and what's more, there'd be lots of people wanting to see her, touch her, steal her even. No, no, David, you can't do that to me, not after you promised.'

'Hang on a minute, John,' said Sir David Otterbury. 'There's something you don't know about. Hear me out while I make you another promise, which is – I will not show any film of your golden goose as long as she is still golden.'

'Whatever do you mean? She always will be.'

'She may not,' said Sir David, and he told the farmer about the Roman legend.

'She may change, you see,' he said. 'Today her droppings are no longer gold. Tomorrow – next week, next month, who knows – it may be her feet or her beak or her eyes that lose their colour, and then her feathers, until she is a golden goose no longer. But John, if only you will allow me to film her now, then we will have a record of her for all time. I promise not to show the film on television till she's lost all her colour.'

'And if she doesn't?'

'Then I won't show it at all. I'll keep it as a private record of her, just for your family and for me.'

Suppose those old Romans were right? Farmer Skint thought. Suppose that before long Joy will be golden no more? It would be dreadful not to have a picture of his beautiful golden goose.

'All right, David,' he said at last. 'You go ahead. I trust you.'

‘Thank you, John,’ said Sir David Otterbury. ‘And just remember that if a film of Joy is ever shown on television, they’ll pay a great deal of money for it and I’ll make sure that a large part of it comes to you.’

Sir David worked fast. Two days later he was out in the orchard at Woebegone Farm with his cameraman and sound recordist, giving a commentary as Joy walked down to the pond between her proud white parents, and the three of them swam together in the morning sunshine.

‘Never,’ he said, ‘has such a bird as this been seen before. Golden from top to toe – feathers, eyes, beak, feet – this goose is a creature hitherto unknown to science,

and is certainly the most amazing discovery of my life as a naturalist. The only reference to it was made by the ancient Romans nearly two thousand years ago, some of whom believed in the magic powers of the bird they called "Anser Aureus", the Golden Goose. To touch it, they said, was to experience instant happiness.'

No sooner had he finished speaking into the microphone than Joy left Misery and Sorrow floating on the sunlit water. She walked up out of the pond

and waddled straight towards the camera and stopped and stood, waiting. And Sir David Otterbury stepped into shot and bent and stroked her golden back.

Then he straightened up and turned to the camera, his face wreathed in smiles.

'The Romans were right!' he said.

Chapter Nine

As they drove away from Woebegone Farm, the cameraman said to the sound recordist, 'What a bird, eh?'

'Never seen anything like it,' replied the other, 'and nor has the old Otter either. Never seen him so pleased. I mean, when we were filming those mountain gorillas, years ago, remember? And they were crawling all over him and he was looking as though he loved it? But today he looked even happier.'

'Yes,' agreed the cameraman. 'I got some lovely shots.'

'And I got some good wild track too,' said the sound recordist. 'Cows mooing, birds singing, and those two old white geese honking away – to show how proud they were of their daughter, I suppose.'

'Someone's going to pay a great deal of money to show this little bit of film we've just made.'

'Not half! Pity it has to be a secret,' said the sound recordist, 'but when the old Otter tells me to keep shtoom, I keep shtoom.'

Sir David Otterbury, meanwhile, had gone back to Galapagos House. Before he left, he said to Farmer Skint, 'Now, John, as soon as that bit of film is processed and edited, you must all come over to my place and see it.'

'See it? On the telly, you mean? But you promised you wouldn't show it while she's still golden!'

'No, not on the telly. I've got my own

little projection room at Galapagos House – a kind of mini-cinema. I'll show you the film there when it's ready. Now please will you promise me something, John, before I go?'

'What?'

'Promise to let me know when there's any further loss of colour from your wonderful golden goose.'

'You think there's bound to be, do you, David?'

'I've a nasty feeling that those old Romans were right. But try not to worry too much, John. They also said that such a bird would still retain its magic gifts.'

A week later the phone rang in Galapagos House.

'Hullo, David Otterbury here.'

'It's John Skint.'

'John, what news?'

'The Romans were right. The colour has nearly gone from her webs and her beak and her eyes.'

'What about her plumage?'

'Not as bright as it was.'

'Thank goodness I persuaded him to let me make that film!' said Sir David to himself as he put the phone down.

Looks like we were only just in time.

A couple of weeks later two things happened: the film of Joy, the golden goose, arrived at Galapagos House, and at Woebegone Farm Joy was golden no longer.

Sir David came over the next day and they all went out into the orchard together, he and John Skint and Janet Skint and Jill Skint and Jack Skint (who was toddling by now). They stood looking at not two but three ordinary white geese.

'Which is Joy?' asked Jill.

‘Joy gone?’ asked Jack.

‘No,’ said Farmer Skint. ‘She hasn’t gone. She’s just changed colour, that’s all. She’s still our lucky magic goose.’ And he called, ‘Come, Joy!’ and one of the three white geese waddled forward and stood before them, and each of them in turn stroked the feathers of her back, feathers that had been brilliant gold and were now dull white.

But all of them, from the oldest to the youngest, felt a thrill of happiness and contentment as they stroked, and little Jack summed the whole thing up.

‘Joy not gone!’ he said happily.

That afternoon the Skints all went over to Galapagos House to see the film. The voice-over, the camerawork, the sound

were all perfect, and no one in the world, seeing the shots of Joy, would ever be able to doubt that there was such a bird as a golden goose.

After tea – with hot buttered crumpets for John and Janet and chocolate-chip ice cream for Jill and Jack – Sir David Otterbury said to Farmer Skint, 'Now then, John, what are we going to do? Are we going to keep this film to ourselves, or are we going to show the golden goose to the world?'

John Skint turned to his wife. 'What do you think, Janet?'

'I think,' said Janet Skint, 'that Sir David would be very disappointed if he couldn't show the film on television. And it would be lovely for other people and their children to see our Joy as she used to be. After all, no one can bother us about it – we haven't got a golden goose any more. But just think how interested thousands of

other people would be to see her.'

'Millions,' said Sir David. 'And as I told your husband, Mrs Skint, the television companies will fight tooth and nail for the rights to screen this film. They will pay a great deal of money for it, I've no doubt, and I will pay John a very fair share of it.'

That goose, thought Janet Skint – she doesn't half earn us money, one way or another.

'I'm happy about it, John,' she said to her husband, 'if you are.'

'I am,' said John Skint.

'And so am I,' said Jill Skint.

As for Jack Skint, it was all a bit confusing for him, but he was very happy because of what he'd just seen.

'Joy gold again!' he said.

Chapter Ten

When that film of the golden goose was shown on television – not just British television but all over the world – it created an enormous sensation. Sir David Otterbury received a huge amount of praise (and indeed a huge amount of money, a very fair share of which went, as had been promised, into

Farmer Skint's pockets).

The cameraman and the sound recordist did very nicely out of it too.

'Let's just hope,' one said to the other, 'that the Skints won't have to put up with masses of people coming to Woebegone Farm to have a look at the bird.'

But he needn't have worried. True, there were newspaper reporters who snooped around a number of farms near Galapagos House, but though Farmer Skint did, they could see, have geese, they were very ordinary ones.

One person who saw the film on TV and was puzzled was the postman.

'Funny, you know,' he said to his wife, 'but about a year ago, at Woebegone Farm, the farmer's little daughter told me they had a golden goose and I mentioned it to Sir David Otterbury and I could swear that orchard in the film was Farmer Skint's orchard. But I was there delivering mail only yesterday and his geese are ordinary white ones. I tell you what I've just realized – the whole thing was a con! They painted one of those geese with gold paint! What a spoof! I'd never have believed Otterbury was so deceitful!'

For Farmer Skint, who had once been a poor, unfortunate man, things were going swimmingly. True, when he cleaned out Joy's litter tray, he still nurtured a

dim hope that perhaps her droppings would turn gold again, but they never did, and in time the Skints decided that, though Joy would always be welcome in the farmhouse, it was now time that she had a home of her own and, what's more, a husband.

So with some of the money he'd got from the film, John Skint bought a brand-new wooden shed. Joy obviously thought it was beautiful, but Misery and Sorrow were too old for change and preferred their original hut.

He then bought a handsome young

gander (whom Joy also thought beautiful), a jolly sort of fellow they named Merriment. Misery was none too keen on having another gander about the place, but Merriment was polite to him and kept out of his way, and the young couple slept happily in the smart new shed.

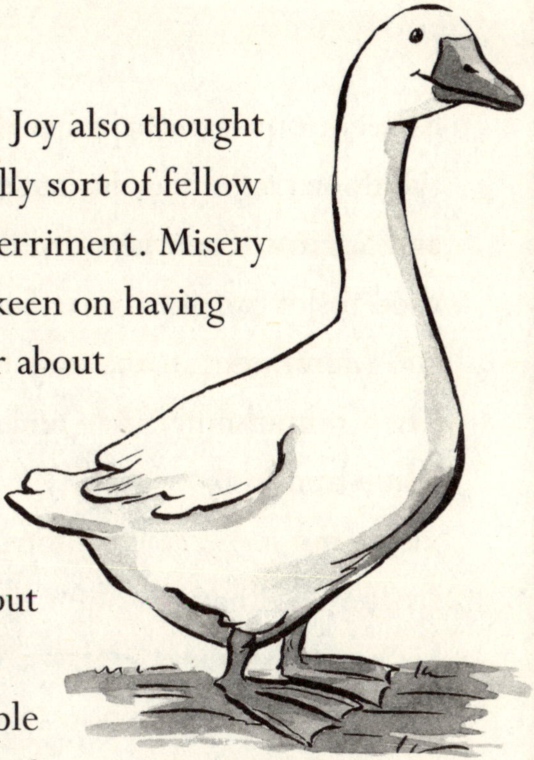

One morning the following spring, Farmer Skint finished the milking and then, before feeding his pigs and his chickens and going for his own breakfast, he went out into the orchard and opened the door of the old hut to let out Misery and Sorrow. Then he went to the new shed to let out Joy and Merriment. Then something made him look inside it.

After he'd had his breakfast (bacon and eggs, a

good lining to the stomach), he said to his wife, 'Guess what, Janet.'

'What?'

'Joy has laid her first egg.'

'Oh, that's wonderful!' she cried.

'It is indeed wonderful,' said Farmer Skint. 'Guess what, Janet.'

'What?'

'It's a golden egg.'

Dick King-Smith

Born: Bitton, Gloucestershire
27 March 1922

Jobs: Soldier, farmer, salesman, teacher, TV presenter and author

When did you start writing?

Started my first book for children, *The Fox Busters*, in 1976, got it published in 1978. Since then I have written so many books that I think I have rather lost count!

Where do you get the ideas for your stories?

Things I've done, people I've met or known, animals I've owned or know, but mostly it's just a question of sitting and thinking.

What are your hobbies?

Writing books for my children. Sitting in the garden on summer evenings with a nice drink. Talking to my dogs. Washing up. You'll never catch me buying a dishwasher; it would take all the fun out of it!

Will you give your three top tips on becoming an author?

- Read as widely as you can. Try not to read rubbish, but soak up all sorts of good stories.
- Practise. No good saying, 'I'm going to be a writer'. Get on with it. Write about whatever you fancy.
- Show what you've done to someone whose opinion you respect – Mum, Dad, your teacher. Listen to their comments: don't get upset by them, think about them.

And finally, if you hadn't been a writer, what do you think you would have been?

A farmer still. I'm glad I'm not now, I'm too blooming old to be humping sacks of corn or pitching bales; and I shouldn't like to go back to milking cows. I wish I still had some pigs though…

A whole barnyard of books!

If you loved *The Golden Goose*, here are just a few of the other titles by Dick King-Smith…

Ace is a very special pig.

He loves watching television and gradually makes himself at home in the farmhouse, much to the annoyance of Megan, the corgi. Megan is determined to keep Ace out, but Ace is the great-grandson of Babe the sheep-pig, and he's full of surprises.

When Babe, the little orphaned piglet, is won at a fair by Farmer Hogget, he is adopted by Fly, the kind-hearted sheep-dog. Babe is determined to learn everything he can from Fly. He knows he can't be a sheep-dog. But maybe, just maybe, he might be a sheep-pig.

Winner of the

Guardian Children's Fiction Prize

Here's what the judges had to say about

The Sheep-Pig

★ 'Perfect'

★ 'Thrilling'

★ 'Funny'

★ 'The Best'

★ 'Charmer'

★ 'Suspense'

★ 'Breathless'

★ 'Delight'

PUFFIN BOOKS

Dinosaur Trouble

Dick King-Smith served in the Grenadier Guards during the Second World War, and afterwards spent twenty years as a farmer in Gloucestershire, the county of his birth. Many of his stories are inspired by his farming experiences. Later he taught at a village primary school. His first book, *The Fox Busters*, was published in 1978. Since then he has written a great number of children's books, including *The Sheep-Pig* (winner of the Guardian Award and filmed as *Babe*), *Harry's Mad*, *Noah's Brother*, *The Hodgeheg*, *Martin's Mice*, *Ace*, *The Cuckoo Child* and *Harriet's Hare* (winner of the Children's Book Award in 1995). At the British Book Awards in 1991 he was voted Children's Author of the Year. He has three children, a large number of grandchildren and several great-grandchildren, and lives in a seventeenth-century cottage only a crow's flight from the house where he was born.

Books by Dick King-Smith

ACE
CLEVER DUCK
THE CUCKOO CHILD
DAGGIE DOGFOOT
DINOSAUR TROUBLE
DRAGON BOY
FIND THE WHITE HORSE
THE FOX BUSTERS
GEORGE SPEAKS
THE GOLDEN GOOSE
HARRY'S MAD
THE HODGEHEG
HOW GREEN WAS MY MOUSE
THE INVISIBLE DOG
THE JENIUS
LADY DAISY
MAGNUS POWERMOUSE
MARTIN'S MICE
THE MERMAN
THE MERRYTHOUGHT
PRETTY POLLY
THE QUEEN'S NOSE
THE ROUNDHILL
SADDLEBOTTOM
THE SCHOOLMOUSE
THE SHEEP-PIG
SMASHER
THE STRAY
THE SWOOSE
TREASURE TROVE
UNDER THE MISHMASH TREES
THE WATER HORSE
THE WITCH OF BLACKBERRY BOTTOM

Dinosaur Trouble

Dick King-Smith

Illustrated by Ben Cort

PUFFIN

PUFFIN BOOKS

Published by the Penguin Group
Penguin Books Ltd, 80 Strand, London WC2R 0RL, England
Penguin Group (USA) Inc., 375 Hudson Street, New York, New York 10014, USA
Penguin Group (Canada), 90 Eglinton Avenue East, Suite 700, Toronto, Ontario, Canada M4P 2Y3
(a division of Pearson Penguin Canada Inc.)
Penguin Ireland, 25 St Stephen's Green, Dublin 2, Ireland (a division of Penguin Books Ltd)
Penguin Group (Australia), 250 Camberwell Road, Camberwell, Victoria 3124, Australia
(a division of Pearson Australia Group Pty Ltd)
Penguin Books India Pvt Ltd, 11 Community Centre, Panchsheel Park, New Delhi – 110 017, India
Penguin Group (NZ), cnr Airborne and Rosedale Roads, Albany, Auckland 1310, New Zealand
(a division of Pearson New Zealand Ltd)
Penguin Books (South Africa) (Pty) Ltd, 24 Sturdee Avenue, Rosebank, Johannesburg 2196,
South Africa

Penguin Books Ltd, Registered Offices: 80 Strand, London WC2R 0RL, England

www.penguin.com

First published 2005
Published in this edition 2005

11

Set in 17/22.5 Perpetua
Made and printed in England by Clays Ltd, St Ives plc

British Library Cataloguing in Publication Data
A CIP catalogue record for this book is available from the British Library

ISBN-13: 978–0–14–131845–5

Chapter One

When he hatched from his egg, the first thing the baby saw was a huge face looking down at him. Above a long, toothless, beaked jaw two large eyes stared into his as he struggled free of the egg. Once the baby was out, he could see that the creature had big leathery wings, stretching from its fingers to its knees, and that it had long, slender, thin legs.

'Hullo!' it said.

'Who are you?' asked the baby.

'Your mother,' the creature replied. 'Nice to see you. Let's go flying,' and she spread her big leathery wings and took off.

Could I do that, wondered the baby?

Only one way to find out. So he spread his very small wings and flew up after his mother.

'Well done!' she cried when he reached her. 'It's nice to be nidifugous, isn't it?'

'What does "nidifugous" mean, Mum?' the baby asked.

'It means to be able to fly as soon as you're hatched. All pterodactyls can.'

'What does "pterodactyl" mean, Mum?"

'Creatures like us,' the baby's mother replied. '"*Pteron*" means a wing and "*daktylos*" means a finger. Each of my wings is attached to each of my fourth fingers, see? And so are yours.'

'So I'm a whatever-you-said, am I?'

'A pterodactyl. Yes, you are, my son. And a very pulchritudinous one too.'

'What does "pulchritudinous" mean, Mum?'

'Beautiful.'

'Oh,' said the baby pterodactyl, and he kicked his little legs happily as he flew high above the rocky land.

'Now,' said his mother, 'there's the matter of nomenclature.'

'What,' said the baby, 'does "nomenclature" mean, Mum?'

'Names. You have to have one.'

'Gosh, you do know a lot of long words, Mum.'

'One has to,' said his mother, 'in these Jurassic days, if one wants to survive. Who knows, one day pterodactyls might become extinct. And before you ask me what "extinct" means, I'll tell you. It means gone, finished, kaput, dead and done for.'

'But, Mum,' the baby said, 'I don't want to be extinct.'

'Don't worry your head about it,' his mother said. 'If it should happen, it won't be for millions and millions of years, my son. Now then, what shall we call you? You ask enough questions. How about Nosy? How d'you like that?'

The baby waggled his small but rather long snout.

'I don't mind,' he said, 'but, Mum, what's your name?'

'Aviatrix,' said his mother.

'What does "aviatrix" mean, Mum?' asked Nosy.

'A female flier. In the skills of flying,

among all pterodactyls I am paramount.'

This time Nosy didn't ask anything. He simply said, 'I suppose that means "the best".'

'It does, Nosy, my boy,' replied Aviatrix. 'It most certainly does.'

Mother and son flew on, side by side. Nosy flapped along as fast as he could, while his mother flew slowly so that he could keep up with her.

'Mum,' said Nosy after a while, 'where are we going?'

'To see your father,' said Aviatrix.

'Oh. What's he called?'

'His name is Clawed. You'll see why when you meet him. Never have there been claws like his.'

Before long they left behind the dry

stony place where Nosy had hatched among the hot rocks, and came to a wood. Here there were quite a number of pterodactyls, hanging upside down as pterodactyls do, each gripping a branch with its taloned feet. The biggest one, Nosy could see as they dropped lower, had the most enormous claws.

'There he is!' cried Aviatrix. 'There's my Clawed! Come on, Nosy, come and meet your daddy!'

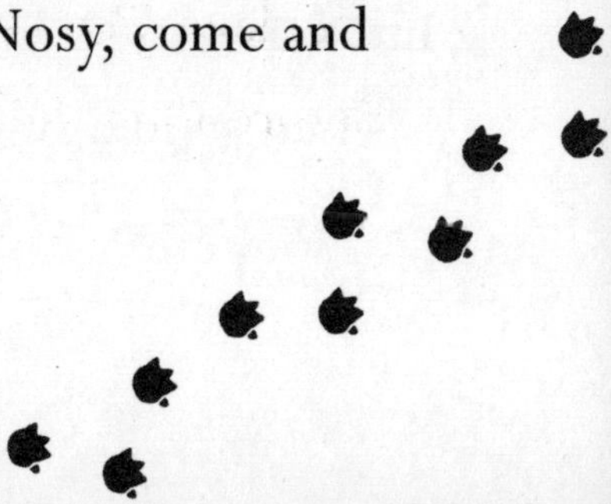

Chapter Two

When they landed, Aviatrix could see that Clawed was fast asleep. She hung herself head down at one side of him. Nosy, copying his mother, hung himself on the other side. He thought of saying, 'Hullo, Daddy,' but there didn't seem much point, so he said nothing.

Then suddenly Clawed said in a loud

deep voice, 'Watch out, everybody!'

'What does Daddy mean?' asked Nosy.

'Haven't a clue,' replied his mother. 'Your father is a somniloquist.'

'What does "somniloquist" mean, Mum?'

'Someone who talks in his sleep. I expect he'll say something else in a minute,' and almost immediately Clawed shouted, 'T. rex approaching! Scramble! Scramble!'

Aviatrix raised a wing and smacked her husband across his face.

'Wake up, Clawed!' she said. 'You're dreaming.'

Clawed opened his eyes and shook his head as though to clear it.

'Oh, hullo, Avy, old girl,' he said. 'I was having a nightmare. Didn't know you were here.'

'I'm not the only one who's here,' said Aviatrix. 'Look on your other side.'

Obediently Clawed turned his huge head, to see a very small head close by.

'Hullo, Daddy,' said Nosy.

'Daddy?' said Clawed. 'What are you talking about, boy? What's he mean, Avy?'

'This is our son, dear,' said Aviatrix proudly. 'Our firstborn. Only hatched this morning, but already he's a good flier.'

'Because I'm nidifugous, Daddy,' said Nosy.

Clawed shook his head in puzzlement.

'Sounds like one of those long words your mother uses,' he said. 'Half the time I never understand what she's on about.'

'You never were very bright, dear,' said Aviatrix, 'but I think our son is an infant prodigy.'

'What does "infant prodigy" mean, Mum?' asked Nosy.

'A highly intelligent child,' replied his mother.

Nosy felt very pleased at this. He couldn't kick his little legs because he was hanging by them, but he flapped his little wings instead.

'Don't suppose he even knows what he is,' said Clawed grumpily. 'What are you, boy, eh?'

'I'm a pterodactyl, Daddy,' said Nosy. 'Like you. Though I don't suppose I'll ever be as big as you.'

Or as silly, said Aviatrix to herself, fond as I am of him.

'What's your name, boy?' asked

Clawed. 'If I know your mother, she'll have given you a very long one.'

'No, Daddy,' said Nosy. 'I'm just Nosy.'

'Are you indeed?' said Clawed. 'Poking your snout into other people's business, eh? Well, ask me no questions and I'll tell you no lies.'

'No, I mean, my name is Nosy.'

'Oh,' said Clawed. 'Oh, I see. By the way, my name's Clawed.'

'I know,' said Nosy, 'but I can't call you that. You're my father.'

Clawed hung in silence for a while, deep in thought. Then he said 'You're right, my son. You'd better stick to "Daddy". Take him away now, Avy. I haven't had enough sleep,' and he closed his eyes.

'Come on, then, Nosy,' said his mother. 'Daddy's tired,' and she dropped from the branch and spread her wings and flew off.

Nosy followed.

'Where are we going now, Mum?' he asked.

'To get some breakfast.'

'What sort of breakfast?'

'Bugs.'

'What does that mean?'

'Flies and beetles and gnats and midges and things. We are carnivores, you see.'

'What does that mean?'

'We eat meat, including insects. There should be lots flying about on a nice warm morning like this. Specially if there should be a dead dinosaur lying about somewhere. There'll be masses of flies around it,' said Aviatrix.

Before long she said, 'We're in luck, Nosy. Look down there.'

Nosy looked down and on the ground below he saw a simply enormous body, with clouds of flies buzzing upon and around it.

'Whatever is that, Mum?' he asked.

'Brachiosaurus.'

'But it's so huge! Whatever could have killed it?'

'T. rex, I expect.'

'T. rex? That's what Daddy shouted out in his nightmare. What does it mean, Mum?'

'Tyrannosaurus rex,' said his mother. 'The fiercest, fastest flesh-eating dinosaur of all. A truly nightmarish creature.'

'What does it look like, Mum?' asked Nosy.

'Oh, stop your everlasting questions, Nosy, do! Tuck in to these flies,' said Aviatrix.

She swooped down upon the swarm of insects hovering above the dead brachiosaurus and snapped up the largest. Nosy, copying, began to catch the smallest.

Then his mother dropped down and landed upon the enormous dinosaur. Nosy followed her. All kinds of delicious little creatures were crawling over the brachiosaurus.

Nosy said, 'But, Mum, what does T. rex look like?'

'Well,' said Aviatrix, with her mouth full, 'it's got a massive body and a short, thick neck and a large head and a battery of long, sharp teeth. It has tiny forelegs but very big muscular back legs on which it stands upright.'

'Oh,' said Nosy. 'Mum?'

'What now?'

'There's one coming.'

Chapter Three

A terrifying roar split the air. Aviatrix looked up from her meal of fat flies.

'So there is,' she said.

'Mum,' said Nosy, 'hadn't we better push off before it arrives?'

Every time T. rex roared, Nosy could see those long, sharp teeth, and they looked very sharp indeed.

'No hurry,' said Aviatrix. 'Time for a bit of fun. Do you remember what my name means?'

'Yes, Mum. Female flier.'

'And what else did I tell you?'

'You said you were paramount among all pterodactyls in the skills of flying.'

'Quite right, Nosy. Watch this,' said Aviatrix, and she took off and flew directly at the approaching tyrannosaurus.

Seeing her coming, it reared up to its full height and opened wide that huge mouth crammed with sharp teeth. It thought this was going to be an easy meal.

Now Aviatrix showed just how skilled a flier she was. As she neared that open mouth, she suddenly shot straight up into the air. And, as she zoomed over the head

of T. rex, she sank her sharp claws into its snout.

T. rex let out a loud bellow, not of pain (for its skin was too thick to be much harmed by a scratch from a pterodactyl) but of rage at the cheek of the creature. It watched in fury as Aviatrix now put on a show of aerobatics.

First she looped the loop, high above the great flesh-eater, then she dived back down, straight at it, so that the watching Nosy felt sure that his mother's last moment had come.

But no, gracefully she side-slipped past the open mouth and then began to sweep round and round T. rex's neck in tight circles, while it snapped furiously at her. It rocked unsteadily on its hind feet, becoming quite giddy in its vain efforts to catch this pest.

Shooting skywards once more in the steepest of climbs, Aviatrix hovered for a moment high above the tyrannosaurus. Then, folding her leathery wings, she dropped, twisting and turning like a falling leaf, apparently totally out of control.

It looked to Nosy as though his mother was going to go straight down the throat of T. rex. But all its last snap at her earned it was a mouthful of fresh air and another scratch on the nose.

Once more Aviatrix slipped past those gaping jaws and then climbed high, to perform one last magnificent feat of aerobatics. She spread her wings wide and rolled, with first her right wing pointing skywards, then her left, over and over and over, before she finally flew back to the body of the brachiosaurus, towards which the raging T. rex was now rushing at top speed.

'Scramble, Nosy!' she called down. 'I think our friend is a bit upset.'

'Gosh, Mum, you really are a paramount

flier!' said Nosy as they flew away together. 'What was that last thing you did?'

'That,' said his mother, 'was the Victory Roll.'

When Clawed eventually woke up, he remembered that something nice had happened. What was it? Oh yes, he was

a father, he had a son, Avy had brought the boy along to see him. What was he called? Oh yes, Nosy, that was it.

Clever little chap too, thought Clawed, knows some long words already, just like his mother. I don't know any long words. Oh no, wait a minute, I do know some. Pterodactyl to begin with, and – let's see now – diplodocus and iguanodon and allosaurus and stegosaurus and triceratops.

Not bad, eh? What have I left out? Oh, I know, horrible old Tyrannosaurus rex. Had a nightmare about it, didn't I? Sooner call it T. rex, though – short names are easier. Could shorten the others, I suppose. Dip. Ig. Al. Steg. Tri. No, it doesn't quite work.

Clawed yawned, tired by so much thinking. He was about to doze off again when he heard two voices.

'Clawed!' said one, and, 'Daddy!' said the other, and the branch creaked as his wife and his son landed to hang upside down on either side of him.

'Hullo,' he said. 'Where have you two been?'

'Nosy will tell you,' replied Aviatrix.

'Oh, Daddy!' cried Nosy. 'We've had

ever such an exciting time! We were feeding on a brachiosaurus –'

'What, eating it?' interrupted Clawed. 'How did you manage that?'

'Don't be silly, Clawed,' said Aviatrix. 'Nosy means we were on a brachiosaurus, feeding. On flies. Don't interrupt the boy.'

'Oh, sorry,' said Clawed. 'Go on, Nosy.'

'And then,' went on Nosy, 'what d'you think we saw, Daddy?'

'Haven't a clue,' said Clawed.

'Have a guess.'

'One of our relations, perhaps? Haven't seen my brother for a while. You'd like your Uncle Eggbert, Nosy. He's nearly as big as me.'

And nearly as silly, said Aviatrix to herself, smiling fondly at her husband.

'No, Daddy,' said Nosy. 'It wasn't a pterosaur we saw, it was a dinosaur.'

Dip? Ig? Al? Steg? Tri? thought Clawed. I don't know.

'I give up,' he said.

'We saw a T. rex!' said Nosy. 'And Mum did some absolutely fantastic, superlative aerobatics.'

'Which you will probably be able to do just as well when you're grown up, Nosy,' said Aviatrix. 'Thanks to your primogeniture.'

'What does that word mean, Avy?' asked Clawed.

'Literally,' replied Aviatrix, 'it means the circumstance of being firstborn. If you comprehend the purport of my prognostication.'

Clawed looked blank.

'Mum means I'm going to be a good flier, Daddy,' said Nosy.

Clawed looked pleased.

'You're bound to be, my son,' he said, 'with a father like me.'

Chapter Four

Aviatrix looked at her large husband with a mixture of amusement and pride. He may be silly, she thought, but he is a good flier. Not as good as me, of course, but faster, I have to admit. With that enormous wingspan of his and his great strength, I reckon he could beat any pterodactyl on earth in a race. I bet Nosy

would be surprised. Shall I get old Clawed to show off his speed? Why not!

'Let's get airborne, Clawed,' she said to her husband, 'and then you'll be able to see how well Nosy is doing. Anyway, you need some exercise. You're always hanging about.'

Clawed looked doubtful.

'Come on, Daddy,' said Nosy. 'I'd love to fly with you. Mum is a bit too fast for me.' But you won't be, he thought. You're too big and heavy and lazy.

Clawed yawned.

'Oh, all right,' he said. 'If I must, I must,' and he unclasped his huge claws and dropped down till he was clear of all the branches of the tree. Then he glided out into the open, where the others joined him, and the three of them set off in line, Nosy in the middle, one parent on either side of him.

'Mum! Daddy! Where are we going?' he asked.

'Let's go to the lake,' said Clawed. 'I'm thirsty.'

'All right,' said Aviatrix, 'and then we can go on to the Great Plain. Now then, Nosy, we'll give you a start. Show Daddy how fast you can fly.'

Nosy beat his little wings as hard as he could and pulled away ahead of his parents.

'Good boy!' he heard them shout, and then came the flap of much much larger wings as Aviatrix caught him up and passed him. A moment later Clawed came thundering by. His wings, Nosy could see, were even bigger, much much bigger, and although he beat them more slowly, they carried him along at such a rate that he in turn caught up with Aviatrix and swept past her.

Gosh! He's fast! He must be the fastest pterodactyl in the world, thought Nosy.

In front of and below him now, he could see a great sheet of water. His parents were gliding down towards it. First his father and then his mother skimmed the surface of the lake, wings splayed wide, mouths wide open. They drank as they flew, and Nosy copied as best he could.

At the far side of the lake were trees that hung out over the water. The family settled there, to hang upside down on a convenient branch.

Nosy shook himself.

'I'm wet, Mum,' he said.

'You have to learn the trick of it,' said Aviatrix, 'but you did well.'

'And you flew well, my boy,' said Clawed.

'Gosh! You're fast, Daddy!' said Nosy.

Clawed looked pleased.

'You must be the fastest pterodactyl in the world,' said Nosy.

Clawed looked very pleased.

'He is,' said Aviatrix.

'Oh, I don't know,' said Clawed.

'Yes, you are,' said Aviatrix. 'Don't argue. Now then, let's go on to the Great Plain.'

'But, Mum,' said Nosy, 'I'm tired. Can't we rest for a bit?'

'Good idea,' said Clawed.

'No,' said Aviatrix. 'But I'll tell you what. You can have a piggyback.'

'What does that mean, Mum?' asked Nosy.

'You can have a ride on Daddy's back. That'll give you a good rest.'

'Can I really?'

'Of course you can.'

'But, Avy,' said Clawed, 'I wouldn't mind a rest too.'

'Nonsense,' said Aviatrix. 'Jump on now, Nosy. Oops-a-daisy!'

Nosy never forgot the thrill he felt when, clinging tightly to his father's back, he looked down and saw the Great Plain for the first time.

In the land where the pterodactyls lived there were three different kinds of country.

Firstly, there was the dry stony desert, where Nosy had hatched. Here, each female would lay her solitary egg among the hot rocks.

Secondly, there were the woods, full of convenient trees for pterodactyls to hang upon.

And thirdly, there was the Great Plain: miles and miles of grassland, where all the great plant-eating dinosaurs lived.

Now, as Nosy looked down in wonder, he saw herds of huge creatures such as diplodocuses and ankylosauruses and stegosauruses.

Nosy's parents dropped lower and hovered above a single enormous dinosaur that was moving very slowly, grazing on the coarse grasses.

'Gosh! What's that, Daddy?' he cried.

'Apatosaurus,' said Clawed.

'It's so *big*!' cried Nosy. 'They're all so big, all these beasts below us!'

'Second-class creatures, the lot of them,' said his mother scornfully.

'Not a patch on us,' said his father proudly.

'Why not?'

'Because,' said his parents with one voice, 'they can't fly!'

At that moment something came out from beneath the giant dinosaur. Something which had been sheltering there and had been alarmed by the flying creatures overhead.

It was a baby apatosaurus.

Chapter Five

'Ma,' said the baby apatosaurus, 'what were those funny things in the sky?'

'Pterodactyls,' replied her mother, whose name was Gargantua.

'I was frightened,' said the baby.

'No need,' said Gargantua. 'Pterodactyls are fourth-rate creatures, much inferior to us.'

'Why?'

'They've only got two legs. They can't walk about like we dinosaurs can. Just remember that of all creatures dinosaurs are the best and that of all dinosaurs apatosauruses are the greatest.'

'Yes, Ma,' said the baby.

'One day,' said Gargantua, 'you'll grow up to be a big girl, a very big girl, as big as me.'

'And then I won't be frightened of anything, Ma?'

Gargantua looked down at her small daughter.

'Certainly not,' she said.

No point in worrying her, she thought. With a bit of luck she may never meet a T. rex.

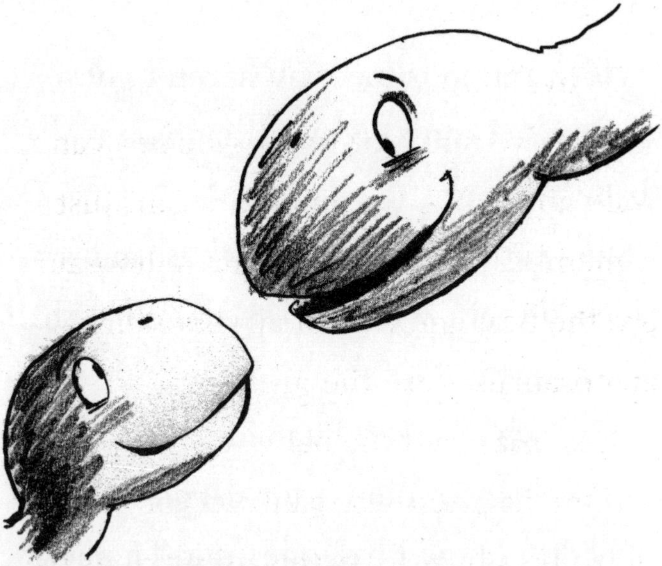

Just then another apatosaurus, even bigger than Gargantua, plodded heavily towards them.

'Oh, look!' said Gargantua. 'Here comes your father,' and she called, 'Titanic!'

'What does that mean, Ma?' asked the baby.

'It's his name, dear,' replied Gargantua.

'Which reminds me, you haven't got a name yet. I can't go on calling you "baby".'

She waited until her huge husband reached them and then asked, 'What shall we call her?'

'Call who?' asked Titanic.

'This baby of ours. Your daughter.'

'Didn't know I had one,' said Titanic.

'Well, now you do. Say hullo to your father, baby.'

'Hullo, Pa,' said the little apatosaurus.

'Hullo, Wotsyername,' said Titanic. 'What's she called, Gargy?'

'She hasn't got a name yet. Can you think of one?'

'She's very small,' said Titanic.

'She's very young,' said Gargantua.

'She'll be big one day.'

'Suppose so,' said Titanic. 'But just now she looks a bantamweight. Tell you what, Gargy, let's call her Banty.'

Gargantua turned to her daughter.

'How about that, baby?' she said. 'Shall we call you Banty? How would you like that?'

'I don't mind,' said the little apatosaurus.

She looked up at her enormous parents. Shall I really be as big as them one day, she thought? Shall I have four great legs like pillars and a very long tail and a very very long neck?

She looked carefully at their heads.

'Why are your nostrils so high up?' she asked.

'So that we can stand in very deep water, almost completely submerged, and yet still be able to breathe,' said her mother.

'But why would you want to stand in very deep water?'

'To get cool,' replied her father.

And to escape from a T. rex, he thought, but no point in worrying the child with that. With a bit of luck she may never meet one.

'Talking of which,' he went on, 'I could do with a dip. I'm hot and I'm hungry. I could murder a good meal of waterweed.'

So they plodded off towards the lake, where Banty stood in the shallows, watching as Titanic and Gargantua plunged their long necks deep under the water to pull up great mouthfuls of weed.

She looked up into the sky, remembering the flying creatures she had seen. I wonder why Ma was so nasty about pterodactyls, she said to herself. I thought they were interesting, specially the little one. It was rather sweet.

Meanwhile Nosy and Clawed and Aviatrix had arrived back at their perch in the woods. Upside down, Nosy looked at the ground below, remembering the apatosaurus and its baby. It was rather sweet, he thought. Wonder why Mum and

Daddy were so nasty about apatosauruses. I thought they were interesting. I'd like to meet that little one again.

Early next morning, while his parents were still asleep, Nosy dropped off the branch and flew away in the direction of the Great Plain. Which is beyond the lake, he said to himself, and I can't miss that.

Sure enough, before long he saw beneath him the great sheet of water. Round its edges a number of dinosaurs were drinking – diplodocuses, ankylosauruses, stegosauruses and many others – but Nosy could not see the apatosaurus family.

This was not surprising, since all that was showing of them were, in deep water, the nostrils of Gargantua and

Titanic, and in the shallows, where she was practising going underwater, the very small nostrils of their child.

By a lucky chance, Banty popped her head up as the young pterodactyl was flapping by.

That's it, thought Nosy, that's the one, I'm sure, and he dropped lower and called out, 'Good morning!'

Banty waded out of the water and stood looking up at him.

'Good morning,' she said. 'You're a pterodactyl, aren't you?'

'Yes,' replied Nosy. 'And you're an apatosaurus. Excuse me asking, but what's your name?'

'Banty. What's yours?'

'Nosy.'

'Oh. Are you a girl or a boy?'

'Boy. And you?'

'Girl.'

'It's strange,' said Nosy, 'but my mum and daddy are very rude about apatosauruses.'

'Why?'

'Because you can't fly.'

'Oh,' said Banty. 'Well, funnily enough

my ma and pa are very rude about pterodactyls.'

'Why?'

'Because you've only got two legs, so you can't walk.'

'But I don't want to walk,' said Nosy. 'Flying's nicer.'

'And I don't want to fly,' said Banty. 'Walking's nicer.'

They looked at one another with interest.

'Talking's nice too,' said Nosy.

'Yes, it is,' said Banty, 'but it must be tiring for you to keep flapping about, Nosy, while I'm standing comfortably.'

'No problem, Banty,' said Nosy. 'If you'll just walk over to this tree that overhangs the water,' and he grasped a convenient branch with his little claws and swung over to hang upside down.

'Wow! That's cute!' said Banty, and she stretched up her little neck and pulled a bunch of leaves off the branch.

'Gosh! That's clever!' said Nosy. 'You must be a herbivore.'

'What's that mean?' asked Banty.

'A creature that eats grass and leaves. Me, I'm a carnivore.'

'Where did you learn long words like those?'

'From my mum. She knows lots of long words. She's clever, my mum.'

'So's my ma,' said Banty.

'What about your father?' asked Nosy.

'He's not all that bright.'

'Nor's my daddy. Perhaps females are always cleverer than males. What do you think?'

'I don't think that's true,' said Banty. 'It's obvious to me that you are a much brighter dinosaur than I am.'

'Well, actually,' said Nosy, 'I'm not strictly a dinosaur. I'm a pterosaur. "*Pteron*" means a wing and "*saurus*" means a lizard.'

'Oh. Well, what does the "*dino*" bit of dinosaur mean?'

'Huge and terrible.'

‘Wow! I like it!’ said Banty.

She looked round at the sound of a mighty splashing in the lake.

‘Here come Ma and Pa,’ she said. ‘You better beat it, Nosy, before they start being rude about you. But come back another day, won’t you?’

‘I will,’ said Nosy as he dropped off his branch.

‘See you, my friend!’ he squeaked as he flew away.

Chapter Six

Gargantua and Titanic came lumbering up towards their daughter. They were dripping wet, and covered in mud and waterweed.

'Whatever was that you were talking to, Banty?' her mother asked.

'A pterodactyl, Ma. A young one. He's nice.'

'Nice!' said Gargantua. 'I'm surprised

at you, speaking to such a creature. You don't know where it's been.'

'Dirty things they are,' rumbled Titanic.

'Nosy isn't dirty, Pa,' said Banty.

'Oh,' said Gargantua, 'so we're on first-name terms already, are we?'

'He can hang upside down, Ma,' said Banty.

'Hang upside down!' said her mother in

tones of horror. 'Well, there you are! How can it possibly keep clean?'

'What d'you mean, Ma?'

'Well, goodness me, Banty, you're old enough now to know that all creatures have to . . . um, er . . . make themselves comfortable. No one can digest everything that is eaten. Some of it is, er, wasted. It has to be got rid of.'

'What d'you mean, Ma?'

'Droppings,' said Titanic heavily. 'We all do 'em.'

'But,' said Gargantua, 'we do them on the grass.'

'Or in the water,' said Titanic.

'But just imagine,' said Gargantua, 'a creature that is hanging upside down and suddenly needs to do its, er . . .'

'. . . droppings,' said Titanic.

'. . . and you can easily realize that it is going to make itself filthy. I very much hope, Banty, that you will have nothing more to do with it.'

Nosy's a 'he', not an 'it', thought Banty, and we're friends, and if I want to see him again, I *shall*, Ma, so there.

Meanwhile, back in the woods, Aviatrix and Clawed were waking up to find that Nosy was absent.

'Where's he gone?' said his mother.

'Don't know,' said his father.

'What are we going to do?'

'Don't know.'

'Wherever he's gone, he'll come back, won't he?'

Clawed, hanging by his huge talons, stretched his huge wings and yawned a huge yawn.

'Don't know,' he replied.

You don't know anything, thought Aviatrix angrily, but before she could say more Nosy came flying in at speed.

In one fluent movement he turned on his back, reached up with his little legs, caught the branch with his little claws and hung there, swinging to and fro.

Aviatrix turned her anger on her son.

'Wherever have you been, you naughty boy?' she cried.

'To the lake, Mum.'

'To the lake? Whatever for?'

'A drink, I expect,' said Clawed. 'That's why I go there. I like a drink, now and again.'

'No, Daddy,' said Nosy. 'I went to meet a friend.'

'A friend?' said his mother. 'Another pterodactyl, you mean?'

'No, Mum.'

'What, then?'

'A young apatosaurus. The one we saw yesterday. On the Great Plain. She's called Banty. She's nice.'

'Well!' said Aviatrix. 'I'm dumbfounded!'

'What's that mean, Mum?'

'Reduced to silence.'

'But you're talking.'

'Hold your tongue, child. I am utterly flabbergasted.'

'What's that mean?'

'Oh, stop your endless questions. I cannot tell you how surprised I am that you should be speaking to such a creature.'

'But you are telling me, Mum,' said Nosy.

'You don't know where it's been,' said Clawed. 'They're dirty things, they are.'

He did a huge poo, which, by a stroke of luck, missed his head and fell to the ground below.

'They're not dirty, Daddy,' said Nosy.

'They come off the Great Plain and go and bathe in the lake. Banty certainly isn't dirty.'

'Banty!' said Aviatrix. 'What a silly name for a silly flightless creature. I trust you'll have nothing more to do with it.'

Banty's a 'she', not an 'it', thought Nosy. She's my friend and I hope I'm hers, and I *shall* see her again, Mum, so there.

Chapter Seven

Of all the creatures that lived on the Great Plain, the nastiest was Tyrannosaurus rex, and of all tyrannosauruses the biggest and most bloodthirsty was the one that Aviatrix and Nosy had met when they were fly-catching on the body of the dead brachiosaurus. His name was Hack the Ripper.

What he liked best was to hunt a dinosaur – any one of the many kinds of grass-eaters that roamed the plain – and kill it, and eat it, or as much of it as he could stomach. Hack's favourite prey was baby dinosaur, not because it was too slow to escape him – they were all too slow, whatever their age – but because a baby made such a lovely meal: so tender, so tasty, so mouth-watering.

On one particular morning he was walking upright across the plain, scanning the various herds of animals with his cold, hard eyes, looking to see if there was a nice fat baby nearby.

As soon as they saw him, diplodocuses, iguanodons and the rest all moved away, slowly of course, turning small heads on the end of long necks to see if he was following.

Hack the Ripper was hungry, but not ravenously hungry. He decided he would have a drink – it was a hot day – before beginning his hunting.

It so happened that Titanic and Gargantua were standing at the edge of the lake, at the very spot indeed to which Hack was heading.

They had been out grazing on the plain since first light and their huge stomachs were packed full of grass. Now, when they saw T. rex approaching, they splashed as hastily as they could out into deep water and submerged. Only their nostrils showed.

Some minutes passed, and then, slowly, Titanic put his head up and then so did Gargantua.

'It's all right, Gargy,' said Titanic. 'The brute is going,' and they watched as Hack strode away back to the grasslands.

'Horrible thing!' said Gargantua. 'I wonder what wretched animal will die today to feed its disgusting appetite?'

'They say it likes baby dinosaurs best,' said Titanic.

The two great apatosauruses stretched up their long necks and stared, first at one another and then, as the same thought struck them, all around the lake and its shore, and with one voice, a horrified voice, they cried, 'Where's our Banty?'

Chapter Eight

Thinking about his new friend, Nosy had become worried about her. He knew all about T. rex – he'd seen one, close up, after all – but he was pretty sure that Banty did not.

Obviously her parents had never told her, never warned her of the danger of the plain's fiercest flesh-eater. They just hope, he supposed, that she'll never meet one.

She should be told, he thought. I'll get Mum and Daddy to tell her, and I might even be able to persuade them to fly over and have a chat with Banty's ma and pa.

With all this in mind, he had flown off very early that morning in search of his friend. By luck, he found her at the lake's edge. He glided down.

'Hullo, Banty!' he called.

Banty looked up.

'Oh, hullo, Nosy!' she cried. 'Where are you off to?'

'I've just come to see you,' Nosy said. 'I wanted to ask you something.'

'What?'

'Well, how would you like to come and

see where I live with my mum and my daddy?'

'Where's that?'

'In the woods. It's not far. You wouldn't be scared, would you?'

'Scared?' said Banty. 'Of what?'

'Oh, of . . . um . . . leaving your ma and pa for a while.'

'No,' said Banty. 'They probably won't even notice I'm gone.'

'Well, come on, then,' said Nosy. 'I'll fly very slowly above to show you the way.'

And to keep a good lookout for You-Know-Who, he thought.

Before long, Banty was standing in the pterodactyls' wood, looking up at Clawed and Aviatrix as they hung, still asleep,

above her. They were on a fresh branch because, the previous evening, Nosy had persuaded his parents to move. He didn't want Banty to have to stand in a bed of deep, pongy poo.

'Mum, Daddy, wake up!' he called, hitching on to the branch beside them. 'I've brought my friend Banty to meet you.'

Aviatrix opened her eyes and looked down in horror at the baby apatosaurus. The shock rendered her speechless.

'Good morning, Nosy's mum,' said Banty in the politest of tones. 'I'm very pleased to meet you. Nosy thought I might like to see the wood where you live. It's beautiful, isn't it?'

'It's pulchritudinous,' said Nosy.

'Nosy tells me,' said Banty, 'that you have taught him a great many long words. You must be very clever.'

'Sagacious,' said Nosy.

'That too,' said Banty.

'The epithets are synonymous,' said Aviatrix.

Quite a nice little thing, she thought. Well, not little, but nice. Good manners.

At this point Clawed woke up. He was about to do a poo, always his first act of the day, but seeing what stood below him, he refrained.

'Who's this?' he said.

'My friend, Daddy,' said Nosy.

'Good morning, sir,' said Banty.

Clawed was so astonished at being addressed with such respect that he almost fell off the branch.

'Morning,' he said.

'Her name is Banty, Daddy,' said Nosy, 'and I've brought her to see you and Mum for a very special reason. Knowing how clever you both are.'

Aviatrix looked very pleased at this, Clawed very puzzled.

'And what is this very special reason?' asked Aviatrix.

'I want you to warn her,' said Nosy.

'Warn her? Against what?'

'T. rex.'

'What's that?' asked Banty.

'Tyrannosaurus rex,' replied Aviatrix. 'The fiercest of the carnivores.'

'Please, Nosy's mum – what is a carnivore?'

'A meat-eater. And stop calling me

"Nosy's mum". My name is Aviatrix.'

'And mine's Clawed,' said Clawed, 'but you can go on calling me "sir" if you like – I quite fancy it.'

'Hang on a minute,' said Nosy.

'We all are,' said Clawed, taking a fresh grip on the branch with his large talons.

'No, Daddy, I mean, let me tell you what's worrying me. You can see that Banty's parents have never told her about T. rex, though I don't know why. Which means she's in terrible danger if she ever comes across one.'

'She is vulnerable,' said Aviatrix.

'What's that mean, Avy?' asked Clawed.

'Capable of being physically wounded or injured or, in Banty's case, killed and eaten.'

Banty shuddered (and when an

apatosaurus, even a small one, shudders, it's quite a sight).

'What does this awful thing look like?' she said, and the two adult pterodactyls told her, each in its own way.

Aviatrix's description was full of long words like 'formidable', 'terroristic', 'repulsive' and 'unprepossessing'.

Clawed, who understood none of these adjectives, simply said, 'Big and scary.'

'But surely, sir,' said Banty, 'this T. rex creature couldn't kill something as big as an apatosaurus?'

'Easily,' said Clawed.

'And you're only a baby one,' said Aviatrix.

By now she had warmed to this odd-looking, innocent young animal.

'You must take great care, Banty, dear,' she said. 'We can always escape by flying, but you can't.'

'Mum, Daddy,' said Nosy, 'please could you do my friend here a big favour?'

'Indubitably,' said his mother, 'and before you ask me, Clawed, that means without a doubt.'

'What d'you want?' asked Clawed.

'Could you both come over to the lake with me so that you can meet Banty's parents? Neither of us knows why, but they don't seem to like pterodactyls and you don't like apatosauruses. Banty and I are friends, but wouldn't it be nice if we were all friends – both families, I mean?'

'Would you like us to come, Banty?' Nosy's mother asked.

'Oh yes, I would, please!'

'Then we will,' said Clawed. 'I could do with a drink anyway.'

Chapter Nine

'Banty! Banty!' called Gargantua and Titanic as they lumbered round the rim of the lake, but there was no response.

When they stopped to get their breath, at a point that chanced to be the nearest to the distant woods, Gargantua gasped, 'It couldn't have taken her, could it?'

Titanic looked puzzled.

'What couldn't have taken who?' he asked.

'That T. rex we've just seen, you fool,' said Gargantua. 'Could it have taken our Banty?'

Titanic considered.

'Don't think so,' he said. 'It didn't have anything in its mouth and we weren't submerged long enough for it to have time to –'

'Stop!' cried Gargantua. 'Don't say it!' and she shuddered the most enormous apatosaurian shudder.

Just then they saw, flying towards them from the direction of the woods, three pterodactyls. There was a little one, a big one and a very big one.

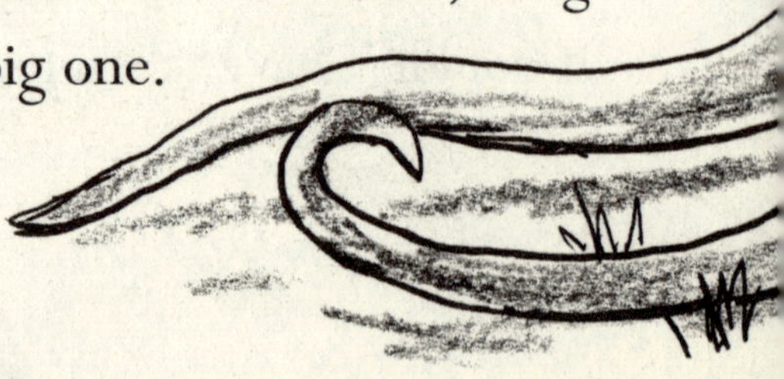

'We could ask those wotchermecallits if they've seen her,' Titanic said.

'Pterodactyls!' said Gargantua scornfully. 'They wouldn't know the difference between an iguanodon and a triceratops. Stupid things! I've no use for them.'

At that moment the small pterodactyl detached itself from the two much larger ones, which were flying very slowly, and flew, very quickly, towards the apatosauruses.

'Ugh!' said Gargantua. 'One of them is coming straight to us. If it speaks, don't answer, Titanic.'

'Good morning!' squeaked Nosy when he reached them. 'I've a favour to ask you. Could I introduce my mum and my daddy to you?' There was no answer.

'Oh,' said Nosy, 'we've got Banty with us,' he added.

'What?' bellowed both apatosauruses.

'We've got Banty. We've brought her home,' said Nosy. 'Look, you can see her now.'

Titanic and Gargantua stretched up their long necks to the fullest extent, and there was their missing daughter, coming towards them, escorted by the two big pterodactyls, which were flying, very slowly, above her.

'Oh, my Banty!' called Gargantua, waddling forward. 'You're safe!'

'Ma thought you might have been eaten by that T. rex,' said Titanic.

'Oh, you saved her!' cried Gargantua to Aviatrix and Clawed. 'You saved my Banty! Oh, how can we ever thank you enough?'

Clawed looked extremely puzzled.

'Saved her?' he began, but Aviatrix quickly interrupted him.

'We are glad to have been of help,' she said to Gargantua. 'We weren't sure if Banty was aware of certain dangers.'

'Like T. rex,' said Clawed. 'Although actually . . .'

'Be quiet a minute, Clawed,' said

Aviatrix, and, 'Hang on, Daddy,' said Nosy, a suggestion which his father instantly obeyed, on a branch of the nearest tree.

Aviatrix and Nosy, hovering above, looked down at Banty, and she looked up at them, and each knew exactly what the others were thinking.

Let my ma and pa believe that the pterodactyl family *did* rescue me somehow, thought Banty, just as Aviatrix and Nosy thought, let's pretend we did rescue her. That way they'll be very grateful and we'll all be the best of friends.

When the apatosauruses had finished nuzzling the child they thought they had lost, Gargantua started to make a speech.

'First of all,' she said to Aviatrix and Nosy, 'please do join your, er . . .'

'Husband,' said Aviatrix.

'Daddy,' said Nosy.

'. . . on that branch. So much less tiring than having to beat your wings all the time,' and when they took her advice, she went on to address the three of them.

'I cannot begin to tell you,' she said, 'how grateful Titanic . . .'

'Your husband?' said Aviatrix.

'My daddy,' said Banty.

'. . . how grateful we are to all of you for saving our beloved child. We have met dear little Nosy before and now are honoured to be introduced to his parents, though I fear I do not know your names.'

'Aviatrix,' said Nosy's mother.

'Clawed,' said his father.

'I,' said Banty's mother, 'am Gargantua, and my husband, Titanic, and we are the happiest apatosauruses in the world thanks to your pterodactylic heroism in rescuing our Banty from the clutches of T. rex.'

'But –' said Clawed.

'Hang on, dear,' said Aviatrix.

'I am hanging on.'

'If you will allow me to say so,' went on

Aviatrix, 'I think that perhaps you, as Banty's parents, should have made her more aware of the danger posed by a certain carnivore . . .'

'T. rex,' said Clawed.

'. . . danger,' continued Aviatrix, 'of which she may have known nothing.'

'We should! We should!' cried Gargantua. 'Just think, Titanic, she might have become the prey of that T. rex that came to the lake if this brave pterodactyl family had not somehow rescued her. Oh, how grateful we are to you all!'

Clawed, as so often, looked puzzled.

'We rescued her, did we, Avy?' he asked.

'Of course we did!' said Aviatrix and Nosy.

Now Titanic cleared his very long throat.

‘As head of the family,’ he said to Clawed, ‘I must thank you, sir, from the bottom of my heart.’

Clawed had by now realized that, what with one thing and another, he had not yet performed what was usually his first act of the day, and in some confusion at this thought and at once again being addressed as 'sir', he became muddled and replied, 'It is I who must thank you, from the heart of my bottom.'

Then he spread his huge wings and flew hastily away to a branch on another tree, where he did his morning poo out of sight of the rest.

Chapter Ten

That first meeting, with all its misunderstanding of Banty's 'rescue', did indeed lead to friendship between the two families of dinosaurs and pterosaurs.

The mothers in particular became great friends. They would now meet regularly by the lake or on the near part of the Great Plain. Obviously this was simpler, for the pterodactyls could fly to these meetings. The adult apatosauruses would have had great difficulty in making their way into the woods. Trees would be falling everywhere before the impact of their bulk.

'It will be so much easier for you, Gargantua,' said Aviatrix. 'It's not the least trouble for us to fly to the lake or the Great Plain or wherever we want to meet. We are, after all, aeronauts of remarkable facility and versatility.'

'How I admire the way you have with words, Aviatrix,' said Gargantua. 'It is such a pleasure to talk with you. And you are all such good fliers.'

I just said that, thought Aviatrix. Ah well, maybe I can improve her vocabulary. Which, to some extent, she did.

Gargantua learned to say 'perambulate' instead of 'walk', 'enumerate' instead of 'count', 'cogitate' or 'deliberate' instead of 'think', and many other long words which, though familiar to Aviatrix, were quite new to the apatosaurus.

'Not the most erudite of creatures, those apatosauruses,' said Aviatrix to her husband later.

'Come again?' said Clawed.

'They don't know very much.'

'Oh,' said Clawed. 'Not as much as we do, eh?'

As I do, said Aviatrix to herself.

'She's not too bad,' she said. 'What d'you think of him?'

'Who?'

'Titanic.'

'Oh, him. Well, he's a fine figure of an apatosaurus, I must say.'

And he called me 'sir', he thought. Not a bad start.

'He's all right,' he said. 'Probably not all that clever, like we are.'

If Aviatrix had possessed eyebrows, she would have raised them.

'Perhaps you could teach him a thing or two, Clawed,' she said.

Fat chance, she thought.

Meanwhile, Banty's parents were talking about the pterodactyls.

'I must tell you, Titanic,' said Gargantua, 'that I have changed my mind about little Nosy's mother and father.'

'Have you, Gargy?' said her husband. 'Because they rescued Banty, you mean?'

'Of course. But also because they turned out to be much brighter than I thought they'd be.'

'He was?' asked Titanic.

He too would have raised his eyebrows if he'd had any.

'Well, perhaps not,' replied Gargantua,

'but she seemed quite intelligent.'

Now, when one set of parents met the other, usually by the lake, it was generally mother who talked to mother, and father to father. Because of the great difference between the two species, these conversations were always conducted in the same way. Each pterodactyl would fly to, and hang from, a branch high enough for each apatosaurus to stretch its very long neck to the fullest extent. Then each was able to speak to the other, face to face, one face of course being upside down.

The mothers talked about all kinds of different things. Their conversations were lively – and filled with long words. It was somewhat different when Clawed met Titanic.

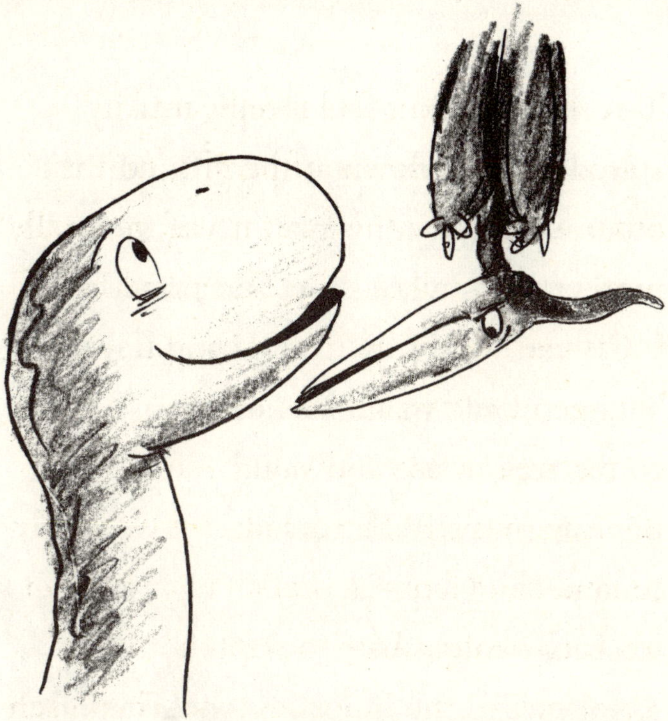

To begin with, neither male quite liked to look the other in the eye. Their faces may have been close, but Titanic tended to look up into the sky or out to the lake or over to the Great Plain, while Clawed, partly because he was upside down and partly because talking to

Titanic made him feel sleepy, usually stared straight down at the ground. In contrast to the conversations of their mates, theirs were short and pretty dull.

Clawed would fly in and hang up, and Titanic would make his heavy way to the tree in use and stand beneath and stretch up his long neck. A typical exchange might be as follows:

Clawed: Morning.

Titanic: Good morning, sir. I trust you're well?

C: Not too bad.

Longish pause.

C: Nice weather.

T: A trifle hot, I fear, for someone of my size. Makes walking tiring.

This last word would make Clawed yawn.

T: How fortunate you are, sir, to have the gift of flight. How pleasant it must be in the upper air.

C: Yes.

T: Your family well?

C: Yes.

Longish pause.

C: Any sign of T. rex?

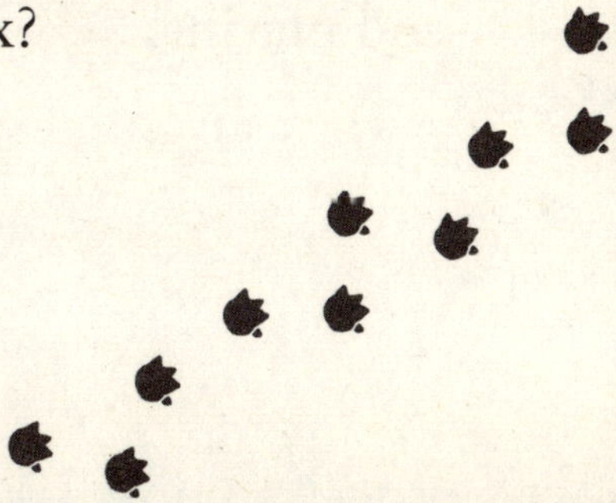

T: No, I think he must be on the other side of the Great Plain.

C: Hope he stays there.

Short pause.

T: If you'll excuse me, sir, I'll go down to the lake for some waterweed, if I may?

C: Please do.

T plods heavily off.

C goes heavily to sleep.

These family meetings between the pterodactyls and the apatosauruses suited Nosy and Banty perfectly. With their parents close by in case of trouble, they could spend time together, chatting and playing.

They invented some games, like

'Hide-and-Seek', where Nosy closed his eyes and counted to a hundred, while Banty went to the lake and submerged. Then, when time was up, Nosy would skim the surface of the water, searching for those two little nostrils which were all that would show of his friend.

Another game was 'Cry T. Rex!' Nosy would wait till Banty was peacefully grazing and then he'd suddenly fly hastily towards her, squeaking, 'T. rex! T. rex! Run, Banty!' and she would run (or rather waddle) as quickly as she could for the safety of the lake, while Nosy watched happily.

To pay him back for frightening her, Banty would sneak up behind a branch on which he was hanging, as quietly as

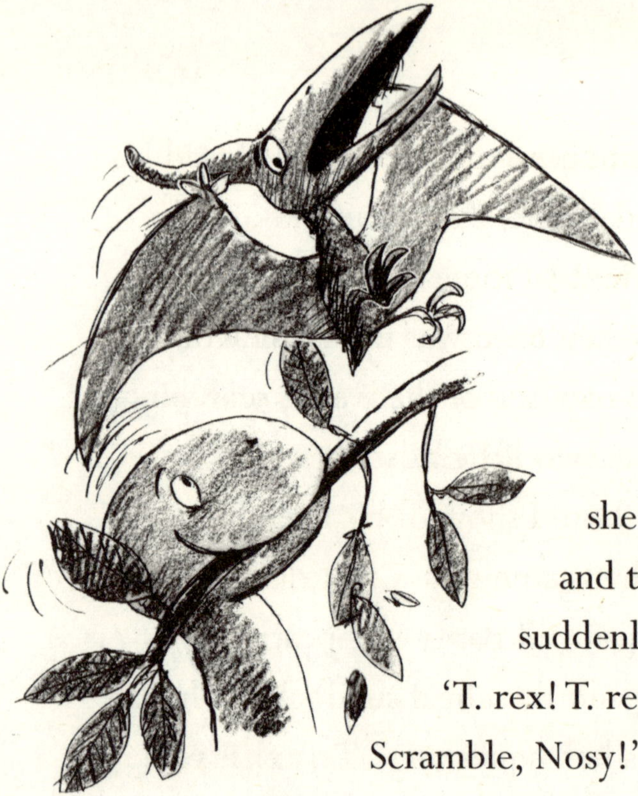

she could, and then suddenly cry, 'T. rex! T. rex! Scramble, Nosy!' She would grasp the branch in her mouth and shake it violently as the awful monster might have done, and then roar with laughter as Nosy flew off in a panic.

The thought of T. rex was in everyone's minds, but for a long time there was mercifully no sign of Hack the Ripper.

He was hunting on the far side of the Great Plain, where many dinosaurs had laid their eggs some months ago. Now there were dozens of nice fat newly hatched babies that made easy and very tasty meals for Hack. A river ran by this side of the plain, so that there was no need for the tyrannosaurus to visit the lake for a drink.

But gradually the slow brains of brachiosaurus or iguanodon or triceratops took in the fact that they were losing a lot of their babies, and that perhaps they had better migrate across the plain.

The herds made for the lake, thinking they would escape from Hack the Ripper.

But they were to be disappointed.

He followed.

Chapter Eleven

Both Nosy's and Banty's families noticed that there were a great many more dinosaurs about the place. Though there was as yet no sign of the Tyrannosaurus rex, they became worried that Hack might come to hunt there again.

The three pterodactyls took it upon themselves to do regular aerial surveys of that part of the Great Plain nearest to the lake. Flying up to a good height, they had a fine pterosaur's-eye view, and would be able to give warning, in time for the apatosaurus family to take cover under water, save for their nostrils.

Aviatrix then arranged a duty roster. Each morning she would fly out first, to be relieved later by Nosy, who in turn gave way to his father. (Clawed did not like early rising.)

One mid-morning, Nosy left the woods and flew off to take over from his mother. He saw no sign of her in the skies, but then caught sight of her as she skimmed low over the part-eaten body of a stegosaurus. Clouds of insects were busy about it, and she was busy about them.

She flew up when she saw Nosy approaching.

'Well,' she said, 'what d'you think killed that, my son?'

'T. rex?'

'Exactly. He's back. I haven't seen any sight of him yet, he's probably busy digesting this breakfast of his. But you keep your eyes skinned. Daddy will be along later.'

After his mother had gone, Nosy flew up high to scan the plain below. A number of herds of different sorts of dinosaurs were grazing below him, but then, suddenly, they all began to move about nervously, and then, in a kind of mass panic, to hurry away, to left or to right, as though some fearful enemy was coming.

T. rex, thought Nosy?

He flew lower over the hustling herds,

and, sure enough, there, marching forward towards the lake on his two great hind legs, his tiny forelegs held against his massive chest, his jaws agape to show those long dagger-like teeth, was Hack the Ripper. He was growling, and soon his growls turned to roars.

There's nothing I can do to save any of these wretched beasts below me, thought Nosy, but I must alert Banty and her ma and pa, so that they can get into the water, and he set off towards the lake. Halfway there he saw a solitary figure, its head buried in the grass of the plain, quietly eating. It was a apatosaurus. It was a young apatosaurus. It was Banty!

Quickly he flew towards her and hovered above her.

'T. rex! T. rex! Run, Banty!' he squealed.

Banty did not even look up.

'Not now, Nosy,' she said, 'not while I'm having my lunch. Anyway, I'm a bit bored with playing "Cry T. Rex!" We'll have to think of another game to play.'

'But this isn't a game, Banty, this is real!' squeaked Nosy. 'Can't you hear him? Look, you can see him now, and he's coming straight for you!'

At this Banty raised her head, stretched her neck and saw Hack.

He was no more than ten apatosaurus-lengths away, and the lake was about the same distance from Banty. She would never reach it in time, he was so much faster on his two legs than she was on her four. At the sight of her, Hack roared even louder.

If only Mum were here, thought Nosy, she could fly at him and scratch his snout like she did before. There's only one thing for it – I'll have to try to do the same.

But at that moment he saw his father come flying from the woods, across the lake and over the fleeing apatosaurus.

'Daddy, Daddy!' he squealed. 'It's T. rex! He's going to kill Banty! Can you do something? Please!'

Clawed may have been slow-witted, but now he showed how quick he could be in action.

'Out of the way, boy!' he cried, and he dived upon the fast-approaching Hack the Ripper.

Then, spreading his great wings wide,

he hovered directly in front of the tyrannosaurus so as to obscure the creature's view of the way ahead.

Snap and snarl as he might, Hack could not shift Clawed out of his path. So he didn't see Banty reach the lake, splosh into it and submerge.

As Clawed wheeled away, Hack dashed on down to the water's edge, but there was nothing to be seen except, some way out, a small pair of nostrils. These, of course, Hack the Ripper did not notice, as he stood knee-deep, cursing the pterodactyl that had blocked his view of the prey.

'Gosh, Daddy!' said Nosy as they circled above. 'You played a blinder!'

Chapter Twelve

Hack the Ripper was furious. Roaring and snarling, he strode back to the body of the stegosaurus, hacking at it to stuff himself full of meat. All the dinosaurs on that part of the Great Plain moved as hastily as they could out of sight of the angry tyrannosaurus. Once again, had they known it, they were in fact quite safe for a while. He would not hunt till he was hungry again.

Gargantua and Titanic had been out in the lake, gathering their daily ration of waterweed, and had seen the drama of Banty's escape.

'Again!' cried Gargantua. 'Again our friends the pterodactyls have saved our Banty!'

'Old Clawed,' said Titanic, 'was pretty good, wasn't he, Gargy?'

'Magnificent,' said his wife. 'Let us collect Banty and then we will all walk to the woods to thank him.'

Later that afternoon, Nosy and his parents were hanging from a favourite branch when they heard a lot of noise in the distance. It sounded like branches breaking, which it was.

Banty could have walked among the trees without damaging them, but Titanic and Gargantua, who were much of a size – enormous – could not.

As they neared the pterodactyls' roost, Titanic attempted to make his way between two very large trees that were growing close together, too close for a apatosaurus to pass. He became stuck.

‘I’m stuck, Gargy!’ he called. ‘What shall I do?’

‘Use your brains,’ Gargantua called back.

Titanic thought about this advice for a while, with no result. Then, growing annoyed, he began to lean sideways, first against one tree, then against the other, until, with a tremendous crash, first one and then the other tree fell, torn up by the roots.

Titanic walked on till he caught up with his wife and his daughter, and all three dinosaurs stood below the high branch from which the three pterosaurs were hanging.

‘Aviatrix, dear,’ Gargantua called up, ‘we have come, Titanic and I, to thank your husband for his heroic efforts in once again saving our child. What do you say, Banty?'

'Thank you, sir,' said Banty.

'And please, sir, accept my grateful thanks,' said Titanic.

Daughter and father both calling me 'sir', thought Clawed. I wish the mother would too, but you can't have everything.

'My dear Gargantua,' said Aviatrix, 'once again we are only too glad to have been of service. Had I been on duty at the time, I should no doubt have flummoxed the dastardly curmudgeon.'

Gargantua looked pleased.

Titanic and Clawed looked puzzled.

Banty and Nosy looked at one another with amusement.

'Well,' said Gargantua, 'we must be

getting back to the lake. Why don't you all come and have a drink with us? To celebrate.'

'Shall we, Clawed?' said Aviatrix.

'Good idea, Avy,' said Clawed.

As the pterodactyls, flying very slowly above their friends, followed the path by which the apatosauruses had reached them, they noticed the two great trees that had been felled.

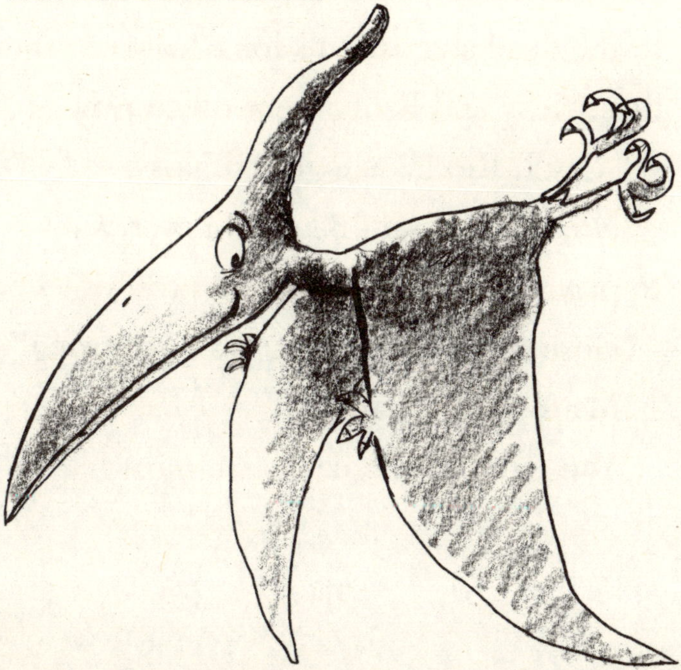

Titanic stopped and stretched up his long neck to address Clawed hovering above.

'I must apologize, sir,' he said. 'I got a bit stuck between those trees, I'm afraid.'

'Don't worry, old lad,' replied Clawed. 'Plenty more trees about.'

When they had all reached the lake and Aviatrix had flown up on a quick reconnaissance patrol to make sure the coast was clear, she and Clawed went off to the dead stegosaurus for a feast of flies. Nosy and Banty went off to play.

'"Cry T. Rex!"?' suggested Nosy.

'No, thanks,' said Banty. 'I never want to play that game again.'

'Gosh!' Nosy said. 'Your pa is so strong!'

'Ma too,' said Banty.

'You will be, one day.'

'Suppose so.'

Nosy let himself down gently on to his friend's neck. They had invented this position, which gave him a rest from flying and still allowed her, if she wished, to graze. One leg on either side of her neck meant that there was no danger of his claws scratching her.

'I've been thinking,' he said.

'Oh yes?'

'Sooner or later we've got to do something about T. rex.'

'What can we possibly do? Your mum and daddy couldn't do anything, nor could Ma and Pa.'

'True,' said Nosy. 'But you and I might, between us. There must be a way to rid us of T. rex.'

'How?'

'Give him a fright,' said Nosy. 'He's always roaring about, attacking baby dinosaurs. I bet he's really a coward. And if *we* attack *him*, he'll get the fright of his life and run away. We'll scare him off.'

Chapter Thirteen

'You must be joking,' said Banty.

'No,' said Nosy, 'I'm not. Think what we saw, just now, when we were walking or flying back through the woods.'

'What?'

'Those two great trees your pa pushed down.'

'Well?'

'Suppose,' said Nosy, 'that T. rex had been under one of those trees when it fell. That would have given him a tremendous fright – and a real bump on the head. Serve him right.'

'Wow!' said Banty. 'But how do we get him in the right place at the right time?'

'Decoy him.'

'Decoy him?'

'Yes,' said Nosy. 'Select a tree, a really big one, for your pa to push over just as T. rex goes past. He could even loosen it a bit before, to make sure it would fall. It would be a kind of trap, you see, and all we have to do is to lure the beast into it.'

'And how do we do that?' asked Banty.

'Like I say, by using a decoy, so that he's chasing it and, as he goes by the tree, your pa gives it a good push and down it comes – straight on to T. rex.'

'I see,' said Banty. 'This decoy isn't one of you, is it? He knows you could just fly away.'

'That's right.'

'And it isn't going to be Pa, who'll be waiting behind the tree. Ma too, probably.'

'That's right.'

'So,' said Banty, 'I am to be the decoy, am I, Nosy?'

'That's right.'

'Just suppose I can't go fast enough. Just suppose he catches me.'

'He won't. Mum and Daddy and I will fly in his face so he can't see where he's going. You'll be all right, Banty.'

'Thanks,' said Banty. 'Glad to know that.'

*

When they got back, they found their parents chatting, the pterodactyls hanging from a branch of a large lakeside tree, the apatosauruses standing below, long necks upstretched.

Nosy hung, Banty stood.

'Nosy has a plan,' she said to them all.

'A plan?' said Aviatrix. 'What about?'

'T. rex.'

'What are you going to do to him?' asked Gargantua.

'Frighten him,' said Nosy. 'Scare him away.'

'Don't be silly, Nosy,' said his mother. 'Run away and play. Scare T. rex indeed!'

'Hang on a minute, Avy,' said Clawed.

'I *am* hanging on!'

'Yes, but let's hear what the boy's got to say. I could do with a good laugh.'

So Nosy outlined his scheme, as he had to Banty.

'She'll have to be the decoy, of course,' he finished up.

‘It’s so simple, isn’t it?’ said Aviatrix sarcastically to the three adults. ‘Titanic just drops a tree on the brute. A tree which is in the woods, which are on the other side of the lake, which means that T. rex will be chasing Banty for a long way, which means he’ll catch her. I never heard of anything more injudicious.’

‘What’s that mean, Mum?’ asked Nosy.

‘Unwise.’

‘I quite agree, Aviatrix,’ said Gargantua. ‘How perspicacious you are!’

Aviatrix looked very pleased. I only taught her that word quite recently, she thought. There’s hope for her yet.

Titanic, standing looking up at the three pterodactyls on their branch, looked further up still.

‘I quite agree with your good lady, sir,’ he said to Clawed. ‘To go all the way to your woods might not be wise. But this tree here is a very large one, which I make bold to say I could, I think, push over, especially with the assistance of my good lady. As close to the lake as we are, it seems to me that Banty could easily escape into the water.’

'No! No!' cried Gargantua. 'Forget about T. rex. We must not put our daughter's life at risk.'

'If we forget about T. rex, Gargy,' said Titanic, 'our daughter may pay for it with her life.'

There was silence for a while as they all thought about Nosy's plan, a silence broken only by a small snore as Clawed, tired by all the talk, dozed off.

'Well, Mum,' said Nosy at last, 'what do you think?'

Aviatrix looked at her son. She suddenly felt very proud of him. Fancy him thinking up such a scheme all by himself. And this was the right spot, no doubt of it, this was where T. rex came to drink, in the shade of this great tree. But wouldn't he see Titanic and Gargantua waiting behind the tree? No, because she and Clawed would pester him all the time. She would use her aerobatic skills to scratch his beastly snout, and Clawed would spread his great wings before him, to confuse him, and Nosy – could Nosy do anything when T. rex came?

'I think it is a fine plan, my son. But tell me, what will you do?' she asked.

Nosy had a sudden brainwave.

'I,' he said, 'will be the first decoy. When T. rex comes down for a drink, I'm going to flutter about on the ground in front of him, as though I were sick or had been hurt, and I'll keep doing that until he catches sight of Banty. I may not be much of a mouthful, but he won't be able to resist chasing me. Then Banty gets into the lake and her pa and ma fell the tree and I'll get out of the way and it will be "Bye-bye, T. rex." You'll see. You'll all see.'

Chapter Fourteen

The best-laid schemes often go wrong, sometimes badly wrong, and it is rare for a plan to succeed completely, turning out in every detail exactly as the planner had hoped.

But this is what happened for Nosy.

By now each member of the two families knew exactly what to do when the time came. They even rehearsed it, pretending that a triceratops, who happened to come down for a drink, was T. rex, and taking up their positions accordingly.

Titanic leaned on the tree quite a bit, so that it was now not as strongly rooted as it had been.

Aviatrix went out on regular long-distance patrols so as to have early warning of the approach of the tyrannosaurus.

One morning, she flew back to the lake at top speed, crying, 'Action stations!' and by the time Hack the Ripper came striding down for a drink, everyone was ready.

Clawed and Nosy took off to join Aviatrix.

Banty stood by the water's edge, looking inviting.

Titanic stood quite still behind the great tree, with Gargantua standing behind him.

Now Nosy flew down and flopped about upon the ground in front of the T. rex, who had by this time caught sight of Banty and was making for her. But he took his eye off her, thinking that he would first kill and eat this annoying flapping, flopping and seemingly flightless thing in his path.

Then Aviatrix flew in at full speed and scratched his snout, and he was blinded by rage, and by Clawed, who had spread his wide wings to spoil his view – of Banty, of Aviatrix, of Titanic and of Gargantua.

The harassed tyrannosaurus was totally bemused. He roared in rage.

'Now!' screamed Nosy at the top of his voice, and then everything happened at once, just as it was meant to.

Banty plunged into the lake, the three pterodactyls winged their way out of danger, Titanic pushed his great weight against the trunk of the tree, and Gargantua pushed her great weight against him.

With an almighty crash, the tree fell, right on top of Hack.

Then all was still, save for one small movement, the movement of something that stuck out from beneath the wreckage.

It was the tip of the tail of Hack the Ripper.

It twitched once, twice, a third time, and then it was still, forever.

Between them, the apatosauruses rolled the tree trunk off the body of the T. rex for all to see, as Banty came dripping out of the lake.

'We've given him more than a fright,' said Nosy.

'He won't hurt us any more. He's as dead as he can be.'

'Well done, Titanic, old chap!' cried Clawed.

'I thank you too, sir,' Titanic replied.

And, 'Well done, Gargantua!' cried Aviatrix. 'Such potency!'

'There's one person,' said Banty, 'that deserves all our thanks. If it hadn't been for him, none of this would have happened.'

'Who's that, then?' asked Clawed.

'Your son, sir,' said Banty. 'My friend. Our hero. Nosy!'

Everyone looked at him and thought what a jolly fine young pterodactyl he was.

Then Titanic and Gargantua lumbered off on to the Great Plain, and Clawed and Aviatrix flew back to the woods.

‘You must be tired, Nosy,’ said Banty. ‘Take a break.’

Gently, Nosy let himself down to sit astride his friend’s neck and together they gazed reflectively at the great broken body of Hack the Ripper.

‘We need never be afraid of him again,’ said Banty.

‘Or,’ said Nosy, ‘as my mum would have put it, there is no longer any necessity to regard him with trepidation.’

‘But,’ said Banty, ‘he can’t be the only T. rex in the world. Another might come, one day.’

‘Not to worry, Banty,’ said Nosy. ‘If it does, I’ll fix it. But you never know, this brute here may be the last of them. Neither Mum nor Daddy nor your ma and pa have ever set eyes on another one. T. rex may now be extinct.'

'What does "extinct" mean, Nosy?' asked Banty.

Remembering exactly what his mother had told him when he was a tiny baby, Nosy replied, 'It means gone, finished, kaput, dead and done for.'

'Wow!' said Banty. 'I like it!'

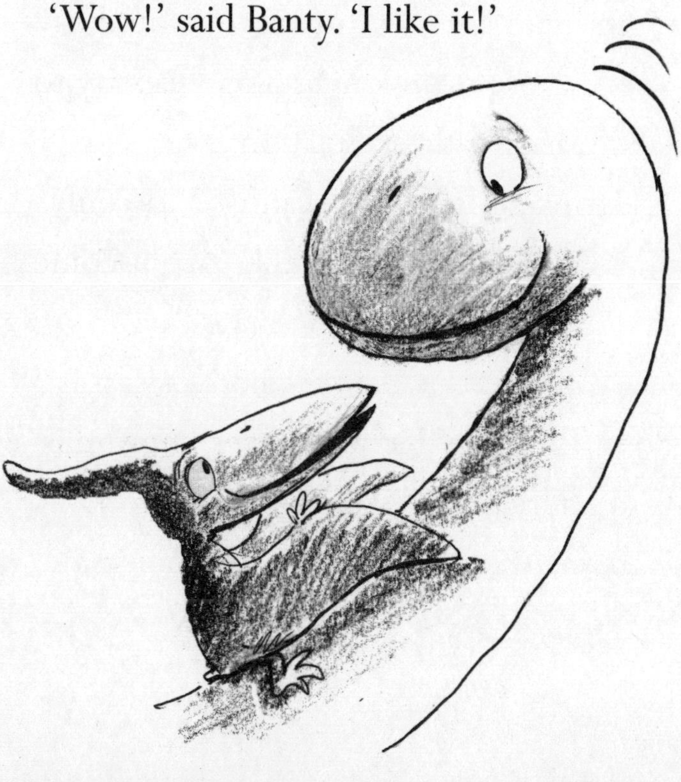

PUFFIN BOOKS

Smasher

Dick King-Smith served in the Grenadier Guards during the Second World War, and afterwards spent twenty years as a farmer in Gloucestershire, the county of his birth. Many of his stories are inspired by his farming experiences. Later he taught at a village primary school. His first book, *The Fox Busters*, was published in 1978. Since then he has written a great number of children's books, including *The Sheep-Pig* (winner of the Guardian Award and filmed as *Babe*), *Harry's Mad*, *Noah's Brother*, *The Hodgeheg*, *Martin's Mice*, *Ace*, *The Cuckoo Child* and *Harriet's Hare* (winner of the Children's Book Award in 1995). At the British Book Awards in 1991 he was voted Children's Author of the Year. He has three children, a large number of grandchildren and several great-grandchildren, and lives in a seventeenth-century cottage only a crow's flight from the house where he was born.

Some other books by Dick King-Smith

ACE
THE CUCKOO CHILD
DAGGIE DOGFOOT
DODOS ARE FOREVER
DRAGON BOY
FIND THE WHITE HORSE
THE FOX BUSTERS
THE GOLDEN GOOSE
HARRY'S MAD
THE HODGEHEG
HOW GREEN WAS MY MOUSE
LADY DAISY
MAGNUS POWERMOUSE
MARTIN'S MICE
THE MERMAN
THE MERRYTHOUGHT
THE MOUSE BUTCHER
NOAH'S BROTHER
PADDY'S POT OF GOLD
PRETTY POLLY
THE QUEEN'S NOSE
THE ROUNDHILL
SADDLEBOTTOM
THE SCHOOLMOUSE
THE SHEEP-PIG
THE STRAY
TREASURE TROVE
THE WATER HORSE
THE WITCH OF BLACKBERRY BOTTOM

Dick King-Smith

Smasher

Illustrated by Ann Kronheimer

PUFFIN BOOKS

PUFFIN BOOKS

Published by the Penguin Group
Penguin Books Ltd, 80 Strand, London WC2R 0RL, England
Penguin Putnam Inc., 375 Hudson Street, New York, New York 10014, USA
Penguin Books Australia Ltd, 250 Camberwell Road, Camberwell, Victoria 3124, Australia
Penguin Books Canada Ltd, 10 Alcorn Avenue, Toronto, Ontario, Canada M4V 3B2
Penguin Books India (P) Ltd, 11 Community Centre, Panchsheel Park, New Delhi – 110 017, India
Penguin Books (NZ) Ltd, Cnr Rosedale and Airborne Roads, Albany, Auckland, New Zealand
Penguin Books (South Africa) (Pty) Ltd, 24 Sturdee Avenue, Rosebank 2196, South Africa

Penguin Books Ltd, Registered Offices: 80 Strand, London WC2R 0RL, England

www.penguin.com

First published by Viking 1996
Published in Puffin Books 1998
Published in this edition 2003
9

Set in 15/18.5 Perpetua

Made and printed in England by Clays Ltd, St Ives plc

British Library Cataloguing in Publication Data
A CIP catalogue record for this book is available from the British Library

ISBN-13: 978–0–14–131639–0

www.greenpenguin.co.uk

One
The Ugly Puppy

'Kindest thing I could do for you,' said Farmer Buzzard, 'would be to knock you on the head.'

He stood in the stable looking down into a shallow wooden box filled with straw, where his collie bitch Kay lay nursing her litter of newborn puppies.

He was not talking to Kay, though she

wagged at the sound of his voice.

He was not talking to three of the four puppies, who were all black-and-white miniatures of their mother.

He was talking to the fourth puppy.

The fourth puppy looked nothing like the others. It was bigger, it was the colour of milky coffee, and it had a very large blunt head with a wrinkled face. It looked, in short, like a freak.

Farmer Buzzard bent down and picked up the fourth puppy in one large hand and held it in front of his face.

'Good job your eyes is closed, my son,' he said to it, 'because if you was to catch sight of yourself in a mirror, you'd have a fit, you would. I never seed anything so ugly in all my born days. You're not going

to be no use to no one. I got to do away with you. I'll be doing you a favour.'

As though she could understand his words, Kay whined softly.

'All right, all right,' said Farmer Buzzard. 'Keep un for now, old girl.' And he put the fourth puppy back with the rest and walked out of the stable.

In the kitchen of the farmhouse, Mrs Buzzard had breakfast ready. As some married couples do, the Buzzards looked strangely alike, so that they might have been taken for brother and sister. Both were tall and angular with strong curved noses, and strangers sometimes thought them well named, so much did they put them in mind of a pair of big birds of prey. Oddly, Mrs Buzzard had been a Miss Hawk before she got married.

Now she said, as she had said every mealtime for the past thirty years, 'Wash your hands.'

Farmer Buzzard washed them. As he stood drying them, he said, 'Kay's whelped.'

'How many pups?' asked Mrs Buzzard.

'Four.'

'All right, are they?'

'Three are. Look just like Kay.'

'What's up with t'other?'

'Martha,' said Farmer Buzzard solemnly,

'he's the ugliest puppy you ever did see. Who the father of them is I do not know, but to see this puppy you'd think his dad was the Hound of the Baskervilles. I shall have to knock him on the head.'

Mrs Buzzard smiled. She knew how tender-hearted her husband was, and she put a plate of bacon and eggs in front of him and said, 'Eat your breakfast, Ken, and then you can go and put the poor little creature out of his misery. A little runt, is he?'

'No,' said Farmer Buzzard. 'He's the biggest.'

'Weakly, then?'

'No, the strongest.'

'Just ugly?'

'Aye,' said Farmer Buzzard. 'Ugly as sin.'

'Dear, dear,' said Mrs Buzzard.

At the end of the morning, when her husband came in for his midday meal, she said, 'Done it then?'

'Done what?' said Farmer Buzzard.

'Put that puppy down.'

'Oh no, I forgot. Been that busy.'

In the afternoon Mrs Buzzard went out with a bucket of corn and a basket, to feed her hens and collect their eggs. On her way back she went into the stable to see Kay and her litter. The three black-and-white puppies were all asleep, full fed, but the big brown puppy was still nursing busily, and the look of pride on the collie bitch's face told Mrs Buzzard

just what the mother thought of
this hideous child.

'Don't you fret, my girl,' she said to the dog. 'He won't never harm un. He's too soft.'

That evening after tea she said to her husband, 'Treat

yourself to a glass of beer, I should. 'Twill make you feel better. It must have been a hard thing to do.'

'Feel better?' said Farmer Buzzard. 'Hard thing? What are you on about?'

'Killing that puppy, of course.'

Farmer Buzzard grinned sheepishly.

'I never,' he said.

'Why ever not?'

'Not his fault he looks like he does. You never know, he might get better-looking when he's growed.'

'Can't fail to,' said Mrs Buzzard.

'You know what, Martha?' said her husband. 'I think I'll have that glass of beer. You like anything?'

'I shouldn't mind a drop of port,' said Mrs Buzzard, and when her husband had

fetched the glasses, she said, 'We'll drink his health, shall us?'

'What, that puppy?'

'Yes. And he ought to have a name, now

that you've decided to keep him.'

'Don't know about keeping him,' said Farmer Buzzard. 'I shall be selling all the puppies once they're old enough.'

'Reckon anyone will want him? Seeing he's so ugly? Perhaps that's what we'd better call him. "Ugly." After all, even if he does improve in looks, he's never going to be a smasher, is he?'

'"Smasher"!' said Farmer Buzzard. 'That's it! That's what we'll call him!' and they touched glasses and drank.

Two
Chicken Chasing

Eight weeks later, Farmer Buzzard put an advertisement in the local paper, which read:

**COLLIE PUPPIES FOR SALE, TWO DOGS,
ONE BITCH, FROM GOOD WORKING MOTHER
STEADY ON SHEEP OR CATTLE.**

When Mrs Buzzard read it, she said,

'I see you've only advertised three.'

'That's right,' said her husband.

'Well, well,' said Mrs Buzzard.

Over the next few days several people came to look at the puppies.

The first was another farmer, a neighbour of the Buzzards, and he knew exactly what he wanted.

'I'll have the bitch puppy, Ken,' he said. 'I've always fancied having a daughter of your Kay's. She's a good un, she is.'

He squatted on his heels and patted the three black-and-white pups.

'Nice level lot,' he said. 'Who's the father?'

'Oh, you wouldn't know him,' said Farmer Buzzard.

At that moment Smasher, who had been

playing by himself in a far corner of the stable, came bumbling up, pushing his rather smaller brothers and sister out of his way, and licked the neighbour's hand with a large slobbery tongue.

'What's this then?' said

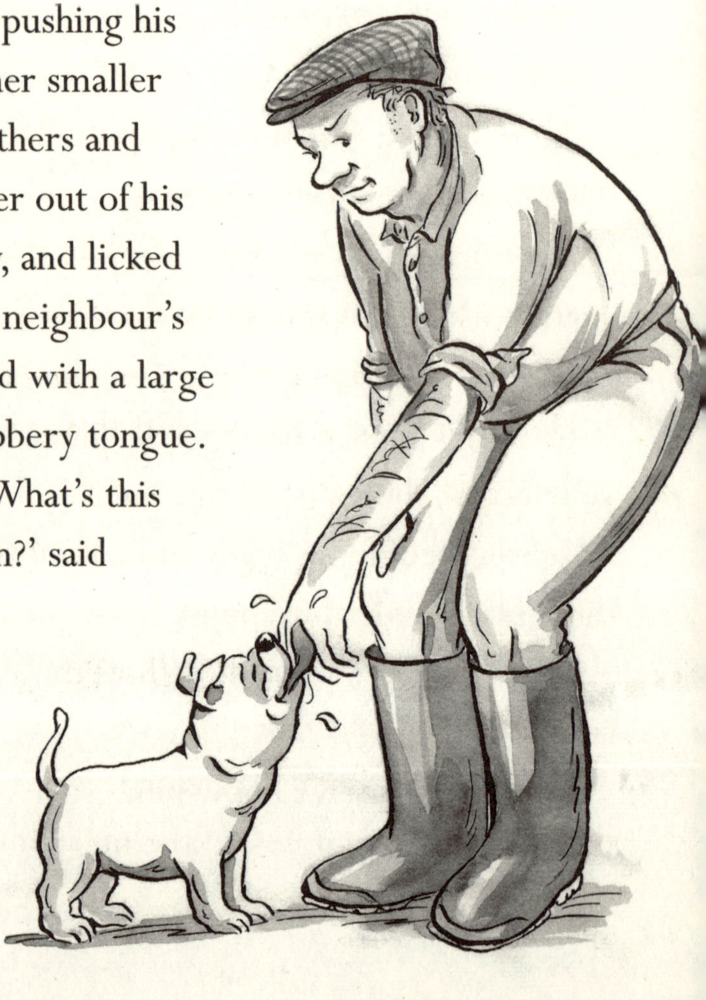

the neighbour. 'He's never out of the same litter, is he?'

Farmer Buzzard nodded.

'Throwback,' he said.

'Throwback!' said the neighbour. 'I reckon I'd have thrown him out.'

He looked at the brown puppy, noting the size of his feet and the folds of loose skin on his big face.

'He's more like a bull mastiff than a collie, he is,' he said. 'Puts me in mind of that guard dog that Fred Selman used to have, up at Hollybush Farm. What an object! However did your Kay come to have one like that?'

'Dunno,' said Farmer Buzzard.

'Ain't he ever ugly!' said the neighbour, and when there was no reply to this, added, 'Well, he's no beauty, Ken, is he?'

'Not pertickerly,' said Farmer Buzzard. 'You going to keep him?'

'Dunno. I might.'

The second man to come in search of a puppy was obviously short-sighted. He wore a pair of thick spectacles, and when he was shown the three remaining puppies, pointed straight at Smasher and said, 'I'll have the brown one.'

For a split second Farmer Buzzard was tempted. Here was the one chance of a home for the ugly puppy (which he didn't need to keep – Kay did all the work of the farm with no trouble). Nobody but the half-blind man would have picked him.

The farmer looked at Smasher's large wrinkled face, turned up to him with a sort of grin on it.

'Sorry,' he said, 'the brown un's not for sale. There's two other dog puppies to pick from.'

'You choose one of them for me then,' said the short-sighted man. 'My sight's not so good these days. Pity about the brown one though. A fine-looking little chap, from what I can see.'

That same day the other black-and-

white dog puppy was sold to another farmer, and Smasher was left alone with his mother.

That night, as he lay beside her in the stable, he said, thoughtfully, 'I don't look much like you, Mum, do I?'

Kay surveyed her remaining child. Poor little chap, she thought.

‘No, dear,’ she said. ‘Not a lot.’

‘And I don’t look like my brothers or my sister did.’

‘No, dear. You must take after your father.’

‘What was he like, Mum?’

‘Tall. And dark.’

‘And handsome?’

‘Oh yes,’ said Kay.

'So when I grow up, I'll be tall, dark and handsome, shall I, Mum?'

'Of course you will, dear,' said Kay. 'Of course you will.'

That night as she lay in bed beside her husband, Mrs Buzzard said, thoughtfully, 'What are you going to do with him then, Ken?'

'Who?' said Farmer Buzzard sleepily.

'Smasher. Going to train him to work sheep?'

'No. He got no gift for that,' said Farmer Buzzard, for he had noticed that, while the other three puppies had begun to try to herd his wife's chickens about the farmyard, Smasher had taken no part in this instinctive sheepdog behaviour. His only occasional contribution had been to rush at a hen, open-mouthed, and try to grab hold of

it. The farmer had not told his wife this.

'Well, what have you kept him for then?' asked Mrs Buzzard. 'Not for his looks, surely? Come on, admit it, you've just got a soft spot for him, haven't you?'

'Not pertickerly,' said Farmer Buzzard.

But he had.

It was just as well that he had, because, some weeks later, Smasher went looking for trouble. Not only was he growing fast, he was also faster on his feet, and he started to chase chickens in earnest.

Feathers began to fly, and, fearing that blood would soon be spilled, Kay gave her son a good talking-to.

'Smasher,' she said (for, hearing his

name on the farmer's lips, she had learned it, just as, long ago, she had learned her own), 'you are *not* to chase chickens. Do you understand?'

'Why not, Mum?'

'Because if my master catches you doing it, he will beat you.'

'Why, Mum?'

'Because dogs are not allowed to chase chickens.'

'Why not, Mum?'

'Because people don't like that.'

'Why, Mum?'

Kay lost patience.

'Oh be quiet!' she growled. 'And don't you dare say, "Why, Mum?"' and she walked away.

'Why not, Mum?' said Smasher under his breath. Chicken chasing is fun, he thought, and next day he waited until his mother had left the yard with the farmer to go round the sheep, and then he went into action.

Mrs Buzzard was making bread, when she heard through the open kitchen

window a frantic chorus of shrieks and squawks, and, looking out, saw hens flapping madly everywhere as the big brown puppy galloped clumsily among them. Some birds in their panic fluttered into the duckpond, and after them rushed Smasher, and after him ran Mrs Buzzard on her long thin legs, a rolling-pin in her floury hand and a string of angry words on her lips.

Smasher fled and the waterlogged hens floundered to safety and Mrs Buzzard fumed. She had quite a temper and she was very angry.

'What d'you think your dog's been up to?' said Mrs Buzzard when she next saw her husband.

'My dog?' said Farmer Buzzard. 'She's been with me, all morning.'

'No, not Kay. Your puppy, that Smasher. Only chasing my chickens, that's all. Drove some of them into the duckpond and half drowned them.'

'Oh,' said Farmer Buzzard.

'No good you standing there saying "Oh",' said Mrs Buzzard. 'He wants a beating, he does, teach him a lesson.'

Farmer Buzzard went to find Smasher.

No good beating him now, he thought, he won't understand what it's for. Have to catch him in the act.

Smasher was lying beside his mother in the stable with his ugly head on his paws, looking as though butter wouldn't melt in his big mouth.

'He's been a bad boy, Kay,' said Farmer Buzzard softly. 'You ought to have learned him better.'

Then he picked up a length of rope, and with it he struck six hard blows on an old canvas tarpaulin that was hung from the roof beam to dry.

'Naughty dog!' shouted Farmer Buzzard loudly as he whacked the tarpaulin, while Kay and Smasher looked on in astonishment.

'Sounds like you gave him what for,' said

Mrs Buzzard when her husband returned. 'Didn't hit him too hard, I hope? He's only little.' She was already regretting making the farmer punish Smasher.

'No,' said Farmer Buzzard.

'He's a brave one though,' said his wife. 'I could hear you beating him plain as plain, yet he never made a sound.'

'No,' said Farmer Buzzard.

'The master sounded angry,' said Smasher to his mother when Farmer Buzzard had gone.

'Yes,' said Kay, thoughtfully.

She looked carefully at her son. Stuck to the corner of his mouth, she could see, was a single small wet white feather.

'You've been chasing those chickens again,' she said.

'Just for fun, Mum,' said Smasher. 'I won't do it again,' he said.

Or not while you're around, he thought.

'You better not,' Kay said.

Because, she thought, puppies that chase chickens could well end up as dogs that chase sheep. And dogs that chase sheep could well end up dead.

Three
As Good as Gold

Up till now, Smasher had not been allowed into the farmhouse. Once or twice he had tried to follow Kay in, but Mrs Buzzard had always shooed him out again.

'You stop out in the stable, my lad,' she had said. 'You can make as much mess as you like out there.'

But then she changed her mind, for two reasons. One was on account of her hens. He needs watching, that puppy does, she thought, while Ken and Kay are out round the farm. That's when he gets into mischief. Better if he's with me, then I can keep my eye on him.

The second reason was that she felt guilty. I never should have told Ken to beat him, she said to herself (and that hard too, it's not like him). After all, he's only a puppy even though he's growed so big, as big as his mother he is already.

So one morning, when the farmer and the collie bitch had gone out on their rounds, Mrs Buzzard opened the back door and called, 'Smasher!'

She called, had she known it, in the nick

of time, for Smasher was just about to have a go at one of her hens, which had most unwisely wandered into the stable.

Smasher was lying quite still, pretending to be asleep. I'll corner this one, he thought. I know Mum said I shouldn't but this is too good a chance to miss.

Then he heard his name called.

What a great thing he's getting, thought Mrs Buzzard as she watched him lumbering across the yard towards her. He's not got any better looking but maybe he's got more sensible. He hasn't bothered the hens lately. She reeled as, unable to stop in time, he bumped into her legs.

'Steady!' she said. 'Clumsy great elephant,' and she turned back into the house.

Smasher sat down outside the open back door. He did not expect to be invited in. He had discussed this with his mother.

‘Why don’t they want me in the house, Mum?’ he had said.

'Because you're a yard dog,' said Kay. 'Not a house dog.'

'But you go in, and you're a sheepdog, not a house dog.'

'I'm both, dear,' said Kay. 'I know how to behave properly indoors.'

So now it was with surprise that he heard Mrs Buzzard calling, 'Smasher. Come along in. Good boy.'

Ears cocked, he hurried through the door and along a passage that led to the kitchen. The passageway was dark, and Smasher did not see that at one side of it there was a tall old-fashioned umbrella-stand holding a clutch of walking-sticks and hung with many mackintoshes and coats and hats – until he barged straight into it.

It fell down with a great clatter, and the mass of clothing buried him.

'Clumsy as a *herd* of elephants, I should have said!' cried Mrs Buzzard as she put everything in order again.

While she was doing this, she heard a loud racket in the kitchen. Smasher had upset a large tin basin full of dog's drinking-water which now streamed across the floor.

'What next!' cried Mrs Buzzard. Her question was soon answered.

As ill luck would have it, Mrs Buzzard was preparing to make jam that day, and had put ready, on a low wooden bench close to the stove, a double rank of glass screwtop jars.

As she knelt on the kitchen floor, mopping up the water, Smasher, seeing her for the first time down at his own level on hands and knees, thought she was playing some sort of game. Eagerly he bounded forward to lick her face, his long thick tail whipping madly from side to side. Each stroke of it sent jam-jars tumbling off the bench to smash to pieces on the flagged floor.

How aptly was he named at that moment.

'Smasher!' screamed Mrs Buzzard. 'You bad dog, you!' And she stood up and grabbed a mop. She aimed a furious blow at the puppy, a blow which broke the remaining jam-jars, while Mrs Buzzard slipped on the wet floor and fell flat on her back.

When she got to her feet once more, Smasher was nowhere to be seen.

'Only meself to blame,' grumbled Mrs Buzzard as she went down the passage to shut the back door.

'And you can stop out!' she shouted down the yard as she closed it. 'Should have had more sense than to let you in in the first place!'

*

Smasher, however, was still in the house.

Bewildered by the crash of breaking glass and the sound of Mrs Buzzard's angry voice and the fact that she was trying to hit him, he had bolted out of the kitchen through the nearest door, into another of the many passageways that threaded the rambling old farmhouse. A little way along it was a small room from which a most attractive smell came to Smasher's blunt nose.

Curious, he looked into the larder and saw, upon a marble slab, a large piece of meat. Carefully, for he could still hear Mrs Buzzard's angry voice in the distance, he took the leg of lamb in his mouth, and proceeded down the passage till he came to another room.

This was Mrs Buzzard's front parlour, a room which was her pride and joy, never used except when there was special company. It contained two large armchairs and a sofa, all upholstered in a kind of pale blue velvet, and a number of small slender-legged tables on which stood a great many china ornaments.

Something told Smasher he had better lie low for a bit.

Earlier that morning he had been down to the duckpond for a drink and a little paddle. His large feet (though Mrs Buzzard had not noticed this) had on their pads a good deal of mud, mostly composed of duck muck. It had dried, but now the water spilled on the kitchen floor had wetted it again.

Smasher padded across the room, carrying the leg of lamb, and the carpet, which was a cream colour, acquired a brand-new pattern.

He hoisted himself up on to the sofa and tucked in to the meat.

This is more comfortable than the stable, he thought, when only the bone was left. I'll have a nap now.

After a while Smasher woke suddenly. He felt an urgent need. He had drunk a great deal of water from the duckpond, and now he needed to get rid of some of it.

Only a few days ago he had, for the first time ever, not squatted as puppies do but cocked his leg against the stable doorpost.

'Watch me, Mum,' he had said. 'You can't do that, can you?'

'I don't do that,' said Kay.

Now he cocked his leg against the side

of the blue velvet sofa and then, for luck, against each of the armchairs.

Handy trick that is, he said to himself with a sigh of relief. Better than squatting in the middle of the carpet. She might not have liked that. Now then, if I'm going to be a house dog, I'd better have a good look round the place.

He wandered out of the parlour and along the passage till he came to the foot of a flight of stairs. Smasher humped himself up these and saw, facing the head of the stairs, an open bedroom door.

It was the Buzzards' bedroom, and on the Buzzards' bed, as yet unmade, was a candlewick bedspread, fringed with rows of little round bobbles. After trying unsuccessfully to jump up on the bed,

Smasher contented himself with chewing off a great many of the bobbles.

Then he turned his attention to the bottom of the curtains and altered their shape a good deal. Then he found Mrs Buzzard's mules and chewed up the left one. Then he came across Farmer

Buzzard's bedroom slippers and chewed up one of those (the right one, as it happened).

After that, bored with chewing things, Smasher decided to go downstairs again. They were quite steep, and he fell most of the way.

Passing the parlour door once more, he looked in. There, on the sofa, sniffing at the lamb bone, *his* lamb bone, was one of Mrs Buzzard's cats.

Furiously, Smasher rushed at it, overturning a couple of little tables on his way into the room

and another couple on his way out after the fleeing cat, while china ornaments flew everywhere.

The cat dashed out through the back door, which Mrs Buzzard had left open while she went down the yard to make sure that Smasher wasn't after her hens.

Smasher followed, but the cat was much too quick for him and he gave up the chase.

Smasher made his way to the stable and lay down, full of lamb and tired out by his morning's work.

A few minutes later Mrs Buzzard looked in and saw him lying there.

'Bless him,' she said as she made her way back to the farmhouse.

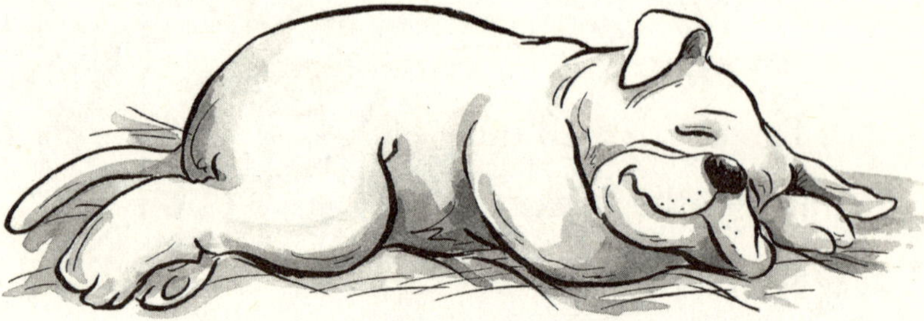

'There's me thinking the worst of him and all the time he's lying there as good as gold.'

In the kitchen she looked up at the clock on the wall, and said, 'Now then, I must make the bed and dust the front parlour and then I'll put that nice leg of lamb on to cook . . .'

Four
The Field-barn

'And on top of all that,' said Mrs Buzzard, 'he wetted on my three-piece suite!'

She had just finished detailing to her husband the damage done by the puppy, his puppy. She was absolutely furious.

'Add it all together,' she said, 'and you're looking at a hundred pounds' worth and more. You named him well, you did.'

'Oh,' said Farmer Buzzard.

'No good you standing there saying "Oh",' replied Mrs Buzzard. 'What are you going to do about it? That's what I'm asking.'

'Dunno.'

'Well, I do. That animal is never coming inside my house again, never. Which I dare say he'll try to do unless I keeps every door shut from now on. Which I'm not prepared to do, this fine weather. So there's only one answer.'

'What's that, Martha?' said Farmer Buzzard.

'You got to get rid of him.'

'Sell him, you mean?'

'Don't know about sell him,' said Mrs Buzzard. 'Nobody would buy such an ugly creature, not unless 'twas a half-blind man.'

'You surely don't mean,' said Farmer Buzzard, 'that you want me to . . .' He stopped, unable to complete the sentence.

'I don't care what you does, Ken,' said Mrs Buzzard, her eyes flashing, 'just so long as he's gone. After today, I never wants to set eyes on him again.'

Meanwhile, in the stable, Smasher was saying, 'Guess what, Mum.'

'What, dear?'

'I think I'm going to be a house dog. I was invited into the house today.'

'Did you enjoy it?'

'Oh yes!' said Smasher. 'It was smashing.'

'I hope you behaved yourself,' said Kay.

At that moment they saw the farmer coming across the yard towards them. He carried his gun in the crook of his arm.

He picked up the length of rope with which he had once whacked the tarpaulin, and tied it round Smasher's neck. Then he set off with the two dogs, Smasher cavorting excitedly on the end of the rope, Kay trotting soberly at heel. Out through the yard gate they went and off across the fields.

Some time afterwards Mrs Buzzard, sitting at her sewing-machine repairing her tattered bedroom curtains, heard the bang of a distant gun.

'Oh, no!' she said. 'He's surely never been and gone and . . .' she stopped, unable to complete the sentence.

'I heard a shot,' she said when her husband returned.

'Rabbit,' said Farmer Buzzard. 'Missed him.'

That evening Mrs Buzzard had no cause to go into the stable, but if she had, she would have found Kay there alone.

So busy was Mrs Buzzard with curtain mending, and bedspread mending, and the cleaning of carpet and furniture, and the repair of broken ornaments, and the collecting of replacement jam-jars that it was not until twenty-four hours later that she found time to say, 'That Smasher. What have you done with him?'

'Found him a good home,' said Farmer Buzzard.

'That's quick, then,' said Mrs Buzzard with relief. 'Difficult, was it, to place him?'

'Not pertickerly,' said Farmer Buzzard.

At the far end of the farm there stood, in the middle of a field, an old stone barn with a walled yard in front of it. Here, in winter, Farmer Buzzard kept a dozen or so store cattle.

Now it contained one animal only – Smasher.

This was where the farmer had gone the previous day, gun in hand, one dog at heel, the other on a rope, while slung across his back was his gamebag. In it was a feeding-dish and a supply of dog food.

When they reached the field-barn, Farmer Buzzard shut the gate of the yard behind them and let Smasher off the rope.

He checked that there were some straw bales inside the building, that the cattle-trough was low enough for Smasher to drink from and that the bars of the gate were too close together for him to squeeze between. The walls were too high to be jumped.

It was a prison certainly, but a roomy

and comfortable one nevertheless, and a perfect hiding-place. No one ever came there but the farmer. Mrs Buzzard certainly wouldn't. No one would know.

Farmer Buzzard sat down on a bale of straw, and Smasher bumbled up and shoved his wrinkled face into his master's lap.

Farmer Buzzard did his best to explain the position to the exile.

'Now you listen here, my boy,' he said, 'while I puts you in the picture. You've blotted your copybook proper, you have, and my missus wants to see the back of you for good and all. She'd like me to take you to the Dogs' Home, I dare say. Or worse. Which I'm not going to do. And why not? Because I've growed fond of you, ugly and clumsy and destructive as you are. There's good in you somewheres, I'm sure of it. So you've got to stop here whether you likes it or not, and your mum and me, we'll come and visit you every day, to exercise you and to feed you, while we give things time to settle down at home.'

'What was all that about, Mum?' asked Smasher as the farmer stood up and, cutting the strings of the straw bale he'd been sitting on, began to strew it about to make a bed.

Kay had not of course understood Farmer Buzzard's actual words, but she knew instinctively what was going to happen. Smasher, for some reason, was going to be kept down here in the field-barn for the time being. He must have done something wrong. He's in the dog-house, she thought to herself.

'I think, dear,' she said, 'that the master was telling you that now you're a big boy – not a puppy any more but a dog – he's giving you your very own place to live. See, he's brought your feeding-dish and he's going to give you your supper now and a lovely supper it looks.'

Farmer Buzzard put the loaded

feeding-dish down on the floor, and Smasher tucked in.

Quietly the farmer said, 'Come, Kay,' and quickly they slipped out of the barn, through the yard, and out of the gate, which Farmer Buzzard latched behind them.

It's only for a few days, he said to himself as they walked home. Till the storm blows over.

But all the same he was worried at the thought of the dog left all alone, so much so that when a rabbit popped up right in front of them, he completely missed his shot.

When Smasher had finished his food, he went to the gate, through which, his nose

told him, his mother and the master had gone. But it was closed. He tried to squeeze between the bars, but he was too big.

Oh well, he thought, they'll be back in a

minute. He was quite used to being on his own during the daytime, in the stable. He had a drink at the cattle-trough, went into the barn, lay down on his straw bed, and went to sleep.

When he woke again it was getting dark, and still they hadn't come back. Mum's always back by dark, he thought. Never in his short life had Smasher slept a night on his own.

He went to the gate again and looked out, but there was nothing to be seen except the distant lights of the farmhouse.

That's where I should be if I'm going to be a house dog, thought Smasher, not stuck out here, and he pointed his blunt snout at the sky and let out a long doleful howl.

In the stable Kay heard it. Poor boy, she thought, he's lonely.

In the house Mrs Buzzard heard it.

'What's that?' she said.

'Dog howling somewhere,' said Farmer Buzzard.

'Not Kay, is it?'

'No, she's in the stable.'

'Well, it can't be that Smasher,' said Mrs Buzzard. 'He's in his new home, I'm thankful to say. He'll soon settle down there.'

'I hopes,' said Farmer Buzzard.

Five
A Stifled Sneeze

'Only a few days,' Farmer Buzzard had said to himself, but two months later, Smasher was still living in the field-barn.

The more he thought about it, the more the farmer was sure that there was no point in bringing the dog back to the farm yet, much less in hoping that Smasher would be allowed in the house again.

Mrs Buzzard was still so cross she would never allow it.

The return from exile could only possibly happen when Smasher was a fully trained animal.

'So,' said Farmer Buzzard to Kay, 'we must set about training this son of yours. He must have some of your brains, whoever his father was. And he's anxious to please, which is half the battle.'

On this last point he was right. Smasher was indeed keen to be in the farmer's good books, and when, after that first evening, his mother told him that howling at night (or at any other time) was not a good idea, he did not howl again.

At first he thought of the field-barn as a prison with its own exercise yard, but as time went on, and Kay kept telling him how lucky he was to have such a place all to himself, Smasher began first to accept and then quite to enjoy his solitary life.

Nor was it all that solitary, for the master came with Kay three times every day. They came in the morning, on their rounds of the sheep and cattle, and again in the evening, when Smasher was fed. And in the middle of each day, in the early afternoon, Farmer Buzzard set aside a couple of hours for a training session.

He was by nature a good trainer of dogs, knowledgeable and firm and above all patient, and he was determined that this ugly dog of his should become a model pupil. Tearing things up in the house and making messes was puppy stuff, never to be repeated.

To put his teeth to proper use, he gave Smasher big marrow bones to gnaw, but the teaching of cleanliness was a more difficult problem.

The only way open to him, Farmer Buzzard decided, was to pretend that the field-barn was a house and teach Smasher to do

everything he had to do in the yard outside. Barn-trained equalled house-trained, he reckoned.

It took time, because Smasher couldn't see the point of it, but Kay encouraged him and the farmer rewarded him, and soon it became habit.

In the meantime Smasher was taken around the farm (always out of sight of the house) on a leash, and taught to walk at heel, and then (off the leash) to sit, and

at the command 'Down!' to lie down, and at 'Stay!' to remain lying down, even though the master should move away from him. At first Farmer Buzzard only took a few steps away, but before too long he could walk half across a field and stop and look back to see Smasher still lying where he had been put. After the earlier business with the chickens, Farmer Buzzard was concerned that Smasher might chase the cattle, or worse, the sheep. But he need not have worried. Smasher showed no interest in either.

The credit for this was Kay's.

The very first time that Smasher had gone among the flock of sheep while off the leash, he had made a little rush at a lamb while the farmer's back was turned.

Farmer Buzzard looked round at the sound of a sudden growl followed by a sharp yelp of pain, to see Smasher holding up a paw and looking very sorry for himself. Kay, he saw, had her hackles up.

Perhaps he trod on her, he thought. He's clumsy enough and a lot bigger than her too.

‘What’s up, Kay?’ he said, but she could not of course answer.

‘Ow!’ cried Smasher. ‘That hurt, Mum! What did you want to do that for?’

‘To teach you a lesson, I hope,’ said Kay angrily. ‘I told you before what happens to dogs who chase sheep. I never want to see you chasing an animal on this farm again, ever, whether it’s chickens or bullocks or sheep, do you understand?’

‘Yes, Mum,’ said Smasher, licking his bitten paw.

‘You’re doing very well in your training,’ said Kay, ‘so don’t go messing it up now.

Say to yourself, whatever happens, I must always act sensibly.'

'Yes, Mum,' said Smasher. 'If I do,' he said, 'd'you think I'll be a house dog in the end?'

'I don't know,' said Kay.

She looked up at the farmer and whined a little, which meant, 'D'you think he will be?' but he could not of course answer.

When two months had gone by, a major problem arose.

The time was fast approaching when Farmer Buzzard would need the field-barn and yard to house a dozen bullocks through the winter months. Then there would be no way that Smasher could stay. He might be barn-trained but the bullocks certainly weren't.

'I got no choice,' said the farmer to Kay. 'He'll have to come back up the farm. Can't take him in the house, Martha won't have it, but she might just put up with him being in the stable again. After all, time's passed since he did all that damage, and what's more, he's well-trained now.'

Farmer Buzzard left things as late as he could, but it had been a wet autumn, and already the heavy bullocks were beginning

to poach the fields, to tread the grass, especially around the gateways and water-troughs, into a muddy mess.

'Anyways,' he said to Kay, 'with the cold weather coming we can't leave Smasher down here all through the winter. He needs to come in by the fire night times, like you do.'

So he decided that the following

Saturday he would yard the bullocks and bring Smasher back to the farm.

He did not try to prepare the way for this by any mention of his plan to his wife. She, after all, believed that the dog had been living with a new master for almost three months now.

'We'll just have to take a chance,' he said to Smasher. 'One thing's certain, I'm not getting rid of you.' And he patted his ugly brown dog.

As he did so, it struck him how much Smasher had grown, what a big strong animal he now was, and he remembered the words of his neighbour who had bought Smasher's sister.

'He's more like a bull mastiff than a collie,' he had said.

'You are, too,' he said now. 'And as for ugly, well, I don't know so much about that. Maybe I've just got used to the way you look, with that wrinkly pushed-in face of yours, but I wouldn't call you ugly.

True, you're not as handsome as some but all the same you've growed into a fine strong dog. You look – what's the word I want? – noble. Yes, that's it, noble.'

On the Saturday that he was going to yard the bullocks, Farmer Buzzard said to Smasher, 'You don't know it, my son, but you'll be spending this night in the stable.'

What he did not know was that Smasher would be spending that night in the farmhouse.

Fate, in the shape of another dog, took a hand in the matter.

Just as the farmer was about to set off with Kay to take the bullocks down to the field-barn, the phone rang.

Mrs Buzzard answered it.

'Yes?' she said. 'Oh, no! Oh dear, oh

dear! Oh, yes. Of course. Yes. No. Yes. No. Straight away.'

'What was all that about, Martha?' asked her husband.

'That was our Bertha,' said Mrs Buzzard.

Mrs Buzzard's unmarried sister Bertha lived in the nearby town, alone save for her dog, a much-spoiled Spaniel.

'That Trixibelle of hers,' went on Mrs Buzzard, 'tripped her up and she fell down the stairs. Nothing broken, doctor says, but she's ever so bruised and she wants me to come for a few days and look after her. You could manage, couldn't you, Ken?'

'I dare say,' replied Farmer Buzzard.

'You'll have Kay for company.'

Not only Kay, thought the farmer.

'You don't mind, then?'

'Not pertickerly,' said Farmer Buzzard.

That evening, when Mrs Buzzard had gone to her sister's and the bullocks were safely yarded down at the field-barn, Farmer Buzzard sat comfortably in his favourite chair, watching the telly. At his feet lay his dogs.

Farmer Buzzard enjoyed television. Recently he had treated himself to a brand-new set, the latest model, with a very big screen.

When it had arrived, Mrs Buzzard had said, 'You want to put a rug or summat over that thing night times.'

'Whatever for?' said Farmer Buzzard.

'Burglars,' said Mrs Buzzard. 'There's been a lot of it about, breaking into people's houses and taking their tellies and video recorders and that. They look through the window and see that great thing, they'll have it.'

'That's in town,' said Farmer Buzzard. 'They don't come out here.'

Now, at bedtime, he pointed the remote control at his pride and joy and switched it off.

Then he put the dogs out for a run.

Then he shut Kay up in the stable.

'I hopes your feelings won't be hurt, old

girl,' he said, 'but I want Smasher to be on his own in the house for the night. If he's going to do anything naughty, it's better done while Martha's away.'

Inside the house, he put an old blanket on the floor beside his chair and made Smasher lie down on it.

'Now you be a good boy,' he said. 'You're not a pup any more, you're a dog, so you behave yourself.' And he climbed the stairs to bed.

This is the life, thought Smasher drowsily, at last I'm a house dog, and he fell happily asleep.

He slept so soundly that he did not hear stealthy footsteps outside the window in the middle of the night. Nor did he hear the slight scraping noise as the window was expertly forced. What woke him was in fact a stifled sneeze.

The burglar had shone his torch upon the television set and had just unplugged it, when he felt the sneeze coming on and hastily pressed a forefinger above his upper lip.

For a moment he stood stock still, listening in case the slight noise should have woken anyone upstairs. But then he in turn heard a slight noise.

Turning round, he shone his torch, and there, standing directly between him and the open window, was the largest, ugliest dog he had ever seen.

Six
New Dog

Hullo, said Smasher to himself, who's this then? Must be a pal of the master's, come to stay, and, being a friendly dog, he advanced towards the man, tail wagging, ugly mouth agape in what was actually a smile but looked in the torchlight like an angry snarl.

'Good dog,' whispered the burglar in a

shaky voice, and Smasher, encouraged by this, leapt up and put his large paws on the man's chest.

The burglar was a small man, and he fell backwards under the weight of the dog, and began to shout 'No! No! Get him off me! Help!'

Good game this, Smasher thought, and he began to bark loudly with excitement.

Woken by the hubbub, Farmer Buzzard hurried downstairs, snatching his gun from its cupboard on the way. He opened the door of the room and switched on the lights, to see Smasher standing on the man's chest and giving his face a thorough washing with a large slobbery tongue, while the burglar still cried, indistinctly now, for help.

Farmer Buzzard looked at the open window and then at the unplugged television set.

Martha was right, he thought.

He pointed to Smasher's blanket and said 'Down!' and Smasher obeyed.

Then he waved his gun towards the

prostrate burglar and said, 'And you stay down too, or my dog'll tear your throat out.'

Then he rang the police.

'The master was ever so pleased with me, Mum,' said Smasher to Kay when they met the next morning.

'What happened, dear?' asked Kay. 'I heard you barking in the middle of the night, and then later on I heard a car drive up, and then voices. What was it?'

'I don't really know, Mum,' said Smasher. 'A man came and I thought he was a friend of the master's and I had a bit of a game with him. But then some other men came dressed in blue and wearing funny hats, and they took him away in a

car with his hands sort of tied together.'

'Handcuffs,' said Kay. 'Policemen! He must have been a burglar. He came to steal something, and you stopped him, dear!' And, just as her master had done, she said, warmly, '*What* a good boy!'

One evening a week later Mrs Buzzard returned. She found her husband sitting watching the telly, the remote control in his hand, the collie at his feet. In the next room there was, though she did not know

it, another dog, lying still and silent as he had been told to do.

'Well, Ken,' she said, kissing the top of his head. 'You been all right?'

Farmer Buzzard nodded.

Conversation was not possible with him, Mrs Buzzard knew, while he was watching television, so she waited until the programme had ended and then said, 'Everything been all right here?'

Farmer Buzzard switched off.

'You were right, Martha,' he said.

'What about?'

'Burglars. We had one, the first night you was away.'

'Never!'

'Yes. After my telly, he was.'

'I told you!' Mrs Buzzard said. 'I said you ought to cover it up night times. But he never got it then?'

'No,' said Farmer Buzzard.

'You caught him?'

'No. My dog caught him.'

'Oh, Kay!' cried Mrs Buzzard. '*What* a good dog!' And she bent to stroke the collie.

'No, not Kay,' said her husband. 'My new dog.'

'New dog?'

'Yes. The very day you went to Bertha's, it was. After what you said about burglars, I thought to meself – what we need is a proper house dog, a big strong animal that will guard the place, one that no burglar would face.'

'So you went out and got one?'

'I went out,' said Farmer Buzzard truthfully, 'and I got one. And by the time I got downstairs that night, he'd knocked the burglar down and he was standing on him. "He'll tear your throat out," I said to the man. We needn't worry about burglars any more.'

'Well, I never!' said Mrs Buzzard. 'Where is he then, this new dog?'

For answer Farmer Buzzard stood up and opened the connecting door and said 'Come!' and in walked Smasher.

'Sit!' said the farmer, and he sat.

'Down!' said the farmer, and he lay down, tail gently wagging, a big grin on his wrinkly, pushed-in face.

'He won't tear my throat out, will he?' said Mrs Buzzard, a trifle nervously.

Farmer Buzzard laughed.

'Never!' he said. 'He's a soft old thing, he is.'

Like you, thought Mrs Buzzard, as she

took a proper look at the dog.

'It's a funny thing,' she said, 'but I tell you who he reminds me of. I know I haven't got my proper spectacles on, but he puts me in mind of that puppy we got rid of, you know, the one that did all that damage, that Smasher.'

'That's what I call this dog, too,' said Farmer Buzzard.

'You're right, he is a big strong dog,' said Mrs Buzzard. 'We'll be all right with him in the house. Though he's no beauty, mind. How would you describe him? What's the word?'

'Noble,' said her husband.

Mrs Buzzard nodded.

'But doesn't he remind you of that ugly puppy too?' she asked, innocently.

'Not pertickerly,' said Farmer Buzzard.

Winner of the

Guardian Children's Fiction Prize

Here's what the judges had to say about

The Sheep-Pig

★ 'Perfect'

★ 'Thrilling'

★ 'Funny'

★ 'The Best'

★ 'Charmer'

★ 'Suspense'

★ 'Breathless'

★ 'Delight'

Ace

Ace is a very special pig.

He loves watching television and gradually makes himself at home in the farmhouse, much to the annoyance of Megan, the corgi. Megan is determined to keep Ace out, but Ace is the great-grandson of Babe the sheep-pig, and he's full of surprises.

The Hodgeheg

The story of Max, the hedgehog who becomes a hodgeheg, who becomes a hero!

Max's family dreams of reaching the Park. But no one has ever found a safe way of crossing the very busy road. Can Max really solve the problem?

PUFFIN BOOKS

The Sheep-Pig

Dick King-Smith served in the Grenadier Guards during the Second World War, and afterwards spent twenty years as a farmer in Gloucestershire, the county of his birth. Many of his stories are inspired by his farming experiences. Later he taught at a village primary school. His first book, *The Fox Busters*, was published in 1978. Since then he has written a great number of children's books, including *The Sheep-Pig* (winner of the Guardian Award and filmed as *Babe*), *Harry's Mad*, *Noah's Brother*, *The Hodgeheg*, *Martin's Mice*, *Ace*, *The Cuckoo Child* and *Harriet's Hare* (winner of the Children's Book Award in 1995). At the British Book Awards in 1991 he was voted Children's Author of the Year. He has three children, a large number of grandchildren and several great-grandchildren, and lives in a seventeenth-century cottage only a crow's-flight from the house where he was born.

Some other books by Dick King-Smith

ACE
THE CUCKOO CHILD
DAGGIE DOGFOOT
DODOS ARE FOREVER
DRAGON BOY
FIND THE WHITE HORSE
THE FOX BUSTERS
HARRY'S MAD
THE HODGEHEG
HOW GREEN WAS MY MOUSE
LADY DAISY
MAGNUS POWERMOUSE
MARTIN'S MICE
THE MERMAN
THE MERRYTHOUGHT
THE MOUSE BUTCHER
NOAH'S BROTHER
PADDY'S POT OF GOLD
PRETTY POLLY
THE QUEEN'S NOSE
THE ROUNDHILL
SADDLEBOTTOM
THE SCHOOLMOUSE
THE STRAY
TREASURE TROVE
THE WATER HORSE
THE WITCH OF BLACKBERRY BOTTOM

Dick King-Smith

The Sheep-Pig

Illustrated by Ann Kronheimer

PUFFIN BOOKS

PUFFIN BOOKS

Published by the Penguin Group
Penguin Books Ltd, 80 Strand, London WC2R 0RL, England
Penguin Putnam Inc., 375 Hudson Street, New York, New York 10014, USA
Penguin Books Australia Ltd, 250 Camberwell Road, Camberwell, Victoria 3124, Australia
Penguin Books Canada Ltd, 10 Alcorn Avenue, Toronto, Ontario, Canada M4V 3B2
Penguin Books India (P) Ltd, 11 Community Centre, Panchsheel Park, New Delhi – 110 017, India
Penguin Books (NZ) Ltd, Cnr Rosedale and Airborne Roads, Albany, Auckland, New Zealand
Penguin Books (South Africa) (Pty) Ltd, 24 Sturdee Avenue, Rosebank 2196, South Africa

Penguin Books Ltd, Registered Offices: 80 Strand, London WC2R 0RL, England

www.penguin.com

First published by Victor Gollancz 1983
Published in Puffin Books 1985
Published in this edition 2003
19

Set in 15/18.5 Perpetua

Made and printed in England by Clays Ltd, St Ives plc

British Library Cataloguing in Publication Data
A CIP catalogue record for this book is available from the British Library

ISBN-13: 978-0-141-31600-0

www.greenpenguin.co.uk

Contents

One
'Guess My Weight'

'What's that noise?' said Mrs Hogget, sticking her comfortable round red face out of the kitchen window. 'Listen, there 'tis again, did you hear it, what a racket, what a row, anybody'd think someone was being murdered, oh dearie me, whatever is it, just listen to it, will you?'

Farmer Hogget listened. From the usually quiet valley below the farm came a medley of sounds: the oompah oompah of a brass band, the shouts of children, the rattle and thump of a skittle alley, and every now and then a very high, very loud, very angry-sounding squealing lasting perhaps ten seconds.

Farmer Hogget pulled out an old pocket-watch as big round as a saucer and looked at it. 'Fair starts at two,' he said. 'It's started.'

'I knows that,' said Mrs Hogget, 'because I'm late now with all theseyer cakes and jams and pickles and preserves as is meant to be on the Produce Stall this very minute, and who's going to take them there, I'd like to know, why you are, but afore you does, what's that noise?'

The squealing sounded again.

'That noise?'

Mrs Hogget nodded a great many times. Everything that she did was done at great length, whether it was speaking or simply nodding her head. Farmer Hogget, on the other hand, never wasted his energies or his words.

'Pig,' he said.

Mrs Hogget nodded a lot more.

'I thought 'twas a pig, I said to meself that's a

pig that is, only nobody round here do keep pigs, 'tis all sheep for miles about, what's a pig doing, I said to meself, anybody'd think they was killing the poor thing, have a look when you take all this stuff down, which you better do now, come and give us a hand, it can go in the back of the Land Rover, 'tisn't raining, 'twon't hurt, wipe your boots afore you comes in.'

'Yes,' said Farmer Hogget.

When he had driven down to the village and made his delivery to the Produce Stall, Farmer Hogget walked across the green, past the Hoopla Stall and the Coconut Shy and the Aunt Sally and the skittles and the band, to the source of the squealing noise, which came every now and again from a small pen of hurdles in a far corner, against the churchyard wall.

By the pen sat the Vicar, notebook in hand, a cardboard box on the table in front of him. On the hurdles hung a notice – 'Guess my weight. Ten pence a go.' Inside was a little pig.

As Farmer Hogget watched, a man leaned over and picked it out of the pen. He hefted it in both hands, frowning and pursing his lips in a considering way, while all the time the piglet struggled madly and yelled blue murder. The moment it was put down, it quietened. Its eyes, bright intelligent eyes, met the farmer's. They regarded one another.

One saw a tall thin brown-faced man with very long legs, and the other saw a small fat pinky-white animal with very short ones.

'Ah, come along, Mr Hogget!' said the Vicar. 'You never know, he could be yours for ten pence. Guess his weight correctly, and at the end of the day you could be taking him home!'

'Don't keep pigs,' said Farmer Hogget. He stretched out a long arm and scratched its back. Gently, he picked it up and held it before his face. It stayed quite still and made no sound.

'That's funny,' said the Vicar. 'Every time so far that someone has picked him up he's screamed his head off. He seems to like you. You'll have to have a guess.'

Carefully, Farmer Hogget put the piglet back in the pen. Carefully, he took a ten pence piece from his pocket and dropped it in the cardboard box. Carefully, he ran one finger down the list of guesses already in the Vicar's notebook.

'Quite a variation,' said the Vicar. 'Anything from twenty pounds to forty, so far.' He wrote down 'Mr Hogget' and waited, pencil poised.

Once again, slowly, thoughtfully, the farmer picked the

piglet up.

Once again, it remained still and silent.

'Thirty-one pounds,' said Farmer Hogget. He put the little pig down again. 'And a quarter,' he said.

'Thirty-one and a quarter pounds. Thank you, Mr Hogget. We shall be weighing the little chap at about half past four.'

'Be gone by then.'

'Ah well, we can always telephone you. If you should be lucky enough to win him.'

'Never win nothing.'

As he walked back across the green, the sound of the pig's yelling rang out as someone else had a go.

'You do never win nothing,' said Mrs Hogget at tea-time, when her husband, in a very few words, had explained matters, 'though I've often thought I'd like a pig, we could feed un on scraps, he'd come just right for Christmas time, just think, two nice hams, two sides of bacon, pork chops, kidneys, liver, chitterling, trotters, save his blood for black pudding, there's the phone.'

Farmer Hogget picked it up.

'Oh,' he said.

Two
'There. Is That Nice?'

In the farmyard, Fly the black and white collie was beginning the training of her four puppies. For some time now they had shown an instinctive interest in anything that moved, driving it away or bringing it back, turning it to left or right, in fact herding it. They had begun with such things as passing beetles, but were now ready, Fly considered, for larger creatures.

She set them to work on Mrs Hogget's ducks.

Already the puppies were beginning to move as

sheep-dogs do, seeming to creep rather than walk, heads held low, ears pricked, eyes fixed on the angrily quacking birds as they manoeuvred them about the yard.

'Good boys,' said Fly. 'Leave them now. Here comes the boss.'

The ducks went grumbling off to the pond, and the five dogs watched as Farmer Hogget got out of the Land Rover.

He lifted something out of a crate in the back, and carried it into the stables.

'What was that, Mum?' said one of the puppies.

'That was a pig.'

'What will the boss do with it?'

'Eat it,' said Fly, 'when it's big enough.'

'Will he eat us,' said another rather nervously, 'when we're big enough?'

'Bless you,' said his mother. 'People only eat stupid animals. Like sheep and cows and ducks and chickens. They don't eat clever ones like dogs.'

'So pigs are stupid?' said the puppies.

Fly hesitated. On the one hand, having been born and brought up in sheep country, she had in fact never been personally acquainted with a pig. On the other, like most mothers, she did not wish to appear ignorant before her children.

'Yes,' she said. 'They're stupid.'

At this point there came from the kitchen window a long burst of words like the rattle of a machine-gun, answered by a single shot from the stables, and Farmer Hogget emerged and crossed the yard towards the farmhouse with his loping stride.

'Come on,' said the collie bitch. 'I'll show you.'

The floor of the stables had not rung to a horse's hoof for many years, but it was a useful place for storing things. The hens foraged about there, and sometimes laid their eggs in the old wooden mangers; the swallows built their nests against its roof-beams with mud from the duckpond; and rats and mice lived happy lives in its shelter until the farm cats cut them short. At one end of the stables were two loose-boxes with boarded sides topped by iron rails. One served as a kennel for Fly and her puppies. The other sometimes housed sick sheep. Here Farmer Hogget had shut the piglet.

A convenient stack of straw bales allowed the dogs to look down into the box through the bars.

'It certainly looks stupid,' said one of the puppies, yawning. At the sound of the words the piglet glanced up quickly. He put his head on one side and regarded the dogs with sharp eyes. Something about the sight of this very small

animal standing all by itself in the middle of the roomy loose-box touched Fly's soft heart. Already she was sorry that she had said that pigs were stupid, for this one certainly did not appear to be so. Also there was something dignified about the way it stood its ground, in a strange place, confronted with strange animals. How different from the silly sheep, who at the mere sight of a dog would run aimlessly about, crying

'Wolf! Wolf!' in their empty-headed way.

'Hullo,' she said. 'Who are you?'

'I'm a Large White,' said the piglet.

'Blimey!' said one of the puppies. 'If that's a large white, what's a small one like?' And they all four sniggered.

'Be quiet!' snapped Fly. 'Just remember that five minutes ago you didn't even know what a pig was.' And to the piglet she said kindly, 'I expect that's your breed, dear. I meant, what's your name?'

'I don't know,' said the piglet.

'Well, what did your mother call you, to tell you apart from your brothers and sisters?' said

Fly and then wished she hadn't, for at the mention of his family the piglet began to look distinctly unhappy. His little forehead wrinkled and he gulped and his voice trembled as he answered.

'She called us all the same.'

'And what was that, dear?'

'Babe,' said the piglet, and the puppies began to giggle until their mother silenced them with a growl.

'But that's a lovely name,' she said. 'Would you like us to call you that? It'll make you feel more at home.'

At this last word the little pig's face fell even further.

'I want my mum,' he said very quietly.

At that instant the collie bitch made up her mind that she would foster this unhappy child.

'Go out into the yard and play,' she said to the puppies, and she climbed to the top of the straw stack and jumped over the rail and down into the loose-box beside the piglet.

'Listen, Babe,' she said. 'You've got to be a brave boy. Everyone has to leave their mother, it's all part of growing up. I did so, when I was your age, and my puppies will have to leave me quite soon. But I'll look after you. If you like.' Then she licked his little snout with a warm rough tongue, her plumed tail wagging.

'There. Is that nice?' she said.

A little while later, Farmer Hogget came into the stables with his wife, to show her his prize. They looked over the loose-box door and saw, to their astonishment, Fly curled round the piglet. Exhausted by the drama of the day, he lay fast asleep against his new-found foster-parent.

'Well, will you look at that!' said Mrs Hogget. 'That old Fly, she'll mother anything, kittens, ducklings, baby chicks, she's looked after all of they, now 'tis a pig, in't he lovely, what a picture, good job he don't know where he'll finish up, but he'll be big then and we'll be glad to see the back of him, or the hams of him, I should say,

shan't us, wonder how I shall get it all in the freezer?'

'Pity. Really,' said Farmer Hogget absently.

Mrs Hogget went back to her kitchen, shaking her head all the way across the yard at the thought of her husband's soft-heartedness.

The farmer opened the loose-box door, and to save the effort of a word, clicked his fingers to call the bitch out.

As soon as Fly moved the piglet woke and

followed her, sticking so close to her that his snout touched her tail-tip. Surprise forced Farmer Hogget into speech.

'Fly!' he said in amazement. Obediently, as always, the collie bitch turned and trotted back to him. The pig trotted behind her.

'Sit!' said Farmer Hogget. Fly sat. Babe sat. Farmer Hogget scratched his head. He could not think of anything to say.

Three
'Why Can't I Learn?'

By dark it was plain to Farmer Hogget that, whether he liked it or no, Fly had not four, but five children.

All the long summer evening Babe had followed Fly about the yard and buildings, aimlessly, it seemed to the watching farmer, though of course this was not the case. It was in fact a conducted tour. Fly knew that if this foster-child was to be allowed his freedom and the constant reassurance of her company for which he obviously craved, he must quickly learn (and patently he was a quick learner) his way about the place; and that he must be taught, as her puppies had been taught, how to behave like a good dog.

'A pig you may be, Babe,' she had begun by saying, 'but if you do as I tell you, I shouldn't be a bit surprised if the boss doesn't let you run about with us, instead of shutting you up. He's a kind man, the boss is.'

'I knew that,' said Babe, 'when he first picked me up. I could feel it. I knew he wouldn't hurt me.'

'You wait . . .' began one of the puppies, and then stopped suddenly at his mother's warning growl. Though she said nothing, all four of her children knew immediately by instinct what she meant.

'Wait for what?' said Babe.

'Er . . . you wait half a tick, and we'll take you round and show you everything,' said the first puppy hastily. 'Won't we, Mum?'

So Babe was shown all round the yard and the farm buildings, and introduced to the creatures who lived thereabouts, the ducks and chickens and other poultry, and the farm cats. He saw no sheep, for they were all in the fields.

Even in the first hour he learned a number of useful lessons, as the puppies had learned before him: that cats scratch and hens peck, that turning your back on the turkey-cock means getting your bottom bitten, that chicks are not for chasing and eggs are not for eating.

'You do as I do,' said Fly, 'and you'll be all right.'

She thought for a moment. 'There is one thing though, Babe,' she said, and she looked across at the back door of the farmhouse, 'if I go in there, you stay outside and wait for me, understand?'

'Aren't pigs allowed in there?' asked Babe.

'Not live ones,' said one of the puppies, but he said it under his breath.

'No, dear,' said Fly. Well, not yet anyway, she thought, but the way you're going on, I shouldn't be surprised at anything. Funny, she thought, I feel really proud of him, he learns so quick. Quick as any sheep-dog.

That night the loose-box in which Babe had first been put was empty. In the next-door one, all six animals slept in the straw together. Though he did not tell his wife, Farmer Hogget had not had the heart to shut the piglet away, so happy was it in the company of the dogs.

At first the puppies had not been equally happy at the idea.

'Mum!' they said. 'He'll wet the bed!'

'Nonsense,' said Fly. 'If you want to do anything, dear, you go outside, there's a good boy.'

I nearly said 'there's a good pup' she thought. Whatever next!

In fact, in the days that followed, Babe became so doglike, what with coming when Fly came and sitting when Fly sat and much preferring dog's food to anything else he was offered, that Farmer Hogget caught himself half expecting, when he patted the piglet, that it would wag its tail. He would not have been surprised if it had tried to accompany Fly when he called her to go with him on his morning rounds, but it had stayed in the stables, playing with the puppies.

'You stop with the boys, Babe,' Fly had said, 'while I see to the sheep. I shan't be long.'

'What's sheep?' the piglet said when she had gone.

The puppies rolled about in the straw.

'Don't you know that, you silly Babe?' said one.

'Sheep are animals with thick woolly coats.'

'And thick woolly heads.'

'And men can't look after them without the help of the likes of us,' said the fourth.

'Why do they need you?' said Babe.

'Because we're sheep-dogs!' they all cried together, and ran off up the yard.

Babe thought about this matter of sheep and sheep-dogs a good deal during the first couple of weeks of his life on the Hoggets' farm. In that time Fly's puppies, now old enough to leave home, had been advertised for sale, and Fly was anxious to teach them all she could before they went out into the world. Daily she made them practise on the ducks, while Babe sat beside her and watched with interest. And daily their skills

improved and the ducks lost weight and patience.

Then there came, one after another, four farmers, four tall long-legged men who smelt of sheep. And each picked his puppy and paid his money, while Fly sat and watched her children leave to start their working life.

As always, she felt a pang to see each go, but this time, after the last had left, she was not alone.

'It's nice, dear,' she said to Babe. 'I've still got you.'

But not for all that long, she thought. Poor little chap, in six months or so he'll be fit to kill. At least he doesn't know it. She looked fondly at him, this foster-child that now called her 'Mum'. He had picked it up, naturally enough, from the puppies, but it pleased her to hear it, now more than ever.

'Mum,' said Babe.

'Yes, dear?'

'They've gone off to work sheep, haven't they?'

'Yes, dear.'

'Because they're sheep-dogs. Like you. You're useful to the boss, aren't you, because you're a sheep-dog?'

'Yes, dear.'

'Well, Mum?'

'Yes, dear?'

'Why can't I learn to be a sheep-pig?'

Four
'You'm a Polite Young Chap'

After the last of the puppies had left, the ducks heaved a general sigh of relief. They looked forward to a peaceful day and paid no attention when, the following morning, Fly and Babe came down to the pond and sat and watched them as they squattered and splattered in its soupy green depths. They knew that the old dog would not bother them, and they took no notice of the strange creature at her side.

'They'll come out and walk up the yard in a

minute,' said Fly. 'Then you can have a go at fetching them back, if you like.'

'Oh yes please!' said Babe excitedly.

The collie bitch looked fondly at her foster-child. Sheep-pig indeed, she thought, the idea of it! The mere sight of him would probably send the flock into the next county. Anyway he'd never get near them on those little short legs. Let him play with the ducks for a day or two and he'd forget all about it.

When the ducks did come up out of the water and marched noisily past the piglet, she half expected him to chase after them, as the puppies usually did at first; but he sat very still, his ears cocked, watching her.

'All right,' said Fly. 'Let's see how you get on. Now then, first thing is, you've got to get behind them, just like I have to with the sheep. If the boss wants me to go round the right side of them (that's the side by the stables there), he says "Away to me". If he wants me to go round the left (that's the side by the Dutch barn), he says

"Come by". OK?'

'Yes, Mum.'

'Right then. Away to me, Babe!' said Fly sharply.

At first, not surprisingly, Babe's efforts met with little success. There were no problems with getting round the ducks – even with his curious little see-sawing canter he was much faster than they – but the business of bringing the whole flock back to Fly was not, he found, at all easy.

Either he pressed them too hard and they broke up and fluttered all over the place, or he was too gentle

and held back, and they waddled away in twos and threes.

'Come and have a rest, dear,' called Fly after a while. 'Leave the silly things alone, they're not worth upsetting yourself about.'

'I'm not upset, Mum,' said Babe. 'Just puzzled. I mean, I told them what I wanted them to do but they didn't take any notice of me. Why not?'

Because you weren't born to it, thought Fly. You haven't got the instinct to dominate them, to make them do what you want.

'It's early days yet, Babe dear,' she said.

'Do you suppose,' said Babe, 'that if I asked them politely . . .'

'Asked them politely! What an idea! Just imagine me doing that with the sheep – "please will you go through that gateway", "would you kindly walk into that pen?" Oh no, dear, you'd never get anywhere that way. You've got to tell 'em what to do, doesn't matter whether it's ducks or sheep. They're stupid and dogs are intelligent, that's what you have to remember.'

'But I'm a pig.'

'Pigs are intelligent too,' said Fly firmly. Ask them politely, she thought, whatever next!

What happened next, later that morning in fact, was that Babe met his first sheep.

Farmer Hogget and Fly had been out round the flock, and when they returned Fly was driving before her an old lame ewe, which they penned in the loose-box where the piglet had originally been shut. Then they went away up the hill again.

Babe made his way into the stables, curious to meet this, the first of the animals that he planned one day to work with, but he could not see into the box. He snuffled under the bottom of the door, and from inside there came a cough and the sharp stamp of a foot, and then the sound of a hoarse complaining voice. 'Wolves! Wolves!' it said. 'They do never leave a body alone. Nag, nag, nag all day long, go here, go there, do this, do that. What d'you want now? Can't you give us a bit of peace, wolf?'

'I'm not a wolf,' said Babe under the door.

'Oh, I knows all that,' said the sheep sourly. 'Calls yourself a sheep-dog, I knows that, but you don't fool none of us. You're a wolf like the rest of 'em, given half a chance. You looks at us, and you sees lamb-chops. Go away, wolf.'

'But I'm not a sheep-dog either,' said Babe, and he scrambled up the stack of straw bales and looked over the bars.

'You see?' he said.

'Well I'll be dipped,' said the old sheep, peering up at him, 'no more you ain't. What are you?'

'Pig,' said Babe. 'Large White. What are you?'

'Ewe,' said the sheep.

'No, not me, you – what are you?'

'I'm a ewe.'

Mum was right, thought Babe, they certainly are stupid. But if I'm going to learn how to be a sheep-pig I must try to understand them, and this might be a good chance. Perhaps I could make a friend of this one.

'My name's Babe,' he said in a jolly voice. 'What's yours?'

'Maaaaa,' said the sheep.

'That's a nice name,' said Babe. 'What's the matter with you, Ma?'

'Foot-rot,' said the sheep, holding up a foreleg. 'And I've got a nasty cough.' She coughed. 'And I'm not as young as I was.'

'You don't look very old to me,' said Babe politely.

A look of pleasure came over the sheep's mournful face, and she lay down in the straw.

'Very civil of you to say so,' she said. 'First kind word I've had since I were a little lamb,' and she belched loudly and began to chew a mouthful of cud.

Though he did not quite know why, Babe said nothing to Fly of his conversation with Ma. Farmer Hogget had treated the sheep's foot and tipped a drench down its protesting throat, and now, as darkness fell, dog and pig lay side by side, their rest only occasionally disturbed by a rustling from the next-door box. Having at last set eyes on a sheep, Babe's dreams were immediately filled with the creatures, all lame, all coughing, all, like the ducks, scattering wildly before his attempts to round them up.

'Go here, go there, do this, do that!' he squeaked furiously at them, but they took not a bit of notice, until at last the dream turned to nightmare, and they all came hopping and hacking and maa-ing after him with hatred gleaming in their mad yellow eyes.

'Mum! Mum!' shouted Babe in terror.

'Maaaaa!' said a voice next door.

'It's all right, dear,' said Fly, 'it's all right. Was it a nasty dream?'

'Yes, yes.'

'What were you dreaming about?'

'Sheep, Mum.'

'I expect it was because of that stupid old thing in there,' said Fly. 'Shut up!' she barked. 'Noisy old fool!' And to Babe she said, 'Now cuddle up, dear, and go to sleep. There's nothing to be frightened of.'

She licked his snout until it began to give out a series of regular snores. Sheep-pig indeed, she thought, why the silly boy's frightened of the things, and she put her nose on her paws and went to sleep.

*

Babe slept soundly the rest of thc night, and woke more determined than ever to learn all that he could from their new neighbour. As soon as Fly had gone out on her rounds, he climbed the straw stack.

'Good morning, Ma,' he said. 'I do hope you're feeling better today?'

The old ewe looked up. Her eyes, Babe was glad to see, looked neither mad nor hateful.

'I must say,' she said, 'you'm a polite young chap. Not like that wolf, shouting at me in the middle of the night. Never get no respect from they, treat you like dirt they do, bite you soon as look at you.'

'Do they really?'

'Oh ar. Nip your hocks if you'm a bit slow. And worse, some of them.'

'Worse?'

'Oh ar. Ain't you never heard of worrying?'

'I don't worry much.'

'No no, young un. I'm talking about sheep-worrying. You get some wolves as'll chase sheep and kill 'em.'

'Oh!' said Babe, horrified. 'I'm sure Fly would never do that.'

'Who's Fly?'

'She's my m . . . she's our dog here, the one that brought you in yesterday.'

'Is that what she's called? No, she bain't a worrier, just rude. All wolves is rude to us sheep, see, always have been. Bark and run and nip and call us stupid. We bain't all that stupid, we do just get confused. If only they'd just show a bit of common politeness, just treat us a bit decent. Now if you was to come out into the field, a nice well-mannered young chap like you, and ask me to go somewhere or do something, politely, like you would, why, I'd be only too delighted.'

Five

'Keep Yelling, Young Un'

Mrs Hogget shook her head at least a dozen times.

'For the life of me I can't see why you do let that pig run all over the place like you do, round and round the yard he do go, chasing my ducks about, shoving his nose into everything, shouldn't wonder but what he'll be out with you and Fly moving the sheep about afore long, why dussen't shut him up, he's running all his flesh off, he won't never be fit for Christmas, Easter more like, what d'you call him?'

'Just Pig,' said Farmer Hogget.

A month had gone by since the Village Fair, a month in which a lot of interesting things had happened to Babe. The fact that perhaps most concerned his future, though he did not know it, was that Farmer Hogget had become fond of him. He liked to see the piglet pottering happily about the yard with Fly, keeping out of mischief, as far as he could tell, if you didn't count moving the ducks around. He did this now with a good deal of skill, the farmer noticed, even to the extent of being able, once, to separate the white ducks from the brown, though that must just have been a fluke. The more he thought of it, the less Farmer Hogget liked the idea of butchering Pig.

The other developments were in Babe's education. Despite herself, Fly found that she took pleasure and pride in teaching him the ways of the sheep-dog, though she knew that of course he would never be fast enough to work sheep.

Anyway the boss would never let him try.

As for Ma, she was back with the flock, her foot healed, her cough better. But all the time that she had been shut in the box, Babe had spent every moment that Fly was out of the stables chatting to the old ewe. Already he understood, in a way that Fly never could, the sheep's point of view. He longed to meet the flock, to be introduced. He thought it would be extremely interesting.

'D'you think I could, Ma?' he had said.

'Could what, young un?'

'Well, come and visit you, when you go back to your friends?'

'Oh ar. You could do, easy enough. You only got to go through the bottom gate and up the hill to the big field by the lane. Don't know what the farmer'd say though. Or that wolf.'

Once Fly had slipped quietly in and found him perched on the straw stack.

'Babe!' she had said sharply. 'You're not talking to that stupid thing, are you?'

'Well, yes, Mum, I was.'

'Save your breath, dear. It won't understand a word you say.'

'Bah!' said Ma.

For a moment Babe was tempted to tell his foster-mother what he had in mind, but something told him to keep quiet. Instead he made a plan. He would wait for two things to happen. First, for Ma to rejoin the flock. And after that for market day, when both the boss and his mum would be out of the way. Then he would go up the hill.

Towards the end of the very next week the two things had happened. Ma had been turned out, and a couple of days after that Babe watched as Fly jumped into the back of the Land Rover, and it drove out of the yard and away.

Babe's were not the only eyes that watched its departure. At the top of the hill a cattle-lorry stood half-hidden under a clump of trees at the side of the lane. As soon as the Land Rover had disappeared from sight along the road to the market town, a man jumped hurriedly out and opened the gate into the field. Another backed the lorry into the gateway.

Babe meanwhile was trotting excitedly up the hill to pay his visit to the flock. He came to the gate at the bottom of the field and squeezed under it. The field was steep and curved, and at first he could not see a single sheep. But then he heard a distant drumming of hooves and suddenly the whole flock came

galloping over the brow of the hill and down towards him. Around them ran two strange collies, lean silent dogs that seemed to flow effortlessly over the grass. From high above came the sound of a thin whistle, and in easy partnership the dogs swept round the sheep, and began to drive them back up the slope.

Despite himself, Babe was caught up in the press of jostling bleating animals and carried along with them. Around him rose a chorus of panting protesting voices, some shrill, some hoarse, some deep and guttural, but all saying the same thing.

'Wolf! Wolf!' cried the flock in dazed confusion.

Small by comparison and short in the leg, Babe soon fell behind the main body, and as they reached the top of the hill he found himself right at the back in company with an old sheep who cried 'Wolf!' more loudly than any.

'Ma!' he cried breathlessly. 'It's you!'

Behind them one dog lay down at a whistle, and in front the flock checked as the other dog steadied them. In the corner of the field the tailboard and wings of the cattle-lorry filled the gateway, and the two men waited, sticks and arms outspread.

'Oh hullo, young un,' puffed the old sheep. 'Fine day you chose to come, I'll say.'

'What is it? What's happening? Who are these men?' asked Babe.

'Rustlers,' said Ma. 'They'm sheep-rustlers.'

'What d'you mean?'

'Thieves, young un, that's what I do mean. Sheep-stealers. We'll all be in thik lorry afore you can blink your eye.'

'What can we do?'

'Do? Ain't nothing we can do, unless we can slip past theseyer wolf.'

She made as if to escape, but the dog behind darted in, and she turned back.

Again, one of the men whistled, and the dog pressed. Gradually, held against the headland of the field by the second dog and the men, the flock began to move forward. Already the leaders were nearing the tailboard of the lorry.

'We'm beat,' said Ma mournfully. 'You run for it, young un.' I will, thought Babe, but not the way you mean. Little as he was, he felt suddenly not fear but anger, furious anger that the boss's

sheep were being stolen. My mum's not here to protect them so I must, he said to himself bravely, and he ran quickly round the hedge side of the flock, and jumping on to the bottom of the tailboard, turned to face them.

'Please!' he cried. 'I beg you! Please don't come any further. If you would be so kind, dear sensible sheep!'

His unexpected appearance had a number of immediate effects. The shock of being so politely addressed stopped the flock in its tracks, and the cries of 'Wolf!' changed to murmurs of 'In't he lovely!' and 'Proper little gennulman!' Ma had told them something of her new friend, and now to see him in the flesh and to hear his well-chosen words released them from the dominance of the dogs. They began to fidget and look about for an escape route. This was opened for them when the men (cursing quietly, for above all things they were anxious to avoid too much noise) sent the flanking dog to drive the pig away, and some of the sheep began to slip past them.

Next moment all was chaos. Angrily the dog ran at Babe, who scuttled away squealing at the top of his voice in a mixture of fright and fury. The men closed on him, sticks raised. Desperately he shot between the legs of one, who fell with a crash, while the other, striking out madly, hit the rearguard dog as it came to help, and sent it yowling. In half a minute the carefully planned raid was ruined, as the sheep scattered everywhere.

'Keep yelling, young un!' bawled Ma, as she ran besidc Babe. 'They won't never stop here with that row going on!'

And suddenly all sorts of things began to happen as those deafening squeals rang out over the quiet countryside. Birds flew startled from the trees, cows in nearby fields began to gallop about, dogs in distant farms to bark, passing motorists to stop and stare. In the farmhouse below, Mrs Hogget heard the noise as she had on the day of the Fair, but now it was infinitely louder, the most piercing, nerve-tingling, ear-shattering burglar alarm. She dialled 999 but then talked for so long that, by the time a patrol car drove up the lane, the rustlers had long gone. Snarling at each other and their dogs, they had driven hurriedly away with not one single sheep to show for their pains.

'You won't never believe it!' cried Mrs Hogget when her husband returned from market. 'But we've had rustlers, just after you'd gone it were, come with a girt cattle-lorry they did, the police said, they seen the tyremarks in the gateway, and a chap in a car seen the lorry go by in a hurry, and there's been a lot of it about, and he give the alarm, he did, kept screaming and shrieking enough to bust your eardrums, we should have lost every sheep on the place if 'tweren't for him, 'tis him we've got to thank.'

'Who?' said Farmer Hogget.

'Him!' said his wife, pointing at Babe who was telling Fly all about it. 'Don't ask me how he got there or why he done it, all I knows is he saved our bacon and now I'm going to save his, he's stopping with us just like another dog, don't care if he gets so big as a house, because if you think I'm going to stand by and see him butchered after what he done for us today, you've got another think coming, what d'you say to that?'

A slow smile spread over Farmer Hogget's long face.

Six
'Good Pig'

The very next morning Farmer Hogget decided that he would see if the pig would like to come, when he went round the sheep with Fly. I'm daft, he thought, grinning to himself. He did not tell his wife.

Seeing him walk down the yard, crook in hand, and hearing him call Fly, Babe was about to settle down for an after-breakfast nap when to his surprise he heard the farmer's voice again.

'Come, Pig,' said Farmer Hogget and to his surprise the pig came.

'I expect it's because of what you did yesterday,' said Fly proudly, as they walked to heel together up the hill. 'The boss must be very pleased with you, dear. You can watch me working.'

When they reached the lower gate, Farmer Hogget opened it and left it open.

'He's going to bring them down into the home paddock, away from the lane,' said Fly quickly. 'You be quiet and keep out of the way,' and she went to sit waiting by the farmer's right side.

'Come by!' he said, and Fly ran left up the slope as the sheep began to bunch above her. Once behind them, she addressed them in her usual way, that is to say sharply.

'Move, fools!' she snapped. 'Down the hill. If you know which way "down" is,' but to her surprise they did not obey. Instead they turned to face her, and some even stamped, and shook their heads at her, while a great chorus of bleating began.

To Fly sheep-talk was just so much rubbish, to which she had never paid any attention, but Babe, listening below, could hear clearly what was being said, and although the principal cry was the usual one, there were other voices saying other things. The contrast between the politeness with which they had been treated by yesterday's rescuer and the everlasting rudeness to which they were subjected by this or any wolf brought mutinous thoughts into woolly heads, and words of defiance rang out.

'You got no manners! . . . Why can't you ask nicely? . . . Treat us like muck, you do!' they cried, and one hoarse voice which the pig recognized called loudly, 'We don't want you, wolf. We want Babe!' whereupon they all took it up.

'We want Babe!' they bleated. 'Babe! Babe! Ba-a-a-a-be!'

Those behind pushed at those in front, so that

they actually edged a pace or two nearer the dog.

For a moment it seemed to Babe that Fly was not going to be able to move them, that she would lose this particular battle of wills; but he had not reckoned with her years of experience. Suddenly, quick as a flash, she drove in on them with a growl and with a twisting leap sprang for the nose of the foremost animal; Babe heard the clack of her teeth as the ewe fell over backwards in fright, a fright which immediately ran through all. Defiant no longer, the flock poured down the hill, Fly snapping furiously at their heels, and surged wildly through the gateway.

'No manners! No manners! No ma-a-a-a-anners!' they cried, but an air of panic ran through them as they realized how rebellious they had been. How the wolf would punish them! They ran helter-skelter into the middle of the paddock, and wheeled as one to look back, ears pricked, eyes wide with fear. They puffed and blew, and Ma's hacking cough rang out. But to their surprise they saw that the wolf had dropped by the gateway, and that after a moment the pig came trotting out to one side of them.

Though Farmer Hogget could not know what had caused the near-revolt of the flock, he saw clearly that for some reason they had given Fly a hard time, and that she was angry. It was not like her to gallop sheep in that pell-mell fashion.

'Steady!' he said curtly as she harried the rearguard, and then 'Down!' and 'Stay!' and shut the gate. Shepherding suited Farmer Hogget – there was no waste of words in it.

In the corner of the home paddock nearest to

the farm buildings was a smallish fenced yard divided into a number of pens and runways. Here the sheep would be brought at shearing-time or to pick out fat lambs for market or to be treated for various troubles. Farmer Hogget had heard the old ewe cough; he thought he would catch her up and give her another drench. He turned to give an order to Fly lying flat and still behind him, and there, lying flat and still beside her, was the pig.

'Stay, Fly!' said Hogget. And, just for fun, 'Come, Pig!'

Immediately Babe ran forward and sat at the farmer's right, his front trotters placed neatly together, his big ears cocked for the next command.

Strange thoughts began to stir in Farmer Hogget's mind, and unconsciously he crossed his fingers.

He took a deep breath, and, holding it . . . 'Away to me, Pig!' he said softly.

Without a moment's hesitation Babe began the long outrun to the right.

Quite what Farmer Hogget had expected to happen, he could never afterwards clearly remember. What he had not expected was that the pig would run round to the rear of the flock, and turn to face it and him, and lie down instantly without a word of further command spoken, just as a well-trained dog would have done. Admittedly, with his jerky little rocking-horse canter he took twice as long to get there as Fly would have, but still, there he was, in the right place, ready and waiting. Admittedly, the sheep had turned to face the pig and were making a great deal of noise,

but then Farmer Hogget did not know, and Fly would not listen to, what they were saying. He called the dog to heel, and began to walk with his long loping stride to the collecting-pen in the corner. Out in the middle of the paddock there was a positive babble of talk.

'Good morning!' said Babe. 'I do hope I find you all well, and not too distressed by yesterday's experience?' and immediately it seemed that every sheep had something to say to him.

'Bless his heart!' they cried, and, 'Dear little soul!' and, 'Hullo, Babe!' and, 'Nice to see you again!' and then there was a rasping cough and the sound of Ma's hoarse tones.

'What's up then, young un?' she croaked.

'What be you doing here instead of that wolf?'

Although Babe wanted, literally, to keep on the right side of the sheep, his loyalty to his foster-mother made him say in a rather hurt voice, 'She's not a wolf. She's a sheep-dog.'

'Oh all right then,' said Ma, 'sheep-dog, if you must have it. What dost want, then?'

Babe looked at the army of long sad faces.

'I want to be a sheep-pig,' he said.

'Ha ha!' bleated a big lamb standing next to Ma. 'Ha ha ha-a-a-a-a!'

'Bide quiet!' said Ma sharply, swinging her head to give the lamb a thumping butt in the side. 'That ain't nothing to laugh at.'

Raising her voice, she addressed the flock.

'Listen to me, all you ewes,' she said, 'and lambs too. This young chap was kind to me, like I told you, when I were poorly. And I told him, if he was to ask me to go somewhere or do something, politely, like he would, why, I'd be only too delighted. We ain't stupid, I told him, all we do want is to be treated right, and we'm as bright as the next beast, we are.'

'We are!' chorused the flock. 'We are! We are! We a-a-a-a-are!'

'Right then,' said Ma. 'What shall us do, Babe?'

Babe looked across towards Farmer Hogget, who had opened the gate of the collecting-pen and now stood leaning on his crook, Fly at his feet. The pen was in the left bottom corner of the paddock, and so Babe expected, and at that moment got, the command 'Come by, Pig!' to send him left and so behind the sheep and thus turn them down towards the corner.

He cleared his throat. 'If I might ask a great favour of you,' he said hurriedly, 'could you all please be kind enough to walk down to that gate where the farmer is standing, and to go through it? Take your time, please, there's absolutely no rush.'

A look of pure contentment passed over the faces of the flock, and with one accord they turned and walked across the paddock, Babe a few paces in their rear. Sedately they walked, and steadily, over to the corner, through the gate, into the pen, and then stood quietly waiting. No one broke ranks or tried to slip away, no one pushed or shoved, there was no noise or fuss. From the oldest to the youngest, they went in like lambs.

Then at last a gentle murmur broke out as everyone in different ways quietly expressed their pleasure.

'Babe!' said Fly to the pig. 'That was quite beautifully done, dear!'

'Thank you so much!' said Babe to the sheep. 'You did that so nicely!'

'Ta!' said the sheep. 'Ta! Ta! Ta-a-a-a-a-a! 'Tis a pleasure to work for such a

little gennulman!' And Ma added, 'You'll make a wunnerful sheep-pig, young un, or my name's not Ma-a-a-a-a-a.'

As for Farmer Hogget, he heard none of this, so wrapped up was he in his own thoughts. He's as good as a dog, he told himself excitedly, he's better than a dog, than any dog! I wonder . . . !

'Good Pig,' he said.

Then he uncrossed his fingers and closed the gate.

Seven
'What's Trials?'

Every day after that, of course, Babe went the rounds with Farmer Hogget and Fly. At first the farmer worried about using the pig to herd the sheep, not because it was a strange and unusual thing to do which people might laugh at – he did not care about that – but because he was afraid it might upset Fly and put her nose out of joint. However it did not seem to do so.

He could have spared himself the worry if he had been able to listen to their conversation.

'That *was* fun!' said Babe to Fly that evening. 'I wonder if the boss will let me do some more work?'

'I'm sure he will, dear. You did it so well. It was almost as though the sheep knew exactly what it was you wanted them to do.'

'But that's just it! I asked them . . .'

'No use asking sheep anything, dear,' interrupted Fly. 'You have to *make* them do what you want, I've told you before.'

'Yes, Mum. But . . . will you mind, if the boss uses me instead of you, sometimes?'

'Mind?' said Fly. 'You bet your trotters I won't! All my life I've had to run round after those idiots, up hill, down dale, day in, day out. And as for "sometimes", as far as I'm concerned you can work them every day. I'm not as young as I was. I'll be only too happy to lie comfortably in the grass and watch you, my Babe.'

And before long that was exactly what she was doing. Once Farmer Hogget could see by her wagging tail and smiling eyes that she was perfectly happy about it, he began to use Babe to do some of her work. At first he only gave the pig simple tasks, but as the days and weeks went by, Hogget began to make more and more use of his new helper. The speed with which Babe learned amazed him, and before long he was relying on him for all the work with the flock, while Fly lay and proudly watched. Now, there was nothing, it seemed, that the pig could not do, and do faultlessly, at that.

He obeyed all the usual commands immediately and correctly. He could fetch sheep or take them away, move them to left or right, persuade them round obstacles or through gaps, cut the flock in half, or take out one individual.

To drench Ma, for instance, there was no need for Hogget to bring all the sheep down to the collecting-pen, or to corner them all and catch her by a hindleg with his crook. He could simply point her out to the pig, and Babe would gently work her out of the bunch and bring her right to the farmer's feet, where she stood quietly waiting. It seemed like a miracle to Hogget, but of course it was simple.

'Ma!'

'Yes, young un?'

'The boss wants to give you some more medicine.'

'Oh not again! 'Tis horrible stuff, that.'

'But it'll make your cough better.'

'Oh ar?'

'Come along, Ma. Please.'

'Oh all right then, young un. Anything to oblige you.'

And there were other far more miraculous

things that Babe could easily have done if the farmer had only known. For example when it was time for the ewes to be separated from their lambs, now almost as big and strong as their mothers, Farmer Hogget behaved like any other shepherd, and brought the whole flock down to the pens, and took a lot of time and trouble to part them. If only he had been able to explain things to Babe, how easy it could have been.

'Dear ladies, will you please stay on the hill, if you'd be so kind?'

'Youngsters, down you go to the collecting-pen if you please, there's good boys and girls,' and it could have been done in the shake of a lamb's tail.

However, Babe's increasing skill at working sheep determined Farmer Hogget to take the next step in a plan which had begun to form in his mind on the day when the piglet had first penned the sheep. That step was nothing less than to take Pig with him to the local sheep-dog trials in a couple of weeks' time. Only just to watch, of course, just so that he could have a look at well-trained dogs working a small number of sheep, and see what they and their handlers were required to do. I'm daft, he thought, grinning to himself. He did not tell his wife.

Before the day came, he put a collar and lead on the pig. He could not risk him running away, in a strange place. He kept him on the lead all one morning, letting Fly do the work as of old. He need not have bothered – Babe would have stayed tight at heel when told – but it was interesting to note the instant change in the atmosphere as the collie ran out.

'Wolf! Wolf!' cried the flock, every sheep immediately on edge.

'Move, fools!' snapped Fly, and she hustled them and bustled them with little regard for their feelings.

'Babe! We want Babe!' they bleated. 'Ba-a-a-a-a-a-be!'

To be sure, the work was done more quickly, but at the end of it the sheep were in fear and trembling and the dog out of patience and breath.

'Steady! Steady!' called the farmer a number of times, something he never had to say to Babe.

When the day came for the local trials, Farmer Hogget set off early in the Land Rover, Fly and Babe in the back. He told his wife where he was going, though not that he was taking the pig. Nor

did he say that he did not intend to be an ordinary spectator, but instead more of a spy, to see without being seen. He wanted Pig to observe everything that went on without being spotted. Now that he had settled on the final daring part of his plan, Hogget realized that secrecy was all-important. No one must know that he owned a . . . what would you call him, he thought . . . a sheep-pig, I suppose!

The trials took place ten miles or so away, in a curved basin-shaped valley in the hills. At the lower end of the basin was a road. Close to this was the starting point, where the dogs would begin their outrun, and also the enclosure where they would finally pen their sheep. Down there all the spectators would gather. Farmer Hogget, arriving some time before them, parked the Land Rover in a lane, and set off up the valley by a roundabout way, keeping in the shelter of the bordering woods, Fly padding behind him and Babe on the lead trotting to keep up with his long strides.

'Where are we going, Mum?' said Babe excitedly. 'What are we going to do?'

'I don't think we're going to do anything, dear,' said Fly. 'I think the boss wants you to see something.'

'What?'

They had reached the head of the valley now, and the farmer found a suitable place to stop, under cover, but with a good view of the course.

'Down, Fly, down, Pig, and stay,' he said and exhausted by this long speech, stretched his long frame on the ground and settled down to wait.

'Wants me to see what?' said Babe.

'The trials.'

'What's trials?'

'Well,' said Fly, 'it's a sort of competition, for sheep-dogs and their bosses. Each dog has to fetch five sheep, and move them through a number of gaps and gateways – you can see which ones, they've got flags on either side – down to that circle that's marked out in the field right at the bottom, and there the dog has to shed some sheep.'

'What's "shed" mean?'

'Separate them out from the rest; the ones to be shed will have collars on.'

'And then what?'

'Then the dog has to gather them all again, and pen them.'

'Is that all?'

'It's not easy, dear. Not like moving that bunch of woolly fools of ours up and down a field. It all has to be done quickly, without any mistakes. You lose points if you make mistakes.'

'Have you ever been in a trial, Mum?'

'Yes. Here. When I was younger.'

'Did you make any mistakes?'

'Of course,' said Fly. 'Everyone does. It's very difficult, working a small number of strange sheep, in strange country. You'll see.'

By the end of the day Babe had seen a great deal. The course was not an easy one, and the sheep were very different from those at home. They were fast and wild, and, good though the dogs were, there were many mistakes made, at the gates, in the shedding-ring, at the final penning.

Babe watched every run intently, and Hogget watched Babe, and Fly watched them both.

What's the boss up to, she thought, as they drove home. He's surely never thinking that one day Babe might . . . no, he couldn't be that daft! Sheep-pig indeed! All right for the little chap to run round our place for a bit of fun, but to think of him competing in trials, even a little local one like today's, well, really! She remembered something he had said in his early duck-herding days.

'I suppose you'd say,' she remarked, 'that those dogs just weren't polite enough?'

'That's right,' said Babe.

Eight
'Oh Ma!'

Fly's suspicions about what the farmer was up to grew rapidly over the next weeks. It soon became obvious to her that he was constructing, on his own land, a practice course. From the top of the field where the rustlers had come, the circuit which he laid out ran all round the farm, studded with hazards to be negotiated. Some were existing gateways or gaps. Some he made, with hurdles, or lines of posts between which the sheep had to be driven. Some were extremely difficult. One, for example, a plank bridge over a stream, was so narrow that it could only be crossed in single file, and the most honeyed words were needed from Babe to persuade the animals to cross.

Then, in the home paddock, Hogget made a rough shedding-ring with a circle of large stones, and beyond it, a final pen, a small hurdle enclosure no bigger than a tiny room, with a gate to close its mouth when he pulled on a rope.

Every day the farmer would send Fly to cut out five sheep from the flock, and take them to the top of the hill, and hold them there. Then, starting Babe from the gate at the lower end of the farmyard, Hogget would send him away to run them through the course.

'Away to me, Pig!' he would say, or 'Come by, Pig!' and off Babe would scamper as fast as his trotters could carry him, as the farmer pulled out his big old pocket watch and noted the time. There was only one problem. His trotters wouldn't carry him all that fast.

Here at home, Fly realized, his lack of speed didn't matter much. Whichever five sheep were selected were only too anxious to oblige Babe, and would hurry eagerly to do whatever he wanted. But with strange sheep it will be different, thought Fly. If the boss really does intend to run him in a trial. Which it looks as though he does! She watched his tubby pinky-white shape as he crested the hill.

That evening at suppertime she watched again as he tucked into his food. Up till now it had never worried her how much he ate. He's a growing boy, she had thought fondly. Now she thought, he's a greedy boy too.

'Babe,' she said, as with a grunt of content he licked the last morsels off the end of his snout. His little tin trough was as shiningly clean as though Mrs Hogget had washed it in her sink, and his tummy was as tight as a drum.

'Yes, Mum?'

'You like being a . . . sheep-pig, don't you?'

'Oh yes, Mum!'

'And you'd like to be really good at it, wouldn't you? The greatest? Better than any other sheep-pig?'

'D'you think there are any others?'

'Well, no. Better than any sheep-dog, then?'

'Oh yes, I'd love to be! But I don't really think that's possible. You see, although sheep do seem to go very well for me, and do what I ask . . . I mean, do what I tell them, I'm nothing like as fast as a dog and never could be.'

'No. But you could be a jolly sight faster than you are.'

'How?'

'Well, there are two things you'd have to do, dear,' said Fly. 'First, you'd have to go into proper training. One little run around a day's not enough. You'd have to practise hard – jogging, cross-country running, sprinting, distance work. I'd help you of course.'

It all sounded fun to Babe.

'Great!' he said. 'But you said "two things". What's the second?'

'Eat less,' said Fly. 'You'd have to go on a diet.'

Any ordinary pig would have rebelled at this point. Pigs enjoy eating, and they also enjoy lying around most of the day thinking about eating again. But Babe was no ordinary pig, and he set out enthusiastically to do what Fly suggested.

Under her watchful eye he ate wisely but not too well, and every afternoon he trained, to a programme which she had worked out, trotting right round the boundaries of the farm perhaps, or running up to the top of the hill and back again, or racing up and down the home paddock. Hogget thought that Pig was just playing, but he couldn't help noticing how he had grown; not fatter, as a sty-kept pig would have done, but stronger and wirier. There was nothing of the piglet about him any more; he looked lean and racy and hard-muscled, and he was now almost as big as the sheep he herded. And the day came when that strength and hardness were to stand him in good stead.

*

One beautiful morning, when the sky was clear and cloudless, and the air so crisp and fresh that you could almost taste it, Babe woke feeling on top of the world. Like a trained athlete, he felt so charged with energy that he simply couldn't keep still. He bounced about the stable floor on all four feet, shaking his head about and uttering a series of short sharp squeaks.

'You're full of it this morning,' said Fly with a yawn. 'You'd better run to the top of the hill and back to work it off.'

'OK, Mum!' said Babe, and off he shot while Fly settled comfortably back in the straw.

Dashing across the home paddock, Babe bounded up the hill and looked about for the sheep. Though he knew he would see them later on, he felt so pleased with life that he thought he would like to share that feeling with Ma and all the others, before he ran home again; just to say 'Hullo! Good morning, everybody! Isn't it a lovely day!' They were, he knew, in the most distant of all the fields on the farm, right away up at the top of the lane.

He looked across, expecting that they would be grazing quietly or lying comfortably and cudding in the morning sun, only to see them galloping madly in every direction. On the breeze came cries of 'Wolf!' but not in the usual bored, almost automatic, tones of complaint that they used when Fly worked them. These were yells of real terror, desperate calls for help. As he watched, two other animals came in sight, one large, one small, and he heard the sound of barking and yapping as they dashed about after the fleeing sheep. 'You get some wolves as'll chase sheep and kill 'em' – Ma's exact words came back to Babe, and without a second thought he set off as fast as he could go in the direction of the noise.

What a sight greeted him when he arrived in the far field! The flock, usually so tightly bunched, was scattered everywhere, eyes bulging, mouths open, heads hanging in their evident distress, and it was clear that the dogs had been at their worrying for some time. A few sheep had tried in their terror to jump the wire fencing and had become caught up in it, some had fallen into the ditches and got stuck. Some were limping as they ran about, and on the grass were lumps of wool torn from others.

Most dreadful of all, in the middle of the field, the worriers had brought down a ewe, which lay on its side feebly kicking at them as they growled and tugged at it.

On the day when the rustlers had come, Babe had felt a mixture of fear and anger. Now he knew nothing but a blind rage, and he charged flat out at the two dogs, grunting and snorting with fury. Nearest to him was the smaller dog, a kind of mongrel terrier, which was snapping at one of the ewe's hindlegs, deaf to everything in the excitement of the worry.

Before it could move, Babe took it across the back and flung it to one side, and the force of his rush carried him on into the bigger dog and knocked it flying.

This one, a large black crossbred, part collie, part retriever, was made of sterner stuff than the terrier, which was already running dazedly away; and it picked itself up and came snarling back at the pig. Perhaps, in the confusion of the moment, it thought that this was just another sheep that had somehow found courage to attack it; but if so, it soon knew better, for as it came on, Babe chopped at it with his terrible pig's bite, the bite that grips and tears, and now it was not sheep's blood that was spilled.

Howling in pain, the black dog turned and ran, his tail between his legs. He ran, in fact, for his life, an open-mouthed bristling pig hard on his heels.

The field was clear, and Babe suddenly came back to his senses. He turned and hurried to the fallen ewe, round whom, now that the dogs had gone, the horrified flock was beginning to gather in a rough circle. She lay still now, as Babe stood panting by her side, a draggled side where the worriers had pulled at it, and suddenly he realized. It was Ma!

'Ma!' he cried. 'Ma! Are you all right?'

She did not seem too badly hurt. He could not see any gaping wounds, though blood was coming from one ear where the dogs had bitten it.

The old ewe opened an eye. Her voice, when she spoke, was as hoarse as ever, but now not much more than a whisper.

'Hullo, young un,' she said.

Babe dropped his head and gently licked the ear to try to stop the bleeding, and some blood stuck to his snout.

'Can you get up?' he asked.

For some time Ma did not answer, and he looked anxiously at her, but the eye that he could see was still open.

'I don't reckon,' she said.

'It's all right, Ma,' Babe said. 'The wolves have gone, far away.'

'Far, far, fa-a-a-a-a-ar!' chorused the flock.

'And Fly and the boss will soon be here to look after you.'

Ma made no answer or movement. Only her ribs jumped to the thump of her tired old heart.

'You'll be all right, honestly you will,' said Babe.

'Oh ar,' said Ma, and then the eye closed and the ribs jumped no more.

'Oh Ma!' said Babe, and 'Ma! Ma! Ma-a-a-a-a-a!' mourned the flock, as the Land Rover came up the lane.

Farmer Hogget had heard nothing of the worrying – the field was too far away, the wind in the wrong direction – but he had been anxious, and so by now had Fly, because Pig was nowhere to be found.

The moment they entered the field both man and dog could see that something was terribly wrong. Why else was the flock so obviously distressed, panting and gasping and dishevelled?

Why had they formed that ragged circle, and what was in the middle of it? Farmer Hogget strode forward, Fly before him parting the ring to make way, only to see a sight that struck horror into the hearts of both.

There before them lay a dead ewe, and bending over it was the pig, his snout almost touching the outstretched neck, a snout, they saw, that was stained with blood.

Nine
'Was It Babe?'

'Go home, Pig!' said Farmer Hogget in a voice that was so quiet and cold that Babe hardly recognized it. Bewildered, he trotted off obediently, while behind him the farmer picked up the dead ewe and carried it to the Land Rover. Then with Fly's help he began the task of rescuing those sheep that were caught or stuck, and of making sure that no others were badly hurt. This done, he left Fly to guard the flock, and drove home.

*

Back at the farm, Babe felt simply very very sad. The sky was still cloudless, the air still crisp, but this was a very different pig from the one that had cantered carefree up the hill not half an hour ago. In those thirty minutes he had seen naked fear and cruelty and death, and now to cap it all, the boss was angry with him, had sent him home in some sort of disgrace. What had he done wrong? He had only done his duty, as a good sheep-pig should. He sat in the doorway of the stables and watched as the Land Rover drove into the yard, poor Ma's head lolling loosely over the back. He saw the boss get out and go into the house, and then, a few minutes later, come out again, carrying something in the crook

of one arm, a long thing, a kind of black shiny tube, and walk towards him.

'Come, Pig,' said Farmer Hogget in that same cold voice, and strode past him into the stables, while at the same moment, inside the farmhouse, the telephone began to ring, and then stopped as Mrs Hogget picked it up.

Obediently Babe followed the farmer into the dark interior. It was not so dark however that he could not see clearly that the boss was pointing the black shiny tube at him, and he sat down again and waited, supposing that perhaps it was some machine for giving out food and that some quite unexpected surprise would come out of its two small round mouths, held now quite close to his face.

At that instant Mrs Hogget's voice sounded across the yard, calling her husband's name from the open kitchen window. He frowned, lowered the shiny tube, and poked his head around the stable door.

'Oh there you are!' called Mrs Hogget. 'What

dost think then, that was the police that was, they'm ringing every farmer in the district to warn 'em, there's sheep-worrying dogs about, they killed six sheep t'other side of the valley only last night, they bin seen they have, two of 'em 'tis, a big black un and a little brown un, they say to shoot 'em on sight if you do see 'em, you better get back up the hill and make sure ours is all right, d'you want me to fetch your gun?'

'No,' said Farmer Hogget. 'It's all right,' he said.

He waited till his wife had shut the window and disappeared, and then he walked out into the sunlight with Babe following.

'Sit, Pig,' hc said, but now his voice was warm and kindly again.

He looked closely at the trusting face turned up to his, and saw, sticking to the side of Babe's mouth, some hairs, some black hairs, and a few brown ones too.

He shook his head in wonder, and that slow grin spread over his face.

'I reckon you gave them summat to worry about,' he said, and he broke the gun and took out the cartridges.

Meanwhile Fly, standing guard up in the far field, was terribly agitated. She knew of course that some dogs will attack sheep, sometimes even the very dogs trained to look after them, but surely not her sheep-pig? Surely Babe could not have done such a thing? Yet there he had been at the centre of that scene of chaos, bloodstained and standing over a dead ewe! What would the boss do to him, what perhaps had he already done? Yet she could not leave these fools to find out.

At least though, she suddenly realized, they could tell her what had happened, if the shock hadn't driven what little sense they had out of their stupid heads. Never before in her long life had Fly sunk to engaging a sheep in conversation.

They were there to be ordered about, like soldiers, and, like soldiers, never to answer back. She approached the nearest one, with distaste, and it promptly backed away from her.

'Stand still, fool!' she barked. 'And tell me who chased you. Who killed that old one?'

'Wolf,' said the sheep automatically.

Fly growled with annoyance. Was that the only word the halfwits knew? She put the question differently.

'Was it the pig that chased you? Was it Babe?' she said.

'Ba-a-a-a-abe!' bleated the sheep eagerly.

'What does that mean, bonehead?' barked Fly. 'Was it or wasn't it?'

'Wolf,' said the sheep.

Somehow Fly controlled her anger at the creature's stupidity. I *must* know what happened, she thought. Babe's always talking about being polite to these woolly idiots. I'll have to try it. I must know. She took a deep breath.

'Please . . .' she said. The sheep, which had

begun to graze, raised its head sharply and stared at her with an expression of total amazement.

'Say that agai-ai-ai-ain,' it said, and a number of others, overhearing, moved towards the collie.

'Please,' said Fly, swallowing hard, 'could you be kind enough to tell me.'

'Hark!' interrupted the first sheep. 'Hark! Ha-a-a-a-ark!' whereupon the whole flock ran and gathered round. They stood in silence, every eye fixed wonderingly on her, every mouth hanging

open. Nincompoops! thought Fly. Just when I wanted to ask one quietly the whole fat-headed lot come round. But I must know. I must know the truth about my Babe, however terrible it is.

'Please,' she said once more in a voice choked with the effort of being humble, 'could you be kind enough to tell me what happened this morning? Did Babe . . . ?' but she got no further, for at the mention of the pig's name the whole flock burst out into a great cry of 'Ba-a-a-a-abe!'

Listening, for the first time ever, to what the sheep were actually saying, Fly could hear individual voices competing to make themselves heard, in what was nothing less than a hymn of praise. 'Babe ca-a-a-aame!' 'He sa-a-a-a-aved us!' 'He drove the wolves awa-a-a-a-ay!' 'He made them pa-a-a-a-ay!' 'Hip hip hooray! Hip hip hooray! Hip hip hoora-a-a-ay!'

What a sense of relief flooded over her as she heard and understood the words of the sheep! It had been sheep-worriers, after all! And her boy had come to the rescue! He was not the villain, he was the hero!

Hogget and Babe heard the racket as they climbed the hill, and the farmer sent the pig ahead, fearing that perhaps the worriers had returned.

Under cover of the noise Babe arrived on the scene unnoticed by Fly, just in time to hear her reply.

'Oh thank you!' she cried to the flock. 'Thank you all so much for telling me! How kind of you!'

'Gosh, Mum,' said a voice behind her. 'What's come over you?'

Ten
'Get It Off By Heart'

Because Babe had now saved the flock not only from rustlers but also from the worriers, the Hoggets could not do too much for him.

Because he was a pig (though Farmer Hogget increasingly found himself thinking of Pig as Dog and fed him accordingly), they gave him unlimited supplies of what they supposed he could not have too much of – namely, food.

Because he was strong-minded and revelled in his newfound speed, he ate sparingly of it.

Because there was always a lot left over, Fly became fat and the chickens chubby and the ducks dumpy, and the very rats and mice rolled happily about the stables with stomachs full to bursting.

Mrs Hogget even took to calling Babe to the back door, to feed him some titbit or other that she thought he might particularly fancy; and from here it was but a short step to inviting him into the house, which one day she did.

When the farmer came in for his tea, he found not only Fly but also Pig lying happily asleep beside the Aga cooker. And afterwards, when he sat down in his armchair in the sitting-room and switched

on the television, Babe came to sit beside him, and they watched the six o'clock news together.

'He likes it,' said Hogget to his wife when she came into the room. Mrs Hogget nodded her head a great many times, and as usual had a few words to say on the subject.

'Dear little chap, though you can't call him little no longer, he've growed so much, why, he's big enough to you-know-what, not that we ever shall now, over my dead body though I hopes it ain't if you see what I do mean, just look at him, we should have brought him in the house long ago, no reason why not, is there now?'

'He might mess the carpet,' said Farmer Hogget.

'Never!' cried Mrs Hogget, shaking her head the entire time that she was speaking. 'He's no more likely to mess than he is to fly, he'll ask to go out when he wants to do his do's, just like a good clean dog would, got more brains than a dog he has, why 'twouldn't surprise me to hear he was rounding up them old sheep of yourn, 'twouldn't honestly, though I suppose you think I'm daft?'

Farmer Hogget grinned to himself. He did not tell his wife what she had never yet noticed, that all the work of the farm was now done by the sheep-pig. And he had no intention of telling her of the final part of his plan, which was nothing less than to enter Pig in that sternest of all tests, the Grand Challenge Sheep Dog Trials, open to all comers! Never in his working life had he owned an animal good enough to compete in these Trials. Now at last he had one, and he was not going to be stopped from realizing his ambition by the fact that it was a pig.

In a couple of weeks they would be competing against the best sheep-dogs in the country, would be appearing, in fact, on that very television screen they were now watching.

'No, you're not daft,' he said.

But you won't half get a surprise when you sit here and watch it, he thought. And so will a lot of other folks.

His plan was simple. He would appear at the Grand Challenge Trials with Fly, and at the last possible moment swap her for Pig. By then it would be too late for anyone to stop him. It didn't matter what happened afterwards – they could disqualify him, fine him, send him to prison, anything – as long as he could run Pig, just one glorious run, just to show them all!

And they couldn't say they hadn't been warned – the name was there on the entry form.

He had been worried, for he was a truthful man, that the heading might say 'Name of Dog', and then whatever he put would be a lie. But he'd been lucky. 'Name of Competitor' (the form said) . . .

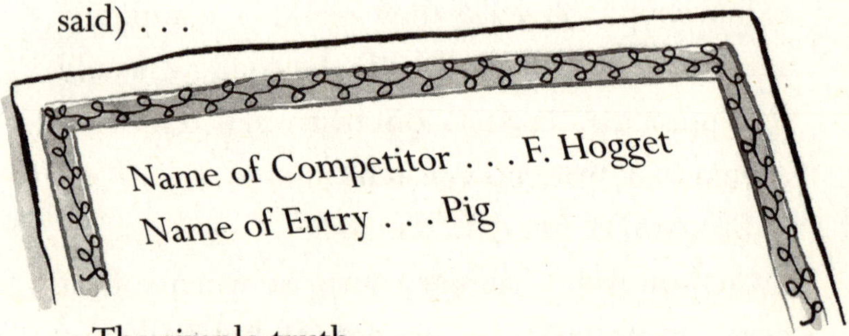
Name of Competitor . . . F. Hogget
Name of Entry . . . Pig

The simple truth.

Shepherds usually give their dogs short names, like Gyp or Moss – it's so much quicker and easier than shouting 'Bartholomew!' or 'Wilhelmina!' – and though someone might say '"Pig"? That's a funny name,' no one in their wildest dreams would guess that simple truth.

The two weeks before the Grand Challenge Trials were two weeks of concentrated activity. Apart from Mrs Hogget who as usual was busy with household duties, everyone now knew what was going on. To begin with, Hogget altered the practice course, cutting out all the frills like the plank bridge over the stream, and building a new course as like as possible to what he thought they might face on the day.

As soon as Fly saw this, she became convinced that the plan which she had suspected was actually going to be put into operation, and she told the sheep, with whom she was now on speaking terms.

Every night of course she and Babe talked endlessly about the coming challenge before they settled to sleep (in the stables still, though the Hoggets would have been perfectly happy for Babe to sleep in the house, so well-mannered was he).

Thoughtful as ever, Babe was anxious, not about his own abilities but about his foster-mother's feelings. He felt certain she would have given her dog-teeth to compete in the National Trials, the dream of every sheep-dog, yet she must sit and watch him.

'Are you *sure* you don't mind, Mum?' he asked.

Fly's reply was as practical as ever.

'Listen, Babe,' she said. 'First of all it wouldn't matter whether I minded or not. The boss is going to run you, no doubt of it. Second, I'm too old and too fat, and anyway I was only ever good enough for small local competitions. And lastly, I'll be the happiest collie in the world if you win. And you can win.'

'D'you really think so?'

'I'm sure of it,' said Fly firmly, but all the same she was anxious too – about one thing.

She knew that the sheep-pig, speedy as he now was, would still be much slower than the dogs, especially on the outrun; but equally she was confident that he could make this up by the promptness with which the sheep obeyed his requests. Here, at home, they shot through gaps or round obstacles as quick as a flash, never putting a foot wrong; the ones to be shed nipped out of the ring like lightning; and at the final penning, they popped in the instant that the boss opened the gate. But that was here, at home. What would strange sheep do? How would they react to Babe? Would he be able to communicate with them, in time, for there would be none to waste?

She determined to ask the flock, and one evening, when Babe and the boss were watching television, she trotted off up the hill. Since that first time when she had been forced to speak civilly to them, they no longer cried 'Wolf!' at her, and now they gathered around attentively at her first words, words that were carefully polite.

'Good evening,' said Fly. 'I wonder if you could

be kind enough to help me? I've a little problem,' and she explained it, speaking slowly and carefully (for sheep are stupid, she said to herself: nobody will ever persuade me otherwise).

'You see what I mean?' she finished. 'There they'll be, these strange sheep, and I'm sure they'll do what he tells them . . . asks them, I mean . . . eventually, but it'll all take time, explaining things. The last creature they'll be expecting to see is a pig, and they might just bolt at the sight of him, before he even gets a chance to speak to them.'

'Password,' said several voices.

'What do you mean?' Fly said.

'Password, password, pa-a-a-assword!' said many voices now, speaking slowly and carefully (for wolves are stupid, they said to themselves: nobody will ever persuade us otherwise).

'What our Babe's got to do,' said one, 'is to larn what all of us larned when we was little lambs.'

‘’Tis a saying, see,’ said another, ‘as lambs do larn at their mothers’ hocks.’

‘And then wherever we do go . . .’

‘. . . to ma-a-a-arket . . .’

‘. . . or to another fa-a-a-arm . . .’

‘. . . we won’t never come to no ha-a-a-arm . . .’

‘. . . so long as we do say the pa-a-a-assword!’

‘And if our Babe do say it to they . . .’

‘. . . why then, they won’t never run away!’

Fly felt her patience slipping, but she controlled herself, knowing how important this information could be.

‘Please,’ she said quietly, ‘please will you tell me the password?’

For a long moment the flock stood silent, the only movement a turning of heads as they looked at one another. Fly could sense that they were nerving themselves to tell this age-old secret, to give away – to a wolf, of all things – this treasured countersign.

Then ‘’Tis for Babe,’ someone said, ‘’tis for his sa-a-a-ake.’

'Ah!' they all said softly. 'A-a-a-a-a-a-ah!' and then with one voice they began to intone:

'I may be ewe, I may be ram,
I may be mutton, may be lamb,
But on the hoof or on the hook,
I bain't so stupid as I look.'

Then by general consent they began to move away, grazing as they went.

‘Is that it?’ called Fly after them. ‘Is that the password?’ and the murmur came back ‘A-a-a-a-a-a-a-a-a-a-ar!’

‘But what does it all mean, Mum?’ said Babe that night when she told him. ‘All that stuff about “I may be you” and other words I don’t understand. It doesn’t make sense to me.’

‘That doesn’t matter, dear,’ said Fly. ‘You just get it off by heart. It may make all the difference on the day.’

Eleven
'Today Is the Day'

The day, when it dawned, was just that little bit too bright.

On the opposite side of the valley the trees and houses and haystacks stood out clearly against the background in that three-dimensional way that means rain later.

Farmer Hogget came out and sniffed the air and looked around. Then he went inside again to fetch waterproof clothing.

Fly knew, the moment that she set eyes on the

boss, that this was the day. Dogs have lived so long with humans that they know what's going to happen, sometimes even before their owners do. She woke Babe.

'Today,' she said.

'Today what, Mum?' said Babe sleepily.

'Today is the day of the Grand Challenge Sheep Dog Trials,' said Fly proudly. 'Which you, dear,' she added in a confident voice, 'are going to win!' With a bit of luck, she thought, and tenderly she licked the end of his snout.

She looked critically at the rest of him, anxious as any mum that her child should be well turned out if it is to appear in public.

'Oh Babe!' she said. 'Your coat's in an awful mess. What have you been doing with yourself? You look just as though you've been wallowing in the duck-pond.'

'Yes.'

'You mean you have?'

'Yes, Mum.'

Fly was on the point of saying that puppies

don't do such things, when she remembered that he was, after all, a pig.

'Well, I don't know about Large White,' she said. 'You've certainly grown enormous but it's anyone's guess what colour you are under all that muck. Whatever's to be done?'

Immediately her question was answered.

'Come, Pig,' said Hogget's voice from the yard, and when they came out of the stables, there stood the farmer with hosepipe and scrubbing brush and pails of soapy water.

Half an hour later, when a beautifully clean shining Babe stood happily dripping while Hogget brushed out the tassel of his tight-curled tail till it looked like candy-floss, Mrs Hogget stuck her head out of the kitchen window.

'Breakfast's ready,' she called, 'but what in the world bist doing with thik pig, taking him to a pig show or summat, I thought you was going to drive up and watch the Trials today, anybody'd think you was going to enter 'e in them the way you've got un done up, only he wouldn't be a sheep-dog, he'd be a sheep-pig wouldn't 'e, tee hee, whoever heard of such a thing, I must be daft though it's you that's daft really, carrying him about in the poor old Land Rover the size he is now, the bottom'll fall out, I shouldn't wonder, you ain't surely going to drive all that way with him in the back just so's he can watch?'

'No,' said Farmer Hogget.

Mrs Hogget considered this answer for a moment with her mouth open, while raising and lowering her eyebrows, shaking her head, and drumming on the window-sill with her finger-tips. Then she closed her mouth and the window.

After breakfast she came out to see them off. Fly was sitting in the passenger seat, Babe was comfortable in a thick bed of clean straw in the back, of which he now took up the whole space.

Mrs Hogget walked round the Land Rover, giving out farewell pats.

'Good boy,' she said to Babe, and 'Good girl,' to Fly. And to Hogget, 'Goodbye and have you got your sandwiches and your thermos of coffee and your raincoat, looks as if it might rain, thought I felt a spot just now though I suppose it might be different where you'm going seeing as it's a hundred miles away, that reminds me have you got enough petrol or if not enough money to get some if you haven't if you do see what I do mean, drive carefully, see you later.'

'Two o'clock,' said Hogget. And before his wife had time to say anything, added, 'On the telly. Live,' and put the Land Rover into gear and drove away.

When Mrs Hogget switched the television on at two o'clock, the first thing in the picture that she noticed was that it was raining hard. She dashed outside to fetch her washing in, saw that the sun was shining, remembered it wasn't washing-day anyway, and came back to find the cameras showing the lay-out of the course. First there was a shot of a huge pillar of stone, the height of a man, standing upright in the ground.

'Here,' said the voice of the commentator, 'is where each handler will stand, and from here each dog will start his outrun; he can go left or right, to get into position behind his sheep; today each dog will have ten sheep to work; they will be grouped near that distant post, called the

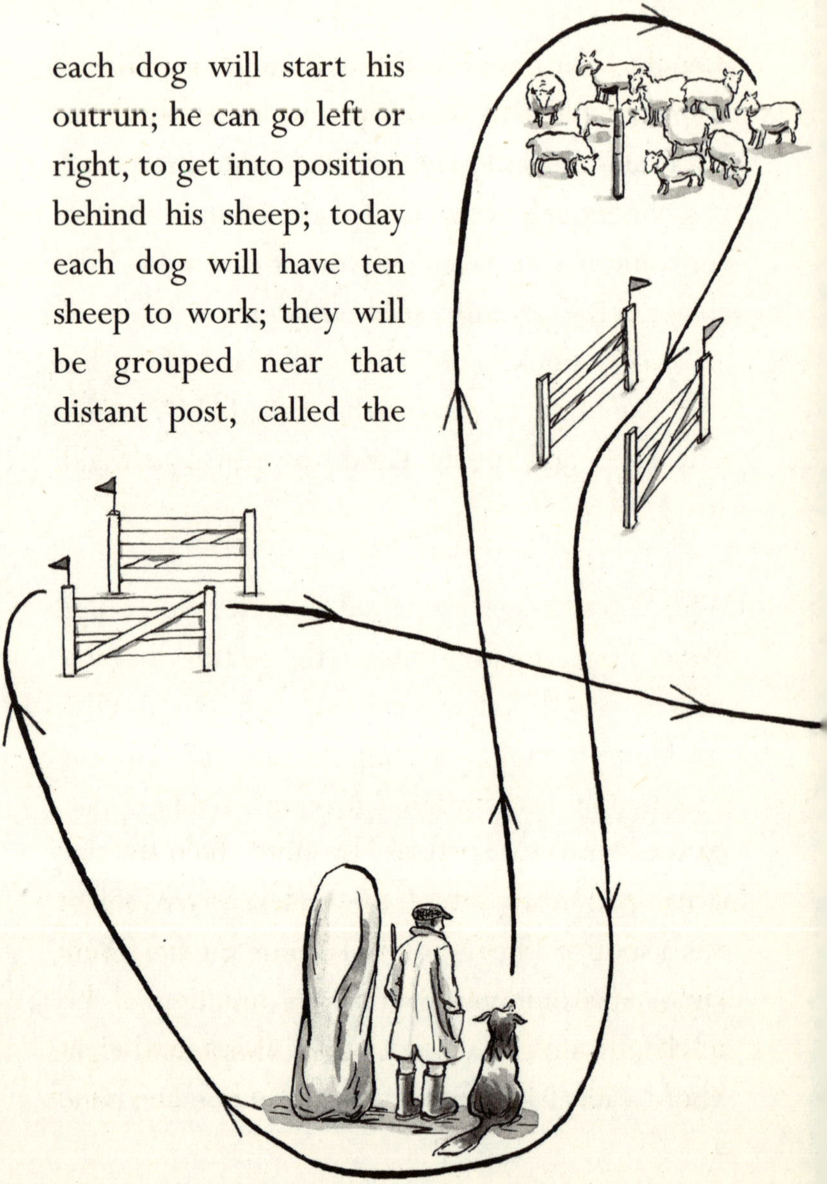

Holding Post,' (all the time the cameras followed his explanations), 'and then he must fetch his sheep, through the Fetch Gates, all the way back

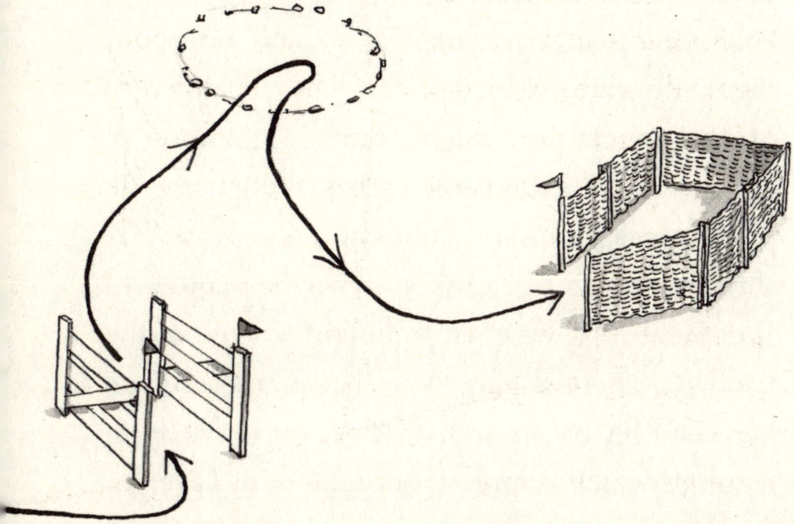

to the Handler's Post, and round it; then the dog drives the sheep away – to the left as we look at it – through the Drive Away Gates, turns them right again and straight across the line of his fetch, through the Cross Drive Gates, and right again to the Shedding Ring, and when he's shed his sheep and collected them again, then finally he must pen them here.'

'Mouthy old thing!' said Mrs Hogget, turning the sound off. 'Some folk never know how to hold their tongues, keeping on and on about them silly gates, why don't 'e show us a picture of the spectators, might catch a glimpse of Hogget and Fly, you never knows, though not the pig, I hopes, he's surely not daft enough to walk about with the pig, can't see why he wanted to take un all that way just to lie in the back of the Land Rover, he'd have done better to leave un here and let un sit and watch it on the telly in comfort which is more than some of us have got time for, I got work to do,' and she stumped off into the kitchen, shaking her head madly.

On the silent screen the first handler walked out and took up his position beside the great sarsen-stone, his dog standing by him, tense and eager in the pouring rain.

Twelve
'That'll Do'

Hundreds of thousands of pairs of eyes watched that first dog, but none more keenly than those of Hogget, Fly and Babe.

The car-park was a big sloping field overlooking the course, and the farmer had driven the Land Rover to the topmost corner, well away from other cars. From inside it, the three so different faces watched intently.

Conditions, Hogget could see immediately, were very difficult. In addition to the driving rain, which made the going slippery and the sheep more obstinate than usual, there was quite a strong wind blowing almost directly from the Holding Post back towards the handler, and the dog was finding it hard to hear commands.

The more anxious the dog was, the more the sheep tried to break from him, and thus the angrier he became. It was a vicious circle, and when at last the ten sheep were penned and the handler pulled the gate shut and cried 'That'll do!' no one was surprised that they had scored no more than seventy points out of a possible hundred.

So it went on. Man after man came to stand beside the great sarsen-stone, men from the North and from the West, from Scotland, and Wales, and Ireland, with dogs and bitches, large and small, rough-coated and smooth, black-and-white or grey or brown or blue merle. Some fared better than others of course, were steadier on their sheep or had steadier sheep to deal with. But still, as Farmer Hogget's turn drew near (as luck would have it, he was last to go), there was no score higher than eighty-five.

At home Mrs Hogget chanced to turn the sound of the television back up in time to hear the commentator confirm this.

'One more to go,' he said, 'and the target to beat is eighty-five points, set by Mr Jones from Wales and his dog Bryn, a very creditable total considering the appalling weather conditions we have up here today. It's very difficult to see that score being beaten, but here comes the last competitor to try and do just that,' and suddenly there appeared on the screen before Mrs Hogget's astonished eyes the tall long-striding figure of her husband, walking out towards the great stone with tubby old Fly at his heels.

'This is Mr Hogget with Pig,' said the commentator. 'A bit of a strange name that, but then I must say his dog's rather on the fat side . . . hullo, he's sending the dog back . . . what on earth? . . . oh, good heavens! . . . Will you look at that!'

And as Mrs Hogget and hundreds of thousands of other viewers looked, they saw Fly go trotting back towards the car-park.

And from it, cantering through the never-ending rain, came the long, lean, beautifully clean figure of a Large White pig.

Straight to Hogget's side ran Babe, and stood like a statue, his great ears fanned, his little eyes fixed upon the distant sheep.

At home, Mrs Hogget's mouth opened wide, but for once no sound came from it.

On the course, there was a moment of stunned silence and then a great burst of noise.

On the screen, the cameras showed every aspect of the amazing scene – the spectators pointing, gaping, grinning; the red-faced judges hastily conferring; Hogget and Babe waiting patiently; and finally the commentator.

'This is really quite ridiculous,' he said with a shamefaced smile, 'but in point of fact there seems to be nothing in the rule book that says that only sheep-dogs may compete. So it looks as though the judges are bound to allow Mr Hogget to run this, er, sheep-pig I suppose we'll have to call it, ha, ha! One look at it, and the sheep will disappear into the next county without a doubt! Still, we might as well end the day with a good laugh!'

And indeed at that moment a great gale of laughter arose, as Hogget, receiving a most unwilling nod from the judges, said quietly, 'Away to me, Pig,' and Babe began his outrun to the right.

How they roared at the mere sight of him running (though many noticed how fast he went), and at the purely crazy thought of a pig herding sheep, and especially at the way he squealed and squealed at the top of his voice, in foolish excitement they supposed.

But though he was excited, tremendously excited at the thrill of actually competing in the Grand Challenge Sheep Dog Trials, Babe was nobody's fool. He was yelling out the password: 'I may be ewe, I may be ram, I may be mutton, may be lamb, but on the hoof or on the hook, I bain't so stupid as I look,' he hollered as he ran.

This was the danger point – before he'd met his sheep – and again and again he repeated the magic words, shouting above the noise of wind and rain, his eyes fixed on the ten sheep by the Holding Post. Their eyes were just as fixed on him, eyes that bulged at the sight of this great strange animal approaching, but they held steady, and the now distant crowd fell suddenly silent as they saw the pig take up a perfect position behind his sheep, and heard the astonished judges award ten points for a faultless outrun.

Just for luck, in case they hadn't believed their ears, Babe gave the password one last time. '. . . I bain't so stupid as I look,' he panted, 'and a very good afternoon to you all, and I do apologize for having to ask you to work in this miserable weather, I hope you'll forgive me?'

At once, as he had hoped, there was a positive babble of voices.

'Fancy him knowing the pa-a-a-a-assword!'

'What lovely ma-a-a-anners!'

'Not like they na-a-a-asty wolves!'

'What d'you want us to do, young ma-a-a-a-aster?'

Quickly, for he was conscious that time was ticking away, Babe, first asking politely for their attention, outlined the course to them.

'And I would be really most awfully grateful,' he said, 'if you would all bear these points in mind. Keep tightly together, go at a good steady pace, not too fast, not too slow, and walk exactly through the middle of each of the three gates, if

you'd be good enough. The moment I enter the shedding-ring, would the four of you who are wearing collars (how nice they look, by the way) please walk out of it. And then if you'd all kindly go straight into the final pen, I should be so much obliged.'

All this talk took quite a time, and the crowd and the judges and Mrs Hogget and her hundreds of thousands of fellow viewers began to feel that nothing else was going to happen, that the sheep were never going to move, that the whole thing was a stupid farce, a silly joke that had fallen flat.

Only Hogget, standing silent in the rain beside the sarsen-stone, had complete confidence in the skills of the sheep-pig.

And suddenly the miracle began to happen.

Marching two by two, as steady as guardsmen on parade, the ten sheep set off for the Fetch Gates, Babe a few paces behind them, silent, powerful, confident. Straight as a die they went towards the distant Hogget, straight between the exact centre of the Fetch Gates, without a moment's hesitation, without deviating an inch from their unswerving course. Hogget said nothing, made no sign, gave no whistle, did not move as the sheep rounded him so closely as almost to brush his boots, and, the Fetch completed, set off for the Drive Away Gates.

Once again, their pace never changing, looking neither to left nor to right, keeping so tight a formation that you could have dropped a big tablecloth over the lot, they passed through the precise middle of the Drive Away Gates, and turned as one animal to face the Cross Drive Gates.

It was just the same here. The sheep passed through perfectly and wheeled for the Shedding Ring, while all the time the judges' scorecards showed maximum points and the crowd watched in a kind of hypnotized hush, whispering to one another for fear of breaking the spell.

'He's not put a foot wrong!'

'Bang through the middle of every gate.'

'Lovely steady pace.'

'And the handler, he's not said a word, not even moved, just stood there leaning on his stick.'

'Ah, but he'll have to move now – you're never going to tell me that pig can shed four sheep out of the ten on his own!'

The Shedding Ring was a circle perhaps forty yards in diameter, marked out by little heaps of sawdust, and into it the sheep walked, still calm, still collected, and stood waiting.

Outside the circle Babe waited, his eyes on Hogget.

The crowd waited.

Mrs Hogget waited.

Hundreds of thousands of viewers waited.

Then, just as it seemed nothing more would happen, that the man had somehow lost control of the sheep-pig, that the sheep-pig had lost interest in his sheep, Farmer Hogget raised his stick and with it gave one sharp tap upon the great sarsen-stone, a tap that sounded like a pistol-shot in the tense atmosphere.

And at this signal Babe walked gently into the circle and up to his sheep.

'Beautifully done,' he said to them quietly. 'I can't tell you how grateful I am to you all. Now, if the four ladies with collars would kindly walk out of the ring when I give a grunt, I should be so much obliged. Then if you would all be good enough to wait until my boss has walked across to the final collecting pen over there and opened its gate, all that remains for you to do is to pop in. Would you do that? Please?'

'A-a-a-a-a-ar,' they said softly, and as Babe gave one deep grunt the four collared sheep detached themselves from their companions and calmly, unhurriedly, walked out of the Shedding Ring.

Unmoving, held by the magic of the moment, the crowd watched with no sound but a great sigh of amazement. No one could quite believe his eyes. No one seemed to notice that the wind had dropped and the rain had stopped. No one was surprised when a single shaft of sunshine came suddenly through a hole in the grey clouds and shone full upon the great sarsen-stone.

Slowly, with his long strides, Hogget left it and walked to the little enclosure of hurdles, the final test of his shepherding. He opened its gate and stood, silent still, while the shed animals walked back into the ring to rejoin the rest.

Then he nodded once at Babe, no more, and steadily, smartly, straightly, the ten sheep, with the sheep-pig at their heels, marched into the final pen, and Hogget closed the gate.

As he dropped the loop of rope over the hurdle stake, everyone could see the judges' marks.

A hundred out of a hundred, the perfect performance, never before matched by man and dog in the whole history of sheep-dog trials, but now achieved by man and pig, and everyone went mad!

At home Mrs Hogget erupted, like a volcano, into a great lava-flow of words, pouring them out towards the two figures held by the camera, as though they were actually inside that box in the corner of her sitting-room, cheering them, praising them, congratulating first one and then the other, telling them how proud she was, to hurry home, not to be late for supper, it was shepherd's pie.

As for the crowd of spectators at the Grand Challenge Sheep Dog Trials they shouted and yelled and waved their arms and jumped about, while the astonished judges scratched their heads and the amazed competitors shook theirs in wondering disbelief.

'Marvellous! Ma-a-a-a-a-arvellous!' bleated the ten penned sheep. And from the back of an ancient Land Rover at the top of the car-park a tubby old black-and-white collie bitch, her plumed tail wagging wildly, barked and barked and barked for joy.

In all the hubbub of noise and excitement, two figures still stood silently side by side.

Then Hogget bent, and gently scratching Babe between his great ears, uttered those words that every handler always says to his working companion when the job is finally done.

Perhaps no one else heard the words, but there was no doubting the truth of them.

'That'll do,' said Farmer Hogget to his sheep-pig. 'That'll do.'

A whole barnyard of books!

If you loved *The Sheep-Pig*, here are just a few of the other titles by Dick King-Smith…

A golden goose!
There's no such thing!
Oh yes, there is, and she's living on Farmer Skint's farm.He was a poor unfortunate man but now the golden goose has brought him good luck and happiness. But what will happen if other people find out about his golden bird?

When Babe, the little orphaned piglet, is won at a fair by Farmer Hogget, he is adopted by Fly, the kind-hearted sheep-dog. Babe is determined to learn everything he can from Fly. He knows he can't be a sheep-dog. But maybe, just maybe, he might be a sheep-pig.

Winner of the

Guardian Children's Fiction Prize

Here's what the judges had to say about

The Sheep-Pig

★ 'Perfect'

★ 'Thrilling'

★ 'Funny'

★ 'The Best'

★ 'Charmer'

★ 'Suspense'

★ 'Breathless'

★ 'Delight'

PUFFIN BOOKS

The Jenius

Dick King-Smith served in the Grenadier Guards during the Second World War, and afterwards spent twenty years as a farmer in Gloucestershire, the county of his birth. Many of his stories are inspired by his farming experiences. Later he taught at a village primary school. His first book, *The Fox Busters*, was published in 1978. Since then he has written a great number of children's books, including *The Sheep-Pig* (winner of the Guardian Award and filmed as *Babe*), *Harry's Mad*, *Noah's Brother*, *The Hodgeheg*, *Martin's Mice*, *Ace*, *The Cuckoo Child* and *Harriet's Hare* (winner of the Children's Book Award in 1995). At the British Book Awards in 1991 he was voted Children's Author of the Year. He has three children, a large number of grandchildren and several great-grandchildren, and lives in a seventeenth-century cottage only a crow's flight from the house where he was born.

Books by Dick King-Smith

ANIMAL STORIES
BACK-TO-FRONT BENJY
CLEVER DUCK
GEORGE SPEAKS
THE GHOST AT CODLIN CASTLE AND OTHER STORIES
THE HODGEHEG
THE INVISIBLE DOG
JULIUS CAESAR'S GOAT
THE JENIUS
THE MAGIC CARPET SLIPPERS
KING MAX THE LAST
A NARROW SQUEAK AND OTHER ANIMAL STORIES
PHILIBERT THE FIRST AND OTHER STORIES
MR POTTER'S PET
SMASHER
THE SWOOSE

Colour Young Puffins

BLESSU
DINOSAUR SCHOOL
DUMPLING
FAT LAWRENCE
POPPET
THE GREAT SLOTH RACE

Dick King-Smith

The Jenius

Illustrated by Ann Kronheimer

PUFFIN

PUFFIN BOOKS

Published by the Penguin Group
Penguin Books Ltd, 80 Strand, London WC2R 0RL, England
Penguin Group (USA), Inc., 375 Hudson Street, New York, New York 10014, USA
Penguin Books Australia Ltd, 250 Camberwell Road, Camberwell, Victoria 3124, Australia
Penguin Books Canada Ltd, 10 Alcorn Avenue, Toronto, Ontario, Canada M4V 3B2
Penguin Books India (P) Ltd, 11 Community Centre, Panchsheel Park, New Delhi – 110 017, India
Penguin Books (NZ) Ltd, Cnr Rosedale and Airborne Roads, Albany, Auckland, New Zealand
Penguin Books (South Africa) (Pty) Ltd, 24 Sturdee Avenue, Rosebank 2196, South Africa

Penguin Books Ltd, Registered Offices: 80 Strand, London WC2R 0RL, England

www.penguin.com

First published by Victor Gollancz Ltd 1988
Published in Puffin Books 1998
Published in this edition 2004
8

Set in 17/22.25pt Perpetua

Made and printed in England by Clays Ltd, St Ives plc

British Library Cataloguing in Publication Data
A CIP catalogue record for this book is available from the British Library

ISBN 978-0-14-131286-6

www.greenpenguin.co.uk

Mixed Sources
Product group from well-managed forests and other controlled sources
www.fsc.org Cert no. SA-COC-1592
© 1996 Forest Stewardship Council
FSC

Penguin Books is committed to a sustainable future for our business, our readers and our planet. The book in your hands is made from paper certified by the Forest Stewardship Council.

Contents

1
Guinea Pigs Aren't Stupid

'If I was the Queen,' Judy said, 'I wouldn't have corgis.'

'What sort of dogs would you have, Judy?' said her teacher.

The class were talking about pets and which were their favourites.

'I wouldn't have dogs at all.'

'What would you keep then,' said

Aa Bb Cc Dd
Ee Ff Gg Hh
Ii Jj Kk Ll
Mm Nn Oo Pp
Qq Rr Ss Tt
Uu Vv Ww Xx
Yy Zz
Pets
stick insects
rabbits

Judy's teacher, 'if you were the Queen?'

'Guinea pigs,' said Judy.

Everybody burst out laughing and Judy went very red.

'They're my favourite animals,' she said defiantly. 'If I was the Queen I'd keep lots of them.'

'In hutches, you mean?'

'No. In Buckingham Palace.'

'But Judy,' said her teacher, 'wouldn't it look rather odd if someone very important came to call, like, say, the President of the United States of America, and the Queen, I mean you, said "Do take a seat, Mr President", and there was

a guinea pig lying in the armchair?'

'And there'd be messes all over the carpet,' someone said.

'And the President would step in them,' said someone else.

Everybody giggled.

'My guinea pigs would be house-trained,' muttered Judy, close to tears.

'Palace-trained, you mean,' said a voice, and now there was so much sniggering that the teacher said

'That's enough, children.'

She put her hand on Judy's shoulder and said: 'It's a nice idea, but even if you were the Queen you wouldn't be able to train a guinea pig like you can train a dog. Only certain animals are intelligent enough to be taught things by humans, and I'm afraid guinea pigs are not among them. They're dear little creatures, Judy, but they haven't got a lot of brains.'

2
An Unexpected Arrival

'You *have* got a lot of brains,' said Judy.

As always, she had run down to the shed at the bottom of the garden the moment she arrived home from school, to see her own two guinea pigs. One was a reddish rough-haired boar called Joe and the other was a smooth-coated white sow by the name of Molly. Judy had had them ever since her sixth birthday, nearly two years ago now, and they were very dear to her. Her only regret was that, surprisingly, they had never had babies.

'You *have* got brains,' she said, 'I'm sure of it. It's just that no one's ever taught you to use them. Now, if I'd had you when you were tiny, I bet I could have taught you lots of things. If only you'd had children of your own. I'd have chosen one of them and kept it and really trained it, from a very early age. I bet I

could have done.'

As usual, the guinea pigs responded to the sound of her voice by beginning a little conversation of their own. First Joe made a grumbling sort of chatter (which meant 'Molly, you're as lovely now as the day I first set eyes on you'), and then Molly gave a short shy squeak (which meant 'Oh Joe, you say the nicest things!').

Then they both squealed long and loudly at Judy. She knew what that noise meant. They were telling her to cut the cackle and dish up the grub.

'Greedy old things,' she said, and she picked up the white one, Molly.

'Molly!' said Judy. 'You look awfully fat. Whatever's the matter with you?'

Molly didn't reply. Joe grunted in a self-satisfied sort of way.

'I'll have to put you on a diet,' said Judy firmly, 'starting tomorrow.'

But next morning, when she went to feed the guinea pigs, the white one, she found, looked quite different.

'Molly!' said Judy. 'You look awfully thin. Whatever's the matter with you?'

This time they both answered,

Molly with a series of small happy squeaks and Joe with a low proud grumble, as they moved aside to show what had happened. There between them was a single, very large, baby guinea pig, the child of their old age. It was partly white and smooth like its mother and partly red and rough like its father.

To Judy's delight it stumbled forwards on feet that seemed three sizes too big, until it bumped the wire of the hutch-front with its huge head. Its eyes were very bright and seemed to shine with intelligence. Then it spoke a single word in guinea pig language. Anyone could have told it meant 'Hullo!'

'Oh!' said Judy. 'Aren't you beautiful!'

'He gets it from his mother,' chattered

PERFECT LAWN
ROSE
POISON
GUINEA DINNER
PIG

Joe in the background.

'And aren't you brainy!'

'He takes after his dad,' squeaked Molly.

Judy stared into the baby's eyes.

'You,' she said, 'are going to be the best-trained, most brilliant guinea pig in the whole world. And you're going to start lessons right away. Now then. Sit!'

Of course, when you're only a few hours old, standing can be tiring, but was that the reason why Joe and Molly's son immediately sat down?

3
Training

That night, before she went to bed, Judy wrote the great news in her diary. She was very faithful about putting something in it every day, even if sometimes it was only a bit about the weather. But that Joe and Molly should have had a baby – that was great news and deserved a lot of space.

JUDY'S DIARY. PRIVIT.

JUNE 10th: Great surprise! Molly had a baby! Found him first thing this morning and I am going to train him. Alreddy he sits when he is told. He is briliant. He is mostly white like Molly but he has a sort

of main like a horse running all down his back and that is reddish like Joe.

I asked Dad what you call someone who is really briliant and he said 'A jenius. Why?' and I said 'because that is what I'm going to call my new baby guinea pig' and he laughed but I said 'You just wait. One day the World will know June 10th is the birthday of Jenius.'

June 10th was in fact a very good time for Jenius to have been born, because it meant that he was around six weeks old by the time the long summer holidays began. Now his trainer would be able to

concentrate on him without the interruption of school.

During those six weeks Jenius had grown amazingly. All baby guinea pigs do, of course, but he had benefited particularly, first from being an only child and so getting all his mother's milk, and secondly from Judy's spoiling.

Ordinary guinea pigs, for example, might get the occasional piece of stale bread. Jenius got regular digestive biscuits.

So that Judy's diary, which had contained daily reports of the progress of the wonder child, read . . .

JULY 22nd: Begining of Summer Hollidays. Today I took Jenius away from his parents and put him in the spare hutch, he is reddy to start his training, he is alreddy half as big as Joe, he is alreddy very good at sitting when he is told because that is what I have consentrated on but now I am going to teach him 'Come' and 'Stay' and 'Down'. Joe and Molly don't seem to miss him.

Joe and Molly were actually quite glad to see the back of Jenius.

Molly was thankful not to be nagged for the milk she no longer had, and Joe, though at first proud of the obvious cleverness of his son, was growing tired of being patronized.

'Thinks he knows it all,' he grumbled to Molly, 'with his "No, Dad, you've got that wrong" or "No, Dad, you don't understand". I said to him: "When you've

been around as long as I have, my boy, then maybe you'll know a thing or two".'

'Quite right, dear,' murmured Molly. 'What did he say then?'

'He said: "When I've been around as long as you have I'll know hundreds of things". Cheeky young devil!'

'Ah well,' sighed Molly. 'He's only young, Joe dear. We're all of us only young once.'

'Molly,' said Joe, 'you're as lovely now as the day I first set eyes on you.'

'Oh Joe,' said Molly, 'you say the nicest things!'

4
A Great Team

'Mum! Mum!' cried Judy, bursting in from the garden with Jenius in her arms. 'Guess what!'

'Not now, Judy,' said her mother. 'I haven't got time for guessing games this morning what with the washing and the ironing, and I've got a lot of cooking to do, never mind the housework. Off you

run and play, out of my way, please.'

'But Mum, Jenius comes when he's told!'

'Very clever, dear. Now you go when you're told, there's a good girl.'

'She just didn't listen to what I was saying,' said Judy as she sat on the lawn with Jenius on her lap.

Jenius replied with a small sympathetic

whistle which meant, Judy felt sure, 'Grown-ups are hopeless, aren't they? I expect it'll be just the same when you tell your dad.'

And it was.

'Comes when you call him, does he?' said her father from behind his evening paper.

'Yes, Dad! Honest! Don't you want to see?'

'Not now, pet, I've had a long day. You go and teach your precious genius something else.'

'What like?'

'Oh, reading, writing, some sums. Start with the two-times table – guinea pigs are good at multiplying. Buzz off now, there's a good girl.'

JULY 23rd: I think Mum and Dad grew up in Vicktorian days, they think that childeren should be seen and not herd. I am not going to bother to tell them anything about Jenius any more but only write about him in this dairy so that the World will know how clever he is when I am ~~DED~~ Dead and Gone.

In the darkness of the garden shed Jenius squeaked from the spare hutch: 'Mum! Dad! Guess what!'

'Not now, dear,' said Molly.

'But guess what I learned today!'

‘Hundreds of things, I imagine,’ said Joe sourly.

‘No, only one. I learned to come when called.’

‘Well, now learn to shut up,’ said Joe. ‘It’s late.’

‘Your father’s right, dear,’ said Molly. ‘Go to sleep now, there’s a good boy.’

Throughout those fine sunny summer holidays the flowering of Jenius came into full bloom.

Judy was the ideal trainer, patient and hard-working, and her new pet was the perfect pupil. He enjoyed his lessons, he learned quickly, and what he had learned he seldom forgot. They made a great team.

AUGUST 15th: Here is a list of the things I have trained Jenius to do:

1. COME
2. SIT
3. STAY
4. DOWN
5. WALK ON A LEED

(I do not make him walk to heal because I might tred on him so he walks a little bit in front of me.)

Before the end of the Hollidays I am going to teach him three speshial tricks

(A) 'Speak.' That is to make a noise when he is told (I suppose I should call this 'SQUEAK').

(B) 'Trust'. That is balancing a bit of biskit on his nose.

(C) 'Die For Your Country'. He has to lie quite still with his eyes shut pretending to be Dead. If I can teach him all these things before the begining of Term I will take him to school and show them all just what a <u>Jenius</u> can do.

Every day trainer and trainee worked at their lessons. And every night Jenius kept his aged parents awake long after their proper bedtime, telling them all the clever things he had learned to do. He had become, it must be said, a bit of a bighead.

Molly, who was rather vague by nature, did not listen very carefully to her son's boasting, and only yawned and said, 'Very nice, dear,' now and then, but Joe became irritable.

‘You must be the most brilliant guinea pig there has ever been,’ he would say sourly, but this did not improve matters, for Jenius always replied: ‘I am, Dad, I am,’ in a voice so smug that it made Joe’s teeth chatter with rage.

‘Cocky young blighter,’ he would mutter to Molly. ‘One of these fine days he’s going to be too clever for his own good.’

And Joe was right. One of those fine days came quite soon.

5
Die For Your Country!

Jenius had woken early. He looked out of the shed door (which Judy always left open on warm nights) and saw a number of attractive things outside in the garden. There were lettuces and cabbages and the feathery tops of carrots and the shiny dark leaves of beetroot – all very appealing to a growing lad. Why wait to

be fed, he thought. I'll feed myself.

'Mum!' he called. 'I'm going for a walk.'

Molly came to the front of her hutch and looked across the shed.

'Don't be silly, dear,' she said. 'You can't.'

Joe joined her.

'In case you hadn't noticed,' he said sarcastically, 'there's a door on the front of your hutch.'

'Dad,' said Jenius in a patient tone of voice, 'doors are meant to be opened.'

'I know that, boy. By humans. From outside. Not by us from inside. If you can open the door of that hutch from inside, I'll eat my hayrack.'

Each hutch had an outward-opening wire door, kept shut by a two-inch turn button, a simple device capable of keeping prisoner every guinea pig that had ever lived. Except the Jenius.

Sitting up on his bottom as he had learned, he reached a forepaw through the wire mesh and turned the button vertically. The door swung open, and down he hopped.

He paused at the entrance to the shed.

'Dad,' he called, 'don't forget to eat your hayrack,' and off he trotted.

What happened next was recorded by a short dramatic entry in the diary.

AUGUST 26th: Jenius got out and was nearly killed! I am keeping the door of the shed shut in case he esscapes again.

Jenius was sitting happily in the sunlit vegetable garden, nibbling a tender young lettuce plant and thinking what a

clever chap he was, when he heard his name called. He looked up and saw Judy leaning out of her bedroom window.

'Whatever are you doing out there?' she said, and since Jenius made no reply, she issued two commands.

‘Sit!’ she said, and ‘Stay!’

Jenius obediently sat down, quite content to remain where he was, in easy reach of such nice food.

Judy was just turning away from her window when to her horror she saw the big tabby tom cat from next door drop down from the dividing wall. Slowly, stealthily, he began to stalk the lettuce-eater.

Judy thought frantically. If she left Jenius dutifully sitting and staying, he was a goner. If she called ‘Come!’ the cat would surely overtake him before she could get downstairs.

There was only one thing to be done, only one order she could give that might perhaps puzzle the hunter for long enough for her to rush to the rescue.

'Jenius!' she yelled in the fiercest, most commanding voice she could manage. 'Die For Your Country!'

6

A Nightmare

Jenius, accustomed as he now was to receiving odd orders at odd times, instantly collapsed flat on his back. He stopped chewing his mouthful of lettuce, he closed his eyes, and even the rise and fall of his ribs seemed to have stopped, so lightly did he breathe. He lay, slack and still, looking every inch as he was meant

to look. Dead.

'Dead!' said a voice in his ear suddenly.

Jenius's blood ran cold at the sound of this harsh, cruel voice, at the smell of hot, rank breath, at the tickle of long whiskers as something sniffed him all over.

'Pity,' said the cat. 'Could have had a bit of sport if you'd been alive. Ah well, a dead tail-less rat is better than no rat at all,' and with that he began to lick at his victim's head.

Try as he would, Jenius could not keep his upper eye shut. Under the rasp of the cat's tongue the eyelid was pulled back, and he saw, only inches away, a nightmare face. A merciless face it was, with glowing yellow eyes and a wide mouth

filled with sharp white teeth. Despite himself, Jenius gave a little shudder.

'Aha!' hissed the cat. 'Not dead after all!' and he opened that wide mouth. But before he could close it again, a clod of earth hit him on the ear and a furious voice yelled, 'Scat!' as Judy came galloping to the rescue. She knelt among the lettuce plants beside the motionless figure of the Jenius.

'It's all right!' she cried. 'He's gone. You can get up now.'

As always she used the system of praise-and-reward by which she had trained him.

'*What* a good boy!' she said, and from the pocket of her dungarees she took one of his favourite digestive biscuits and broke off a bit.

Jenius did not move. Now it was Judy's blood that ran cold. Fearfully she lifted the limp body. There was no mark upon it, no blood to be seen.

Could he have died of shock?

'Jenius!' cried Judy frantically in his ear. 'Speak to me. Speak!'

Even though he had fainted with fear at the sheer horror of the experience, the sound of a familiar command was enough to bring him to his senses.

Feebly, through that unchewed mouthful of lettuce, the Jenius obediently uttered a single strangled squeak.

It was a much-reduced Jenius that Judy replaced in his hutch, and when Molly asked: 'Had a nice walk, dear?' he did not answer.

'What's the matter, son?' said Joe. 'Cat got your tongue?'

7
A Bit of a Bighead

AUGUST 26th: Jenius escaped a horribel Death!

Jenius had no intention of escaping again. He had had the fright of his life and, for a little while, his parents were spared their son's bragging and they could enjoy some early nights.

But before long he forgot, and his natural cockiness returned, particularly when he at last mastered the most difficult trick of the exercises that Judy set him. This was the ending to the trick called 'Trust'.

Not only had he to balance a piece of biscuit on the end of his nose, but then, when Judy said 'Paid for!', he had to toss up the food with a jerk of his head and catch it in his mouth.

Jenius never tired of telling his mother and

father how easy this trick was.

'Mind you,' he said, 'I'm the only guinea pig in the world who can do it, I'm sure of that.'

'Very nice, dear,' said Molly absently.

'Pride,' muttered Joe darkly, 'comes before a fall.'

SEPTEMBER 3rd: Jenius has quite recovered. Tomorrow is the last day of the Hollidays and I am going to give him a Test. I am going ~~the~~ to make him do all the things he has been taut and he has got to do them correcktly and I shall give him marks for his performants in each one.

SEPTEMBER 4th: Jenius lived up to his name! He performed perfictly and got Full Marks and I am going to ask my teacher if I can take him to school and show them how briliant he is and how briliantly I have trained him. I'm the only person in the World who could have done it, I'm sure of that.

Jenius, it must be said, was not the only one who had become a bit of a bighead, and by the end of the first day back at school everyone in the class was fed up with hearing how clever both he and Judy were. Before long Judy's teacher too had had enough.

'Judy,' she said. 'You don't really expect us to believe all this, do you?'

'Yes,' said Judy. 'It's true.'

'Well, I'll tell you what. You bring this amazing animal of yours into school and then you can show us all these tricks that you say he can do.'

At once everyone wanted to get in on the act and bring their pet to school.

'Oh, can I bring my rabbit?'

'. . . my gerbil?'

'. . . my hamster?'

'. . . my budgie?'

Until the teacher said: 'All right. We'll have a Pets' Day. You can each bring a pet in to school, provided you bring it in a cage or a box – we don't want anything too big, mind, no Shetland

Ponies or Great Danes. Who knows, Judy, someone else may have a clever animal too.'

Judy laughed. 'Not as clever as Jenius,' she said scornfully. 'Not possibly. You just wait and see.'

8
Pets' Day

Like most people who keep diaries, Judy wrote in hers each evening. But as soon as she woke on the morning that had been chosen for Pets' Day, she opened it.

SEPTEMBER 11th: Today it is Pets' Day at school! Jenius will tryumph! * Watch this space! *

At breakfast time she could not contain herself. Till now she had said nothing to her parents – as she had sworn on July 23rd – of the progress of the Jenius, but she just knew she would not be able to resist describing the success that was to come before another hour had passed.

'What d'you think is happening today?' she said.

'You're going to be late for school,' said her mother, 'if you don't hurry up. And clean your shoes before you go. And take your anorak – it looks like rain.'

‘I’m taking Jenius to school,’ said Judy.

‘Very nice, dear,’ said her mother. ‘Now, do you want an apple or a banana in your lunch box?’

‘Apple,’ said Judy. ‘Dad, did you hear what I said?’

‘I did,’ said her father from behind his morning paper. ‘Will he have to start in the Infants or is he clever enough to go straight into your class?’

‘Oh Dad!’ cried Judy. ‘Honestly, I really have trained him,’ and she rattled off a list of the things that Jenius could do.

‘Judy,’ said her father. ‘You don’t really expect us to believe all this, do you?’

‘Yes,’ said Judy. ‘It’s true.’

Her father folded his newspaper.

'Now look here,' he said. 'Playing pretend games with your precious pet is one thing. But you mustn't confuse fantasy with truth.'

There was hardly room to move in Judy's classroom that morning.

Everywhere there were hutches and cages and baskets and boxes containing pets. Only the Jenius was free, sitting perfectly still in front of Judy.

Judy's teacher saw what seemed to her a rather odd-looking whitish guinea pig, with a crest of reddish hair sticking up along its back, and said: 'Is this the genius we've heard such a lot about?'

'Yes,' said Judy proudly. 'Shall I show you what he can do?'

Pets
dogs
stic
inse
cats
rabb
mice
rats
ham
frogs
snakes
tortoises

'All right,' said her teacher. 'Put him on that big table in the middle of the room where everyone can see him.'

Ranged around the edges of the big table were several pet-containers: a couple of hamster-cages, a glass jar that held stick insects and a square basket that had one open side barred with metal rods.

Fate decreed that Judy should put the Jenius down quite near to this basket and facing it, and though no one else could see what was in it, he could. He looked through the bars and saw a face, a merciless face, with glowing yellow eyes and a wide mouth filled with sharp white teeth.

In fact the occupant of the basket was

only a half-grown kitten, but the sight of it turned Jenius's legs to jelly and scrambled his brains. He was so frightened that he promptly Died For His Country, and there he lay, quite still and barely breathing. He could hear Judy's

voice
saying, 'Come!'
and then, more
loudly, 'Jenius! Come!!' Then he heard a rising tide of noise which was the whole class first sniggering, then giggling, and finally laughing their heads off at clever Judy and her clever guinea pig, about

which she had boasted so loud and long. But he could not move a muscle.

'The great animal trainer!' someone said, and they laughed even more.

'Perhaps that will teach you a lesson, Judy,' said the teacher at last. 'He doesn't

seem to be quite the genius you told us he was. You mustn't confuse fantasy with truth.'

9

Eat Your Hat

'How did you get on, dear, your first day at school?' said Molly that evening.

'Need you ask?' growled Joe. 'You were top of the class, weren't you, son? Got full marks for everything? Performed perfectly, eh?'

'No,' said the Jenius in a small choked voice. 'I didn't do anything.'

'Well well well,' said Joe. 'The only guinea pig in the world who can do all those tricks and he didn't do anything. I quite expected you to tell us you did something fantastic . . . Hopping like a rabbit perhaps. Or flying like a bird, I shouldn't be surprised.'

Judy came in at that moment with a bunch of dandelions, to hear Joe and Molly making an awful racket. She thought they were yelling for food as usual but actually they were in fits of laughter.

'Flying! Oh Joe, you are a scream!' squealed Molly, and Joe, snorting with mirth, chuckled, 'Pride comes before a crash-landing!'

A few minutes later Judy's father, home from work, put his head in at the door of the shed.

'Well?' he said. 'And did our genius perform all his amazing tricks?'

'No,' said Judy. 'He wouldn't do anything.'

'Perhaps that will teach you a lesson, Judy,' said her father.

Judy took a deep breath.

'Perhaps it has, Dad,' she said. 'But I wouldn't like you to think I was a liar.'

'It's difficult for me not to think that,' said her father, 'when you tell me such

fantastic things. For instance, that your guinea pig can balance something on his nose and then throw it up and catch it. If

he can do that, I'll eat my hat, I promise you.'

'Watch,' said Judy. She took a digestive out of her pocket and broke a piece off. She opened the door of Jenius's hutch.

'Come!' she said, and he came.

'Sit!' she said, and he sat.

Carefully she placed the fragment of biscuit on top of Jenius's snout.

'Trust!' she said, and he remained sitting bolt upright and stock-still for perhaps ten seconds, till Judy cried, 'Paid for!'

Up in the air sailed the bit of digestive and down it came again, straight into the open mouth of the Jenius.

'*What* a good boy!' said Judy. 'Now you can eat it up.'

She turned to her father, who was bending down, hands on knees, watching in open-mouthed

amazement, hat in hand. She took it from him.

'And you,' she said, 'can eat that.'

PUFFIN BOOKS

Harry's Mad

Dick King-Smith served in the Grenadier Guards during the Second World War, and afterwards spent twenty years as a farmer in Gloucestershire, the county of his birth. Many of his stories are inspired by his farming experiences. Later he taught at a village primary school. His first book, *The Fox Busters*, was published in 1978. Since then he has written a great number of children's books, including *The Sheep-Pig* (winner of the Guardian Award and filmed as *Babe*), *Harry's Mad*, *Noah's Brother*, *The Hodgeheg*, *Martin's Mice*, *Ace*, *The Cuckoo Child* and *Harriet's Hare* (winner of the Children's Book Award in 1995). At the British Book Awards in 1991 he was voted Children's Author of the Year. He has three children, a large number of grandchildren and several great-grandchildren, and lives in a seventeenth-century cottage only a crow's flight from the house where he was born.

Books by Dick King-Smith

ACE

THE CUCKOO CHILD

DAGGIE DOGFOOT

DODOS ARE FOREVER

DRAGON BOY

FIND THE WHITE HORSE

THE FOX BUSTERS

HARRY'S MAD

HOW GREEN WAS MY MOUSE

JUST BINNIE

LADY DAISY

MAGNUS POWERMOUSE

MARTIN'S MICE

THE MERMAN

THE MERRYTHOUGHT

THE MOUSE BUTCHER

NOAH'S BROTHER

PADDY'S POT OF GOLD

PRETTY POLLY

THE QUEEN'S NOSE

THE ROUNDHILL

SADDLEBOTTOM

THE SCHOOLMOUSE

THE SHEEP-PIG

THE STRAY

TREASURE TROVE

THE WATER HORSE

THE WITCH OF BLACKBERRY BOTTOM

Dick King-Smith

Harry's Mad

Illustrated by Robert Bartelt

PUFFIN

PUFFIN BOOKS

Published by the Penguin Group
Penguin Books Ltd, 80 Strand, London WC2R 0RL, England
Penguin Group (USA) Inc., 375 Hudson Street, New York, New York 10014, USA
Penguin Group (Canada), 10 Alcorn Avenue, Toronto, Ontario, Canada M4V 3B2
(a division of Pearson Penguin Canada Inc.)
Penguin Ireland, 25 St Stephen's Green, Dublin 2, Ireland (a division of Penguin Books Ltd)
Penguin Group (Australia), 250 Camberwell Road, Camberwell, Victoria 3124, Australia
(a division of Pearson Australia Group Pty Ltd)
Penguin Books India Pvt Ltd, 11 Community Centre, Panchsheel Park, New Delhi – 110 017, India
Penguin Group (NZ), cnr Airborne and Rosedale Roads, Albany, Auckland 1310, New Zealand
(a division of Pearson New Zealand Ltd)
Penguin Books (South Africa) (Pty) Ltd, 24 Sturdee Avenue, Rosebank, Johannesburg 2196,
South Africa

Penguin Books Ltd, Registered Offices: 80 Strand, London WC2R 0RL, England

www.penguin.com

First published by Victor Gollancz Ltd 1984
Published in Puffin Books 1986
This edition with new illustrations published in 1999
22

Set in 15/18.5pt Perpetua
Made and printed in England by Clays Ltd, St Ives plc

British Library Cataloguing in Publication Data
A CIP catalogue record for this book is available from the British Library

ISBN-13: 978–0–14–130257–7

www.greenpenguin.co.uk

Mixed Sources
Product group from well-managed forests and other controlled sources
www.fsc.org Cert no. SA-COC-1592
© 1996 Forest Stewardship Council
FSC

Penguin Books is committed to a sustainable future for our business, our readers and our planet. The book in your hands is made from paper certified by the Forest Stewardship Council.

CHAPTER 1

Most people walk down stairs, putting one foot more or less carefully in front of the other, and perhaps holding on to the banisters. Not Harry Holdsworth, oh no, not he!

Long hours of practice had made Harry expert in unusual methods of getting from the upper to the ground floor of the Holdsworths' house.

Some were comparatively simple – sliding down the banisters for example, or rolling down the stairs, or hopping down them, feet together, one step at a time. Hopping down but missing out every other step was a good deal more difficult, and could be made harder still by doing it with hands in pockets, or even – the real test – with hands in pockets and eyes shut.

Harry only attempted this last combination when something told him it was going to be a very special sort of day. On this particular morning, something told him.

As an Olympic athlete, a jumper perhaps, stands poised, breathing deeply, swaying gently back and forth, tensing himself for that indefinable moment when he knows that he is exactly ready to make the

attempt, Harry stood at the head of the stairs. His feet were neatly together on the edge of the top step, his hands rammed deep into his trouser pockets, his eyes wide, as though to photograph in his mind the other thirteen steps stretching away below him. Seven jumps to make. Harry shut his eyes.

He was about halfway down the staircase when suddenly it all happened. Below him he heard his mother's voice calling 'Breakfast!' as she came from the kitchen with a loaded tray; behind him he heard his father say 'Mind out of the way, Harry, I'm late already,' and, right in the middle of Jump Number Five, the postman rang the doorbell, the dog barked madly (as it always did when the doorbell rang), and the cat dashed upstairs (as it always did when the dog barked madly) just in time to receive Jump Number Six on the end of its tail. Jump Number Seven took Harry straight into the breakfast tray.

As the yells of the departing cat and the crash and tinkle of breaking china died away, there reigned for a moment a horrid silence, interrupted only by the slurping of the dog licking up raspberry jam.

The breath knocked out of him, Harry lay flat upon the hall floor, as his parents gazed resignedly down at him. Then, through the letter-flap, there sailed a large envelope, which settled, like a bird landing, on Harry's chest. It was a heavy official-looking envelope, bearing a number of stamps. The stamps were American ones. It was addressed to: MR HARRY HOLDSWORTH.

'It's from America,' said Harry, when at last they were all sitting down to a hastily-eaten breakfast. 'I don't know anybody in America.'

'Must be from Uncle George,' said Mr Holdsworth, with his mouth full.

'Who's he?'

'My father's eldest brother, went out there as a young man, finished up as a university professor, must be ninety-something by now, you'll have to tell me about it this evening, Harry, I'm going to be late, I must go,' and he drained his coffee and went.

Harry slit open the envelope with a buttery knife. He took out a sheaf of papers. On the top sheet was written WILL. HOLDSWORTH.

'Funny,' said Harry. 'I thought Dad said his name was George.'

'It is,' said his mother. 'Can I see?' She held out her hand for the papers. 'It was,' she said. 'This is a copy of his Last Will and Testament.'

She skimmed hastily through a covering letter from a firm of New York attorneys, then glanced at her watch.

'There's a clause in it somewhere that refers to you, but honestly we haven't got time to look at it now, you must get off to school. We'll go through it when Dad comes back this evening, and see what it's all about. I expect he's left you some little keepsake.'

All through that day at school, Harry's imagination, always fertile, ran riot. 'Some little keepsake' indeed! The fact of the matter is, he told himself, that I have been left something in the Will of my very old, very important American great-uncle. Well to begin with, all Americans are rich, everyone knows that, and as he lived to ninety-something, he would have had all that time to build up a huge store of wealth, thousands and thousands of pounds, dollars I mean, in fact he'd be pretty well bound to be a millionaire, a multi-millionaire, I should think, probably got three or four big houses, all with swimming-pools, and a ranch, and his own power-boat, and his own private jet – perhaps he's left me that, I bet I could soon learn to fly one.

He stretched out both arms wide, and began to make warming-up jet noises deep in his throat. Waiting for a voice from the control tower to give him clearance for take-off, he was quite surprised to hear instead his name called sharply.

'Harry!' said his teacher. 'Just what exactly do you think you're doing?'

'I was . . . um . . . I was just stretching.'

'Stretch your mind for a change, you dreamy boy. I want all those sums finished by break time.'

Around him the other children in the class giggled.

'Harry's mad,' someone said.

'Sums!' said Harry to himself as he bent low over the desk, grasping with expert hands the imaginary wheel of Great-Uncle George's (now his) power-boat as it roared across the finishing line in a cloud of spray to the cheers of the watching crowds. 'The only sums I'm going to need to bother about is adding up all the money he's left me.'

By the end of the school day Harry had convinced himself that this fabulously rich great-uncle had by some quirk of fate left him everything that he possessed. Harry was not by nature a particularly greedy boy but he was a fanciful one, and by now he had gone beyond the three great houses and the speed boat and the executive jet. In addition, he thought, he might well receive the largest custom-built Cadillac ever made, and a couple of Rolls Royces (for occasional use). And of course the wealth wouldn't consist only of boring old dollar bills. There would probably be an actual treasure chest, overflowing with diamonds and rubies and emeralds and showers of gold and silver coins.

He stopped outside the sweet shop on his way home, and looked in at the window. I'll be able to buy every single thing in there and never notice the cost, he thought. He put his hand in his pocket. There were two pennies and a two pence piece in it.

'Well anyway, tomorrow I'll be able to,' he said.

Once home, he looked again at his letter from America, but the language of the Will was so full of whereases and heretofores and hereuntos and aforesaids that he decided to leave it till his father came back from work.

He filled in the time by adding to Great-Uncle George's stable a 1000 cc Harley-Davidson bike (well, an old model – that he rode when he was younger) and making a noisy circuit of the house.

'Harry,' his mother said as he roared along the passage between kitchen and sitting-room, 'could you do that up in your room, please?' She spoke with the infinite patience acquired from ten years' experience of being Harry's mother.

'Vroom, vroom!!' shouted Harry as he twisted the throttle wide open and set the Harley-Davidson at the stairs. Don't worry, Mum, he thought, I'll soon buy you a bigger house. And Dad can have one of the Rolls Royces.

When at last he heard the sound of his father's five-year-old Ford, he came downstairs the fastest way (banisters) in a fever of excitement.

'Dad! Great-Uncle George is dead! What d'you think, that letter, it was a Will! I can't understand what it's about, can you read it for me? Come on, Mum, Dad's going to read it!'

Mr Holdsworth sat down at the table and spread

out the papers. For a while he read in silence, and then he began to chuckle.

'What is it?' asked Mrs Holdsworth. 'Has he left Harry something?'

'Yes, he has.'

'His fortune?' cried Harry.

'His fortune?' said his father. 'No such luck, Harry. The old boy didn't have a lot of money, and what he did have he's left to his university library. No, he's left you what appears to have been his most cherished possession.'

'What's that?' said Harry.

'His parrot.'

CHAPTER 2

'To my great-nephew Harry Holdsworth, whom I have never had the pleasure of meeting, I hereby bequeath my faithful companion of these past forty years, the African Grey Parrot answering to the name of Madison.

'I make this bequest to the aforesaid Harry Holdsworth because he chances to be my only known male relative of an age that I consider suitable, bearing in mind that Madison *a)* may live to twice his present span, and *b)* like me, has not been used to females.'

So ran the early part of Clause 15 of the otherwise conventional Last Will and Testament in witness whereof Professor George Holdsworth had thereunto set his hand.

It went on to detail the provisions that Great-

Uncle George had made to ensure that Harry should not be out of pocket by reason of his legacy. 'The air fare's paid,' said Mr Holdsworth, 'and there's a sum of money to cover the purchase of a large parrot-cage and the cost of the creature's food for a year by Uncle George's reckoning. After that time, you're on your own.'

'For another forty years?' said Harry in a voice of horror. 'You mean I've *got* to keep this bird, and it might live till I'm fifty?'

'Perhaps it'll die before then, darling,' said his mother soothingly.

'You never know,' said his father. 'You may actually like the thing. Perhaps it'll talk. Uncle George was a pretty brilliant sort of chap in his day, I believe. Linguistics – that was his line.'

'What's linguistics?' said Harry.

'The study of language. All about words in fact – the parrot's sure to have picked up a few.'

'Perhaps I could take it to school,' Harry said, brightening up, 'on my shoulder. Like that man in *Treasure Island*.'

He began to stump around the room keeping one leg stiff, mouthing 'Ar! Jim lad! Ar!' and leering dreadfully.

'You're not taking it anywhere,' said his mother. 'This weekend you and Daddy can go and buy a proper parrot-cage. I'm not having the thing make a filthy mess all over the house.'

'It might be house-trained,' said Harry hopefully.

'Don't be silly, Harry. Birds can't . . .'

'Can't what?'

'Well, birds have to . . .'

'They have to do it when they feel like it, your mother means,' said Mr Holdsworth. 'Anyway, let's wait and see what . . . what's he called?' he looked again at the Will, '. . . Madison, that's right, let's wait and see what Madison's like. He should arrive before long.'

And a couple of weeks later, on a Saturday, he did.

News had come from New York of the parrot's time of arrival at London Airport, and now the Holdsworth family waited, with mixed emotions. The whole business, both parents felt, was a great nuisance. Why on earth couldn't old Uncle George have left the bird to a zoo or something? It wouldn't be so bad, they said to each other, if Harry was wildly excited about it, or even moderately happy. As it was, he just looked gloomy. And gloomy Harry was, as he waited for that ring on the doorbell that would herald the delivery van, bringing his companion of the next forty years.

Buying the cage had been quite fun. There was plenty of money allowed for it, Dad said, so they'd bought a huge one like a miniature aviary, that hung on a spring from a tall stand. But the more Harry looked at it that morning, its hoppers filled with seed and water, its floor sanded, its door open in readiness, the more he worried.

I bet it bites me, he thought. And it'll probably smell. And I don't suppose it'll say a word, just screech all day long or say stupid stuff like 'Hullo' and 'Pretty Polly'. And just keep on saying it – till I'm an old man! It isn't even as though I liked birds, and I'm certainly not going to like this one.

The doorbell rang.

Peering into the travelling-box, standing now on a table in the sitting-room, they could see through the ventilation grille a shadowy shape. No sound came from within but a scrape of claws on the floor of the box.

'He's alive,' said Harry. He sounded disappointed.

'Let's get the poor old thing out of it,' said his father. 'He's had a long trip. Open the lid, Harry.'

'He might fly away.'

'Shouldn't think so. After all, he's just flown three thousand miles. Must be tired. Go on, open it up.'

Doubtfully Harry undid the catch and raised the lid. He pulled his hand away sharply, as though the travelling-box contained not a parrot but a poisonous snake.

For a minute or so nothing happened. Then out of the box, in silent slow motion, there rose a round grey head with a sharp hooked beak. On either side of the head was a bright, considering, straw-coloured eye.

One of these eyes considered Harry carefully, noting his smallish rather skinny frame, his mop of bright red hair, his jug-handle ears. Then, levering itself up by gripping the rim of the box with its bill, the parrot climbed out and walked across the table towards him with a rolling, sailor's gait. Harry backed away.

'It seems to know you,' his mother said.

'Don't be frightened,' his father said. 'It won't hurt you.'

'How do you know?' said Harry.

'Put your hand out. See if it'll walk up your arm.'

'You put your hand out,' said Harry.

'No, it's your parrot.'

'Speak to it,' said his mother. 'Say its name.'

Harry looked at the bird, which had now stopped at the edge of the table and was standing, looking up at him, its head cocked to one side. All he could think of was what a large sharp beak it had and what cruel curved talons on its scaly feet. He shut his eyes tight, and put his hand on the table top.

'Hello, Madison,' he gulped nervously.

Very gently, the parrot stepped on to Harry's arm. Very gently, it climbed slowly up and perched on his shoulder. Very gently, it nibbled at the lobe of his ear.

Harry opened his eyes, and a grin of relief spread over his face.

'He likes you,' his mother said.

'He's nice,' his father said.

'Hello, Madison,' said Harry again, this time in a much more confident voice.

The parrot said nothing.

'Perhaps he'll talk once he's had something to eat,' said Mr Holdsworth. 'Stick him in the cage, Harry. He must be hungry.'

And indeed as soon as Harry moved to the parrot-cage and stood beside its open door, the bird stepped off his shoulder and waddled inside. It drank thirstily and then settled down to eat, cracking up sunflower seeds in that powerful beak, and watching them all with one or other pale intelligent-looking eye.

But despite all their efforts to encourage it during the remainder of that first day, it uttered no sound.

'Pity,' said Mr Holdsworth that evening. 'You'd have thought Uncle George would have taught it to say something in all those years he had it.'

'I suppose it's just one of those ones that doesn't,' said Harry's mother.

'Must be. Just a dumb animal. Well, time you were in bed, Harry. Goodnight, old chap.'

'Goodnight, darling,' his mother said.

He was halfway up the stairs when he thought he heard a voice calling, 'G'night, Harry.'

'Goodnight, Dad,' he called back, and then it struck him that the voice was somehow different from his father's, more nasal, more twangy.

He went back down and into the sitting-room, but his parents had left it and it was empty. Only the parrot sat motionless on its perch. 'Madison?' said Harry. 'Did you say something?'

CHAPTER 3

I suppose it must have been Dad's voice, was Harry's last thought before he drifted into a dream-filled sleep where parrots gabbled at him in a language he could not understand, and he could make no reply.

The dreams turned at last into a nightmare in which he became very tiny – the size of a sunflower seed – and he knew that at any moment a parrot would pick him up in its great hooked bill and crack him open.

Harry woke with a start. He looked at the luminous face of his watch. It was five-thirty. Outside the day was thinking of getting light.

He lay still for a minute, enjoying the relief of his escape from the nightmare parrots and thinking about the real one downstairs. OK, Great-Uncle George doesn't seem to have taught Madison anything but there's no reason why I shouldn't. They're only mimics after all, not intelligent creatures, just good at copying. All you have to do is keep on saying the same thing, over and over again, and sooner or later they catch on. About a hundred times should be enough, I should think. And then when they've got it, you teach them something else. I'll start now, it's Sunday, Mum and Dad won't be getting up for ages, it's a good time. What shall I start with? I know, I'll teach him to say his name. But then it's no good just getting him to say 'Madison'. That'd be like me going about saying 'Harry' to people. No, I know, I'll train him to say 'My name is Madison'.

Harry jumped out of bed, put on his dressing-gown, opened the door and (for once) went down the stairs very slowly and quietly. Closing the sitting-room door behind him, he went over to the parrot-cage and stood beside it. It was on a level with his head.

Harry put on his sneering Gestapo interrogator face.

'Ve haf vays of making you talk!' he said between clenched teeth.

The parrot said nothing.

Harry took a deep breath. A hundred times, he said to himself, I'll say it a hundred times. He leaned forward till his lips were almost against the wire bars of the cage, as close as possible to where he thought the bird's ear must be, and, speaking slowly and clearly, as you would to a foreigner or to someone rather deaf, he said, '*My . . . name . . . is . . . Madison.*'

The parrot scratched the side of his bare, scaly face with one foot.

'If you say so, buddy,' he said clearly, 'but that would be a re-markable coincidence. Seeing that my name is Madison also.'

Harry's mouth fell open. He felt amazement, embarrassment, wild excitement, all at the same time.

'What's the matter?' said Madison pleasantly. 'Cat got your tongue?'

'You can talk?' said Harry at last in a kind of hoarse whisper.

'Uh-huh.'

'Properly!'

'Sure. Mebbe a mite differently from you, seeing I was raised in America, but boy, I sure can talk.'

'But . . . I thought parrots could only say a few words.'

'Depends how well they've been taught. I've spent all my life with a professor of linguistics. Dead now, but what a guy!'

'Great-Uncle George!'

'George Holdsworth was your great-uncle? You're a Holdsworth?'

'Yes. He left you to me. In his Will.'

Madison scratched the other side of his face.

'Gee!' he said. 'That explains it all. They shoved me in that box, drove me to the airport, and next thing I know, I'm at Heathrow. Madison Holdsworth, I said to myself, it's London Zoo for you, I guess. Instead of which I'm back with the family. Boy, am I glad to be here!'

He cocked an eye at the ceiling.

'Thanks, George,' he said.

'Why did Great-Uncle George call you "Madison"?' Harry asked.

'James Madison, fourth President of the United States of America, from 1809 to 1817. Came after Thomas Jefferson and before James Monroe.'

'Oh,' said Harry. 'Why did he call you after the fourth president?'

'Simple,' said Madison. 'I was his fourth parrot.

Washington died in his sleep, Adams got pneumonia, and Jefferson tangled with the cat.'

Harry opened the cage door, and the parrot climbed out and up on to his shoulder.

'So it *was* you last night,' Harry said. 'Saying goodnight to me, I mean.'

'Yeah. Kinda slipped out. And then I thought, sleep on it, we'll see what the morning brings. But just now when you came out with that "My . . . name . . . is . . . Madison" bit, I simply couldn't keep my big beak shut.'

'How did you know my name was Harry?'

'Because I heard your mommie and daddy call you that.'

'Oh, silly of me – sorry, I haven't got used to the idea that you can understand everything that's said. What else can you do, Madison?'

'I can read, Harry. And, let's see, I can play the piano a bit, "Camptown Races", "Swannee River", that kind of thing.'

'With your feet?'

'With my beak. Oh, and I can use the telephone. One thing I can't do is write. Never been able to hold a pen or pencil properly.'

'Gosh!' said Harry. 'Wait till I tell them at school!'

He felt the parrot's claws tighten a little on his shoulder, and then Madison said, 'Listen, Harry. Something tells me we're going to get along real fine.

But I guess there's a little matter we gotta get straight right now. This business of me being . . . different from the average parrot.'

'Yes?'

'Keep it to yourself, Harry. George did, all those years, never told a living soul. He reckoned if it ever got out, we'd have every newspaper man and television interviewer in the States down on us, not to mention scientists wanting to test me or showmen trying to steal me. We just kept it to ourselves. Waddya say you and I do the same?'

'Ye-es,' said Harry. He sounded doubtful. 'You sound doubtful,' Madison said.

'Well it's just that . . . it was just the two of you, wasn't it, you and Great-Uncle George?'

'Uh-huh.'

'Well, you see, there's Mum and Dad. They live here too.'

'Oh sure,' said Madison. 'We'll let them into the secret, sure we will. They can keep a secret, I imagine?'

'Oh yes,' Harry said. He grinned, and without really thinking what he was doing, reached up to his shoulder and stroked the round grey head with his finger-tips. 'But let's not tell them straightaway. Let's have a bit of fun first. OK, Madison?'

'Sure, Harry. I'll play it any way you want.'

'Thanks, Madison.'

'And by the way, George always used to call me "Mad" for short. You're welcome to do the same.'

'Thanks, Mad. You must miss him a lot. I do hope you're going to like it here.'

'You bet your life,' the parrot said. He nibbled gently at the boy's ear.

'Are you sure?'

'Sure I'm sure,' said Harry's Mad.

CHAPTER 4

Sunday mornings followed a regular routine in the Holdsworth house. Breakfast was always boiled eggs. Afterwards, it was Harry's job to clear the table and wash up, while his mother and father went to the sitting-room, she to read her book, he to do the *Sunday Times* crossword. Harry was only allowed to interrupt the quiet of what Mrs Holdsworth called 'my morning off' to make and bring them coffee. Otherwise, he was expected to leave his parents in peace and amuse himself.

On the whole Harry was fairly good at amusing himself, but there were often times, especially on Sunday mornings, when he thought that to have a friend, to talk to, to play with, would be nice.

Now, he was thinking as he finished the washing-up, I've got one. He made the mugs of coffee and took them to the sitting-room.

On the sofa, his mother turned the pages of her book. In his favourite chair, his father frowned at the crossword puzzle, his pencil tap-tapping against his teeth. In his cage, Madison sat silent.

'Thank you,' said Mrs Holdsworth. 'Have you done the washing-up, darling?'

'Yes.'

'Thanks,' said Mr Holdsworth. 'You any good at anagrams, Harry?'

'No.'

Madison gave a loud squawk.

'I hope that bird's not going to make a filthy row all morning,' Mr Holdsworth said. 'I shan't be able to concentrate on this crossword.'

'I'll take him up to my room, shall I, Dad?' said Harry quickly.

'Good idea.'

Harry's mother looked worried.

'But he might . . .'

'No, he won't,' Harry said.

Madison made a small rude noise.

Struggling not to burst out laughing, Harry hastily opened the cage door, and then, with the parrot perched on his shoulder, fled from the room.

For the rest of that morning, and at every possible opportunity during the days that followed – there were plenty, it was half-term – Harry and Mad talked and talked and talked. In the safety of Harry's bedroom or whenever they were sure they could not be overheard, they jabbered away nineteen to the dozen. Forty years in the company of Professor George Holdsworth had given Madison a great liking for the art of conversation.

Harry learned a lot about baseball and American football and life in Cambridge, Massachusetts, and a little about Madison.

Madison learned a little about cricket and soccer and life in Greenwich, England, and a lot about Harry.

There were so many questions to be asked.

'How old are you, Harry?' was one of the first from Madison.

'Ten.'

'Ten, eh? That's great, that's swell!'

'Why?'

'Well, you gotta appreciate that your Great-Uncle George was over fifty years of age when I first chipped my way outa my egg. So I've spent all my grown-up life with an old man. Don't get me wrong, Harry – George was a great guy, I'll never forget him, but he'd slowed up a lot towards the end. It's gonna be a whole heap of fun living with someone your age. Incidentally, why aren't you at school? You on vacation?'

'No, it's half-term. We get a week's holiday.'

Madison rolled his eyes.

'Guess I gotta learn the language,' he said. 'What kinda school you go to?'

'Primary.'

'Primary, huh? I guess that figures. You like it?'

'It's all right.'

'Hm. I was lucky, of course. Born with a natural way of learning.'

'How?'

'Parrot-fashion,' said Madison gravely.

'Oh Mad, you are funny.'

'And I had the best possible teacher, an emeritus professor of applied linguistics. Not many parrots could say that.'

'Not without a lot of practice,' said Harry straight-faced.

'Gee, Harry, you're the wackiest.'

And as well as talk, there was play.

'What sort of games d'you like playing, Mad?' Harry asked.

'You mean football and stuff? Guess I ain't built for that, Harry.'

'No, no, I mean games that you and I can play together, you know, like cards.'

'Now cards,' said Madison, 'are real tricky. Trouble is, my foot ain't designed for holding a playing card any more than a pencil. Let alone managing a deck of cards, or shuffling, or dealing. No, what I like are board games, you know? Where I can use my beak to pick up the pieces? George and I used to play a lot.'

'You mean, like dominoes?'

'Yeah.'

'Draughts?'

'Draughts? Never heard tell of that.'

Harry fetched a box of draughtsmen and a board from the cupboard where he kept all his toys.

'These.'

'Oh, checkers! That's what we call it. Yeah, sure we played checkers.'

'I don't suppose you know how to play chess?'

Madison put his head on one side and looked quizzically at Harry.

'Why not, boy?'

Because, Harry was thinking, it's crazy to imagine a bird playing chess, it's just too difficult.

'There's nothing too difficult about the rules of chess, Harry,' chuckled Madison. 'It's playing the game well that's hard.'

'I'm not much good,' said Harry quickly.

'Aw, boloney – you'll beat the feathers off of me. C'mon, let's have a game now.'

A couple of days later Mrs Holdsworth came suddenly into the room when Madison had that instant picked up his Queen. Quick as a flash he juggled the piece into his mouth.

'Anyone would think you were playing chess with Madison!' said Harry's mother.

'They would, wouldn't they, Mum?'

'You haven't swallowed the thing, have you, Mad?' said Harry when she had gone. 'You'd better check.'

'Exactly what I'm gonna do,' said Madison, producing the Queen from her hiding-place and making his move. 'And what's more, Harry boy, I kinda think that that is checkmate.'

'I found Harry playing chess against himself

today,' his mother said later to his father. 'He'd even stood that bird at the other side of the board, pretending it was his opponent, I suppose.'

'Harry spends his time in a land of make-believe,' his father said.

'Well, it's because he's so much on his own.'

Madison saw it a little differently.

Typical only child (like me, he thought) – expects everything done for him, thinks washing up Sunday breakfast is a week's work, and, from the sound of things, doesn't do a lot at school. But I guess he's a real nice kid at heart. Just needs someone to shake him up a bit (like me, he thought). And I kinda like his screwball sense of humour.

For the whole of that first week Harry derived enormous enjoyment from the concealment of the parrot's powers of speech. Part of him longed to see the look on his parents' faces when the secret was revealed, but it was such fun fooling them. At the end of each day he would lie in bed hugging himself with glee at the memory of things that had been said.

'How's your talkative friend, Harry?'

'Oh fine, Dad. Of course it's strange for him after living in America so long, but he's settling in nicely. He really likes it here.'

'I imagine he told you all that himself?'

'Yes, of course.'

'Honestly, Harry!'

Or:

'Why don't you try to teach that bird something, Harry? Just a word or two.'

'Oh I don't think there's much I could teach him, Mum.'

'Why not? Is he too stupid, d'you think?'

'He's absolutely bird-brained.'

And off Harry would go into fits of giggles, falling about clutching his tummy and crying with laughter.

Afterwards, on more than one occasion, Mr Holdsworth said to his wife, 'Sometimes I really do think that Harry's mad.'

'Oh, if they only knew!' said Harry, after Madison had been with them a week.

'Don't you reckon it's time they did, Harry boy? A joke's a joke, but I'm getting kinda tired of sitting around acting the dumb cluck in front of your mommie and daddy. What say we blow the gaff?'

Harry thought. Mad probably knew best. Come to think of it, Mad probably knew best about most things. He stroked his friend's head.

'OK,' he said. 'Tomorrow.'

CHAPTER 5

On the following morning, Mr and Mrs Holdsworth woke to the sound of music, of a kind.

Dimly there came to their ears 'The Battle Hymn of the American Republic' played, correctly but very slowly, on the piano, while Harry's voice informed them that John Brown's body lay a-mould'ring in the grave.

'I've never heard Harry play a tune before,' said his mother.

'Huh. He plays better than he sings,' growled his father, and he pulled the bedclothes over his head.

In the kitchen, at breakfast time, he said, 'Didn't know you were a musician, Harry.'

'Didn't you, Dad?'

'Had you practised that before?' his mother asked.

'Oh no. It's easy if you know how.'

Madison, sitting on Harry's shoulder, gave a loud whistle, and Harry began to giggle helplessly. His father looked at him over the top of the Sunday newspaper.

'Harry,' he said. 'As I've told your mother, sometimes I think you are mad.'

Harry's giggles got worse. He began to splutter and snort, and tears ran down his face.

'No, no,' he gasped, 'that's the one with the feathers!'

'Eat your egg,' said his mother, 'and don't be so silly.'

Madison looked disapprovingly around at the breakfasting family. Not that he had the slightest objection to seeing humans eat or indeed, generally, to what they ate; much of their food, he knew from experience, was delicious, and he must make it clear to young Harry that plain common parrot-seed was only for plain common parrots. But if there was one thing that really turned him up, it was to see them eating boiled eggs. It seemed to him that to do such a thing in front of any bird was in the worst possible taste.

Despite himself, however, he watched with a shudder their different methods.

The woman set her egg in its cup big end up, tapped it carefully with a spoon, and peeled off the shell from its top, leaving a bare white crown like a monk's tonsure.

The man stood his egg narrow end up and, with one brutal sweep of a knife, he beheaded it.

The boy did not use an egg-cup. He peeled all the shell from his egg, laid its defenceless body on his plate, and then with a fork he squashed it into a horrid pulp.

'Yuk!' said Madison loudly.

Mr Holdsworth put down his newspaper.

'That bird actually made a noise,' he said, 'that sounded almost like a word.'

Opposite him Harry was grinning all over his face.

'Now what's the joke?' said his father.

'Say "Good morning",' Harry said.

'I've already said it, when I first came downstairs.'

'No, not to me, Dad. Say "Good morning" to Madison.'

'Don't be so silly, Harry,' his mother said. 'Let Daddy read his paper in peace.'

'Oh go on, Dad.'

Mr Holdsworth shook his head resignedly.

'Well, if I must,' he said. He looked at the parrot.

'Good morning,' he said.

'Good morning,' said Madison.

'Well I'm blowed,' said Mr Holdsworth. 'When did you learn to say that?'

Madison had opened his bill to say 'Oh, about forty years ago' when he saw Harry put his finger to his lips, so he shut it again.

'So you have actually begun to teach him things?'

said his mother. 'You just kept saying it to him till he repeated it ? He said it very clearly, didn't he?'

'Yes.'

Mrs Holdsworth leaned forward. 'Good morning, Madison,' she said.

Madison bobbed his head at her.

'Good morning, Madison,' he replied.

'What a clever old bird you are,' she said.

'What a clever old bird you are,' said Madison.

'Amazing,' said Harry's father. 'He's a natural mimic. We might have known that Uncle George wouldn't have bothered with just any old parrot. Isn't it strange, though, here's this creature repeating what we say, word for word . . .'

'Pronouncing everything quite correctly,' interrupted Harry's mother, 'and what's more, if you notice, with a distinct American accent.'

'. . . which he well might,' went on her husband, 'considering that after all Uncle George must often have played this sort of game with him, and yet – and this is the point, of course – when it comes to the actual meaning of what we are saying, the bird hasn't a clue. Isn't that right, my friend,' he said to Madison, 'not a clue?'

'Not a clue,' said Madison gravely.

'It's a pity they haven't got proper brains like us, isn't it, Dad? I mean, he could help you with the *Sunday Times* crossword puzzle.'

'Don't be silly, Harry,' said his mother, and to her husband, 'Off you go and settle down with your precious puzzle. Harry, time for you to do the washing-up, please. Put Madison back in his cage first.'

'Yes, Mum,' Harry said.

In the passage between kitchen and sitting-room he stopped for a moment, out of earshot of both parents.

'Mad,' he said softly.

'Yeah, Harry?'

'Shall we let them in on the secret now?'

'I sure hope so, Harry boy. It's kinda weird, just repeating stuff all the time. Makes me feel a real dope.'

'OK, Mad,' said Harry. 'But wait till I've finished the washing-up. I don't want to miss this.'

He went on into the sitting-room where his father was already settled, pipe in mouth, pencil poised, and put Madison into his cage.

'I hope that bird's going to keep quiet now,' Mr Holdsworth said.

'Oh he will, Dad,' said Harry, grinning. 'I'm sure.'

'Sure,' said Madison.

Time passed, and all was Sunday morning peace and silence. The only small sounds were the occasional scratch of Harry's father's pencil, the noise of a page turning as his mother read a book, and the cracking of seeds in the parrot-cage. Harry came in with the mugs of coffee.

At that moment Mr Holdsworth knocked out his pipe and sighed deeply.

Mrs Holdsworth closed her book. 'Are you stuck?' she said.

'Mm. It's quite a hard one today, really. Listen to this for instance. I can't think of a single word in the English language that fits. Blank S two blanks T blank C blank N blank.'

‘What’s the clue?’

‘“Cat in spite of being a bird”.’

There was a moment’s silence, and then, ‘It’s an anagram, Mr Holdsworth, sir,’ said Madison in a respectful voice. ‘“Psittacine.” Means, “belonging to the parrot family”. You want I should spell it for you?’

CHAPTER 6

Only a week had passed – just the space between one Sunday and the next – and yet it seemed to all the family that there had never been a time without Madison. How had they ever managed before, each of them wondered.

As for the dog and the cat, they could hardly remember what life had been like before the coming of the stocky grey stranger with the human voice, or rather with a variety of human voices, since Madison might, for example, address either one of them in the tones of any of the three Holdsworths. This filled the mind of the dog with awed respect. He never now barked when the doorbell rang, ever since Madison had furiously cursed him for doing so in his master's voice, and he soon learned to obey commands to 'Sit!' or 'Stay!' even though they came from the

parrot-cage. Doing as he was told would, he knew, be rewarded by a loud cry of '*What* a good boy!' which set him happily wagging.

The cat, naturally but unwisely, had begun by believing the newcomer to be simply a pigeon-sized bird, and, unlike those in the streets outside which it stalked but never caught, easy meat.

Observing that the humans soon allowed the parrot out of its cage, the cat waited until they were all out of the way, and then proceeded to creep towards Madison, who was sitting on the arm of a chair with his back turned. Poor cat! How could it have dreamed what lay in store? How could it have known of those dozens of old gangster films (they were George's favourites) that Madison had watched, over the years, on TV? George Raft, Jimmy Cagney, Edward G. Robinson – Madison knew them all, but it was Bogart's voice that suddenly fell upon the hunter's astonished ears. A slow voice it was, and sneering; and all the more startling because it was not raised.

'Hold it right there, sweetheart,' snarled Madison out of the corner of his beak, and the cat, frozen, held it.

Slowly, deliberately, Madison turned to face the animal, and then he spoke again, even more softly.

'Never do that again, feller,' he said. 'Y'unnerstand? Now – beat it!'

Its hair rising, its tail fluffed out like a bottle-brush, the cat began to slink away, and then suddenly to its horror there came from Madison's beak the tunk-a-tunk-a-tunk-a-tunk of a Thompson sub-machine gun and the zing and whine of ricocheting bullets.

'I had to do it, see, kid,' growled Madison afterwards to Harry. 'It was Johnny the Cat, coming to git me. It was him or me, so I let him have it.'

Already Harry's parents had come to rely upon Madison in particular ways.

Mr Holdsworth found him an excellent companion when, arriving home tired from his day's work, he would switch on the television and they would watch the early evening news together. Then afterwards, while Mrs Holdsworth prepared supper and Harry did his homework, they would discuss the main points.

Madison had been trained by Professor Holdsworth to take an intelligent interest in the strange, often crazy, way in which human beings tried to run the world, a world which they considered belonged to them, yet they seemed determined to destroy it and themselves with it. Privately, Madison considered that parrots would have made a much better job of things.

That second weekend the *Sunday Times* crossword never knew what hit it. Together Madison and Mr

Holdsworth made a perfect team, vying with one another as to who could solve a clue first. Madison was especially strong on anagrams.

And indeed his skills were not solely intellectual. He found, rather to his surprise for he had no previous experience, that he was a great help in the garden. That strong hooked beak was the perfect instrument for hoeing out weed seedlings, many of which, Madison discovered, were rather tasty. Side by side, man and parrot worked in the long summer evenings. They did not speak, lest the neighbours should hear.

Mrs Holdsworth had at first been worried over a basic problem. She was not at all keen to have her furniture and carpets splattered with bird-droppings, but, faced with an animal of Madison's intelligence and sophistication, she did not know quite how to approach the subject. She decided to use Harry as a go-between.

Harry was direct.

'Mad,' he said, grinning, 'Mum says, d'you want to go to the lav?'

Madison looked puzzled.

'The lav?' he said. 'Oh, I guess she means, do I want to go to the bathroom.'

Harry looked puzzled.

'That's what we say in America. No, as a matter of fact, I don't. But I read you, Harry boy – your mommie's worried.'

'Yes.'

'I'll have a word with her.'

He found Harry's mother in the kitchen.

'Mrs Holdsworth, ma'am,' he said.

'Yes, Madison?'

'In the matter of what is sometimes referred to as "the personal care area" . . .'

Mrs Holdsworth looked puzzled.

'Have no fears, ma'am, on my account. There is always the garden. And at night my cage undoubtedly merits the title of "the smallest room". Privately, Madison considered that that was all that parrot-cages were fit for.

Tactfully, he changed the subject.

'Those cookies sure look good,' he said.

'Cookies? Oh you mean my biscuits. Try one.'

'Dee-licious,' said Madison presently. 'A shortbread mixture, I always say, should *not* be over-cooked: it ought always to be this pale golden colour.'

'You're interested in cooking?' asked Mrs Holdsworth.

'I surely am, ma'am. It was George's hobby.'

'Oh really!' said Harry's mother. 'It's mine too. Perhaps you know of some recipes from your part of the world?'

Harry, coming into the kitchen later, found them deep in conversation. 'American brownies,' Madison was saying. 'Delicious squidgy nutty chocolate bars. We used special unsweetened chocolate but the plain dessert type will do, and you can use walnuts, almonds, Brazils, whatever you like. You break the chocolate into small pieces and melt it with four ounces of butter in the top of a double saucepan . . .'

'Hang on, Madison,' Mrs Holdsworth said. 'Let me write it all down.'

Madison dictated the recipe, even managing to say 'and take two eggs' without faltering. Experience had taught him that we all have to make sacrifices now and then in a good cause.

'I didn't know you had a sweet tooth,' Mrs Holdsworth said.

'Tell the truth, I don't have a tooth in my head, ma'am, but yes, I'm very fond of that kind of thing. In fact, I like to eat nearly everything that people like to eat, if you understand me.'

'Madison,' she said. 'I think I'm going to learn a lot from you.'

'You haven't eaten much of your seed today, Mad,' said Harry that evening.

'No,' said Madison, indistinctly, because his mouth was full of delicious squidgy nutty American brownie.

CHAPTER 7

One immediate benefit to Harry was in the matter of homework. It did not take him long to realize that it was a much pleasanter business with Madison around.

One evening the parrot had flown upstairs to find the boy chewing his pencil and staring at an empty page.

'I'm stuck, Mad,' Harry said.

Madison hopped on to Harry's shoulder and peered down at the open book.

'What have we here?' he said.

'English.'

'English!' cried Madison in ringing tones. 'The flower of languages, the noblest speech of all, the mother tongue that Shakespeare spake!'

'Spake?'

'Spake. Whatta we gotta do?'

'It's parts of speech,' Harry said. 'You've got to say which word's a noun and all that. In these sentences. Like this one – "John fell off the wall and broke his left leg."'

'Tough on John,' said Madison, 'but not difficult to answer. Here's what you've got: proper noun; – verb; – preposition; – definite article; – noun; – conjunction; – verb; – pronoun; – adjective; – noun. Get it?'

'No,' said Harry.

But by the time that Madison had explained it and dictated it with the words all correctly spelled, Harry had learned quite a lot.

'You've got these all right, Harry,' his teacher said next day in a puzzled voice. 'Your dad help you?'

'No,' said Harry. 'A little bird told me.'

That the little bird's command of language must be kept secret, the family all agreed. It was easy for Harry and his mother, whose conversations with the parrot took place indoors, but more difficult for Mr Holdsworth, who often came very close to speaking to his fellow gardener; once indeed he leaned on his spade and said, 'How's it going, old chap?' but Madison made no reply.

On the other hand they all thought that a completely silent parrot might seem odd to anyone visiting the house.

'Just say "Hello",' suggested Harry's father. 'People expect that.'

'I suppose you could say "Pretty Polly"?' said Harry's mother.

'Begging your pardon, ma'am,' said Madison, 'but I'd be mighty obliged if you'd excuse me from saying those particular words. The name does not fit, nor the description.'

'How about "Handsome Madison"?' said Harry.

'I'll just stick to "Hello" if you don't mind,' said Madison. And so, when friends or relatives came, he did.

He had an uncanny knack, however, for sensing whether visitors were welcome. Those who were received one quiet polite Hello. But tiresome callers never now stayed long. The word of greeting, repeated over and over again, if needs be in a piercing scream, sent them rushing from the house.

There were times, of course, when Harry was at school, Mr Holdsworth at work, and Mrs Holdsworth out. Then, if anyone came to the door, Madison would growl more horribly than the Hound of the Baskervilles, while the dog itself lay admiringly silent.

If the phone rang, Madison could never resist picking up the receiver. But he gave nothing away, as Mr Holdsworth discovered one morning when ringing from his office to speak to his wife, who had in fact just gone out. He dialled the number and was surprised to be answered in his own voice.

'Hello,' said his own voice. 'This is an answering service. If you have a message for the Holdsworths, please state it slowly and clearly, together with your name and address, when you hear the signal. Thank you for calling. State your message *now*.'

There followed three sharp sounds, the noise in fact of a parrot's beak tapping on the mouthpiece.

'Madison?' said Mr Holdsworth.

There was a pause.

'Aw gee, hello, Mr Holdsworth, sir,' said Madison

in his natural tones. 'I didn't expect to hear your voice.'

'I didn't expect to hear my voice either,' said Harry's father. 'Have you done this often?'

'Coupla times. When Mrs Holdsworth's been out, like she is now – buying stuff for tonight's meal.'

'And you give her the message when she comes in?'

'Sure. What's yours, Mr Holdsworth?'

'Tell her I may be late home this evening, Madison. I've got a meeting that may go on a bit.'

'Gee, that's tough, Mr Holdsworth. But we'll try to save some for you.'

'Save some what?'

'New Orleans Shrimps, Maryland Ham, and Strawberry Shortcake,' said Madison happily. 'Pity about the meeting. Have a nice day.'

'I thought you said you'd be late home,' said Mrs Holdsworth that evening, as her husband walked into a kitchen filled with good sights and smells.

'I, um, cancelled the meeting.'

'Good job you did. Between us, Madison and I have cooked up a rather special meal.'

'I know,' said Mr Holdsworth.

'How d'you know, Dad?' asked Harry.

'A little bird told me.'

Harry much enjoyed this, his mother's first attempt at an all-American meal. At the end of it, which was when he couldn't eat another morsel, he watched Madison, who was still peckish.

The parrot now regularly sat up at table, or rather sat on it, next to Harry. Since he was, through no fault of his own, an untidy eater, Mrs Holdsworth provided for him a tin tray, on which he squatted. Bits of dropped food could then be collected later and put in the dog's bowl. To eat, he used a dessert spoon, which Harry loaded for him. Standing on one foot, Madison held the spoon in the other, and dipped his beak in it in quite an elegant manner.

Now he finished the last of the strawberry shortcake, and turned to Mrs Holdsworth.

'That was terrific,' he said.

'It certainly was,' said Harry's father. 'Where did

you get all these recipes from?' he asked his wife.

'A little bird told me.'

Harry sat thinking. Before Madison's arrival, he had got a book on parrots from the library, and one paragraph had worried him.

'Parrots,' it said, 'have strange likes and dislikes. Some are only fond of men, some respond to women, and others prefer children.'

Isn't it nice, he thought now, he gets on so well with Mum and Dad.

'Isn't it nice,' he said to Madison at bedtime. 'You get on so well with Mum and Dad.'

Madison settled himself on his perch in the parrot-cage.

'Blood is thicker than water,' he said.

'Sorry?'

'You gotta remember I am a Holdsworth,' said Madison with pride. 'If not actually by birth, then by adoption. And birds of a feather flock together. OK, George was a naturalized American, but there's a whole lot about your daddy that reminds me of him, even if he hasn't quite got old George's command of language. And as for your mommie – well, George could cook a bit, but I guess she's the greatest. That strawberry shortcake! You sure got the nicest folks, Harry boy.'

Harry made no reply to this speech, and it was a

mark of the closeness which their friendship had already reached that Madison read his thoughts immediately and correctly. '*But*,' said the parrot firmly, 'you and me, Harry – we're buddies.'

'Gosh, Mad,' said Harry. 'I don't know what I'd do without you.'

CHAPTER 8

Time passed, and Madison settled even more comfortably into the bosom of the family. Happy as he had been all those years in America with Professor Holdsworth, life was now so much fuller, more interesting, fun. In the long summer holidays he had spent almost all his time with Harry, some of it in talk, much of it in playing games.

Sometimes in the evening, after supper, Harry's parents would join them in playing Monopoly.

This was Madison's favourite. True, he needed help in handling the awkward, fluttery paper money; but the shaking of the dice, and the movement, by beak, of his chosen symbol presented no problems. He did not care for top hat, car, dog, flat-iron or boot, but liked always to play with the battleship. And, which is why no doubt he liked the game, he almost always won.

The others might go to jail, move directly to jail, not passing GO, not collecting £200, but Madison was seldom behind bars. The Chance and Community Chest cards he drew were usually good ones, but above all he was very particular about the properties he bought.

'Why do you always go for the red set, Madison?' Mrs Holdsworth said one evening. (As so often, Madison already had hotels up, while the others had only built a modest house or two.)

'Just kinda fancy it, ma'am.'

'The colour, you mean?'

'No. I guess mebbe it's on account of Trafalgar Square.'

'What's special about Trafalgar Square?' Harry asked.

'Why, the memory of Lord Nelson, Harry boy, your greatest sailor. George was a great admirer of Lord Nelson, had a whole shelf full of biographies of him. And we parrots have always been keen on seafaring men.'

'I find myself very short of cash,' said Mr Holdsworth, landing on the Strand. 'You can have my railway stations if you like?'

There was a pleading note in his voice.

'You're going to have to sell 'em, sir,' said Madison firmly, 'in order to realize the necessary capital. I'd be obliged if you would pay me £1,100.'

'£1,100?' said Mr Holdsworth. 'Why, that's highway robbery!'

'Talking of robberies,' said Harry's mother, 'did you know there have been several break-ins in the neighbourhood recently? Daytime ones, I mean?'

'I bet they were all at houses where there's no dog. A dog's the best insurance you can get against housebreakers. No one would try to rob this house if they heard ours barking.'

'Well, that's what worries me a bit. He never seems to bark nowadays. I don't think he'd frighten off any burglar. Oh dear, I've got to go to jail again.'

'Mad would scare them off, wouldn't you, Mad?' said Harry.

'You betcha, Harry boy.'

Madison put on his Humphrey Bogart voice.

'Turn around r-e-a-l slow, mister. You move too fast, I'll plug ya, right between the eyes. Just don't tempt me, baby.'

'That ought to fix them,' Harry said, throwing the dice, and landing, to his dismay, in the middle of Trafalgar Square.

'And that,' said Madison, 'ought to fix you.'

For the first few times that Madison was left on his own in the house after that conversation, the thought of burglars did occur to him, but then he forgot all about it.

A couple of weeks went by. The Christmas term had started and Harry was back at school. Mr Holdsworth was at work, and Mrs Holdsworth was going out to do some shopping.

'Anything you need before I go, Madison?' she called.

Madison looked up from the *Daily Mail* which lay on the kitchen table. He was reading Dermot Purgavie's America.

'You remember we're fresh out of lemons?' he said. 'Gonna need juice and grated peel for tonight's Transparent Pie.'

'Yes, I've got them on my list. Anything special you want? For yourself, I mean?'

'Never say no to a Choc Bar,' said Madison, who was extremely fond of ice-cream.

'All right. I'm off then. I'm taking the dog to give him some exercise. See you soon.'

'Sure thing,' said Madison. But it wasn't.

A quarter of an hour passed. Everything was very quiet, and in the warm kitchen Madison dozed on the *Daily Mail.*

Suddenly there was a noise. It sounded as though it came from the sitting-room. It was quite a light, tinkling noise, a noise of something breakable breaking.

'Now what's that lame-brained kittycat up to?' said

Madison, hopping off the kitchen table and making his way down the passage. Smashed one of Mrs H's little ornaments if I ain't mistaken.'

But he was mistaken, as he found when he waddled into the sitting-room.

It was not an ornament that was broken, it was a window. And climbing over the window-sill was not the cat, but a man. He was not a big ugly roughneck as a burglar ought to be, with a striped jersey and a black mask and a sack marked SWAG. He was small and neat and dressed in a smart suit, and he carried a leather grip.

Madison hid behind the door.

Moving quickly and silently on rubber-soled shoes,

the burglar reached out and closed it with a gloved hand.

Madison stood revealed.

Bogey would never have been caught like this, he thought. Me and my big mouth! He opened it.

'Who's a naughty boy, then?' he said in the squawky tones of an ordinary talking parrot.

The burglar did not find it necessary to reply to this question. Instead he opened the zip fastener of his grip, and after one quick practised look about the room, made straight for an old heavy sideboard in the drawers and cupboards of which Mrs Holdsworth kept all the silver.

Knives, spoons, and forks, cream-jugs and sauce-boats, candlesticks, coasters and salvers, and one especially handsome chased silver rose-bowl – Madison had seen them all when they were brought out for cleaning; and he knew that they were much the most valuable things in the house.

'Stop thief!' he said loudly.

The burglar turned from examining the hallmark on the rose-bowl.

'Shut up, you stupid bird,' he said, 'or d'you want me to shut you up?'

Madison did not find it necessary to reply to this question.

Instead he fluttered up on to the sill of the open window, and took a deep breath.

'HELP! BURGLARS! THIEVES! ROBBERS! FOOTPADS! CUTPURSES! FIRE! MURDER! POLICE! HELP!!!!' shouted Madison at the top of his voice.

Behind him he heard a clatter as the burglar dropped the rose-bowl, and then felt hands grasp him. Into the blackness of the leather grip he went, 'Zip' went the fastener, 'bump' went his head against the window-sill as the burglar fled, and Madison, for once in his long life, was reduced to silence.

Dimly he was conscious of a car door slamming, of engine noise, of a bumpy stop/start journey in what sounded like heavy traffic. And later the grip was lifted out, and he felt himself carried up (he could hear stairs being climbed) and put down. The zip was unfastened.

By now Madison's head had cleared, and after a moment he stuck it out.

He was in a small bed-sitting-room, its door shut, its window curtained. The burglar was sitting on the bed regarding him, frowning to himself and rubbing his chin in thought.

'I ought to have knocked you on the head,' he said.

Madison was tempted to say, 'You did,' but preserved silence.

'Messed up my morning's work properly, you have. Still, I can easily pop back another day – there's some nice stuff there. And at least you ought to fetch a bob or two. Parrots are pricey birds, if I'm not mistaken, specially ones that have learned as many words as you seem to have. Which reminds me, don't start any of that yelling again or you will cop it. Not that you can understand a thing I'm saying.'

He stood up and walked to a table with a telephone on it. He dialled a number. Madison listened carefully.

'Mr Lock, please,' said the burglar. 'Mr Ware here.'

There was a pause.

'Hello? That you, Johnny? Silver speaking – Silver Ware. Wonder if you could do me a favour? I've got a little item for sale, Johnny.

'No, not my usual line, it's a parrot, I just happened to pick up a parrot.'

Though he could not distinguish the words, Madison could hear the tone of surprise in the answering voice.

'That's right, a parrot,' said Silver. 'And he's a good talker, and I thought to myself, old Johnny fences for all the burglars in town, whatever their speciality, he's sure to know some guy in the bird business.

'You do?

'Oh that's great, get him to give me a buzz, will you, Johnny? Thanks a million. I might have some nice stuff for you in the next week or so. Bye now.'

Silver Ware put the phone down, wrote (with a

silver pencil) a name and address in a notebook, pulled from his waistcoat a silver pocket-watch on a silver chain, and said thoughtfully, 'Time for a little drink.'

He shot his cuffs to show their silver links, adjusted the silver pin in his tie, and made for the door.

'Shan't be long,' he said to Madison in passing. 'If the phone rings, you can answer it,' and he went out of the room chuckling at the thought.

CHAPTER 9

After the door had closed, Madison waited until the footsteps had died away down the stairs, and then came out of the grip.

The window, he found by climbing up the curtains and peering between them, was firmly latched. He examined the fireplace. In it stood an electric fire of imitation logs, and behind this, screening the chimney, was a sheet of plasterboard.

'To keep out the draught that comes down the chimney,' thought Madison. 'And if draughts can come down, parrots can go up, I guess,' and he set to work on the plasterboard with his beak. Before long he had prised one edge of it away, and, peering up, could see to his joy a distant circle of sky above.

At that moment the phone rang.

Backing out of the fireplace, Madison fluttered up

on to the table and picked up the receiver.

'Hello,' he said in the burglar's voice, 'Silver Ware speaking.'

'Happywings Home for Birds 'ere,' said the caller. 'Johnny Lock said to ring. You got a parrot for sale?'

'That's right.'

'What kind?'

'African Grey.'

'Good talker?'

'Good talker!' said Madison. 'Why, this bird knows words you've never even heard of. This bird, though I say it myself, is the handsomest, most intelligent parrot in the world bar none.'

'Have you got 'im handy?'

'Yes,' said Madison. 'Hang on a minute, I'll put him on the line.'

He waited ten seconds, and then in a parrot's rasp he said, 'God save the Queen! Rule Britannia! Land of Hope and Glory! You've got a face like a chicken's bum.'

'See what I mean?' he said in Silver's voice. 'What's he worth to you?'

'I'd 'ave to have a dekko at 'im first. Where are you?'

I wish I knew, said Madison to himself, and aloud, 'No, I'd sooner bring him over to you. Give me your address.'

The conversation finished, Madison was about to make for the fireplace and freedom when it occurred to him that he must not pass up this opportunity to let Harry know he was safe. He picked up the receiver again with one foot and dialled the Holdsworths' number with the hook of his beak.

The line was engaged.

Madison glanced at a small (silver) carriage-clock that stood on the bedside table. Mr Ware had already been gone for twenty minutes.

At least, thought Madison, I must repay his hospitality before I take my leave. He dialled again, this time 999.

'Which service do you require?' said the operator.

'Police.'

Presently a voice said, 'Police. What seems to be the trouble?'

'I've been kidnapped,' said Madison.

'I see, sir. Where are you speaking from?'

'I don't know.'

'You don't know where you are?'

'No.'

'What number are you speaking from?'

Madison read it off the dial.

'Well we can soon trace that. Now – about this kidnapping, sir. Who has kidnapped you?'

'Listen, buddy,' said Madison, 'and listen good. I'm kinda pushed for time. The guy who snatched me lives here. Trace this number and you'll find him, he's a smalltime hoodlum name of Silver Ware, and I guess you may find some interesting stuff here. And while you're about it, he might lead you to a receiver of stolen property called Johnny Lock. On top of that, if you're interested in valuable missing birds, try the Happywings Home,' and he recited the address. 'Got all that?'

'Yes indeed. Thank you, sir. Very public-spirited of you. You have an American accent, sir, I think?'

'Sure do. Though to tell the truth, I'm African.'

'I see, sir. You're a black American.'

'Well, grey actually.'

'Could I have some more details, sir? You're tied up?'

'No, free as a bird.'

'You're locked in a room?'

'No, door's not locked.'

'Why don't you open it?'

'Can't reach the handle, buster. I ain't tall enough.'

There was a pause, and when the policeman spoke again, there was an edge to his voice.

'Now look here, my friend,' he said sharply. 'You're telling me that you are quite free and unharmed and in a room whose door is not locked, but you're too short to reach the door handle? Suppose you tell me exactly how tall you are.'

Madison by now was tired of being questioned, nettled by the policeman's tone, and anxious to go.

'OK, buddy boy,' he said. 'You asked for it. I'm nine inches.'

At that moment, Madison heard a door close downstairs, and then the sound of footsteps climbing towards him.

'I gotta go,' he said.

'Up the flipping chimney, I suppose,' said the policeman sarcastically.

'You're dead right, mister,' said Madison, and went.

CHAPTER 10

'Would you like a Choc Bar?' Harry's mother said when he came home from school that afternoon.

'Oh yes please, Mum.'

'There's one in the fridge.'

Harry fetched it. 'Mad would like a bit,' he said. 'He loves Choc Bars. Mad! Where are you?'

'Sit down a minute, Harry,' his mother said. 'Just listen while I tell you what's happened. I went out shopping this morning – I wasn't out long, less than an hour – but when I got home I found we'd had a burglar. One of the sitting-room window panes – the one nearest the catch – had been broken from outside, the bits of glass were on the carpet. Someone had smashed it and reached through and opened the window. It was wide open.'

'Has he stolen lots of stuff?'

'No. He'd obviously been after the silver – the sideboard cupboards were open and my rose-bowl was lying on the floor – but that wasn't what he took.'

'What did he take then?'

'Listen to me, Harry. You're going to have to be very grown-up about this. It's Madison who's missing.'

'Oh no, Mum,' said Harry.

'Yes. Now listen. First of all, I'm sure he won't have been harmed. Whoever took him wouldn't want to hurt him.'

'Why would they take him then?'

'Parrots are valuable animals, you know. Priceless, I suppose, in Madison's case if anyone had known how clever he is, but even a parrot that can only say a few words could be worth between two and three hundred pounds, the police said.'

'The police came?'

'Yes. And interviewed the people across the road, who said they'd heard somebody yelling for help. Which must have been Madison.'

'You didn't tell them . . . ?'

'Oh no, I said it must have been a passer-by who'd seen the break-in.'

'Does Dad know?'

'Yes, he should be here soon, he's coming home early, he's putting advertisements in the papers, offering a reward. Try not to worry, darling, I'm sure well find your old Mad. Don't you want that Choc Bar?'

'No,' said Harry miserably.

The evening was not a happy one. Mr Holdsworth watched the six o'clock news alone. It was as usual filled with gloomy items but his mind was on a gloomier one.

Harry's homework was a messy mass of mistakes.

Mrs Holdsworth, laying the table, automatically put out Madison's tray and spoon before she realized what she was doing.

And though at supper they all made a pretence of enjoying the Transparent Pie, anyone could have seen through it.

Afterwards, Harry could bear the sight of the empty parrot-cage no longer. He said his goodnights and went to bed. Never in his life had he felt so wretched.

'Mad,' he said in the darkness, 'where are you?'

In point of fact, at that moment Madison was halfway up a very dirty chimney. Like all parrots, he was using his beak as well as his feet to climb, and his mouth was full of soot. But he clambered doggedly upward, taking some pleasure in the angry cries of Silver Ware below, and a last desperate fluttering saw him free.

Black now as the night around him, Madison perched unsteadily on the rim of one of London's millions of chimney-pots.

'Mad,' he said in the darkness, 'where are you?'

There followed for Madison Holdsworth, bird of letters, cosmopolitan, bon viveur, self-assured sophisticated connoisseur of good food and witty conversation, the most unpleasant night by far that he had ever spent since first, as a hideous naked nestling, he had tottered from the ruins of his egg.

As if to be lost, hungry and filthy were not hardship enough, the puckish gods of the weather now saw fit to play their part in cutting the handsomest, most intelligent parrot in the world bar none down to size.

First came the wind, from somewhere like Siberia, threatening every moment to tear him from his uneasy hold. And then before long it began to pour with rain that soaked his plumage and mingled with the soot that clogged it, to tar-and-feather him into a pitch-dark sticky mess.

Chilled to the bone, black as any crow, and now as flightless as a penguin, Madison fell helplessly from his perch, off the chimney-stack, down the slippery slope of the tiled roof and over the edge to the street below.

Shocked, shaken and shivering, somehow he managed to crawl from the road into the shelter of a

doorway, out of the wind and the rain. There, awaiting the refuse collectors, was a stack of rubbish composed mainly of cardboard boxes, and into one of these Madison crept with the last of his strength.

'Guess I'm done for,' he murmured feebly. 'Goodbye, Harry boy. George, here I come,' and his eyes closed, and his head dropped upon his breast.

CHAPTER 11

Quite early next morning the dustcart came down the street.

At each bin, or in doorways or areas where rubbish was stacked, one or other of three dustmen would pick up a load and shoot it into the back of the vehicle. Inside a giant metal screw rotated endlessly, smashing and squashing to pulp everything that came its way.

Madison came its way, still out to the world in the cardboard box that promised to be his coffin as it jiggled and shuffled towards destruction. Suddenly one of the dustmen spotted him and shouted a warning, and in the nick of time another pulled him clear.

'I thought I seen something live,' shouted the first dustman.

'It's a bird, innit,' said the second dustman. 'A dead bird.'

'Dead, is it? When I seen it jogging about in that box, I thought it was alive. Ah well, chuck it back in then.'

At this point the third dustman came up.

'Wotcha got there then?' he said.

'It's a bird, innit,' said the second dustman. 'A dead bird.'

'Let's have a butchers. Funny kind of bird.'

'Just an old jackdaw.'

'Funny kind of jackdaw, with a beak like that. Show

him to old Claude. He knows about animals, old Claude does.'

Old Claude was the driver of the dustcart, a big, bald, gentle man. He looked down from the window of his cab.

'What's hup?' he said.

'It's a bird, innit,' said the second dustman. 'A dead bird.'

Claude took the limp body in one large hand. With the other he pulled a bunch of rags from under the dash, and began carefully to wipe the sticky blackness from the matted feathers.

Gradually, Madison began to appear in his true colours – the grey of the plumage, the bright red tail-feathers, the white face, until at last only the beak remained, as ever, black. And gradually, in the warmth of Claude's grasp and under the stimulus of his massaging, a little spark of life began to glimmer faintly once again in Madison's body. It was only a tiny spark, just enough to allow one eye to open for a second, but Claude saw and began to smile.

Standing in the road below, the three dustmen could not see the transformation taking place, but only the broad grin that spread gradually over Claude's face.

'Well?' they said.

Claude looked down at them.

'This 'ere bird,' he said, 'is a Hafrican Grey Parrot. Good talkers.'

'That one's never going to talk no more,' they said.

Carefully Claude tucked Madison inside his donkey-jacket.

'Hi 'ope,' said Claude, ''e is.'

*

Afterwards, Madison remembered nothing of that morning. He was unaware, at the end of the round, of the attention he received in the warmth of Claude's cosy kitchen, of the gentle bathing away of the last of the soot from his plumage, of the blanket-wrapped hot-water-bottles that were folded around him, of the heated milk, laced with a drop of brandy, that was tipped down him. He simply slept.

At last, in the evening, a full twenty-four hours since his chimney climb, he opened both eyes to see a face peering down at him. It was a kindly face, Madison

instantly decided, and out of it came a kindly voice.

''Ello,' said the voice. 'Hi 'ope you're better?'

Madison considered how best to answer this courteous enquiry without revealing his gifts. He decided upon a simple polite affirmative.

'Yes, thank you,' he squawked.

''Ungry?' said Claude.

'Yes, thank you,' said Madison again.

'Hi 'aven't got birdseed,' said Claude. 'Like an apple?'

‘Yes, thank you.’

By making use of this reply to anything that was offered, Madison made an excellent supper, eating until he could eat no more.

‘’Ad enough?’ asked Claude.

‘Yes, thank you.’

‘An egg? ’Ow d’you fancy a boiled egg?’

Madison decided this was the moment to extend his vocabulary.

‘No, thank you,’ he said.

And indeed as the days passed and turned into weeks, he found that thank you with or without a yes or a no served to answer most of the questions that the big bald-headed man asked him. Otherwise he kept silent. It was a strain, a severe strain, upon such a natural conversationalist, but he was resolute, set upon three objectives. To regain his health and strength, to fly this nest, and then to find a telephone (Claude hadn’t one) and contact Harry. So, much as he would have loved a chat with his kind host, he resisted the temptation.

Once, he was nearly caught out.

From behind the evening paper which he was reading, Claude had suddenly, quietly, said ‘Madison?’

Despite himself, Madison half-opened his beak to reply, and then quickly closed it again.

Claude peered over the paper.

‘Thought you might be called “Madison”,’ he said.

‘No, thank you,’ said Madison, crossing his toes.

‘There’s an ad ’ere,’ said Claude. ‘“’Oldsworth. Lost. Hafrican Grey Parrot, name of Madison. ’Andsome reward”, and then a box number. Hi’m glad it’s not you, sure as my name’s Claude Clutterbuck.’

But when a month had gone by, Madison decided the time had come to leave. He made his decision with great regret. Not only had the man saved his life and nursed him back to fitness, for which he would be eternally grateful, but he had grown fond of him. ‘Clutterbuck’, it occurred to him, might well derive from ‘Clatterbeak’, a thought that he found pleasing.

You’re a swell guy, he thought, and I wish there was some way I could repay you for all your kindness. One thing’s sure – I’ll make certain you get that ’andsome reward. But home I gotta go.

For some time, while Claude was out driving his dustcart, Madison had been in secret training. He still had no idea where he was and how far he might be required to fly, so he practised hard, round and round the kitchen, twenty, fifty, a hundred circuits a day.

Now he waited for the right weather conditions, listening carefully to the forecasts on Claude’s radio for the combination he wanted. And one evening it came. In the London area, said the weatherman, the following day would be unusually mild for the time of year, windless, and dry.

All that Madison now needed was that Claude, when he finished his rounds in the late morning, should act as he usually acted.

The back door of his house led directly into the kitchen from a little yard outside where Claude kept a number of animals that he had adopted – old rabbits that children had tired of, and ancient hens who had long forgotten how to lay an egg – and where he stored his coal in a bunker. At each homecoming he would fill two battered buckets with coal for the kitchen fire; and once he had opened the back door, the act of coming through it with both hands full meant that it stood open for a few seconds, long enough for escape.

'I sure feel a dirty heel,' muttered Madison, as he waited tensely, listening for Claude's return. 'But it's gotta be done.'

And done it was, the moment those coal buckets were put down on the kitchen floor. As Claude bent, Madison took off, skimming over the bald head and out through the door. He circled around and then swooped low for two last words.

'Thank you!' shouted Madison, and away he flew, higher and higher over the dingy rooftops.

'Good 'eavens!' said Claude as he stared up at the disappearing figure. 'Hi'll eat my 'at!'

CHAPTER 12

For the first couple of weeks after Madison's disappearance, Mr Holdsworth had made every possible effort to find him. The advertisements he had placed brought no replies, so he telephoned every London pet shop in the yellow pages. Quite a number had African Grey parrots for sale, several recently acquired, and these he went to see. He did not tell Harry, preferring to take upon himself the disappointment of saying 'Madison?' and getting either a foolish reply or none.

One bird (in Harrods' zoo) did actually respond to his question sensibly enough to give him momentary hope. It had apparently been brought up in upper-class surroundings by someone who could not sound the letter 'r' correctly.

'Madison?' Mr Holdsworth had said, and without

hesitation it had replied.

'Tebbly tebbly sowwy. 'Fwaid not.'

It was the kind of posh silly-ass accent that Madison could put on with ease, and just for a second he wondered.

'Mad? Is it you? Stop fooling about,' he said, but the parrot only answered, 'Dweadfully sowwy', and turned away, leaving him feeling stupid.

But when three weeks had gone by, Harry's father made up his mind on a course of action that was bold, decisive, well-meant.

He would buy a replacement for Madison.

There were a number of reasons for this. First, he thought it very probable that they had seen the last of Madison. Second, he could no longer bear either the fact of Harry's obvious unhappiness or the sight of the empty parrot-cage. Third, it was shortly to be Harry's eleventh birthday.

Half a loaf's better than no bread, he said to himself.

So, when the day came, he simply went back to Harrods' zoo and bought the parrot. He did not tell his wife, who would certainly have advised against such a plan. He did not tell Harry, wanting to give him a nice surprise.

Harry was certainly surprised, at breakfast, to receive nothing from his parents but good wishes. Not that he had given all that much thought to a birthday present, he was too busy moping about Madison, but it had occurred to him that his bike was very old, and he half expected a new one.

'You'll have to wait until this evening for your present, Harry,' his father said. 'I'm picking it up after work.'

'He wouldn't even tell me what we're giving you,' his mother said, at tea-time, watching Harry, thinking how he had changed since his tenth birthday.

The old pre-Madison Harry would have been in a fever of excitement and impatience by now, showing off, being silly, roaring round the house imagining all sorts of fantastic presents.

But how much more sensible he had grown, trying harder at school, acting more thoughtfully at home. All since Madison had come.

Now he had gone, leaving behind him yet another Harry, quiet and reserved. She watched him picking listlessly at his birthday cake (from a Madison recipe).

'Isn't it nice, Harry?' she said.

'Yes, thanks.'

'Dad'll be home soon.'

'Yes.'

'Cheer up, darling. Things could be worse.'

And before long, they were.

When Mr Holdsworth arrived home, he put his head round the kitchen door and said, 'Stay there a minute, you two. Don't come into the sitting-room till I call.'

In a little while he called and they came. On the table was a box. Harry's father raised the lid.

For a moment or so, nothing happened. Then out of the box, in silent slow motion, there rose a round grey head with a sharp hooked beak. On either side of the head was a bright, considering, straw-coloured eye. Mrs Holdsworth drew in her breath smartly.

'Oh!' she cried. 'It's not . . .'

'No,' said Harry. 'It's not.'

'No, I'm afraid it isn't,' said Mr Holdsworth, 'but I thought you'd like to have him, Harry, he talks a bit and I'm sure you could teach him lots of words, and anyway, well, half a loaf's better than no bread, eh?'

'Yes, Dad. Thanks. Thank you both. It's very kind of you.'

His mother plunged in hastily.

'He looks awfully like Madison, don't you think?'

'Doesn't he?' said his father heartily. 'I mean, all parrots look alike, don't they?'

'Like all Chinese?' Harry said.

There was a long uncomfortable silence.

I've done a stupid thing, Mr Holdsworth thought. But I meant well.

'You'll have to think of a name for it,' he said.

I'm sure he meant well, Mrs Holdsworth thought. But what a stupid thing to do.

'Perhaps it's got one already,' she said brightly. She bent forward. 'Have you got a name, old boy?'

'Tebbly tebbly sowwy,' said the parrot. ''Fwaid not.'

The days passed, and Harry did his best to appear pleased with his birthday present, the last thing in the world he would have chosen.

He realized that his father, with the kindest of intentions, must have spent a great deal of money to try to comfort him for the loss of Mad, and he tried hard not to show how much worse it had actually made things. He looked after his new pet carefully but he could feel nothing for him. He was just a parrot in a cage. Harry could hardly bring himself to speak to the bird, though by now he had a name.

Because of the affected way he spoke, like a chinless wonder, someone suggested 'Fweddy', and for lack of a better idea, it stuck.

Mr and Mrs Holdsworth made attempts to hold conversations with Fweddy but without much success. True, he would speak in reply to their efforts but only to say he was 'tebbly sowwy' or occasionally, by way of a change, 'fwightfully fwilled'. He also had a limited range of comments about the weather which occasionally, by chance, made sense. But he was perfectly capable of saying, on a fine sunny day, that it was 'waining cats and dogs' or 'fweezing cold'; and once, when the heavens opened, and a downpour drummed against the window panes, Fweddy cried cheerfully, 'Gwand weather for the time of year! Woasting hot, quite twopical, what?'

He also responded to the ringing of the telephone, saying, 'Answer the wetched thing, dahling, I'm too weawy to lift the weceiver.'

By chance, one morning about a week after his birthday, Harry was alone in the house. His father was at work, his mother had gone out. It was the half-term holiday, so that there were all sorts of things he could have been doing, but he didn't feel like doing any of them.

If only Mad was here, he thought. We could have a game of something, like Monopoly. What fun we used to have.

Then the telephone rang.

'Answer the wetched thing, dahling,' said Fweddy. 'I'm too weawy to lift the weceiver.'

'Hello,' said Harry in the flat bored tones that now were customary to him.

'I have a call for Harry Holdsworth,' said the operator.

'That's me.'

'It's a reversed-charge call. From a Mr Madison Holdsworth. Will you accept the charges?'

CHAPTER 13

Madison flew higher and higher into the quiet sky of a pleasant sunny late-October morning, and surveyed the bit of London that lay below him. He was looking for landmarks.

The Holdsworths lived in Greenwich, quite close to the Park. Madison knew, because Harry had told him, all about the Park and the observatory and the Queen's House and the bend in the Thames where the *Cutty Sark* lay, and he was nursing a wild hope that he might be able to see some part of all this.

But no, there was no sign of the river, no sign of any park. All he could see was row after row of little houses, with here and there blocks of high-rise flats towering above them, and the traffic crawling, like flies stuck in the web of narrow streets.

Already the effort of gaining height was beginning

to tire him, and so he glided down to the nearest tall building and landed on its roof.

'Mad,' said Mad. 'Take it easy, feller. Get your breath and use your brains. Examine the pros and cons of the situation. Make a plan. Act on it. On the plus side, you are free, you are returned to health, you are somewhere in London, Harry is somewhere in London. On the minus, you're lost. So waddya do? You contact Harry. So waddya say? Hi, Harry, come and get me, I'm somewhere in London? Big deal, there's only about four hundred square miles of it. No, you gotta fix a meeting-place, a rendezvous, some point that you and Harry can both find easy. OK. Let's find a telephone. Hold on, buster, you just gonna walk into some guy's house and say "Howdy, stranger, mind if I use your phone?" No, it's gotta be a public telephone. Oh yeah? You gonna open the door of a telephone box? With your lousy beak, huh? Or you gonna smash one of its windows, like vandals do? Hey, wait a minute, buddy boy – that's it! That's the answer, go find a vandalized public telephone box! Madison Holdsworth, you ain't just a pretty face! Let's go!'

He was not long in discovering his first telephone box – being red made them easy to spot from the air – but when he flew down to it, he found it occupied. And of the next two that he investigated, one was empty but in good repair so that there was no way in for him, and the other had been just too thoroughly vandalized, all its windows broken, the directories ripped up, the coin-box smashed, the instrument torn out. Against one wall was a spray-painted message in large capital letters informing a puzzled Madison that SPURS RULE OK.

But at last, after several more disappointments, his luck turned. He had flown across the green turf of what he knew, from television, was a football stadium, and just beyond it he found what he wanted. Standing beneath a street sign that read 'White Hart Lane' was a box that was both empty and undamaged except that someone had thoughtfully kicked in one of the lowest panes of glass.

Madison crept in, and fluttered up on to the top of the coin-box. He picked up the receiver and dialled 100.

'What number do you require?' said the operator.

'I want to make a reversed-charge call,' said Madison, and he gave the Holdsworths' number and Harry's name.

'And your name, sir?'

'Madison Holdsworth.'

'Just one moment, please. Trying to connect you.' Then there were buzzings and clickings and a ringing tone and, at last, Harry's voice!

'. . . Will you accept the charges?'

'Yes! Oh yes !' said Harry.

'Go ahead, please, caller.'

'Harry?'

'Mad! Mad, is it really you? What's happened? Where have you been? Are you all right?'

'Yeah, I'm just fine. Tell you all about it when we meet. Gee, it's great to hear you, Harry boy.'

'Oh Mad, where are you?'

'In a phone box.'

'Yes, but where? Tell me where. I'll come and fetch you. I'll come straightaway.'

'Somewhere called "White Hart Lane".'

'Oh gosh, that's North London. Miles from here.'

'Then I'll be like the swallows,' said Madison. 'I'll fly south for the winter. I figure all we gotta do is fix a spot to meet.'

'That's a brill idea,' said Harry.

'Yeah, you ain't got a monopoly of brains, kid. But where?'

Monopoly, thought Harry. Of course! Mad's favourite property. That's the place.

'Trafalgar Square,' he said. 'Listen, Mad. You're some way north of the river. Say seven or eight miles as the crow flies.'

'The parrot.'

'Yes. Listen. Just fly south till you see the Thames, you'll see Trafalgar Square just on your side of the river. You can't miss it, there's the Column and the fountains and the four lions, one at each corner. I'll meet you there. I'll leave a note for Mum, and get the first train I can for Charing Cross. It'll probably take me about an hour. We should get there about the same time.'

At this moment, Madison heard the sound of loud tuneless singing. Coming towards the telephone box was a man with a red nose and a bottle in his hand. He was not walking very straight. When he reached the box, he leaned against it and took a long drink. Then he peered inside.

'Harry,' said Madison hastily. 'I gotta go. See you,'

and he put back the receiver and made his exit through the broken pane.

'A parrot,' the man said carefully. 'Shpeaking on the telephone. Time I shtopped,' and he emptied the bottle on to the pavement.

CHAPTER 14

'Harry!' called Mrs Holdsworth, arriving home. 'I'm sorry I'm so late. I'm afraid you've had to wait for your lunch.'

There was no answer.

'Harry!' she said again. 'Are you there?'

''Fwaid not,' said a voice. 'Tebbly tebbly sowwy.'

Propped up on the kitchen table was a note. *Mum. Mad rang. Going into London to fetch him. Back for tea. How about making some American brownies? Love, Harry.*

Now, try not to worry, she told herself. After all, he's eleven years old and pretty sensible and he's often gone in with me on the train.

She got out the double saucepan.

'Oh dear,' she said aloud. 'I hope to goodness he'll be all right.'

*

Harry in fact was quite all right, only a bit out of breath. He had run all the way to Maze Hill Station, hoping that there would soon be a train for Charing Cross, and there was, and he was on it.

Some uncles and aunts had given him quite a lot of money for his birthday, so that he had plenty and to spare for the return fare. He had also put on his anorak (in case it turned very cold), his wellies (in case it rained heavily), and was carrying his satchel (to put Mad in, in case you had to buy tickets for parrots).

He was so excited that the journey passed in a flash. In no time at all, it seemed, he was hurrying along the Strand, dodging his way through the crowds of pedestrians. There's only one individual I'm interested in, thought Harry – one smallish short-legged grey bird!

He entered Trafalgar Square to find it filled with thousands upon thousands of smallish short-legged grey birds, cooing and strutting and bowing and pecking and squabbling, drinking from the fountains, perching on the lions, covering the paving-stones in one great slate-coloured bustling blanket. For a moment Harry's heart sank. How would he ever find Mad amongst this multitude?

He sat down on a bench, while the pigeons chuckled and gobbled around his feet, and stared unhappily at the Column, pointing like a colossal finger into the London sky. His gaze was drawn up the mighty pillar, up, up to the pedestal on its top where stood the figure of the little Admiral, cocked hat on head, his one and only hand resting upon the hilt of his sword.

BUT . . . what was that shape that sat upon the epauletted shoulder of Horatio, Viscount Nelson and Duke of Bronte, KCB, Vice-Admiral of the Blue? That was no silly pigeon!!

'MAD! MAD! MAD!'

And everywhere people stopped and stared at this

yelling, dancing small boy, who shouted endlessly the word that, it seemed to them, he was. And as they watched, a solitary bird came gliding rather clumsily down from the heights, and pitched awkwardly upon the boy's shoulder, and shuffled sideways to nibble, very gently, at the lobe of his ear.

And the boy stopped his shouting, and stood still, only raising one hand to stroke with his finger-tips that round grey head, while all around the pigeons settled again and the noise of their cooing once more filled the Square.

After that everything went like clockwork. They couldn't talk much – there were too many people about, in the crowded streets, on the packed platform, on the journey through Waterloo and the Elephant & Castle on the way to Greenwich and home – but it didn't matter to either of them. They were together again. There would be all the time in the world to talk later.

Harry managed, at a moment when no one seemed to be looking at the strange pair, to mutter his idea for using his satchel, and the parrot popped inside it to avoid the ticket collectors, but otherwise Harry carried his Mad in triumph.

Up the hill from the railway station they went in the gathering dusk, and skirted the edge of the Park, and turned at last into Unduly Road.

'Nearly there,' cried Harry, pointing. 'Look, Mad, 137, that's our house!' And then they were at the door and Harry's mother was opening it and hugging him and stroking Madison's feathers and hurrying them into the kitchen and plying them with delicious squidgy nutty American brownies and endless questions. And they were still all talking away nineteen to the dozen when Harry's father arrived home, astounded to see Madison who then had to tell the story of his adventures all over again. Until at last Mr Holdsworth looked at his watch and said, 'Mad. Nearly time for the six o'clock news.' And they all smiled, because one of Madison's tricks was to balance on top of the TV set, swing his tail up and his head down, and press the on/off switch with the hook of his beak.

'Sure thing, Mr Holdsworth, sir,' said Madison. 'I'm out of touch with what's been going on. No knowing what may have happened while I've been away,' and he got down on to the floor and waddled off along the passage to the sitting-room.

The smile that had been on Harry's face suddenly changed into a look of horror. Not once all day had he thought about Fweddy. Not till that instant, when a combination of what Madison had just said and where he was going filled him with sudden panic. He should have told Mad, explained it all, promised to get rid of the stupid thing right away!

'Mad!' he cried. 'Hang on a minute!' and he dashed out of the kitchen.

'What's biting you, Harry?' asked Madison, turning to face him in the doorway of the sitting-room.

Harry sought desperately for some last-minute means of softening the blow.

'Listen, Mad. I should have told you, it just never crossed my mind, I was so excited at seeing you and hearing all your news, I just never thought to say. It was a present from Dad. I never wanted it. I'm sorry.'

'Tebbly tebbly fwightfully dweadfully sowwy,' said a voice from the sitting-room.

In the silence that followed, you could have heard a parrot's pin-feather drop. Then Madison turned and walked in. He looked up at his cage. Fweddy looked down. Helplessly, Harry looked on. Madison gave a long low whistle. Fweddy replied with a short high screech. Harry was tongue-tied.

'Come on, Harry boy. Make with the introductions,' said Madison pleasantly.

'Um . . . he's called Fweddy,' mumbled Harry. 'Fweddy, this is Madison.'

'Blistewing hot, what?' said Fweddy.

'He doesn't talk sense,' said Harry hastily. 'Honestly, Mad, he's an idiotic bird, we'll get rid of him, we'll sell him, straightaway, tomorrow, we'll take him to a pet shop, Dad won't mind, I'm sure.'

His parents came into the room.

'Dad won't mind what?' said his father. 'Hey, Mad, you haven't switched the news on.'

'Tebbly tebbly sowwy,' said Madison in Fweddy's high affected voice. 'What a silly pawwot I am,' and, to the amazement of the Holdsworths, both birds suddenly burst out laughing.

CHAPTER 15

That was all on a Thursday. For some reason which they did not understand Madison was anxious to know which Thursday in November it was. He seemed satisfied when they told him it was the first one.

When he reached his office on the Friday, Mr Holdsworth rang the police to enquire if anything further had been heard of the thief who had broken into his house, and was told that a character called Silver Ware had indeed been found to be in possession of a quantity of stolen valuables, and had been arrested.

'He might well have been your man, sir,' the officer told him. 'We've recently had information that led us to a couple of other villains. The same information, strangely enough, that we had some while back, though we disregarded it then as it came from some American joker.'

'Joker?'

'Said he'd been kidnapped, was going to escape up a chimney, and, to top it all, was only nine inches tall.'

'He must have been Mad,' said Mr Holdsworth solemnly.

He also made a call to the local authority to trace the address of one of their dustmen, a Mr Claude Clutterbuck; and then he sent him, anonymously, the reward he'd had in mind, of £50.

''Andsome hindeed,' said Madison in Claude's voice when he heard about this. ''E'll heat 'is hother 'at.'

On the Saturday, they had a family game of Monopoly. Madison's battleship was in unbeatable form, collecting no less than three good sets (including of course the red one), and bankrupting them all.

On Sunday, there was the crossword for Mr Holdsworth and Madison to enjoy.

And on Monday, when the second half of the term began, Harry went back to school with a light heart, looking forward to the evening's homework.

As for Harry's mother, she was very keen on the idea of a special meal, a feast in honour of Madison's homecoming, but he said he would rather wait a while.

'When would you like it, then?' she asked.

'If it's all the same to you, ma'am,' said Madison, 'how about the fourth Thursday of November?'

Mrs Holdsworth was puzzled, but agreed. Maybe it's his birthday, she thought.

All this time, nothing had been decided about Fweddy. Mr Holdsworth had asked Harry what he wanted to do, and Harry asked Madison, and Madison, surprisingly, had seemed quite happy with things as they were.

'You can't just show Fweddy the door,' he said. 'The bird's happy here. And it's company for me, night-times.'

And indeed each night they perched side by side in the big parrot-cage in the most companionable way. Harry would say goodnight on his way to bed, and Madison would answer sensibly. Fweddy on the other hand would either offer his usual apology or make some silly remark about the weather.

But before long he surprised Harry one evening by not only saying 'Goodnight', but actually adding 'Sweet dweams'.

'You're teaching that bird a thing or two, aren't you, Mad?' Harry said next morning at breakfast.

Madison paused, his spoonful of porridge sweetened with golden syrup halfway to his beak. He looked smug.

'You'rc gonna be surprised one of these days,' he said.

'But how do you communicate?' asked Mr Holdsworth. 'I mean, it's not as though he can understand English like you. He's just picked up the odd sentence.'

'It's simple if you think about it. I'm bilingual.'

'What's that mean?' said Harry.

'I speak two languages.'

'What's the other one then?'

'Parrot.'

'So you think Fweddy's going to astonish us, do you, Mad?' asked Mrs Holdsworth.

'Given time, ma'am, given time.'

'How long?' said Harry.

'Coupla weeks, I guess.'

A couple of weeks later Mrs Holdsworth looked at the calendar. It was Tuesday November the 26th, and the 28th had a ring round it to remind her it was the fourth Thursday of the month.

'Mad,' she called from the kitchen. 'Can you spare a minute?'

'Sure,' shouted Madison from the parrot-cage. Its door was always open, but Fweddy seldom ventured out, and Madison, the family noticed, seemed quite happy to keep him company for long spells. They would chatter softly together in parrot language.

'About this feast, Mad,' said Harry's mother when he arrived in the kitchen. 'You wanted it on the

fourth Thursday. That's the day after tomorrow. We ought to be thinking about it.'

'Aw gee, ma'am,' cried Madison. 'What with one thing and another it went clean out of my head. Mighty glad you remembered.'

'Is it your birthday?'

'No, no, it's Thanksgiving Day.'

'Oh. An American national holiday, isn't it?'

'Yeah. To commemorate the feast the Pilgrim Fathers had with the Indians, at Plymouth Colony, to celebrate their first harvest on American soil. I just thought it would be kinda nice to celebrate my return home on that particular day.'

'It would,' said Mrs Holdsworth. 'We will.'

So they began to plan the meal, the main part of which would be roast turkey with cranberry sauce.

When Thursday evening came, and the Thanksgiving supper was almost ready, Madison came shuffling into the kitchen.

'We eating in here, ma'am?'

'We always eat in the kitchen, Madison,' said Harry's mother. 'You know that.'

'Sure, sure. It's just that . . . well, I figured Fweddy might like to come along. Seems kinda tough to be left in there while we're all having a good time.'

'Of course, Mad. I'll lay a place for him.'

Madison went back into the sitting-room where Harry and his father were playing a game.

'Supper nearly ready?' asked Mr Holdsworth.

'Yes, sir. Mrs Holdsworth was kind enough to say Fweddy can come along too.'

'D'you hear that, Fweddy?' said Harry. 'You're invited to the Thanksgiving supper.'

''Fwaid I'm not tebbly hungwy,' said Fweddy.

'I must say, Mad, you've done wonders with that bird,' said Harry's father.

Madison scratched the side of his face.

'You ain't seen nothing yet,' he said.

At that moment Mrs Holdsworth called, 'Supper's ready!'

'Come on, Fweddy,' said Harry. 'There are lots of lovely things to eat.'

'Cawwy me, Hawwy,' said Fweddy. 'I'm feeling fwagile.'

When they were all sitting down, Fweddy on a second tray beside Madison's, Mr Holdsworth poured a glass of wine for his wife and one for himself and a Coke for Harry.

'Now then,' he said to his family, 'I ask you to raise your glasses and drink a toast. Let's begin this splendid feast by giving thanks for the safe return of Harry's Mad.'

'To Harry's Mad!' they all cried, and then they fell to work with a will. Only Fweddy seemed to have no appetite.

'Fweddy,' said Harry's mother. 'You're not eating anything.'

'Tebbly sowwy.'

But for Harry and Mad, who both loved sweet things, the best part of the meal was the Thanksgiving pudding (a favourite of Great-Uncle George's) for which Madison had supplied the recipe, full of figs and raisins and masses of brown sugar.

At last everyone had finished eating, and Mrs Holdsworth was just about to ask for help with the washing-up, when suddenly Fweddy, who had hardly spoken a word throughout but had simply sat,

looking rather uncomfortable, upon the tray, gave a kind of a grunt, and stood up.

And there, to the Holdsworths' amazement, was a small, glistening, pearly-white, new-laid egg.

The three Holdsworths looked at Fweddy.

They looked at the egg.

They looked at Madison.

'Call me Fwedewika,' said Fweddy.

'Call me Dad,' said Harry's Mad.